THE BEAUTY OF MURDER

THE BEAUTY OF MURDER

A K Benedict

WINDSOR
PARAGON

First published 2013
by Orion Books
This Large Print edition published 2013
by AudioGO Ltd
by arrangement with
The Orion Publishing Group Ltd

Hardcover   ISBN: 978 1 4713 5177 8
Softcover   ISBN: 978 1 4713 5178 5

British Library Cataloguing in Publication Data available

Printed and bound in Great Britain by
TJ International Ltd

To Mum and Dad

Prologue

The Magician

The beauty queen lies dead on the carpet. Her arm is bent above her head as if still waving to the clapping crowd. Blood blooms beneath her. Her once-white dress is a mess of red.

Kneeling next to her body, I count the stab wounds and am soothed, like a sleep-seeker numbering sheep. Her stomach has been punctured twelve times; her chest slashed seven or more; her palms gape open where she tried to defend herself before life left her and she exsanguinated on the carpet.

The man I have not seen in thirty years stares down at the body. Last time I saw him he had white smile lines etched into his tanned skin. They radiated out like the spines of a sun dial. He is not laughing now. 'Can you help, Jackamore?' he asks.

I stand and fold my arms. He cannot hold my gaze. 'Beg me,' I say.

He chews his lip. He stares at the photos on the mantelpiece.

'You always were a coward,' I say. 'Now beg me.'

'Please hide her, Jackamore,' he says. His eyes drop and I know he is mine. 'I beg you.'

*   *   *

The sky is in livor mortis when I leave the house. Black and blue-bruised clouds pool over the Cambridge skyline. I weave through the streets scouting for where and when to put her. I stop outside

1

Great St Mary's. Evensong soars and beauty dies: this is the time to be alive.

Chapter One

The Philosopher

Two raindrops race down the pane. One straggles behind and I will it to win, pressing my fingertip to the glass and dragging down, but it takes the long route: bumping into other drops, joining them into a constellation, then tearing down and reaching the sill a second too late. Outside, on the grass, a willow tree headbangs in the wind and a girl runs alongside the Cam, the skirts of her ballgown scrunched up in her hands.

Two jabs come from the room below. I stamp twice on the floorboards and wait for the door to slam, boots to clomp up the stone staircase and Satnam to poke his head round the door.

'Thought you'd never finish,' he says, wandering in and dropping two four-packs of lager on my notes. 'It's only a lecture; you've given them before. It's not as if anyone will go.'

'It's my first lecture *here*,' I say. 'I want to make a good impression, prove to the faculty that they were right to take a risk on me.'

'It's Friday night in Freshers' Week, my furrowed friend: we should be out watching newbies stumbling out of the Matriculation dinner and throwing up in the fountain. It's tradition.'

'And what's Cambridge without tradition?'

'Exactly.' Satnam slumps into the baggy sofa and opens a can away from him. A blob of foam flops onto the carpet. 'Whoah, when did you get that?'

3

he asks, pointing at the 'What-the-Butler-Saw' machine against the wall.

'I rescued it from the back of a junk shop in Bridlington. I got it delivered this morning.'

Satnam sidles up to it with some suspicion, slides an old penny off the top of the machine and pops it in the slot. He bends and peers through the peephole. He twists back to me. 'Well, that's not very erotic,' he says.

'No, but it's erratic. You're lucky it worked at all.'

'Don't you have enough crap in here already?' he says, sweeping an arm around my study. 'No wonder you're always losing stuff.'

'Crap?' I look round at the tussle of books and the rocks and stones on top, the collected bones and teapots and other things Da won't have in the house and I can't bear to get rid of. 'These, I'll have you know, are highly sought after, extremely rare artefacts.' That's not true, obviously. Besides, my rooms are too small for all of it, especially the larger pieces, and I like the jumbliness—I get less lonely. Satnam is a minimalist, with a spreadsheet for his bedsheets. He won't even look at Bandit, my one-armed, tufty, badly taxidermied bear, who guards the door to my bedroom.

It's parky in here. I hadn't noticed while working, but now the bottoms of my nails are inky blue. I walk over to the gas fire and twist the knob till the middle bar sparks up.

Walking back to the window to close the curtains, I open my can and watch two more first years hurry under the window. 'Don't you wish you were starting out again?' I ask.

'Are you saying I'm old?'

4

'You're not young.'

'I'm younger than you.'

'I think you can stop counting those eight months now,' I reply.

'When have you ever known me to give up an advantage?'

'Never.' On the first day of school I sat down next to Satnam and accidentally knocked lemon squash over his comic. I took it home, pegged out the pages for him in our back yard and fastened it back together but, thirty years later, he still says I owe him. And *now* he's found me this job: he'll be bringing that up when we're in a retirement home as a ruse to make me fetch his cocoa. And all he did was email me the details.

'Why would you want to go back anyway?' he says. 'I knew nothing when I arrived.'

'And now of course you know . . . '

'Everything.' He grins and plonks his feet on a box of books. 'That, matey, is obvious to all.'

'You can write my lecture for Monday. Seeing as you know everything.'

'I could,' he says, sweeping his can around, loftily. 'But I only bother with subjects that count. Physics, proper physics, none of your *meta*physics crap, and darts. They are the only things you need.'

'Not love, then? Understanding?' I root around in my head for other essentials. 'Parkin? And don't dismiss metaphysics. I'm an empiricist as much as you. I only trust evidence.'

Satnam sniggers. 'Yeah, right. Love is chemistry and therefore not my field, not that I'd say no to love in a field with, say, that girl with the blue hair from Starbucks. Or the sexy librarian in the UL— she's a good eight, nine from the arse of a whiskey glass. But sex is different. Love involves hearts and hammering them. Not even *you* can fix them.' Satnam gestures to my toolbox by the jack-in-the-box with the snapped latch. I like to mend broken things. 'No,' he continues. 'The requirement for love, understanding and parkin can only be felt by poor souls who are crap at darts. Such as you.'

'I managed a nine-dart finish in The Black Heart yesterday.' I also had a nine-dart beginning and a fifteen-dart middle but I won't mention that.

'You got those flights I gave you?' he says.

I search in my desk drawers, pick up folders, flick through books.

Leaning forward, he sighs and plucks a tin out of his back pocket. He holds it open: inside are six darts, a retractable pencil and a gold-plated fountain pen. He hands me three and points to the dartboard he bought me as a moving-in present. 'See if you can beat me, then. Loser goes out for kebabs.'

*   *   *

'Go easy on the chilli sauce,' Satnam shouts down the staircase, his voice rebounding off stone.

I can't resist a bet. I don't even really like kebabs—the meat pillars make me think of a grotesque music box with a lamb ballerina pirouetting and dwindling to tinny hits—but it's the challenge, the surge in adrenaline.

My umbrella bucks and buckles as I turn the corner into Sepulchre College's Great Court. It gives up and twists inside out. The wind has a knife to my throat and is pickpocketing my bones. Satnam warned me that Cambridge greets

6

newcomers with cold open arms but I thought he was being soft. I've lived in Yorkshire, Dublin, San Francisco and Manchester: I can talk about chills and rain in fifty different ways, about dirty rain and light rain and rain that gets you unaccountably wet, about cold winter days that make you feel you'll never be warm again, but Cambridge already has me shivering in my bed. And it's only the beginning of October.

I run, head down, following the yellow reflections of lamp-posts on the wet path, past the chapel, the college hall, the library with its one light on for students up late and alone on a Saturday. I'm at that best stage of drunkenness, where my legs don't feel like they belong to me but somehow they still keep going. I wheel on through the arched walkway that resembles the ribcage of a skeleton lying on its back and, as I look up and see the city's skyline, elation fizzes through me. I'm in a big stone film set and someone has been barmy enough to employ me. Things could be much worse.

Angela, one of the porters, stands by the door within the towering gatehouse. She looks up at me and grins. 'Evening, Dr Killigan; you're in a good mood.'

'I'm on a kebab mission. It's going to be dangerous but I believe I'm the man for the job. Can I get you summat?'

'I'm no fan of kebabs,' she says, stepping from one foot to the other and rubbing her hands. 'Don't go to the Death Van. I know someone whose brother had to have his bowel removed.'

'Ouch.'

She nods. 'I'll get rid of that if you like,' she says. After a moment, she points at the umbrella.

It hangs its head, raggedy and sad.

'I'll keep it, ta,' I reply.

The rain stops, clouds back away to reveal a half-full moon as I walk down Smoke Lane, the narrow passageway that comes out next to the Fitzwilliam Museum. Stumbling, I grab at a bollard. The street takes a while to right itself around me. I may have more drunkness than I thought. At least no one's looking, aside from Miranda, the missing beauty queen. She smiles from the curling posters in the shop windows, holding the skirt of her polka-dotted white dress, the Miss Cambridge crown slightly wonky on her head. She disappeared a year ago, hours after winning the title. The national press has forgotten about her now; so had I till I arrived and spotted the shrine to her in the netted window of The Red Shoes Tea Shop, her picture propped against a cake-stand, a replica of her crown on the top tier. In the window of the newsagents there's a hand-written plea from her parents to remember her. I look closer at the picture. The missing—dead and alive at the same time. My shoulders shrug in a shiver. Images of Ma float in my head and my heart clenches. This is why I shouldn't drink.

In the market square, students and townies with damp hair mill around skeletal stalls; a girl perches at the end of one trestle table with a boy between her legs, his hands on her back, her fist in his hair. I feel a pang that isn't in my stomach.

Two fast-food vans chug away either side of the market: one, apparently, is the Death Van, the other the Van of Life, but no one really knows which. Both smell of burned onions and armpits. I join the one with the shorter queue—it's a risk but

8

at least death may come quickly.

'One burger please, mate, and a doner and chip pitta with extra chillies. And a Flake.' The chocolate's for me—it's affection in a yellow dress. 'I don't suppose you know where I can get some parkin?' This is parkin weather after all, makes me think of eating hot slabs of it out of woolly gloves on Bonfire Night.

The vendor wipes the back of his hand across his head, peels paper from a pale frozen meat patty and slaps it on the hot plate. 'Should be all right, this time of night—I know the warden and he's in the Arms,' he says.

For a moment I wonder if, in East Anglia, a county so flat there must be something going on underneath the surface, ginger cake can only be found at night, and is guarded fiercely by a dragon-clawed warden. Then I twig, and the image bursts. 'Oh, I don't drive,' I say. 'I'd only crash. Thank you, though.'

The man shrugs. He tears pittas and shovels in fries, teases out strands of lettuce from a tub.

I smother Satnam's doner with chilli sauce, then squeeze on some more. The loser's revenge. I place the bottle down and a girl with a dark bob picks it up, dousing her veggie burger as if putting out a fire. A wine bottle peeks out from under her arm.

'I wouldn't,' she says, nodding at the kebab. She screws her nose up and the tiny green stud in her left nostril eases out.

I imagine gently nudging it back. 'Neither would I. Not that I couldn't take it: I've got the constitution of an ox, no twelve of them—twelve oxen. Yes. At least twelve. A box of oxen.' I waggle a finger in my ear, which has suddenly got very itchy. My face is hot. I have an umbrella gripped between my knees.

'It'd have to be a very big box,' she says, nicking a chip and dabbing it in the correct order of sauces: mayonnaise, tomato sauce, then chilli, then garlic.

'I'm Stephen Killigan,' I say.

She nods. 'I think it's a drove, herd, span or team of oxen. Or yoke if there are just two,' she says.

'That's one of the more logical collective nouns. I prefer the absurd ones.'

'Like a sleuth of bears?'

'A murder of crows.'

'A buffoonery of orangutans.' We grin at each other and a spark of excitement flares in my stomach.

Three drunken, blazer-wearing students bray past us, arms slung round each other's shoulders. One stops to vomit in the gutter. 'Should be a buffoonery of students,' I say, stacking up the polystyrene boxes. I pocket the chocolate and tuck the tattered umbrella under my arm. We move to the side of the van, out of the way of its fuming exhaust. 'What are you studying?' I ask.

Her eyebrows jolt. 'I'm not a student.'

'I just thought . . . '

Staring at me, she takes a wide bite of burger and throws the rest in the bin. Then she balances the wine bottle on her palm and walks away.

How did that happen? Brilliant Killigan, brilliant.

Glass smashes behind me. The students in drinking society blazers stand round the girl. One of them loops his scarf around her neck.

The kebab vendor turns his back and rearranges meat in the freezer.

10

When I arrived here I was invited to join the Sceptres, Sepulchre's drinking society. I went to one meeting but it seems to involve getting pissed and doing all the silly things students do, only in striped jackets, and without women. The girl tosses the scarf in a puddle. She looks around, folds her arm tight into her body and steps back onto the neck of the smashed wine bottle. Her shoes are like my sister's ballet slippers.

I walk towards her; my heart starts running.

'I've seen you in the library,' the one with the scarf and the roundest head says.

'Well done,' she replies.

'Come on, come back with us. We've got access to the cellar.'

I tap him on the shoulder. 'Can I come? Sounds like fun.'

He glares round at me, his eyes crazy-paved with blood vessels. He stares at the threads waving out of my coat and smirks. Turning back to her, he says. 'The *wine* cellar. We've got the keys.' He taps his pocket.

'I prefer attics,' she says.

'Go on, you know you want to,' he says.

'Dangerous   business   that,   making presuppositions,' I say, trying to keep the tremor out of my voice. My tongue feels too big for my mouth. 'The trick in my line of work, if you can call it work and that's a question for another day, if you presuppose that days are made up of hours and hours can be trusted and if you presuppose that there's such a thing as trust and not just a series of occasions where it hasn't been proved otherwise, is to challenge presuppositions made in everyday life—such as the knowledge of anything—how can

11

she know that she knows something? How can you know that she knows she knows something? How can you know that I'm not a figment of your limping imagination? What are you left with? I don't know yet so I suspect you don't. See? I told you it was dangerous.'

'And what's it got to do with you?' he asks. His face is plasticine pink. He stretches it into a sneer.

'That's my brother,' she replies.

Ouch.

'Look,' she says. 'Obviously I'd love to come and be fumbled with, inexpertly I suspect, but my ant farm is having a party tonight and I've promised I'll make the mojitos. Maybe another time. Or not.' She backs away, looks over to me. 'Sorry,' she says, then breaks into a run down Petty Cury.

'Your loss, love.' The pinkest one shrugs. 'Probably a lezzer,' he says to his friends. He shifts his weight and turns to me. The other two move closer. The only fight situations I like involve games where I possess a sword of truth, not a pile of polystyrene and an umbrella.

I nod at the sodden scarf. 'Which college are you at?'

Pink boy juts his chin. 'John's.'

'Aaah. I'm new, you see—a Fellow at Sepulchre.' The three of them look at each other; two of them step back. 'I've only been here a week so I'm not big on college scarves. As far as I can gather, you wear them to denote pride in your tribe: like football teams but without the balls. Good of you to give yours away.' I grin at him. My upper lip sticks to my gums. 'Must be a Cambridge ritual. I'm still learning about those. What's the name of your tutor? I'll let them know how kind you were.'

The pink boy's mouth drops open. His eyes flick from his friends' faces to my fist curled up as tight as an ammonite by my side.

'Have a chip while you think about it.' I hold out the polystyrene box.

Picking up a handful, he nods at the others then walks away with the exaggerated swaggers of a man trying to say that was exactly what he had planned all along. Halfway across the market, he chokes on a chillied chip.

My heart is beating hard in my throat. I keep doing that—walking into situations without thinking. That could have gone very wrong. It didn't, but it could have. It wouldn't be the first time.

My legs are wobbly. I need to sit down. Great St Mary's church is to my right, crenellations bearing their teeth at the sky. The gate into the churchyard is open and I slip through, slumping against the side door of the church. Chips spill; kebab slivers slither onto the ground. My head feels like it's been spun on my neck. The hangover must be kicking in early.

Placing my forehead on my knees, I close my eyes. The church bells clang over my head. Half twelve—Satnam will be passed out on my sofa, darts in his hand, cans scattered. I like it that someone is up there in the bell tower, ringing out the signal that you are not alone.

A fox slinks between the railings and stares at me. Its eyes flash yellow. He trots into the bushes where something white shines out of shadow. A plastic bag or something. The kind of something foxes suffocate in. Using the wall to pull myself to standing, I steady myself, still dizzy, then walk over. I reach into the bushes; the brambles bite at my

13

skin. And then I touch it, something cold and rough and flat. Pulling my coat closer round me, I crouch and peer into the brambles.

A face gleams out of the bushes. The mask of a woman's face: large and oval, a gibbous moon with big eyes, curved nostrils, sharp cheekbones, all scored in and painted. The eyes have nothing in them. Dark hair streams out—but the hair isn't attached to the mask; it's underneath.

My hand jerks away.

My knees drop onto a rope snaking out from under a tarpaulin tucked beneath the chin of the mask. I tug.

The tarpaulin crackles toward me. A glimpse of pale material. I keep pulling, gathering the canvas in—

a body
a woman
in a white dress
with black spots
torn tights, red shoes
arms crossed like a saint
around her neck, beneath the mask,
a rope bites at purple skin

The beauty queen's dress. I reach for her hand. Her palm is not cold but nothing beats in her wrist. My fingers are tacky when I lift them away. Holding her arm up nearer to the streetlight, I gently fold back her white cardigan. A letter has been cut out of the pale skin inside her wrist: a curving, embellished 'S', red and raw, the blood sticky. And further up, words have been scratched, jagged and ugly, up to her elbow.

14

THIS IS YOUR FAULT

A chill scrapes cold fingers down my inner arms.

I've heard those words said to me before. This is my fault. All my fault.

I have the same sensation of choked heart-dread as when I fall in a dream and grab at the edges of the bed. Easing my thumb under the mask, my hands shaking, I lift the heavy stone an inch, and place it back. I can't see her. No. I don't want to see her. I know the eyes of the dead and I don't want to look into hers. That's the coward I really am.

I fumble my phone out of my pocket. No signal. Nothing on the screen at all. I take off my coat and tuck it in around her. 'I'm sorry,' I say.

Running out onto King's Parade, I hold tight to the phone and wait for it to seize a signal.

15

Swallowing down a surge of sick, I turn back to but can't see her; the bushes are in the way of her body. Still no signal. Leaning against Ryder and Amies, I fiddle the battery out of the back and click it back in again. 'Come on, come on,' I shout. One bar, then two. My finger trembles as I dial. Behind the glass plate windows of the shop, academic robes are suspended: graduating ghosts.

The operator answers on the sixth ring.

'Police. And ambulance,' I say. My voice comes out cracked as if I haven't talked for days. 'I've found a body, a woman . . . outside Great St Mary's . . . I think she might be the missing girl, you know, the beauty queen. She's been murdered.' The words spill before I stop them. 'This is my fault,' I say.

Chapter Two

The Detective

Stephen Killigan's voice cracks out of the speakers: 'I've found a body, a woman . . . outside Great St Mary's. I think she might be the missing girl, you know, the beauty queen. She's been murdered. This is my fault.'

Inspector Jane Horne presses stop and leans back in her chair. 'This is what I've been called in for? I was in my pyjamas. Do you know how often I actually get into my pyjamas?'

'Not very often, ma'am?'

Jane checks Sergeant Pemberton's face for any sign of amusement—not even a twitch around his mouth. 'Too right, not very often,' she says.

16

'My first day off in . . . fuck knows and I get a lecturer who says he saw Miranda dead. Only she is nowhere to be seen. He told uniform he had to leave her to find a signal, then when he returned to her she had mysteriously disappeared.'

'I wouldn't have bothered you, only the chief said we should follow the lead. I've done an initial interview, kept him waiting as well.'

Jane looks up at Pemberton. 'You talked to the chief before me?'

'He was in the canteen when I got the call, ma'am.' Pemberton's face shows nothing.

Jane steps over the piled files on her floor and hurries down the corridor, Pemberton striding alongside. 'Tell me what you know, then.'

'Stephen Killigan, thirty-five, new senior lecturer at Sepulchre College, British, been in California most recently, says he specializes in metaphysics.'

'Great. A smart arse.'

'Says he found Miranda's body under a tarpaulin outside Great St Mary's, strangled with a rope.'

Jane's fingers curl into the hollow between her collarbones.

Pemberton continues. 'She was wearing a stone mask. With an "S" cut into her inner wrist and a message saying THIS IS YOUR FAULT on the inside of her arm. But when uniform got there they just found him crouched inside, shaking his head like any other Friday-night madman. There was no body, no sign of her having been there at all. He kept on rifling through the bushes and refused to get in the car, saying that she must be there. We've checked out CCTV, sent a dog in. The usual.'

'How did he know it was her?'

'She was wearing the dress. The one she won in.'

17

'The one that the whole country has seen pictures of. How extremely convenient,' Jane says. 'Well, if I have to do this, I may as well have some fun. I won't sleep now anyway.'

They stop outside Interview Room Two. Jane peers through the wired glass.

Stephen Killigan sits with his head in his hands, long fingers tapping at his temples. His hand slips to the table top where he traces an oval shape with his forefinger, over and over again.

'No lawyer?' Jane asks.

'He's happy helping us with our enquiries,' Pemberton replies.

'Can't be that bright, then. Phone call?'

'A friend of his, who didn't answer. Killigan didn't leave a message.'

Jane turns at the sound of DC Millins' clippity steps on the stairs. Belinda Millins holds out a file. Jane skims the pages, jiggles her hair up at the roots and marches into the room. 'Evening, Dr Killigan,' she says.

Stephen follows her with his eyes but doesn't seem to take anything in. He's shivering in jeans and a T-shirt. He puts his elbows on the table, fingers interlocked and digging into the back of his hands; his fingernails are blue.

'Can you fetch Dr Killigan some very sweet tea please, constable, coffee for me, and a jumper out of lost property. We don't want to be guilty of human rights abuses quite yet. Even if we have been called in on a hoax.'

'It's not a hoax,' Stephen says, quietly.

'Well, let's see—so far there has been no evidence of a woman dead, nearly dead, or otherwise compromised in the vicinity of Great St

18

Mary's. Bertie the sniffer dog found no trace of a fresh body, though the church gets him confused— there used to be a graveyard there and presumably there are bones about the place—and then there's CCTV, which my own DC Millins, bless her, viewed and while she picked you out wielding an umbrella that would be better off as a weather vane and chatting in the market square, standing outside Ryder and Amies, phoning us and then poking about in the undergrowth of the church like a madman who's lost his glasses, at no point do we see anyone with a body, or indeed a body at all.' Jane crosses her arms.

Stephen presses the heels of his hands into his eye sockets. 'You must have missed it.'

'There is no footage of you and a dead body. And there is a camera right by the church so no students can dare each other to nick a Freshers' week trophy.'

'I promise I am not making this up.' He looks straight at her.

Jane cocks her head to one side. He's not the usual hoaxer, the attention seeker whose only human contact is with her, the speaking clock and the thong belonging to Marina the stripper. He's attractive for one thing, kind of, and he seems to believe what he is saying. Not that he would be the first delusional Fellow in history; Cambridge has that effect on you. It seduces with its austere beauty and narrows your vision so that all you see is what it wants you to. It happened to Chris, her last proper lover. They usually take longer than a couple of weeks to lose it, though.

'You must be mad, then,' she says.

Belinda Millins comes back in with three paper

19

cups bunched in her hands and a jumper tied round her middle.

Stephen struggles into the huge fisherman's jumper, his head popping through the hole like a mad-haired jack-in-the-box. He sips at the tea and, grimacing, spits it back into the cup. 'Sorry. Funny taste in my mouth,' he says, wiping his hand over his lips. 'Before we get any further: can I have a pen or pencil, please? And some paper? I've been asking—I need to draw the mask—it's there in front of my head and I don't want to lose the details.'

Jane stares at his blue-stained fingers. She's been out with enough academics, i.e. one, to recognise a man in need of an ink-fix—pen and paper take them to a secure place: teddy bears for the tedious. He's a funny one though. 'Maybe later. Before we go any further, I'd like to know a little about you.'

He looks up. 'Me?'

'Have you been in prison?'

'What?'

She points to the tattoo of a teardrop under his right eye, just touching his skin.

'Oh, this?' he says. 'No. It means something different if you've been in prison.'

'So it's for someone who died?'

Stephen nods.

'Someone you lost?'

He nods again.

Jane taps her pen against the desk. 'I'd be stroking my beard and going "Mmmm, inter-est-ing" now, if I were a psychologist, and if I had a beard.'

'It was my mother. And therefore has nothing to do with tonight,' Stephen says.

20

'You don't seem very convinced, if you don't mind me saying.' She nudges Pemberton to take over.

Pemberton sits straighter in his chair. 'You've been drinking this evening.'

'I had three or four cans earlier.'

'The breathalyser states you had considerably more.'

Stephen's forehead folds up. His confusion seems genuine. His pupils are so wide that they're encroaching on his eyeballs.

Pemberton continues. 'Would you say you were drunk enough to hallucinate or drunk enough to make things up?'

'I don't want to be awkward—'

'Too late for that,' Jane says.

'But that's a false choice you've given me. I was a little drunk, yes, but I did not hallucinate. And I'm not lying.' Stephen's nostrils flare.

'Have you hallucinated before?'

'I don't see how that's relevant.' Stephen stares at his hands and picks at a greying plaster on his palm.

Jane takes a gulp of coffee. 'I think we may be straying into professional head doctor territory, so just tell me what happened after you made the call.'

Stephen's eyes close. 'The operator told me to stay where I was, but I couldn't leave her there alone. I ran back, but the gate had been locked. I hadn't noticed anyone leave so whoever shut it must have been inside the churchyard. I climbed over the railings,' he touches the cut on the heel of his hand, 'and went back to where I had left her. But she had gone. And so had my coat, the tarpaulin and the mask. Even the food I dropped,

21

all of it—gone, cleared away by someone. Whoever it was that locked the gate.'

Pemberton looks up from his notes. 'You're sure that she was dead?'

Stephen covers his eyes with his hand. 'She wasn't breathing, and she didn't have a pulse.'

'You *thought* she wasn't breathing and didn't have a pulse, but if you were drunk, and so shocked at what you saw that you were in a state, then how can you be certain?'

'It is possible that she wasn't dead. I hope so.'

'If you aren't certain of that how can you—'

'I am certain that she was there.' He stares at us, defiant.

'And yet there is absolutely no evidence that she was. Or do philosophers not need evidence?' Pemberton is doing what he does best, making people doubt themselves.

Stephen shakes his head and goes quiet. Pemberton breathes in as if about to speak and Jane shakes her head very slightly. *Wait.* Stephen rakes his hand through his hair. 'I'd be thinking the same thing if I were you.'

'And what are we thinking?' Jane replies.

He looks up to the cracked ceiling tiles. 'That she wasn't there because she had never been there.'

'Well at least you admit that,' she says, closing the file.

'But I touched her,' Stephen says. 'I felt her skin cooling. I was there and she was there. I. Did. Not. Make. This. Up.'

'There is no need to raise your voice, sir,' Pemberton says.

'Look.' Stephen scrapes his chair back against the tiles. Swivelling his legs round, he bends and

22

tugs his left trouser leg up over his knee.

It feels too personal here, in this grey room: it feels like she shouldn't be looking. He's got a nice knee, rounded, muscled.

Holding his leg out to one side, he peers below his knee cap and excitedly taps a finger on a faint indentation that runs across, diagonally striped. 'I knelt on the rope. It happened!'

Pemberton sniffs. 'That would only be evidence if we could match the rope to the markings. And if the rope was matched to Miranda. But there is no rope. Is there?'

Stephen is silent, staring from his bare knees to his jeans. He rubs at his forehead with his middle- and fore-fingers. 'Shouldn't I be filthy if I've been on the ground?' he asks. 'I should be soaking—I knelt long enough—and—' Stephen leaps up and slaps his back pockets. His eyes spark up from inside. 'I sat down on the steps; it's been pouring all evening—I should be soaked through. But I'm not.' His accent is getting stronger the more excited he gets. Jane looks back at his notes—Scarborough born. There's something odd about people brought up within the sound of the sea, not sirens and city streets. Jane shudders at the thought of all that water.

'You all right, guv?' Pemberton whispers.

She nods a curt nod.

Stephen paces from one side of the room to the other.

'Sit down, please, Dr Killigan,' she says. 'You're the first man I've met who gets aroused by proving himself wrong.'

'Was there anything on the security tape, anything that would have me kneeling on something that could approximate a rope?' He waves his hands as he talks, the outsize sleeves flapping about his wrists.

Jane shuffles through the notes. There's reference to him stumbling, but not falling to the ground. 'I can't tell you that,' she says.

'And I didn't kneel on anything earlier in the evening, but the marks are there. And fading. I don't know what happened,' he says, spreading his hands on the table, 'but I know that it did.'

'That makes no sense, Dr Killigan. But let us just go along with you for a moment. Let's just say for the sake of argument that you *did* find her body. And that she had been murdered. Can you explain to us what you meant by the phrase "This is my fault"?'

He blushes. 'I said in my statement. Those were the words scratched on her arm. Above the cut out "S".'

'So it wasn't a confession?'

'I was repeating what I saw on her arm.' He shifts in his seat and looks down at his knees.

'It sounds very much like a confession to me. Does it sound like a confession to you, Sergeant Pemberton?'

Pemberton nods his head. There is a mean glint in his eyes.

Jane continues. 'You realise that if we *do* find her body, a statement like that would not look good for you. If you had explained on the phone, then maybe it would be justified. But you didn't, did you?'

Stephen slams a fist on the desk. 'We are wasting time. I don't know what happened to her but I can see only two explanations. Either someone, probably her killer, moved her when I left to call the police, an act I thought would help her, not get in the way, or I made a mistake and she wasn't dead and is now in pain somewhere in the city. Either way you should be out looking for her. Charge me, don't charge me, I don't care: she has to be found.'

Jane stands up, anger blocking her breath. 'We have been looking for Miranda for a year—you couldn't possibly know how much effort and money has gone into trying to find her. I don't know whether you're trying to make a name for yourself or whether you've cracked—either way I've had enough. DC Pemberton, as he is so interested in wasting time, would you please charge him with wasting ours?' She turns back when she reaches the door. 'Actually don't—he's had enough attention already. Put him in overnight to sober up.'

Jane pushes open the door and waits for it to slam before placing her forehead to the cool wall. She kicks at the skirting—a year on and she can't help letting it get to her. An overtime of officers at the festival and Miranda had still disappeared, leaving only her Miss Cambridge crown and a clump of her hair.

Jane watches through the window as Pemberton finishes off the interview. Stephen seems to be pleading. A silverfish of a shiver slinks down her neck as his finger arcs on the table top, sketching over and over the face of an invisible mask.

Chapter Three

Every Murderer Needs a Detective

The telephone insists from the hallway. I will not answer it. I do not like telephones. Calling cards are preferable. I should get some made up, but I cannot find the enthusiasm. I am so terminally bored that I am considering eating this apple with its skin on. Even the thought of murder exhausts me. Yesterday I hovered by the self-help section of Heffers, flicked through bright-jacketed paperbacks by people with suspect letters after their names. I moved away when a woman smiled encouragement at me, while she held a guide to keeping a man. Everyone needs challenge, a reason to live, one book said, and recognition by others. I cannot disagree. But there is little chance of either at this time.

The telephone shrieks again.

'Yes?' I say into the receiver. It has the pockmarks of a confession booth.

'Have you seen the paper today?'

'I told you not to call me.'

'I'm sorry, I didn't know what to do.' His voice sounds like it did when we first met—unsure and weak. A glass with a crack in its stem.

'What is the problem, exactly?'

I hear him rustling the newspaper. 'Someone's found her. He lost her again, but he found her first.'

I sit down on the Louis XVI that I stole from the seventeenth. 'That is not possible.'

'You always said that more was possible than I thought. And what am I supposed to believe? You refuse to tell me what you did with her.'

'I told you that you didn't need, or want, to know. How do you know it is her?' It cannot be her. There is no way it can be.

'I contacted a friend at the station. They think it was a hoax; there is no evidence that she was there. The thing is, she was wearing the mask.'

I wrap the cord round my wrist. 'Now that is interesting. Who found her?'

'A colleague of mine, a new lecturer at the college. In philosophy. He found her outside Great St Mary's.'

'Did he? Well, that is not where she is supposed to be.' I open my notebook to double check the dates. 'If it is her then something has gone very awry.' I have not been surprised in a very long time. A feeling of lightness rises to my lips. They tip up at the ends.

'How can you laugh? You said everything was under control, that all would be fine if I did what you said.'

'And it will be fine. More than fine, perhaps. You could come out of this better than we thought.'

'What? How?' He is growing unfocused, unclever. I am not surprised. Not many people can accustom themselves to death without losing their grip. What they do not realise is that grip, as it were, is overrated.

'Do you know him?'

'I met him very briefly, at the faculty welcome meeting.'

'And what was your initial impression of him?'

'He made me laugh; I can't remember what he said. He never kept still. I liked his face. I would have talked to him more but I had to go home.'

I twist the apple stalk. There is only one way this Fellow could have found the body, and that makes him very interesting indeed. There has never been a *way I could be caught before. I wonder if he is up to the task. I wonder if I am.*

'We can use him to our advantage,' I say to Robert. 'For the next phase. He could be framed.'

'I couldn't do that.'

'Would you prefer a lifetime in prison? Or you know what the other option is. I could make that happen.'

'What would you do to her?' he says.

I replace the receiver, pick up the apple and go into the kitchen. Taking a knife, I peel off its skin in one long twirl. If human skin could be removed so easily then I could make a wig of pre-Raphaelite curls, and sell it. There's always a purchaser for the residue of crime.

Eating the nude fruit, I realise I am still smiling. Someone has achieved the impossible and I thought I was the only one capable. The apple skin lies on top of the bin and I have a challenge to win.

Chapter Four

Warning

I didn't sleep. Couldn't. And not just because of the thin blue mattress or the screams from the cell next to me from a man calling for his mother. I hammered on the steel door all night, demanding to talk to the chief inspector, another detective, the cleaner, anyone who would take me seriously and look for Miranda. All I got was a slammed hatch and a cup of tea that tasted of the sea.

I step out of the police station onto a street slick

with leaves. It's already mid-afternoon; the day is about to give up and go home. After the harsh strip lights of the cell, everything is grey and washed out; from the cars scooting water onto the kerb to the faces of people hurrying into shops, heads down against the mist and rain as if all is normal. To them, all *is* normal, at least as normal as life gets, while for me the silhouette of that stone mask hangs in my mind every time I close my eyes.

I need to go back to the church. There must be something I missed. I cross Parker's Piece, past the siren light of the wrought-iron lamp-post in the centre: the famous 'REALITY CHECKPOINT' named after the words scratched into its base by, it's thought, a University of East Anglia lecturer to mark the point where the pampered world of the ancient university meets the authenticity of the real town.

I switch on my phone and a line-up of texts beeps through from Satnam, starting with 'Where's my kebab, loser?'; progressing to 'If you've pulled then she'd better have a dirty best mate'; and ending with 'The senior tutor's looking for you. On a Saturday. What've you done, mate?' He's also left messages on my voicemail, as has Frank Utter, the senior tutor, requesting that I see meet him at the Mistress's Lodge 'at your earliest possible convenience to discuss, informally at this stage, your Great St Mary's discovery'. The sarcasm in his voice is clear, even over the scratchy line.

Here a fortnight and I'm in trouble already.

Shivering and soggy in a borrowed jumper, I walk until I find a charity shop that's still open. It's a posh one: appliances come with plugs and the correct instructions; the woman behind the counter

29

has a steam-cleaned face and a twin-set that fits; everything costs more than twenty-five pence. A lot more. But it still has the scent of dead men's shoes, despite the air freshener that exhales every minute as if it too is holding its breath because of the smell. You can't Febreeze the in-between out of a charity shop.

'We're closing in five minutes,' the volunteer says. She stares at me then down to her paper and back again.

'I won't be long,' I say.

The men's coats are on a rail at the back. I try on a wax jacket first: it'll keep me dry, or at least no wetter than I am already. I pull back a curtain to see myself in the changing room mirror. I look like a Tory. At any moment I might shoot a duck and stick its head on the wall.

Sorting through the jackets, I find, at the end of the rail, a black coat lined with torn blue silk. It slips on. As I walk around the shop, the tails of the coat slink around my ankles like Midnight, my tomcat when I was a child. I take it over to the counter and the woman glances at the paper on the surface. On the front cover of today's *Cambridge Evening News*, snapped mid-laugh for the faculty noticeboard, is a photo of me, and above that a headline: 'PROFESSOR IN BEAUTY QUEEN HOAX'.

The woman glares, shakes her perm. She takes the money in silence and slams the till tray. The door tuts closed behind me.

*   *   *

The market is civilised by day, with its coloured

30

canvases billowing like sails in a flotilla of stalls and traders selling their cheese and fish and fudge and pumpkins: only the silent fast food vans and remnants of police tape flapping around the ankles of the church suggest that the night brings its own surprises.

I duck under the tape and climb the gate, checking the bushes again for anything that can prove to the college, the police, the press and me that I'm not mad.

'You won't find anything there,' says a man standing in a shabby coat with a metal detector. 'We've already looked, haven't we, Moonie?' he talks towards his feet.

I look down, expecting to see a dog, but there isn't one. At least I am not the only mad man in Cambridge.

$$* \qquad * \qquad *$$

Sweat drips down my back as I wait outside the Mistress's Lodge. I've been fired in my first month of a new job before, but not since I was fourteen and working in a sweet shop where I gave away fistfuls of licorice to Janice Leyter. She didn't live up to her name.

'Stephen Killigan?' a small, bald man asks. I nod and he escorts me through a tall hallway into a room of cream sofas and soft pink walls. You could spend days searching for a lost marshmallow in here. 'Please take a seat,' he asks. 'I'll call you in when they are ready.'

'What's your name?' I ask.

'I'm Anwar,' he says. 'The butler.'

'Nice to meet you, Anwar.'

31

I didn't think butlers existed still; I thought they had gone the way of bowler hats and the British Empire. I hear him on the phone in the hall, mentioning my name.

A grandfather clock ticks outside the door. Its tock is sluggish: a cog is sticking somewhere. If Da were here he'd be in there murmuring to the mechanism, polishing and soothing till it smiled again. Of course if Da were here it would mean I was speaking to him. Or rather he was speaking to me.

The doorbell rings.

Mutters come from the entrance hall. Frank Utter strides into the room. He pauses, and then limply shakes my outstretched hand. I met him at the drinks party for new staff. He talked about lizards all evening to whoever would listen, which was definitely not me. Someone whispered to me over the drinks table that his usual method for interviewing potential undergraduates involves showing the birthmark on the back of his neck and then posing candidates an epidermal Rorschach test. One lass said it resembled a teapot and he rejected her there and then, just because he doesn't like tea. How can you trust a man who doesn't like tea?

'Come through,' Anwar says, holding open one of the double doors. I follow Utter into a conference room that looks out onto the Fellows' Garden. Around a large round table sit Professor Claire Fidster, recently appointed as the first Mistress of Sepulchre College; the bursar, whose name I can't remember because all I can think of is that his head, smooth and ovoid, looks as if it has been kept in a jar of pickled heads; and

Tara Yarrow, a gorgeous Law lecturer up for a professorship this year despite being only in her early thirties. Tara Yarrow is the only one who smiles at me. Utter sits down next to Claire Fidster and pulls his chair nearer hers.

'This is an extraordinary gathering of the disciplinary committee, Dr Killigan,' she says. 'I have been informed that this,' she holds up a copy of the front page of the *Cambridge Evening News*, 'is already being reported online and will be in the national papers tomorrow.' She skims through the article, sucking in air through her teeth. She nods at Utter, shaking her head as if too shocked to continue. I bet she was a hit at the ADC Theatre when she was a student.

Utter clears his throat. 'Now we can all appreciate youthful high-jinks and we tolerate a certain amount from students, first-year students, but not thirty-five-year-old lecturers.'

The bursar takes over. 'You may not be aware, Dr Killigan, but the college is experiencing some financial troubles in this global economic crisis. This is very serious indeed and will affect how we can help our students.' He bobs in his chair. His voice is cracked around the edges. 'We are embarking on a large-scale fundraising drive to complete the cleansing of the college buildings and to repair the roof of the Great Hall. Any adverse publicity could be devastating for the college at this time. I—'

'Aren't you going to ask me how I am?' I say.

'Excuse me?' asks Utter.

'Seeing as I've been through trauma, questioning and an uncomfortable night in a police station, I was just wondering when you were going to ask me

33

how I was. Seems a reasonable thing to do, don't you think?'

Tara Yarrow covers a laugh with a cough, badly. She looks out of the window to avoid catching my eye.

Frank Utter glares at her. 'We have decided to give you a warning, this time, on the understanding and word from you that you admit that it was an ill-judged prank and steer clear of the police and the press. Any further trouble and we will consider invoking the dismissal process of your probation period.'

They all look at me. Anger boils up. 'It was not a prank,' I say, quietly.

They all look at me.

I look out to the garden. A white bird lands on a rockery and for a moment I'm home on Whitby beach, gulls gunning for my chip butty.

'It was not a prank.' I say it louder this time.

'Either that or you are insane, Dr Killigan: which would you rather on your employment record?' Claire says. Her eyes are as tough as the bark on the trees outside.

'I'll take insanity, then.' I say this cheerily but what I really want to do is crawl under this desk and tell everyone to go away. 'Look. I understand that you do not want this in the press. It was not my intention that it would become a drama, and I suspect it wasn't Inspector Horne's intention either. I reported what I thought was a crime. That is the full story. I am sorry if that has caused problems. I feel right honoured to work at the college, but I will not lie for it.'

'That *is* a fair argument,' Tara says, leaning forward. 'And a just apology. He was doing what anyone should do if they found a body. In my opinion it is not right to ask him to do more purely because the college is in financial difficulties. That is not Dr Killigan's fault.'

The bursar turns more yellow.

The Mistress pauses. Then nods. But her mouth twitches.

Utter turns his back on me. I can see his birthmark. It looks like Margaret Thatcher.

*   *   *

Satnam taps his watch when I walk through his door. 'And where do you think you've been, young man? I was up all night combing the streets, calling your name, looking under cars.'

'No you weren't—within minutes of me leaving you were either snoring or looking at porn. I know you.'

He grins. 'Busted. So what's all this about the beauty queen then? Was she up to much?'

'You are—'

'Incorrigible, I know. That's me.' He turns away from his computer screen and blinks. 'You look awful,' he says.

'I've felt better,' I say, sinking down into his old armchair next to a neat pile of shirts. He irons them with a set square to hand.

Satnam walks over to the fridge and takes out two beers. 'What did I tell you about keeping your head down till you were established?'

'You told me to keep my head down till I was established.'

'So how come your stupid face is on the front page?'

'Leave it, would you? I've had enough from Utter and the Mistress. And what's the problem? Shouldn't people be more concerned with finding the girl?' On the wall, next to his dartboard, is a poster of the Circinus Galaxy black hole. I stare into its white-vapour centre.

'So do you want to go out and forget all about it, or what?'

I close my eyes. The mask is still there. 'I've got to find out what's going on. Tomorrow. All I'm good for now is bed.'

'And not much good for that either, from what I've heard. Oh come on, it's a joke. You're no fun anymore. Well, I'm off out, even if you're not. Wait a second—' he hands me a small pile of letters. 'I picked these up for you.' He slaps me on the back as I turn to leave. 'Sleep well, mate. Leave all this alone. Trust me.'

*   *   *

My room is damp and cold. I pull the duvet around me and wait for the electric heater to warm the two-metre semi-circle around my bed before I get changed. I should listen to Satnam, if no one else. I should put last night down to bad beer and shove it in a drawer with other events that make no sense. That would be best for everyone, except for the girl in the mask.

I open the post under my duvet.

The first is from the college chaplain, offering his ear should I ever need to discuss any 'spiritual or psychological matters'; the second is a credit card bill that I'd rather not see and the third one:

Dear Stephen

I read of your shocking experience and would like to extend a consoling hand of friendship, from one philosopher to another. Cambridge is a strange place; strange things have certainly occurred to me.

Do drop in for tea one afternoon. I am often around on Wednesdays as they are, I feel, the middle and measure of a week; days of purpose and potential. I am afraid, for your heart and mine, that my rooms are at the top of the Mill Building. Please come; I give good cake.
Yours etcetera

Dr Robert Sachs
MA (Oxon), DPhil (Cantab)

Post-script: when in doubt, hold things up to the light.

I turn the words over in my head and the letter in my hand. I hold the paper up to the heater. The orange light stares through the paper, picking out the outline and unseeing eyes of the stone mask.

Chapter Five

Reading Room

The University Library looms over the Cam like a silent-movie villain. There's also the whiff of a crematoriun about the dark brick tower in the centre: as I walk up the steps I expect it to puff out the ashes of books and brains, laughing maniacally.

Sitting at one of the search computers, I find the texts and articles I need for the lecture on causality I'm giving next week, and an anthropology text on masks. Halfway through jotting down the locations, I'm poked in the arm by the bloke next to me, someone I recognise but don't know by name. He smirks and nods over to an elderly woman in purple tartan, perching on the edge of her chair. She is staring at me, bobbing her head between monitors for a closer look.

Cocking her head to one side, she scrabbles in her handbag and pulls out a square magnifying glass. She rubs at a mole on her chin and peers through the glass, eyes roaming round my face with the air of Da assessing a broken clock. She nods, and stands up. 'My name is Iris Burton. I'll be seeing you,' she says, winking through the magnifier. She walks away, dragging a wheeled suitcase behind her.

You get all sorts here. A library is a sanctuary, a paper city where the emotionally homeless can find haven between the pages. It is for me.

As I gather the books from different towers, alleys and side streets of the library, avoiding trolleys and third years, the UL undead, as they lurch from shadow to shadowed stack, my heart calms down for the first time since last night. I carry them through into the Reading Room and build a hardback wall around me. The Reading Room gives me goose bumps—it is the Platonic Form of the library: dark, panelled in wood, desks with studded leather and little lamps, encyclopedias and reference works scaling the walls, the shuffle of chairs and pages, the tap of laptops, the shush of heels of hands across paper, a skeletal, spiral staircase going up from the counter to a secret librarian hide where, I imagine, they straighten jackets and Dewey Decimal System their lunch boxes.

I start on the books, pulling out *A Treatise of Human Nature* from the middle of the stack. The pile teeters and topples in book Jenga. Scholars opposite me glare up from their notes. I wink back.

I'm looking for a quote in Hume on necessary connection; it's in here somewhere. I flick through the tightly bound pages, scanning line after line. The image of the girl keeps coming to my mind, lying alone in the bushes.

'Would you stop doing that? Please?' the girl at the next desk says. Her jaw is clenched. She has ink on her lip.

'What?' I ask. 'I'm reading; this is the Reading Room: I am doing exactly as directed, which I'm not happy with, now I come to think about it. Have you thought about going to the Complaining for No Reason Room?'

'You're still doing it.' She points to my hand.

My fingers tap on the leather of the desk—*rat a tat tat. Rat a tat tat.* And now the words in my head:

this is your fault, this is your fault. A familiar surge of guilt floods me. I'm matching the girl with other memories: I know that—I've had enough therapy. Well, maybe not enough. But how could it be my fault? It wasn't a message for me; it couldn't be. But it was for someone.

Moving Hume to one side, I sketch the mask, what I can remember of it anyway. The narrow nose and flat cheekbones, the outline of Miranda's body underneath. But if I can't be sure, what's the point? Maybe I made it all up anyway: a case of a new job, bad beer and a rampant imagination.

'I'd stick to threatening Boaties with umbrellas if I were you.' The girl from last night is standing next to me, looking at my drawing. 'You got yourself in a pickle after I left.' She takes the *Evening News* out from under her arm, picks up my pen and draws a moustache on my photo.

'Pickle is one word for it.'

'Well there are plenty of other words in here if you're looking,' she says, her eyes sweeping the ceiling-high shelves.

'I mean, it was horrific. I think.'

'You think?' she says. She has a library badge with her name on: L. Carver, Restorer.

'Well, I was pissed. What if I didn't find her at all? Because she wasn't there?' Even as I talk I see it happen: the walk to Great St Mary's, the chips, the cold mask on my fingers.

'If you didn't, then you've got psychiatric problems; if you did then you've got a problem anyway as no one believes you. Which is worse?'

'I'm not sure.'

'Sure you're sure. Would you rather be insane or occupy the moral high ground?'

'Difficult one. No one wants to be mad—that would be madness—but I find the moral high ground unnerving: no one knows you're up there if you slip down a crevasse.'

She smiles, on one side of the mouth only, but it's a start. 'That's the mask she was wearing?' she whispers, slinking into the chair next to me.

'Something like it. I'm not much of an artist.'

She leans closer to look at my drawing. Her hair smells of apple shampoo. She places a hand on her neck. 'Why would you kill someone and cover their face?'

'Make it easier to kill them, maybe? Dehumanise them.'

She shivers. 'It sounds terrible, but I hope she was dead before the mask went on. I can't even wear a Halloween mask without panicking. It's too close to my face.'

'SSSSSSHHHHHHHHHHHHHHH,' says the librarian behind the desk. I can only see the back of his head but his hair is gelled back cellophane-slick. He clicks papery fingers at her without looking round.

'Nosferatu calls,' she murmurs and slips off up the staircase. I watch her go. Cambridge so far: on the one hand a dead girl in a mask, on the other hand, a living girl with a knowledge of horror. I try and go back to Hume but it's no good. He keeps mentioning bodies.

'Killigan,' her boss calls out, and I go up to collect the articles I had requested. Paper-clipped to these is a folded note saying 'I can help you find the masks' with a mobile number and a name, Lana Carver.

I join Satnam in the library cafeteria. He's making his way through a baked potato the size of a baby's head. 'I think she likes me,' he says of the woman behind the serving counter spooning cheese onto an even larger potato. 'I might just give her what she wants, if she's lucky.'

'It's a shame that so few women get lucky in that way, Satnam.'

'Enough of your cheek. When was the last time you had a date?'

'I'm not looking too shabby, actually. I met a girl last night, and saw her again today. She works upstairs from the Reading Room.'

Satnam blinks. I know it's serious when he blinks. 'Not the girl with the dark hair? Crystal stud?'

'That's her. She said she'd help me in researching the masks. Then I'll have something to go to the police with.'

Satnam stirs his coffee, round and round. He doesn't even take milk or sugar.

'What's wrong?' I ask.

'There's no need for you to get involved at all. If she *was* dead, and *did* go missing, then the police will find her eventually. Leave it to them.'

'You don't believe me.'

'It's not that. I don't disbelieve you, it's just—' He stops speaking and picks out the cucumber from his salad garnish and lays the slices flat on each other as if trying to put the vegetable back together.

'Satnam—talk or I'll chuck tomatoes at you.'

He doesn't look up from his plate. 'Her name is Lana Carver. I've liked her since I came here. So

42

that's four years now. A bit longer than a day or so.' His voice is quiet, gentle. This is the Satnam I rarely see.

'But she gave me her card; she's going to help.'

'Just don't go out with her,' he says. He glances up and his eyes are pleading. 'Promise?'

'I promise,' I say.

Chapter Six

Biscuits

'Open here' it says on the packet. Jane tugs again at the little blue strip. It doesn't budge. 'I can't be arsed with this today,' she says out loud. The mugshots on the wall stare and say nothing.

Tummy rumbling—she only had a handful of dry cornflakes for breakfast and hasn't had time for lunch—she picks up her scissors and slices at the wrapping. She slots a whole biscuit in her mouth, a trick that still prompts applause at parties but for some reason never helps her pull.

Pemberton's skinny frame looms in the glass. He reaches for the handle. Jane swivels round in her chair and fiddles with the blind till she's eaten most of the biscuit.

Pemberton stands in front of her desk, shifting from foot to foot.

'Do you need the toilet, Paul?' Jane asks. 'You should run to it if you do; you don't want to give yourself a urinary tract infection.' She holds out the packet.

He shakes his head. 'Phone call, ma'am, from

Ruth Pilkington. She wants to know what you are doing about this.' Pemberton gestures to the front page of the paper.

'Who leaked this to the press? Bet it was him. Should've known he was an attention seeker.' Jane fastens back the part of her fringe that was cut too short. She would prefer not to go back to that hairdresser's again, only they give head massages that are the closest thing she's had to affection since a golden retriever licked a Revel out of her hand at New Year's. Unless you count that night in Ely, which she doesn't.

She taps her finger on Stephen's picture. 'It's odd, though. I don't get it.'

'Ma'am?'

'Don't mind me, I was just thinking. Have you heard of it—thinking? Brilliant pastime, better than whatever you get up to when you're not here. Ten-pin bowling?' She looks down at his feet. 'Finding shoes to fit might be an issue.'

Pemberton's knuckles whiten. 'So what should I tell Miranda's mother? She's on hold; she insisted on talking to you personally.'

'God, you should have said.' Jane picks up the phone. 'Can you put Mrs Pilkington through, please?'

Pemberton flattens the pink Post-it note curling up like a fortune fish in the in-tray.

Jane grabs the note as Ryan on reception puts her through to Ruth. 'I'm so sorry to keep you waiting, Mrs Pilkington.'

'Is there any news on—on the sighting?' Ruth Pilkington asks. Her voice is shaky.

Jane closes her eyes, imagining Ruth standing in the brown-tiled kitchen. 'It wasn't a sighting,

44

I'm afraid. Though I am glad we still have hope that Miranda is alive and well. Last night's witness either made a mistake or is a hoaxer. We have no reason to think otherwise. I'm sorry that there has been no news. We're still doing everything we can.' Even if, with nothing to go on for over a year, that is very little.

'How can he say those things if they're not true? It's horrific.'

'I don't know. I'm sorry. He was cautioned for wasting police time but that is all we can do. Some people don't think of the impact they have.'

'It's the not knowing that's so hard,' Ruth says. Her sobs are barely muffled.

Jane waits till she is sure that Ruth has hung up, then replaces the phone. Opening her fist, she looks down at the Post-it. 'Phone Marion. She needs you,' it says, in her handwriting. She wrote it three weeks ago, after finding out that her one-time detective superintendent was going into the hospice. She still hasn't got in touch. But Marion wouldn't want the fuss, and anyway, she's surrounded, probably, by followers and flowers and the sycophants of the sick; and Jane has more paperwork than desk. She'll go next week.

Pemberton is staring at her.

'Don't just stand there like your balls have been hardboiled. Go and do some work, would you?' she says.

45

Chapter Seven

Murder and Mayonnaise

'There are two things all men should achieve once in their lives: the perfect mayonnaise, and the perfect murder. I have done only one so far . . . ' Professor Sachs pauses. His eyes scan the rammed lecture hall and stall when they reach my face. Glancing away, he picks up a glass from the lectern and takes a pursed-lipped swig. 'But then mayonnaise is a bastard to master; murder is altogether easier to crack.'

The students laugh obediently. The ponytails in the row below me jiggle; the boy next to me giggles, twitching like a tweed-coated fish.

Sachs frowns and holds up a big, tanned hand. 'But murder is no laughing matter,' he says. The audience shushes into silence. All that can be heard is the rumbling heating system. 'Its seriousness raises it to an art form, arguably the highest. Aristotle calls tragic characters *spoudaioi*: good, serious, superior people . . . much like myself.' He taps his hand against his corduroys until the deferential titters subside. 'The perfect murderer is serious and noble: he, or she, has a goal, however misguided that goal may be. And the perfect murder is not simply a case of getting away with it.' Sachs makes a microscopic adjustment to his bow tie. 'Anyone can get away with murder, provided he or she has sufficient quicklime and a good relationship with the neighbours.' He winks at a girl in the front row.

46

I rest my elbows on the ledge of the row in front and watch him charming the audience with an ease I'd love to possess. I barely kept twenty people awake in my lecture this morning. Sachs talks publicly about murder with the confidence and arrogance with which I talked about sex privately before I had even touched someone. He couldn't be so relaxed about killing if he *were* a murderer, but still, he keeps looking back to me, as if contemplating the strychnine he would add to my tea, should I be unwise enough to take him up on his invitation. I rustle his note out of the pocket of my new coat and, shining my phone's light through it, make the mask appear and disappear.

Sachs' loafers shush across the stage. 'The ideal, aesthetically speaking, is to compose a murder, or series of murders, with symmetry and the golden mean in mind. Though first you need the perfect initial victim. The perfect subject is physically beautiful. The pity we feel increases, and the sense of public loss deepens. Let's face it: if someone plain of face dies it's fairly sad, but if a stunner goes, it's a tragedy. We can thank the press for reminding us of that.'

Reaching into his satchel, he takes out a newspaper and opens it to the centre pages. The picture of me grins from the left; on the right, the missing beauty queen smiles beneath her crown.

Students gasp. Some cover their mouths. I pick at the holes in the knees of my jeans.

'What? Too soon?' Sachs plunges his hands in his pockets and walks down from the stage and up the steps of the lecture hall. 'Come on, you're all— well, almost all—men and women of the world. You represent the most important element in the

47

art of murder: the audience. And, let's admit it, you can't get enough. If there isn't an audience to observe and appreciate, what is the point? We all want to be seen and appreciated for who we really are; I know I do. And I'm sure each one of you lonely lot longs for it as well.' He stops by my row.

'Talking of attention seekers. Lookey here.' He points to me. The gold ring on his right hand shines under the lights. 'The lecturer who found the missing beauty queen. Only to lose her again. Careless, wouldn't you say?'

Heads crane round to face me.
I lean back and fold my arms.
The heating system plink-plinks and shudders.

After, I lean up against the cold concrete of the Philosophy building, waiting. Across the courtyard, students sit outside the cafe, their hands clamped round coffee cups, cigarette smoke posing in the air. One of them looks over at me, nudges her friend. They stare, covering their mouths as they whisper. I wave to them.

Robert Sachs stalks out, followed by students who hug their folders to their chests like love letters. Seeing me, Sachs nods goodbye to the girls on either side of him. He stops next to me, standing so close I can smell his cigar-smoked coat and violet cologne.

'Dr Killigan! I was expecting you on Wednesday for tea and a Viennese Whirl, but how charming of you to come and see me in action.'

'I couldn't wait. I wasn't expecting a starring role.'

'Sorry about that. I can't stop myself when I get

going—I saw you and couldn't resist. I'm pompous, facetious and obnoxious. But at least I know it.' Close up, his teeth are yellow and lean against each other like drunks.

'I would have been disappointed if you were any different. I've seen you give your expert opinion on *Newsnight*. Or was it *Crimewatch*?'

He laughs. 'One of the few real joys of this job is meeting public expectations of a Cambridge lecturer.' He looks down to my scuffed boots and tugs at my ripped coat pocket. 'You might think of doing the same.'

The wind kicks at a crisp packet. I dig my hands into my one intact pocket. A plant bulb sits on twists of band and twine. They didn't wash the past from its pockets. 'I'm all right as I am, ta.'

'You might think that now, Stephen. But you'll come round. It'll get you more work on the circuit. The public imagination wants us professors buttering crumpets by fires; thinking great thoughts and swishing across forbidden lawns; muttering into handkerchiefs like the eccentric geniuses we are: when really we spend the day trying to get the photocopier to work like everyone else. It's the same with an Oxbridge education: all three years at Cambridge consist of is pulling, punting and bullshitting—the three key elements of high office—but outsiders are impressed all the same. It's all surface. Take me: I might lecture on murder but, really, I'm harmless.' He looks down at the ground. There are pouches of dark skin under his eyes.

The clouds gang up on the sky. I pull my coat tighter around me. 'I'm walking back to college, if you're going that way.'

49

He beams and pats me on the shoulder. 'I would be delighted. I have a supervision with a fatuous lally who can't say "Kant" without giggling, then I've got a seminar with five earnest third years whose essays make me want to hang them by their college scarves, and then shoot myself. I fail them each week on principle. But you'll see. You'll soon lose your bright eyes and enthusiasm. One way or another.'

We walk through the Sidgwick site's soaring glass and sixties blocks on stilts, then take a shortcut through Clare College gardens. A tree leans, its remaining leaves swept into a crisp brown comb-over.

I unfold his letter. 'So what's this all about, then?'

He glances up at me. 'I like you, Stephen; you're direct.'

'I'm not sure I like *you* yet.'

He laughs. 'Very wise. You have seen no reason to, after all, other than my prodigious talent and overwhelming presence.'

'So?' I say.

'Let me say, first off, that I have no doubt you found her body, or that it disappeared. As I said: Cambridge is a curious place. It is no coincidence that so many discoveries, of all kinds, have been made here.' Sachs nods over to the sculpture of the double helix glinting in a clearing. Its Escher-esque staircases twist up and reach into wishbones. 'Seven hundred years of cerebella and their offspring reverberating in this old stone, without reference to the real world.'

'And what has this got to do with anything? You have the mask as a watermark. You obviously know something.'

'I'm trying to explain, Stephen. It's not straightforward.' Stopping by a flowerbed, he points to a red rose still hanging onto its stem. 'Beauty increases with age, don't you think?' He crouches down next to the rose, his knees clicking. Holding one nostril closed, he sniffs with a short, noisy inhalation and closes his eyes. He presses down the other nostril and sniffs again. Gently, his fingers quivering, he brushes the crease running down the centre of a petal. He smiles, softening the etched-in sneer. 'The question is,' he says, 'do I leave the rose and watch it die; or pluck it and preserve it?'

'You can't preserve it. Not for ever,' I say.

'If I protect it, I can.' He takes a pair of secateurs out of his bag and snips at the stem. The rose falls back into the bush; Sachs picks it up, wraps it in a handkerchief and places it in his satchel. He pats it and zips up the bag.

We walk down the towpath by the Cam, the stiff-spined colleges to our left. I stop and turn to him. 'Do you have anything else to say to me? Apart from allusions, that is?'

Sachs stops and scratches his cheek. The river busies itself over stones. 'You're right. I'm procrastinating because it's complicated, and I'm wary of getting you involved.'

'Involved in what?'

'Isn't that a ridiculous phrase? It's complicated. What isn't?'

'A single cell organism.'

He laughs. Beyond the goth-punk spikes of King's Chapel, a siren screams. Robert looks towards Sepulchre's clock tower. He rubs his hand over his face and massages his jowls, his skin

51

folding and ruffling. 'It's to do with my research. You've read my book, I presume.'

'Nope. Sorry.'

He barks a laugh. 'Most would lie and cover themselves, saying they adored the argument in Chapter Four. Or they'd praise the footnotes. You can't go wrong if you stroke someone's footnotes.' He sees my face and stops smiling. 'Fine. One of my areas is the aesthetics of dead things,' he says. 'Have you any interest in that?'

'I used to be a goth if that helps. And I once read poetry to a girl in a graveyard. But I don't think that, in reality, death is particularly beautiful. Or the dead.' Images again—of Grandpops, Mum, Miranda.

'Well maybe I can change your mind about that.'

'I really don't think so.'

'Well, it has always been a matter of theory before, then a colleague of mine, a one-time friend, got involved.'

'Not a . . . *thought* experiment.'

'No,' he says.

'Something to do with Miranda.'

Sachs nods. We stop at the twisting iron gates set into the tall hedge that surrounds Sepulchre. His eyes fix on me, gleaming. They are the blue of gas rings. I feel my face heat up.

Footsteps lumber behind us. Phil Bowles, the Head Porter, pants over the road, trying to knot his tie and run at the same time.

I step back to let him past but Robert holds out a hand, blocking him. 'What's going on, Phil?' he asks.

Phil grabs onto the gate, panting. Black paint flakes off in his meaty hand. 'I've been called in—

emergency—the police—Joel on duty, he let them in. Have words for him after.'

'Make sure they are strong words. Anglo-Saxon imperatives.'

'Why don't you want the police here?' I ask.

They both look at me as if I've said the most ridiculous thing in the world.

'Cambridge colleges prefer to deal with problems internally. That's always been the way.'

'One of the cleaners found something in the chapel,' Phil Bowles says. 'Got to, you know . . .' He nods at Robert and runs down the path and over the bridge.

Robert watches him, twisting off brown leaves from the ivy threaded through the hedge. 'Right, I'm off home.'

'I thought you had a supervision,' I say.

He glances back down the path to the crowd gathering outside Sepulchre chapel. 'Change of mind. It'll do her good to have a Socratic dialogue on her own. Maybe she'll find inner wisdom I've been unable to locate.'

'Are you just going to leave her there?'

'She probably won't turn up anyway. But you could always have a go at teaching her, if you are worried.' Robert's jaw slides from side to side. He's sweating, his dark blond hair clinging to his head. 'It starts here,' he mutters.

'Are you all right?' I ask.

He blinks at me a few times. 'Come and see me tomorrow afternoon,' he says. 'It's easier if I show you rather than tell you.'

'See you then,' I say and walk through the gate, kicking yellow leaves into the flowerbeds on either side of the path. When I get to the bridge, I look back. Robert is still by the gate, staring after me.

Halfway down the path, three police officers stand in a row. 'You'll have to go back,' the shortest one says to me.

'What's going on?' I ask, looking beyond him. Crime scene tape flaps at the stone chapel; the college porters stand with their arms crossed, the dead eyes and frowns they usually keep for students and visitors are turned on the police officers; a woman in a white protective suit toddles out of the chapel like a sexy Tellytubby.

I look for Inspector Horne but can't see her. The panic of feeling guilty, knowing I've done nothing wrong but knowing I must look guilty rises up. I twang the band.

'I'll have to ask you to turn back, sir,' the beauty-spotted officer says.

'Or you could let me through,' I reply.

He points back the way I came. 'Move along please, sir.'

'Seeing as you called me sir, I'll just stay here.' I walk a few metres onto the lawn, turn back and smile at him. His neck goes red. Only graduates and Fellows are allowed to walk on it—all others are warned 'KEEP OFF THE GRASS' in five languages on little plaques stuck around the hospital corners of the lawn; even the police officers keep looking at their feet to check their boots aren't straying. There are no weeds on the lawn, no brave dandelions or nettle leaves. I take the tulip bulb from my pocket, drop it on the grass and, waving to the officer, gently guide it into the ground with my heel.

Chapter Eight

The First Find

Jane leans over and brushes crisp packets, cassette tapes and biscuit crumbs off the passenger seat. 'Get in, then,' she says, looking up at Sergeant Pemberton.

Climbing into the car, Pemberton folds up like a deckchair, his shinbones pressing into the glove box. 'I could drive you, ma'am,' he says.

'I've been driving since before you were a giant, Paul,' she replies, gripping the steering wheel so he can't see her hands are shaking. 'And your job is to tell me everything you know so that by the time we arrive at the college, I know more than you do.'

The car shakes and lurches forward. She pats the dashboard. 'Reminds me of cats,' she says, 'the way they wiggle their bums before they jump. I couldn't have an actual animal; I'd kill it within a month. Think how that'd look: "New Female Police Inspector Neglects Pet to Death". So, what do you know?'

'A cleaner opened Sepulchre College Chapel as usual and found what could be a body part on one of the pews.'

'Do we know which part of the body?'

Pemberton shakes his head. 'Dr Barinder is on her way. But the college nurse says it could be an organ.'

'Human?' The image of Miranda Pilkington seen in papers, on lamp-posts, in shop windows flashes into her mind: in her tiara and sash, smiling

55

for the camera, all straight teeth and no split ends, followed by the face of Miranda's mum at the press conference, dark shadowed, aged ten years in ten days. 'No possibility of it coming from an animal? A student prank or something?'

'No idea. The college nurse didn't think so, but who knows?'

'What was the nurse doing there?'

'The Mistress said it was "So as not to waste our time".'

'I bet he did,' Jane says. 'The last thing colleges want is outsiders poking around.' She taps the window. 'What's with this traffic?'

'Protest, guv. Against the flooding of the fens.'

'Let the place drown; it gives me the creeps,' she says, then remembers someone telling her that Pemberton lives on his family's farm in Dullwater or some such fenland village. 'No offence meant, Paul.'

They pull up next to Hana Barinder's car, parked on a slant, with its rainbow sticker in the window and baby seat in the back. She's never seen the baby but believes it exists, having once sat on a wrapped-up nappy when Hana gave her a lift home. The squish had reminded her why she didn't want children.

A red-faced man greets them outside Sepulchre College. 'We've stopped anyone coming in or out, madam,' he says. His hair clings to his sweaty head and there's something weird about his eyes. 'The students in the area at the time are being kept in the Hindridge Hall. Of course the situation is made more difficult by those.' He points to the group of protestors eating sandwiches from plastic boxes on a wall, placards piled beside them. She nods at

Pemberton and he walks over to them.

'We'll take over now, Mr . . . ' she looks at his badge and resists a grin, 'Mr Bowles. This way is it, to the chapel?' She strides through the front gate and Bowles hurries alongside, his hand on her lower back. Jane walks faster, her eyes flicking round the first court. The lawn is enclosed on all sides by stone buildings, four storeys high, staircases every fifteen metres. There could be more than a hundred students and tutors living in this one area. 'What time do you lock the front and back gates at night?' she asks.

'Nine,' says Bowles. 'And we open them again at seven thirty in the morning for matins. Keyholders can come as they please.'

'And keyholders are students, tutors, anyone with any business in college?'

Bowles nods, the fat on his neck bunching up into folds.

'Do you keep a log of who goes in and out?' Jane asks.

'Not allowed to. Comes under privacy issues.'

'Who was on duty in the hours before the discovery?'

'The night porters, Geoff and Angela. I'll ask them if they saw anything.'

'No, we'll ask them,' Jane replies as they walk under the arch into the Great Court and up to the crowd of babbling students on the steps into the main hall. A lanky man stands on the lawn, with his back to her. It's the lecturer, Killigan. She can tell by that hair, sticking outwards and upways, hair you could lose your rings and watch and fingers in.

An officer jumps forward and lifts up the tape so she can walk into Sepulchre's chapel. It doesn't have the grandeur of King's: you'd barely get a hundred people inside and any prayers would hit the flat ceiling and plummet back into the pews. Resisting the urge to blow out one of the candles standing in sand, Jane walks up to the cluster of boiler-suited people.

Hana raises a gloved hand. 'This isn't pretty,' she says, pointing down at a chair. Two strips of bodily tissue sit on a prayer cushion, like squid rings cut open and laid next to each other. Underneath it is a newspaper clipping, with a picture of Miranda Pilkington.

Jane looks up. 'God. What is it?'

'Don't know.'

Jane raises her eyebrows.

'Well it could be a ventricular fold. That's part of the human vocal cords,' Hana explains. 'The edges look like they've been cut from the larynx and cartilage.' Hana looks around and sees Pemberton and her own assistant listening. 'But it could equally be something else; you know I'll have to check.'

'Could this have been from someone alive?' Jane asks. Hana shrugs. Again that image of Miranda, meshed with the home video of her as a child, singing into a ladle on the kitchen table. Jane blinks. Crouching down by the cushion, she sniffs. 'It's been pickled,' she says, standing. 'Some fucker's preserved it in a jar. I want to know how and when and who.'

Hana raises her hands, palms up. 'The vinegar could make it hard to identify.'

Jane smoothes her hands down her skirt as if trying to remove grease from her palms. 'A bit of vinegar won't get in your way. I'll bug you at the lab later.'

Outside, the crowd has replicated like germs into more students in striped scarves, holding up mobile phones. Barry and Mable from the *Evening News* are chatting with *East Anglia Today*'s John, swapping gossip as usual. John is probably hoping to swell his wages with a sneaky tabloid exclusive. He jostles a microphone in her face. 'Does this relate to the disappearance of Miranda, Inspector? Would you say you were receiving full co-operation from the college? Are you worried about failing your first high-profile case?'

'Can't you keep them away?' she shouts to her officers, Bowles, anyone. Bowles barrels forward and grabs the microphone. Jane stands on tip-toes, her shoes pinching, then bundles into the students, holding her breath and jabbing into waists with her elbows. 'Get back, would you? Haven't you got something pointless to do?' she says, all the time thinking that this might be on camera, that within minutes she would be up on Facebook, pulling a face that makes her look like the dead Les Dawson. The chief'll love that. She fumbles her way round two students, fused together in the middle so she can't get through. Why do people clump together like hair? It's as if they enjoy getting tangled up, dreadlocked.

Out the other side, Pemberton lopes towards her, tapping a notebook against his hip and whistling. 'Two of the protesters were here before dawn, setting up,' he says. 'They say someone left through the side gate.'

'Get statements from them and everyone in that hall Bowles mentioned. We've no idea what to look for at the moment. I want to talk to the cleaner that found it, the night porter, the head of college and…' Jane glances at the lawn and pulls at a piece of crisp skin on her lips. The only person on the grass is a statue of a dead, stone queen.

Chapter Nine

Jackamore Grass

The crowd gives way for me, each person stepping back but not one of them looking at my face or the box held close to my chest. It is the benefit of the uniform. Anyone can obtain a uniform—police officer, builder, vicar—yet put one on and people see Official: buttons and collars, not person. Inspector Horne will insist that a record is taken of everyone present: she knows that murderers cannot resist visiting the scene of the crime. Only this is my scene. I wrote it this way. And I am in control. I need them to know that I am here, for what I am about to do next.

I place a hand on top of the box and shake gently. The knife inside slides. It is the one I used on the subject. My Laundy amputation knife, 1780: brand new and curving like a sickle moon. Made of ivory, silver and steel. With it, in a pouch, Wiseman's Folding Tongue Depressor. Now I wait.

There is something of the guillotine crowd to these events. A child grabs my hand and I feel the pulse in her wrist reach up to a hundred. The couple next to me push forward. I cannot condemn them for the search for sensation. It is not dissimilar to what I seek. My own pulse, dull in my neck, is stable at thirty-five.

A hush nudges the gathered. The chapel door opens again and the pathologist brings out a box draped with a cloth. The crowd do not know what they are seeing yet; no magic show audience does. The police practise the illusionist's tricks—they have placed a cloth over the cushion, the severed folds placed in a sterile box ready for forensics. Last time I saw the vocal cords they were splayed on their cushion, a saint's relics.

The prayer cushion was an excellent detail. Flaubert says that the good God is in the detail and he is wrong. Neither is the Devil in the detail. How could they be when they do not exist? Murder is in the detail, for example the mask-marked paper handmade by a terrified Italian and the carvings in the wrists by my newly-skilled digits. Details are essential to murderers: concentrate on the detail, just as when you concentrate on God, and you only see a fragment of the canvas.

Inspector Horne, hair falling about her face, gestures to the pathologist who nods and gets into her car. The box is in the boot. Horne is too shambolic to be a good detective. She will always miss things. And there he is, the philosopher, loping back to his rooms, away from the police and the press. He has the haunted, hunted, hurt appearance that suggests more years have passed within his mind than within his body—the same look I had when I gazed into the mirror at his age and tried to work out what I was. I searched his room in order to get to know him, and I feel I have. He has a magpie's eye but he is not without interest. Under his bed lies a soft toy bear with a faded pink stomach and a masticated paw. I experience in myself a desire to talk to him: he knows more than he knows. I can help him through this. In my own way, of course. But it is not yet time.

The inspector is searching the crowd, looking at

61

each one of us. Her gaze bounces off me as if I'm double-glazed and she moves on. I reach into my pocket and retrieve the small music box I slipped from the bedroom of a girl who would no longer hear it. Slowly, I crouch and leave it on the path by a woman's feet. Standing now, I turn and walk again through the audience.

I look at my watch. 5,4,3,2 . . . Behind me, the music box will be opening, a tarot card of The Magus stuck inside its lid. A small plastic figure of the magician holds out the wand like a conductor's baton and, as he turns, the smoke pours out and the sparks begin, a second before the shouting kicks in.

The pathologist looks behind her at the fireworks shrieking up from the crowd. People running as she reverses, not noticing or knowing that the box I am now carrying contains the vocal cords, or that hers has been swapped for the knife that cut them.

Chapter Ten

Metaphysics and the Pigeon

'Down here,' I say over my shoulder to the first years, running down the steps.

'Are you sure?' says Felicity, who has taken very seriously my encouragement to question everything. She peers at me from the top of the stairs. 'It's very dark down there.'

I turn the map upside down but it still makes no sense. Maybe if I'd been concentrating when Bill the Porter drew it for me instead of thinking about Miranda I wouldn't have missed the beginning of a speech that ended with 'down here, round there, a smidge to your left and you can't miss it'. Turns out I can.

From the air, Sepulchre College looks like a giant laid out on the ground, a Gulliver with square hips and shoulder pads. The seminar room I've been assigned to sits with several others in the college's colon, a twisting warren that encloses the most sacred of Cambridge spaces: the wine cellar. Only the college crypt is below us. Most of these areas are out of bounds and there is a thrill among my students as we walk our hands along corridors of exposed, crumbling brick, so different from the cream stoned skin of the college.

'Is it the Berryton Room?' Nick shouts from in front.

'That's the one,' I say.

'It smells a bit,' he replies, pushing open the door to the seminar room.

'Yeah, of a tent put away when it's wet,' says Rachel, who spent her gap year backpacking in the rain. Wherever she went, rain went with her. Hopefully she'll be able to talk about something other than tents soon.

I sweep my arm over the table, brushing off dust and what looks like the crumbs of an illicit picnic. The eight of them sit down, arrange their paper and folders and pens. Somewhere down the hall a cello is playing. The low ache of the instrument keens through the walls. There must be so much these walls keep within themselves.

My students are staring at me, expectant. I check my phone to see if Lana Carver has replied to my text yet. Not that I'm expecting a reply this quickly. It's only been an hour and she probably can't have her phone on at work. Plus, it's about the mask, nothing that Satnam would disapprove of: she will have to find the time to research. I should stop looking. I leave my phone on vibrate, just in case.

'Right,' I say, standing up and wiping equations from the board. They still have whiteboards here. 'Metaphysics. What do you think it's all about?'

Silence.

'Come on. Throw anything at me. Preconceptions; ideas; apples; aardvarks; anything.'

'It's to do with ontology,' says Melanie, leaning forward in her chair. She wears John Lennon glasses and I think she just winked at me. Or it could be a tic.

'That's a great place to start. And what do you understand by "ontology"?'

Her face scrunches up. She looks at Felicity, who glances down at a neat page of notes and covers them over. 'Ontology comes from the Greek ων, ωντοσ which means *being*, or *that which is,* and λογια, *study.*' She sneaks a look back down at her notes. 'Ontology is the study of the nature of being, existence or reality.'

'So what is *being*? Or *existence*? Or *reality*?'

Her mouth opens and closes again.

'Don't worry, it's the questions that matter, and finding a secure place to move on to the next question. One philosophical question opens the door to another, and another—a Russian Doll of questions, only the questions may get bigger, not smaller. Oops: I shouldn't be using similes or metaphors to demonstrate.'

'Why not?' Paul asks. He leans his chin on his hand.

'Generally speaking, comparisons are thought

64

to take us further away from what *is*. But I think they sometimes get underneath and show you the workings. Philosophers are contrary, remember that.'

'No,' says Sidney Barnett, grinning.

'If I had gold stars I'd give you one, Sidney,' I say. 'Actually, if I had gold stars I'd keep them to myself and fashion a gold-starred suit out of them. Probably. My point is: philosophers can't even agree among *themselves* about what metaphysics is. If a flounder of philosophers was at a tea party, one would say "that's a lovely slice of cake", someone else "define lovely; I do not trust your terms"; another, "that does not constitute a slice"; another "how do you know it is cake? Just because it looks like cake and smells like cake and tastes like cake does not mean it is cake"; and the last will have eaten the cake and denied it. The last is usually me.'

Paul rummages inside his rucksack. 'I've got cake if you want it.'

'What kind of cake?' I ask.

'It depends how you define "kind". And "cake".'

'That's my boy. Now hand over the cake.' He passes a tin of cupcakes round the table. The smell of damp chocolate replaces that of damp damp.

'In metaphysics we want to know what lies beyond appearance: what *is*, not what *seems* to be.'

'The truth then,' Sadie Jones-Blent says.

'Yes, a metaphysical statement requires that the speaker state the truth.'

'Why did you lie, then, about finding the girl?' Colin asks.

Melanie gasps. 'We're talking about metaphysics, Colin, not my life.'They look at me expectantly.

65

This is what they want to know. I sigh. 'Okay. The truth as I perceive it,' I say, 'is that I found her body.'

'So something is wrong, either with your perception of reality or that of those who do not believe you,' Paul says.

I nod. Down the hall, the cello stretches into the corridors. 'Something is wrong somewhere,' I say.

*   *   *

Satnam stares at the pile of books and the broken accordion I bought on Mill Road after the seminar. 'You only buy crap when you've had a great day, or a shit day.' He looks me up and down. 'I'd say another shit day.' He goes over to the tiny kitchen area where I keep a kettle that I must de-fur and a man-size box of Yorkshire Tea.

He plonks a mug of tea down next to me and assesses my handiwork. 'Have you asked permission to put those up? 'Cos they're not gonna like it. No way.'

'How are they going to know?' I say. I take the nail out from between my teeth and look up at the clock over the mantelpiece. Twenty minutes till I meet Sachs. If he's remembered. I drill the batten into the wall. A chunk of plaster falls behind the chest of drawers. Nothing like a spot of half-arsed DIY to not quite take your mind off things. 'And if they don't like it, I'll find somewhere out of college and everyone will be happy.'

'I wouldn't be. Some spotty post-grad would probably move in above me and I'll have to put up with hearing them wank every night.'

'You're a post-grad.'

'Aah but I've got the complexion of a young plum. 'S why I'm so lucky with the ladies.'

'In all the years I've known you, I've seen you with three girls. What is it, are you worried I'll charm them away from you?'

A moment's hesitation, then Satnam throws a sofa cushion at me. I duck, my hand slips, and the shelf crashes down. I took the wood from the skip behind Heffers—along with a tricycle with two remaining wheels, a ginger wig and a lopsided umbrella plant that now sits on my desk. I start again. 'How's the analysis going?' I ask.

Satnam puts his hands behind his head and stretches out his legs. 'Nothing yet. It's the search for the golden ticket. All around the world people like me—not as fantastic as me, obviously, but they can dream—are running searches on the Collider data for the next mind-blowing discovery. Everyone's desperate for dark matter.'

'Kinky.' I fill in the wound in the wall.

'Leave that. Let's go to The Eagle,' Satnam says, standing up and stretching.

'I'll meet you there. I've got something to do first.'

*   *   *

The smells of cabbage and gravy stalk the staircase that leads up from the dining hall to Robert Sachs's rooms. The door is half open. Raised voices stop me just short of knocking.

'I can't believe you are going anywhere near him, Robert.'

'You have to trust me; it's for the best. I know it sounds bad but there are things I can't tell you about at the moment.' Robert's voice is different, softer.

'You've let me down, Robbie. Again.' Footsteps clip towards the door.

I step back into the bay window. A woman, sixty-ish, tall, stiff-backed and striking, like a stretched Judi Dench, walks out, jaw thrust forward, fists clenched. She sees me and takes off her glasses. Her eyes are the same blue as Robert's.

The anger on her face is swiped away with a smile. 'Are you one of Robert's students? A pleasure to meet you,' she says, holding out her hand.

Sachs appears in the doorway. 'He's a colleague, Julia. Although I understand that everyone seems young compared to us.' She flinches and smoothes her short hair.

'Punctuality is a sign of an unimaginative mind, Stephen,' he says, turning to me. 'You wouldn't want to give the wrong impression. Meet my sister, Julia. She's off to teach the world to screech.' Covering his mouth, in a mock whisper he says, 'She's a peripatetic music tutor. She's been giving lessons to Sepulchre's string section.'

'You say peripatetic like it's an embarrassing disease,' I say.

'It is as far as Robert is concerned.' Julia glances at her brother and back to me. Her eyes disappear into smile lines. She touches him on the arm, nods to me and walks down the staircase.

Robert, a little smile on his face, gestures me through into a large seminar room. 'Wine?' he asks. I shake my head. 'Coffee, then. Make yourself comfortable, would you?' he says, walking into a smaller, adjoining room. 'I won't be long.'

68

An oval table surrounded by a dozen chairs takes up the centre of the room. Two leather seats are placed in the bay window. As I sit down, the armchair croaks like a Mafioso toad.

Sachs comes in with a coffee tray, then returns carrying a plate with a metal cloche on top and places it on the table.

Sachs eases himself down in the chair opposite. 'So, how are you finding Sepulchre?' He crosses his legs and smoothes his crinkle-cut corduroy trousers.

'I like it. And Cambridge. I am not sure the feeling is mutual. If recent events are anything to go by, my reputation's shattered before I've even started.'

Sachs smiles. 'I wouldn't worry. It'll soon blow over. Anyway, notoriety gets you attention. There'll be quick-draw knickers across the city: and I can guarantee you that every one of them will either want to know if you really found her, or to save you if you're making it up. To the ladies of Cambridge you're a tortured soul to untwist.'

'I can untwist myself.' Though part of me would rather not. 'Can we get to the bit where we talk about real things, please.'

His hands form a steeple shape in his lap. 'Of course. I am sorry we were interrupted yesterday. I am afraid I didn't make much sense.'

'You didn't. Well, not much anyway. You said that you were involved in an experiment that had something to do with Miranda.'

'I did. And I am.'

'You still are?'

Robert's cheek twitches. He nods.

'Do you know where she is?'

He shakes his head. 'No. I don't. He keeps many

69

things from me.'

'He?'

Sachs leans forward and places a hand on my knee. 'Look, Stephen. I like you. I don't want you to get involved. It can only go wrong for you from here. If you leave now you can get on with your research, put finding Miranda down to a bad kebab. Or you can stay, I'll show you how I got to this point and you can help me stop my friend from doing more damage. What do you think?'

'Is this the man your sister was talking about?'

'It is.'

'And he is responsible for Miranda's murder?'

Sachs pauses ever so slightly. 'He is.'

I grab Sachs's sleeve. 'Who is he? Do you have any evidence? Anything that we could take to the police?'

He pulls away. 'Why is this important to you?'

I have hardly slept since seeing that night. If I drift off even for a moment, I hear the tarpaulin sighing and crumpling; I see her cut-out flesh. There is a point when climbing the one hundred and ninety-nine steps up to Whitby Abbey that you might as well keep going up, or down, even if you are not halfway there. 'You said you would show me, so show me,' I say.

He shrugs and heaves himself up, moves over to the table, and lifts the cloche with the flourish of a hotel magician. I smell something sweet and metallic. A dead bird lies on a page of *The Times*. A pigeon with a yawning wound in its side, one grey eye open.

'I found it on the window ledge and put it in the fridge.' He pours cream into my coffee.

70

The pigeon's neck is at an angle, ruffled and scraggy. 'Its neck's broken.'

'Cats,' he says.

'Do many cats get up here?'

'Cats and tax inspectors get everywhere, Stephen. You've got to watch them. Don't look like that. The bird's dead. Give it some respect.'

The purple shimmer of the pigeon's feathers gives him a clerical air. I stir brown sugar into my coffee for something to do with my hands. I don't even take sugar. This wasn't what I was expecting. I don't know what I was expecting.

'This is part of an experiment, Stephen. Pick it up, if you want. Consider it from an aesthetic standpoint.'

Standing, I feel unsteady, as if the bubble in my spirit level has been flipped on its side. Sliding my hands under, I lift the pigeon gently until he lies close to my chest, head on palm, body light on my forearm. For a moment I think I feel his heart, then realise it's my pulse beating hard in my wrist.

'How does it feel?' Robert says.

'It feels wrong to be assessing him. I feel I should call him something.' I think for a moment. 'Albert.'

'How does Albert feel?'

'Cold. The way glass is cold. And vulnerable.'

'But he's dead.'

'Yes.'

'Then how can he be vulnerable?'

'He can't defend himself anymore. Like the original owner of whatever they found in the chapel yesterday.'

'Albert wasn't a master of defence when he was alive. What you mean is, you could do anything to his body.'

71

'Not me. And I don't mean that.' I lay Albert down and gently close his little eye. 'Have you heard anything about what happened?'

Robert walks round the table to stand next to me. 'I feel more alive standing next to something dead. Don't you?'

I swallow a memory. 'I'm no more alive than I was an hour ago.'

'That's not true, is it? What were you doing an hour ago? Nothing special, I'd imagine.' He takes a sip of coffee and looks around the room. 'Bookshelves are the ribs of a room, don't you think? And books the lungs. Talking of things breathing. Or, rather, not.' He prods at Albert's black-tipped wing with a fountain pen.

'I don't know what we're talking about anymore,' I say. 'I was asking if you knew anything about what the police found.'

'You are a very curious fellow, Stephen. You like to know what's going on, that's commendable, but the quest for knowledge can begin to look like a hunger for gossip if you are not careful.'

'I'm not interested in gossip. I want to know if the police found anything to do with Miranda.'

He sighs. 'From what I can gather it was a body part. But I don't want to talk about it; it makes me feel queasy. If we could get back to my experiment—I'm trying to explain that beauty is subjective. When I look at Albert here, I see feathers of a colour equal to, I don't know,' he sweeps his hands in an arc, 'to dawn over London. And that is tripled—doubled—I don't know what the formula is yet—but it's dramatically improved by Albert being dead.'

He has a point. Normally I think of pigeons

as ridiculous birds that walk like Egyptians, but Albert's lying there and my stomach is tugged like it's being pulled down a plughole.

'Pathos is an aesthetic experience,' Sachs continues. 'This flying rat is getting far more attention dead than he did when alive. It's what suicides count on.'

'No it isn't.' That came out louder than I wanted. I look out of the window at the live pigeons on the window ledge, squawking and pacing like bad actors rehearsing Shakespeare.

He tips his head on one side and assesses me. 'Maybe. I'm being flippant—I do that. But I stand by my theory—death makes anyone more beautiful.'

'You've no idea what you're talking about. Reading about death: that's an aesthetic experience, it connects with the human condition—wasted years, there's pathos there—an actual body? Rotting? Makes people run screaming out of hospitals. Dead bodies are not beautiful. This isn't a game. I'm not playing.'

'You're right,' Robert says. He seems older, tired, the shadows deeper under his eyes. He picks up the cloche and goes to place it over Albert.

'Don't,' I say, 'I'll bury him.'

*   *   *

Satnam sways into me as I fumble with the lock on the tiny door that's cut into the college's front gate. I feel like Gulliver stepping back into Lilliput. I've left some of my anger and disappointment in the wall beside the dartboard at The Eagle, washing down crisps with pints but as we pass the dining

73

hall, the lights shining through the stained glass, I look up and see Sach's light still on.

'I'm gonna get a tattoo like one of yours,' Satnam says, slapping me on the back.

'I wouldn't. Tattoos are personal. Should be based on something in your life.'

A policeman stands by the chapel. His torch picks out our feet as we stumble past.

Leaving Satnam struggling to open a box of cornflakes, I climb up to my set. There's a brown parcel outside the door. Taking it through to my study, I slump down on the sofa and stare up. The ceiling does a fandance over my head. I go to put my feet up on a box of books, but miss, my boots clumping onto the floor. The books are in a different place: not by much, maybe eight inches or so. Looking around my study, other things have moved: my phrenological head has turned away from me; the striped Victorian bathing costume on the wall has its arms crossed, and Bandit holds a fresh rose between his claws. I search my rooms but there is no one here. I'll kill Satnam if it was him.

I pick up the parcel, untie the twine, slip a finger under the edge of Sellotape running down the centre of the parcel and rip it off. Layers of bubble wrap surround something heavy and hard. In my own game of pass-the-parcel I remove sheet after sheet until the last one folds open and in the centre sits a stone mask. Taped to the painted mouth is a note.

'It doesn't stop at pigeons,' it says.

Chapter Eleven

Hinc lucem et pocula sacra

Stephen Killigan leans out of his window, looking for whoever left his parcel. He does not see me, but then he is not meant to. I am on the bench, sitting under the lamp-post; he stares into shadows instead of light. People assume that trouble lives in darkness; they forget that it is the little twist of light that causes shadows.

He locks the window but does not leave—he is doing something, reaching out to the glass, moving his hand down, and up, and across. I stand, move around the willow tree and across to the wall, approaching the window from the side. Killigan stares at the pane, then walks away. I walk closer. On the window in black pen is a grid, of two vertical lines, and two horizontal crossing them. In the centre square he has made an X. Noughts and crosses. He has left a game for me.

I walk over the road, holding my wrist. My heartbeat has stepped up. A fizzing starts at my sternum and moves upwards. Now THIS is what I have been missing: after years of breathing mist onto mirrors so I know I'm alive; of letting the fire burn to the grate; letting toast burn to black; letting people go unmurdered. I feel a surge. An excitement that has not been there in centuries. I will do this job right; I will make it more beautiful than Robert can imagine. I feel the cold stones with my hand and black certainty removes doubts like Swarfega. I need complexity, and someone who knows what it is to Travel. If he knows yet that he can.

Chapter Twelve

Harry Zappa and The Onion

Harry Zappa and The Onion, the famous tattoo parlour, is at the far end of Mill Road, a street of charity shops, betting shops, pawn shops, junk shops, shuttered shops which cuddle into the warm walls of Caribbean restaurants and greasy spoons, shops that sell bolts and nothing but, shops that sell anything but bolts, bong sellers, curry houses, head shops and halal butchers. In any other British inner city, it'd be a normal road; in Cambridge, compared with the gowns, the ghosts, the Latin susurrations at Formal Hall, Mill Road has all the magic of real life.

Harry Zappa's has a black and white striped frontage and welcomes the tattooed and soon-to-be-so with a painted smile on the window and a motorised sign of a sugar skull and a silver onion that swings and creaks like a haunted house door. I touch my bag for reassurance—the mask is in the front section, swaddled in bubble wrap. I can't put it down. If I leave it in my room, I start getting anxious, so I carry it with me, take it out to lunch and stare into its face.

Inside, the buzzing of needles sounds like a metal insect cleaning its limbs. The whole place smells of Dettol. The walls are blackberry-coloured, the pigment so deep and rich I could stick my hand in to the wrist and pull it out sticky with jam. Gold writing stands out against the purple, listing in twisting letters the famous rules:

1. Go with your first instinct—your second instinct stinks
2. When it hurts, hold on to a tin of halved peaches
3. Never interrupt The Onion when The Onion sings.

There is no one behind the counter, only a faded red leather chair and a skeleton holding a jar marked 'TIPS', in its metacarpals. I crouch and look beneath into the deep glass cabinets filled with parts of dolls, letters from clients, photos of tattoos fading over time. A human skull sits on its own in the centre cabinet, tattooed with roses and briars.

'The needle pedals straight on the bone,' says The Onion, standing in the doorway to the staffroom wearing a dark vest and striped pyjama bottoms. She holds a mug of tea printed with the motto 'Skin King'. 'The skull is the only place in the body where you are guaranteed to keep your tattoo, as long as you have a skull, of course.' The Onion moves behind the counter, arms crossed. As she lifts the mug, a circus tent flexes its flaps over her bicep and a bearded woman with the body of a carousel horse rides out over her breastbone.

She turns and points at the concentric rings covering the back of her bald head. 'They will be with me, even if I am not. Hurts like a particularly pointy Hell, of course. But then, for something to stay with you, you have to hurt.' She grins. Her eyes are the same green as the ink of the serpent that coils around her neck. 'When they dig up my bones, "there lies The Onion", they'll say.'

She sits down behind the counter and plonks

her feet up on the counter. I've seen pictures of her tattoos in magazines, and have the same tingle and thrill of recognition when I see her soles, covered in prime numbers of different sizes and fonts, as when I stood on the stripes outside Abbey Road. I've wanted to come here since I read an interview with her about the philosophy of tattooing: 'of course it is a mind/body issue, you stupid man; your inside becomes your outside,' she said to the interviewer. 'What a ridiculous question.'

'You're Stephen,' she says, running an arrow-tattooed finger down the appointment list. 'Here for Harry.' She glances to the door at the far end of the parlour. 'He won't be long. He had a fainter and had to sit her down with a glass of Coke and a Curly Wurly. Silly girl hadn't had her breakfast.' The Onion cleans her tattooing machine with a cloth. 'I hope you've eaten. He won't be as patient with another wobbler.'

'I had a fry up over the road.'

'Best brekkie this side of Brixton,' The Onion says, nodding slowly. 'What they can't do with some olive oil and a bit of pig isn't worth putting in your mouth.' The phone rings and she places the receiver between her ear and the tattoo of a globe on her right shoulder. 'Harry Zappa and The Onion, how can we hurt you? Oh, hi Mum.'

I could look at The Onion all day, but I step back and turn over the plastic pages of flash from which people select a stock anchor, a heart, a dragon, a pin-up girl; and, in a red leather-bound folder, Harry Zappa's own freehand art. He is a famous totalitarian in the tattooing world—if you want something from him, you shut up and let him get on with it. At the back are examples of his scar tattoos. Miranda's 'S'-shaped scar keeps bugging me. I spoke to Iain from Inklings in Whitby about it last night. Iain gave me my first tattoo: winding the lyrics to 'Fools Gold' by The Stone Roses around my left arm. I asked him how long it would take for the scar to rise up. 'Don't ask me: I like painting flesh,' he said, 'not removing it. But I can put you in touch with someone near you who does.'

A curtain of sandalwood beads is pulled back and a girl with a green-grey face emerges, groping for the wall. She is laughing though, and staring at the dressing strapped to her inner arm. Harry Zappa leads her to the counter and holds out a jam jar of penny sweets. She chooses a rhubarb and custard.

I smile at her. 'What've you had done?'

She looks shyly up at me, the sweet rattling across her teeth, then peels back part of the cotton covering. A peacock pecks at a blue vein, its bright blue and purple feathers fanning out and wrapping round her wrist. Her eyes shine in a smudge of mascara.

Harry Zappa takes me through to the room and sits at the end of a tilting chair. His arms are covered in mermaids twisting through tendrils of seaweed. The back of his hands each have a scarified Gordian knot raised up against his brown skin. 'Let's have a look at you, first,' he says. 'Then you can fire away. Iain said you liked asking questions.'

I take my T-shirt off and stand in front of two fan heaters that rotate and redly glare. Goose bumps don't tattoo well. 'I want to finish the sleeve, have it start with a candle with a blue-black flicker and leading into a full blaze,' I say, holding out my right

79

arm so Harry can see the flames that lick up from my elbow, finishing on my shoulder in five flares that resemble a hand of fire.

Harry Zappa takes a magnifying glass and examines my arm. Sniffs. 'Not bad. Considering. Must be four different artists, there.'

I nod. 'I add to it when I visit a new city.'

Harry Zappa wags his finger. 'It'll be *my* candle. Done my way. You'll have no say.'

I shrug. 'Tell me about scar tattoos.'

'Getting more popular,' Harry says, opening a wooden chest that smells of frankincense and pine. He holds up phials of ink to the light like an apothecary selecting his remedies.

'How is it done?' I ask as he places ink in the machine.

'It's like making a lino cut,' Harry says, wiping my skin with an antiseptic wipe. 'I cut through the skin with a razor blade, taking away a number of layers so that the flesh is raw and red underneath.' He points to a series of photographs of scar tattoos. 'Then the body starts to repair itself, the tissue forming a scar that, depending on the person, stands proud of the skin.' He offers his hand and I run a finger over the twists in the raised knot. The scarring is rough and fibrous; I feel like I'm reading his braille.

'Do you take the photo immediately after doing the tattoo?' I ask, pointing to the picture of a treble clef on a man's chest, near his heart.

'We always do, when it is at its freshest.' He starts the machine and tests the ink on pigskin first, then strokes it over my skin. It tickles to start with, then it feels like someone scratching you with a nail in the same place over and over again. I like the

80

pain: it stands with its hand on its hips in the way of other pain.

I picture the 'S' shape on Miranda's wrist. It was raw, but there was no blood. 'How long would it take for the skin to stop bleeding?'

'Quickly, half an hour or so. And it would be scarred over in a month.'

'What about the day after it was done?' I watch the outline of the candle appear on my arm.

Harry wipes away my blood and begins to score in the colour of the white-yellow candle. 'Blistering starts quickly, when the body rushes in to save the day. Beautiful—the way we heal over. It would only stay fresh like in that photo for a few hours.'

Miranda was cut the day she died; maybe by her killer. I take a drawing of the curling cut from my jeans pocket. 'Have you seen this pattern before?'

He scratches his ear. 'No,' he says. 'I remember everything I machine and I don't remember that. But it's no big deal: people have their initials or someone else's tattooed on themselves all the time.'

'Are there any other tattooists who specialise in scarring in Cambridge?'

'Enough questions,' Harry Zappa says, changing the ink to deep blue. 'Lie down and shut up.'

*   *   *

I buy a bag of marshmallows on the way back, to get my sugar levels up. Biting into one, I remember an ex, Samantha, who ate vegan marshmallows. She said she was vegetarian yet lived on fishfinger sandwiches as 'they weren't really fish'. After college one afternoon, I tipped a packet of icy fish fingers into her pond. They bobbed about,

81

dodgeming into weeds. She cried, shouted 'They look like amputee goldfish', ran into the house and shouted 'You're dumped' through the kitchen window. I learned two things that day: pointing out the flaws in someone's logic leads not to gratitude, remorse nor romance; and also, after leaving her house, trudging up the hill to The Black Heart and bumping into Carla Lander, whom Samantha had accused me of fancying and I had replied 'don't be silly, you're paranoid', that we're all hypocrites.

The wind is up again, pushing me over the grass of Parker's Piece. My phone dings. A message scrolls across the top of the screen. 'I think I've found your mask,' she says. 'Want to talk about it over coffee?'

Yes, yes I do. I don't care what reality I'm in. I'm going to coffee with Lana Carver.

Chapter Thirteen

1635

Pick a year, any year. Taking a pin and closing my eyes, I stick it at random into the chart that stretches across one wall. The red pin points to 1631. Early seventeenth century. No, make that 1635; I haven't been there before.

The gate slams shut and, keeping my eyes closed and my notebook clamped to my chest. I walk out onto the street. I give myself to the feeling. It is as if I'm falling, that sensation in sleep when, believing yourself to be falling, you seize the sides of your bed. Experiencing that is one of the prerogatives of the

Traveller. There are others, most of which I now have under control.

I open my eyes and the world is composed of colours, smells and sounds that kaleidoscope around me. I suck on a humbug until the chaos reforms itself in my mind. Picking my way from one small, clear patch of paving to another, avoiding the bundle of dumped bloodsoaked clothing, the dark human waste, the rivulets of piss that streak the streets, I take in shallow breaths. The air is as thick and as fetid as a sick child's room. I make notes for my masterpiece: '1635: the sun glows off golden Ketton stone while the town is dulled with rubbish.'

Someone runs into me and I stumble against the railings. 'Watch yourself,' says a gruff, muffled voice.

'Alas,' I reply, 'the placement of my eyes makes that only partially possible.'

The man turns away and stoops to pick up his dropped parcels. A wrapped packet of meat wallows in a puddle and an egg leaks out of its shell over the cobbles. I bend down and reach for the broken egg, smiling across at him and he flinches, distracted from my other hand reaching into the bag of eggs in the crook of his arm; I cough, swap it into my other hand and give him the whole egg.

He grabs it and stares at me with bugging eyes before hurrying away, looking back at me once, then spinning his back as if worried he would turn to salt. That would be a valuable commodity in this time. He won't find out till he gets home that where he had three precious eggs, he now has only one, and he is also wanting his coin bag.

The Eagle is dark, pipe smoke suspended in the fust like the ghosts of old drinkers that will not go home. It is one of the few places in the city that *changes little over time: whichever year I am in, men mumble into their drinks and scratch their names into timbers. I, however, come here to think. Sitting in a corner, looking out of buckled glass into the street, I gulp warmed ale that, spiced to cover the taste, reaches down my throat and up into my frontal lobe. So what will be my next project, the one that connects to my work in the twenty-first century? All great works need an overarching theme, a narrative that runs through their bones. I tap my head to hurry up the thinking. Beauty—art—it is too early for a lecturer in art; they are all concerned with mathematics, which does of course have its own beauty. Maybe a mathematician—they would do it methodically, show their workings..*

I lean against the sticky bar. 'Another ale.'

The landlord refills the tankard. 'You selling in the market? Haven't seen you before.'

'Haven't you?' Opening my notebook, I check back. 'No, that is right. I know your successor. Or his successor.'

The landlord awards me the timeless 'appease the drunkard' smile and wipes a rag over the bar.

I finish my second ale. Leaving a coin stuck to the bar, I exit. My head now clear, I pass the corn exchange and round the corner into the market place. Some of the stallholders are already packing away for the day and the rotten leaves around the pillory suggest I have missed the entertainment of the afternoon. I walk into the sweet-rotten pink miasma that shrouds a pack of stalls in the Shambles. Cuts of meat stacked in bloody series. I move over to the nearest stall. The legs of unknown animals, expertly stripped, hang and swing next to me. I am comfortable around meat. Meat is reassuring.

84

'Could you move?' A voice behind me. A young man sits on a wooden box, sheaf of paper on his legs, charcoal in his left hand.

I walk to him, stepping over the thin stream of water and blood being sluiced through the market and stand right in front of his knees so that his view of the stall is completely obscured. 'Is this better?' I ask.

He looks up. 'You are in my way,' he says, gesturing to the ill-composed sketch of the stall. He smudges the shadows in the cavities of a pig's head.

'You like still life?' I ask. I do not move.

'It is not a matter of liking it. Artists need to experience life and death.' He smoothes back his hair, leaving a coal mark on his temple. His skin is untouched and his eyes show that he has known no worse horror than the prospect of a wineless night.

'I am sorry to hear of your loss.'

'My loss?'

'Your bereavement. I assume you have recently experienced death.'

He stands up, straightens his cloak. 'Good afternoon to you,' he says, walking away with a flounce. An artist. Yes, an artist will be my other murderer. There are few people more susceptible.

Back at the stall, I pat the pig's head, pick up a heart and squeeze it. The muscle bulges through my clenched fingers.

'Are you going to buy that?' the butcher says, steadying the leg protectively. He stands a head taller than the other meat sellers. His face is red, as if turned inside out. He looks at me from my hair to my boots, weighing me like the cut of meat he is tossing from hand to hand. Judging from the greying slabs on the trestle table, he has sold little today.

'I am,' I say. 'And I'll take two steaks from you,

85

and those ribs. A bag of kidneys if you have them.'

He grins. His ruddy face is fanned by wrinkles. 'I'll grant you the heart for nothing.' The butcher bustles and whistles, tying packages of meat with string.

'You are very kind,' I say. 'Do you know that young man, the artist who was over there?'

The butcher snorts. The sound echoes in his nasal chamber. 'That's Lord Witt's son, Charlie. He has taken to painting.'

'I've been thinking of finding an artist,' I say.

He looks at me and places his head on one side. His forehead contracts like bacon strips frying.

'I know I do not look rich enough. That is because I am not rich enough. I find paintings and painters on behalf of patrons. And I have a very important patron indeed.'

The red-faced butcher raises his eyebrows and performs the face that I believe means he is impressed, or is pretending to be. 'Well, if you want Sir Charles, or one of the others, they took over my old cutting rooms in Slaughter Lane. The second on your right from this end. I could show you; I'm packing up soon.'

'No. I know the way.' I turn round as I leave. 'Thank you for your help,' I say.

* * *

Slaughter Lane backs onto the old friary and is more pleasant than it sounds, at least to most people. If the red butcher is correct, the artists should be behind this door. I cannot hear anything inside. Perhaps they are immersed in their work, capturing the likeness of a pomegranate or another new fruit.

My knock brings footsteps, and laughter. The door

opens and the young man from the market stands, hands on hips, smiling at me. White paint licks at the hair on his temples, showing how he will look as an older man. I touch my sideboards. They were once a mix of dark brown and black. .

'Are you here for the turnips?' he asks, pointing to a sack slumped against the wall.

I push back my shoulders. I am not a man who would be here, or anywhere, for the turnips. Or anything that grows in the ground. Unless you count bodies, which you should not—they do not grow. It is thought that hair and fingernails continue to grow after a body has died; it is not true—the skin shrinks back from death, but the myth persists. 'I was told that I would find an artist.'

'That is right. You were by the meat stall. Do you want the turnips anyway?' he says, walking over and picking one up. He hands it to me. 'I've had so much turnip soup I may turn into one.'

'If I have come to the wrong place to have my portrait painted then I shall leave,' I say, turning back into the lane. 'I was hoping to provide the king with proof that the English were as gifted as the Dutch.'

'No, please,' he says, stepping out of the house and grabbing my elbow. He transfers his weight from one bare, hairless foot to the other. 'Come inside, you're in exactly the right place. I'm Charlie, Charles Witt. You have heard of me?' He does not seem surprised when I shake my head. 'I can paint you right now if you like.' His tone has changed to a higher pitch.

I follow him through to a bright room. There are rusted hooks on the ceiling. A spaniel sleeps on a pile of rags on the floor. At the other end, a red sheet is strung up. Areas of the sheet have not absorbed the dye and have the pallid pink rim of an anaemic's eye. *A makeshift bed lies to one side and before that stands an easel, the canvas on it already started, the red background rich and consistent.*

'Am I interrupting you?' I ask. 'You seem to be in the middle of a piece.'

'Fate brought you here,' he says, pushing a box of cauliflowers away with his foot. On top of the vegetables lies a petticoat. 'I was readying this surface for a commission, but you are here, so I will do another for . . . ' He searches for something to say. 'The duke.'

'I would not like to step onto another man's picture, especially not the duke's,' I reply.

Charlie flings the canvas away. It skids across the floor and clatters against the wall, causing the dog to lift its head, stare at its master and flop back down. 'I should know your name, sir, but I am not in a position to attend court.'

'Jackamore Grass. I have been appointed to acquire great works for His Majesty's collection. His Majesty is looking for works that demonstrate elegance in composition, nuance, symbolism, in short that reflect his position.'

'I thought he looked abroad.'

'This has previously been the case,' I say.

From a room nearby comes the sound of female laughter. It is high and takes too long to conclude. Charlie strides over, slams a connecting door and picks another canvas to be placed on the easel. The muscles in his neck stand out. 'I apologise. We all take turns to use the space. There is a small studio next door, but this has the best light. The light in Cambridge is unique, do you agree?' He slides his hand round my shoulders and turns me from the sound, pointing outside to the small courtyard and its aquarium light.

'Perhaps I could meet your fellow artists,' I say, shrugging off his hand. I walk to the door. It opens onto a narrow, damp-blackened corridor; to the left is another room, the door wide open. Three men turn as I enter. One, the tallest man I have seen in my life, bends his head to fit under the ceiling. He is thin—all his growing went upwards. The other two—one short, square and dark-haired, the other blond and bland,— stand over easels painting portraits of a woman reclining on a bench. The woman snatches her gown from the floor and lays it over her body. The yellow skirt is rimmed with dirt. The squat man burls forward and helps her to arrange the material.

Charlie pushes past me. 'This is Mr Jackamore Grass. He has asked me to take his portrait. The king sent him.' He stands, legs wide, in front of me, holding his paintbrush out in front of him.

'I have not yet specified the artist,' I say. Charlie turns back. I walk around him. 'I was told that I would find an artist here; that is all.' I tap my pocket and the coin bag jangles. The artists stare at it.

The one with fair hair tucks his shirt into his trousers. 'I would be honoured to take your portrait, sir. And for less than my friends here.'

'You would?' I ask him. There is promise in the situation; where competition exists, so does murder. Possibilities parade in front of me, turning one way, then the next.

'James Montague. My father is—'

'I would not care were your father the Pope. The question is, can you paint?'

James Montague crumples his neck into his chest in indignation, swallows. Before he can speak, the squat man walks forward and offers his hand. His shirt sleeves are folded up to the widest point of his bicep. 'We can all paint; it is more a question of taste,' he says, jerking his arm to the canvases. The girl herself twists to sit on the edge of the bench, arms crossed in front of her, holding on to her dress.

'What are you looking at?' she says to me.

I hold her gaze then turn my back. 'Art is about taste; you are right, Mr . . .' I pause.

'Orion Glynd. And this is Micklesham—he's large but harmless.'

Micklesham says nothing. He twists back to his portrait, his fist bunching round the paintbrush.

I walk over to him. 'This is good,' I say. 'You have her already.' I touch the edge of the canvas where he is blending pigments to find her skin tone. Her inner arm is the blue-white of light that bounces off snow. The paint dulls on my fingertip; on the canvas it pulses. An eruption of joy boils in my chest: there are some things that only art and murder can do for me.

I turn round to face the men, smiling. 'I suggest a competition, gentlemen.' I open my money bag and tip gold and silver coins onto a table. You will each paint a portrait of this beautiful young woman and the winner, selected by myself, will then paint my portrait. This portrait will be presented to the king, among other examples of the artist's work. I cannot say if he will approve, but you will receive the opportunity to impress him, along with a prize of five guineas.'

I pick up a coin from the table and make it vanish from one hand and reappear in the other. The artists watch, eyes wide.

The girl watches the artists and pulls the blanket up to her neck.

Chapter Fourteen

Special Delivery

Jane sits cross-legged on the floor in her office, fanning witness accounts around her. Pemberton stands in the doorway, his arms crossed. He looks around the room at the mess, one eyebrow rising.

'I've devised a filing system beyond your understanding, sergeant,' Jane says.

'I'm sure you have, ma'am. Here's something else for your system.' He hands her the file on Stephen Killigan and she tosses it onto her desk. 'By the way, I saw the chief in the canteen, ma'am. He said he'd pop in later.'

'I bet he did. And I bet he said "pop" as well, didn't he? Like he was dropping in on his mother for weak tea and a slice of Battenberg.' Jane prods a pen at the mound of used tea bags on a saucer. In another life she would lie down on a chaise longue and have oiled men place them over her eyes.

Picking up a witness report, from a man who spotted 'a woman carrying a music box. But it could have been a jewellery box, I suppose. Or something small anyway, I couldn't really see', she waves it at Pemberton.

'You think I'm wasting my time, don't you?' Jane says, stretching out her arms till something clicks in her shoulder. 'You can say. I won't bite your head off. Not all of it. Not all at once.'

Pemberton shrugs. 'The only lead is that postgraduate. And she couldn't swear she saw a tall man walking over to Hana Barinder's car and

91

opening the boot. And even if she could, it is hard to identify a back in a line-up.'

'Not impossible though. I once got a conviction from a witness correctly distinguishing a culprit from a line-up of right legs.'

'So you've said, guv.'

Jane has an urge to reach up, grab his tie and yank. Then maybe he wouldn't look as smug. 'Watch it, Paul. As your superior officer, I can repeat myself as much as I choose.'

'It could be a student hoax. First-year medical students thinking they are being clever. And it might be time to leave the Miranda case and get on with another.'

'You've been talking with Mark Wadhurst, haven't you? He said that this morning. Actually he said "Get on with a real cunting case", because he has a beautiful way with words. As shown by him also saying that "the beauty queen is probably in Dulwich, shacked up with a nobody and knocked up as well".'

Jane sniffs and picks bobbles off the knees of her tights. Her old guv had understood; she had known that Jane would snuff out a problem, given time and inspiration.

What do other people do for inspiration? Go for walks? Stare at the stars? If she were at home, she'd get in the bath. They should have one in the station, for detectives to splash about and cogitate in. That would go down well in the press. The tabloids would get a picture of her tubby belly hanging as she hauled herself out of the bath.

She glances up at Paul, lurking in the doorway. 'Go and do something, would you?'

'What would you like me to do, guv?'

'Don't ask me, go and—' Her mobile buzzes and slides off the desk, toppling into her box of receipts. 'Hana' she answers in a mumble, pulling the lid off her pen with her teeth. 'You'd better have something good for me: I haven't forgiven you yet.'

'That depends on what you mean by good,' Hana says. 'The tissue we found in the chapel has been handed in.'

'Handed in? How can it be fucking handed in? It's not a lost glove.'

Hana audibly inhales, and coughs. Cars streak past in the background. Hana is taking her fag break. 'It came half an hour ago, special delivery. The packaging is being tested for prints, of course, though that may not be of much help. I'll work on the sample later today.'

'You'll work on it sooner today. Any message, or name on the package?'

'It was addressed to you, care of the lab.' Hana pauses. 'There's something else.' Her voice is low, serious.

Jane bites her lip. 'Go on,' she says. She looks over to Pemberton, who picks up papers from the low brown chair in the corner and sits down, his elbows on his knees, chin in his hand.

'We're checking again, but I thought I should tell you now: we've run DNA on the knife and tongue depressor and Miranda Pilkington's blood is on the knife, along with further sets of DNA also on the depressor. We've checked for cross-matches with other missing persons but nothing as yet. No identity yet for the other sample. There's a backlog.'

'When isn't there?'

Footsteps down the corridor. The chief's quick,

heavy gait.

Jane lurches to her feet. 'Thanks Hana, I'll ring you later.' Her left foot fizzes with pins and needles and she stamps on the paper-covered floor. This is not the time for the chief to see her office. If she keeps talking then he can't launch into another tirade. Ushering Pemberton out, she peers down the hall. The chief inspector is checking his reflection in a glass-encased print, smoothing down his hair.

'Breakthrough on the case, sir. I'll tell you about it over tea.' She takes his arm and leads him back the way he came. The chief looks over his shoulder to her office. She walks a little faster. 'What about a nice sausage sandwich? I'll chuck in an iced finger if you're lucky.'

In the canteen, Jane's stomach moans. Eggs spit on the griddle. 'Have you heard, sir? The tissue found in the chapel has turned up and the lab has confirmed that Miranda Pilkington's DNA is on the knife, plus other people's. It is now a possible murder investigation.'

The chief stirs sweetener into his tea. 'And a possible win situation.'

'Don't call this a win, sir.' She'll have to phone Miranda's mum, Ruth Pilkington, after this, or go round to the house. Make tea, offer up words that could not possibly make a difference. And that fucking bastard is laughing at them all. She can use anger. It makes her feel alive.

'You made no progress for a year and then evidence was stolen and compromised: I mean, how likely is it that the tissue will be admissible?'

An answer isn't necessary. Jane stirs white sugar into her hot chocolate.

'You have a chance to show how good you are, Jane,' he says, his tone changing to slippery motivational speaker. 'I took a risk, taking you on.'

'Look at me, sir,' Jane says, opening her arms wide. 'I'm fine.'

'Still.' The chief lets the word hang.

Mandy brings his sandwich over. Grease bleeds through the bread. He folds out a paper napkin so slowly Jane has to stop herself snatching it and stuffing it in her mouth to muffle a scream.

'What do you think I should have done differently, then?' Jane says. 'Seeing as I've spent the last year doing everything possible to locate Miranda, to the detriment of other cases, to the detriment of other missing women who aren't so front page.'

The chief looks around the canteen. 'Keep your voice down please, Jane. I will tell you what I think you should do: you should attend to the public face of things.' He stares at the chocolate muffin stain on her blouse, then, as if realising what, or rather what he's not looking at, turns away. 'Otherwise, when the press call for someone's head then I won't be able to protect you.' The chief stands, takes a large bite of his sandwich and swipes brown sauce from his chin. 'And find Miranda's body, before she goes missing again.'

Jane sticks two fingers up at his back as he walks out. He looks back and she switches her hand round into a wave.

Chapter Fifteen

Duckling

The white-ruffled boys follow their choirmaster in a line through the college, as trusting as ducklings. The boy is third from the back. I wave as he passes. He waves back. Tomorrow. I will stop him on his way from home, crossing through the park. Even though he is always late, running through the trees to catch up with where he should be, he will stop to push the swing so that it swipes forward and back as he sprints away, looking back at his energy being used up after the fact. And then his murderer will emerge.

Tying two centuries into a cat's cradle requires dexterity, mental strength and the skills of legerdemain. Two hundred and eighty years ago, three artists are painting a woman to prove they are worthy of painting my picture; now a boy wanders on his own grave, in weeks a broken beauty queen is found, another lost. Not that it can't all go wrong, because it can. And that's what keeps my heart going.

Chapter Sixteen

Night Terrors and Holes

Standing on the shoreline, I watch Mum wade out. Her dress grows darker, her hair dips deeper, till just her head and shoulders show. A tall man follows her; she tries to swim away from him but there is nowhere to go. She turns towards me and I shove my knuckles in my mouth to stop myself crying out. She's wearing the mask. Her fingers scrape at the edges of the stone, trying to prise it away. The mask is wearing Mum's face. She lifts her head but her chin is sinking into the water. Her screams are eaten up by sea. And I run with my yellow net to the cluster of rock pools by the cliff. Curled up behind the biggest rock, I poke an anemone, watch it swallow my finger, my fist, my arm, my shoulder. As the red mouth gapes at my head, sirens screech towards me and to me they are screaming: 'This is your fault. This is your fault.'

I wake, shivering, sheets sweated through, duvet on the floor. That's the first time I've had that dream in years, not since I left Whitby. And the first time that mum was wearing the mask. I thought the nightmare was attached to the town, and that if I didn't go back, they wouldn't come back. Maybe it's going to bed in the afternoon, but I feel as if I can never get enough sleep. Or that once again I'm not doing enough to help someone who died. I swing my legs round and look up.

The mask stares its empty stare from its nail on the wall.

*   *   *

A rap at my door. Then two more.

Shit.

I'm giving a supervision. Now. To that girl with the brown hair and scowl. God, I've forgotten her name.

'Won't be long,' I shout.

Grabbing my clothes from the floor as I go, I

97

stumble through into my study. It's a mess, even for me. One leg in my jeans and my T-shirt around my neck, I kick a jumble of clothes that *may* be clean under the desk, clear books from the sofa and try to flatten my bed head into something that could resemble the hair of a professional man; no luck: it cockatiels up and won't be stopped.

A louder knock.

'One more minute,' I call, arm stuck in T-shirt. I open the curtains, a window and packet of biscuits. As a last touch, I treat the room to a blast of ocean breeze deodorant.

'Sorry to keep you,' I say. I see her face and the name slots in: 'Maria.'

She gazes round the room, picking up odd objects. She steps back when she sees Bandit the bear.

'He won't hurt you,' I say, patting his head. His glass eyes shine. Sometimes I think I see him wink. 'Please sit down. Though I can't promise the sofa won't harm you. It swallowed a third year last week. I can hear him quoting Derrida down there.'

She gives a quick smile and sits to one side of the two-seater, staring at the gap in the middle.

'So,' I say, putting on the kettle. 'How did you get on with *Holes*? Have you got an essay for me?'

She reaches into her bag and pulls out a plastic file. She has the shadows under the eyes of the all-nighter. 'I'm going to swap to another subject,' she says, handing it over. 'I've decided. Philosophy is talking about obvious things for hours without getting anywhere. I don't want to spend my life doing that.'

'You didn't get on with *Holes* then?' I say,

98

looking down at her essay.

'It's infuriating. Everyone knows that there *are* such things as holes.'

'What are they?' I say, taking a ginger biscuit from the packet and offering her one.

She looks at the piles of bric-a-brac around her, rifles through a tin of assorted things and pulls out a cookie cutter in the shape of a heart. Waggling her finger through the middle she says, 'That's a hole.' She points to a tear in my jeans: 'That's a hole,' and to the round opening in the globe-shaped lampshade above me, 'that's a hole too. To argue that there aren't any is ridiculous.' She pulls her feet up on the sofa and sits cross-legged with folded arms like a belligerent Buddha.

'Well I'm glad that's sorted. Now we can get on to more important things. Tea?' I ask, pouring into my mug.

She nods. 'Two sugars, please. Of course I understand what the whole debate is about,' she says, frowning.

'Oh yes?'

'That what we perceive to be a hole is actually the perception of whatever surrounds the hole, that any truth regarding the hole is truth in regard to the "hole-lining"; that we cannot easily develop ontological criteria for a hole itself: holes are spatio-temporal particular but they are unique—' She keeps talking, rattling off the salient ontological arguments on holes of the last forty years.

'You definitely have a grasp on all the material; well done,' I say, when she finishes at last. 'That's a lot to digest in a week.'

'I've read all this stuff but they don't come

down with an answer, just more things to question. Studies in developmental psychology show how infants are able to perceive and count holes from a very early age, as well as any other object. There *are* holes—why can't we prove it?' Her face is red now, her voice rising.

'I'd like to be that certain about things,' I say. 'What do you think then? Are holes defined by what is around them; or is the thing that surrounds them defined by the hole?'

She shrugs.

'Take a ring,' I say, walking to my desk and carefully picking a ring out of the white box. 'The gold in this ring was made or chosen to fit a woman with fingers of a narrow width. Without the hole it would not be a ring, but the hole was defined by what needed to fill it, and the band surrounds the hole. When it is filled, there is still a hole in the ring—it has something else temporarily filling that hole.'

Maria shakes her head. 'It's just a ring.'

I hold the ring up to the window. It is just a ring. But also it isn't. 'This was my mother's wedding ring. When I look at it I see two things: the thin gold band, and the hole, the emptiness inside it. On one day I may see more of the hole than the band; on another day the band more than the hole; but the ring would not exist as a ring without both.'

She holds out her hand. I lean forward and place the ring on her palm. She holds it to her eye and squints through the window. Then looks at her lap. She looks close to tears.

'I know this is frustrating,' I say, 'but if you came to Cambridge for answers, then you came to the wrong place. There are more questions here than answers.'

'I just want to be able to get it right,' she says.

'Don't we all,' I reply.

Chapter Seventeen

Pathology

'I'm here to harass you,' Jane says, striding into Hana Barinder's lab.

'Sexually?' Hana says, washing her hands at the huge sink in the corner.

'I wouldn't know how,' Jane replies. 'It's been so long I've forgotten what everything is for.'

Usually path labs make the back of Jane's throat close but this one smells of lavender—Hana makes sure of that—and the white tiles shine like celebrities' teeth. Should Jane get *her* teeth de-stained? No point: she practically soaks her molars in coffee every morning; they'd be brown again in days. 'So. You've had more than enough time to identify the tissue. Give me something, anything.'

'Some details need to be verified, I told you, but I can confirm that it is a pair of human vocal cords, cauterised and removed with a knife, preserved for up to a year in white vinegar comprised of precisely 5 per cent acetic acid.' Hana walks over to a drawer and pulls out a jar topped with a round gingham cover, held in place with an elastic band. 'Whoever sent it has a sense of humour. Or maybe you should take an interest in the local W.I.'

'What else can you tell me?' Jane asks, taking the jar. She bites her lip. No copper likes to know some bastard is laughing at her.

'I pulled some strings and, judging from the risque text messages I've received in the last hour, a burly forensics officer called Phil got the results rushed through. The DNA matches the other sample found on the tongue depressor and the knife. There are several confusing factors: the decay rate of the blood stains on the knife suggests that the removal of the folds was in the last seven to twenty days, but the ventricular folds were removed a year ago. The vocal cords most likely belong to a child—'

'So not Miranda?' Jane says, leaning on the stainless steel table in the centre.

'It *is* hard to tell if the folds belonged to a woman or child—they are shorter and thinner than a man's and they are very damaged—but it seems not. Her blood was on the knife but not the tongue depressor. Which could have been used in the removal of the folds. It would be difficult, and excruciating if the victim were still alive.' Hana swallows.

'But it's not impossible?' Jane asks.

'Highly unlikely. The perpetrator would have to possess considerable surgical skills. The problem is that the DNA match on the knife is with a young boy who went missing yesterday.'

'Yesterday?'

Hana holds out her hands, palms up. 'I'm only telling you what we found.'

'Don't get cryptic on me, Barinder.'

'Fine,' Hana says. 'How are you doing, by the way? You look tired.'

'Thanks a lot.'

'I haven't seen you properly in ages. We should meet up. I'm going swimming with the kids later, if you want to come.'

Jane folds her arms and taps her shoe.

Hana winces. 'Sorry. Forgot. Have you seen anyone about it yet?' Hana says, sliding open the chilled cabinet of cadavers and peering inside as if opening an oven to check on a cake. 'You can't go on with hydrophobia for ever.'

'I can. We're in Cambridge which—'

'Has lots of water . . . '

'Which is many miles from the sea, I was about to say, thank you very much. And there are far worse fears to have. I have a friend who's frightened of shoelaces.'

'Is that true?'

'No, but it could be. Anyway, I'm not paying some cooing therapist fifty quid an hour to tell me it's stupid to be afraid of water. It's entirely logical to steer clear of large amounts of water. Ask Virginia Woolf.'

*   *   *

Pemberton is smoking at the side of the building when Jane emerges. 'Filthy habit, that,' she says. 'And you've never so much as offered me one.'

'I didn't know you smoked, guv.'

'On and off. Given current circumstances, I'm thinking "on".'

'I haven't got any left. We can stop at the garage. I've got a Polo though.'

Jane takes the Polo and lets it roll around her lower teeth. She fastens her seatbelt and her phone goes. 'No, I don't want to go swimming, Barinder. I currently prefer aversion therapy to immersion therapy.'

Hana sounds muffled. 'I didn't know whether you'd left yet. You went away without the details on the other sample we've identified.'

'Who is that? You didn't tell me.' And I didn't ask, Jane thought. She wipes her hand over her face. No more mistakes.

'The boy is called Rhys Withins and he didn't come home yesterday, from choir practice. At Sepulchre College.'

Chapter Eighteen

Carbon Dating

'Meet me after work,' Lana Carver had said and here I am, embarrassingly early, in new shoes slightly too small for me, stepping into the North Wing lift of the University Library. Crouching down, I ease my shoe off to give my heel a rest. I haven't told Satnam I'm here, but it's not as if I'm doing anything wrong. It's work, almost.

'Hold it, please, you. The lift.' An elderly woman rushes towards me, wheeling an upright brown suitcase behind her with one hand, waving a book with the other. I recognise her—she was by the computers, the one who said she'd be seeing me again. She nods at me. The white hairs on her top lip shine under the light-bulb.

She places a bookmark in the text on Schrodinger's Cat and looks at me, very slowly, up and down. Her forehead is bunched up into her head, as if she's trying to square the paradox of a cat being both alive and dead at the same time, just to spite Stephen Hawking. I hope she doesn't: I love envelopes lying unopened on the kitchen table, containing two or more versions of my future. All possibilities exist until you observe the result, and then it is the only possible consequence. Exam scores; a Valentine's card that could be from the one you *really* want one from; credit card bills that are less and more than you fear; a stone mask that I don't want to lift as it will make death real. Maybe I'm like Da. That's a terrible thought. Da never looks at his weekly lottery tickets as, that way, he may be a winner. Of course he'll never know if he *has* won: he would rather not win than know himself to be a loser.

The lift fills with the smell of cocoa boiling on a stove.

I lean back against the thin walls of the cage, stairwells falling below me. There are light animal hairs all over the woman's jacket. Maybe she has a Labrador that she discusses discoveries with over port and dog biscuits. There are many pets in science—Schrodinger's kitten, Pavlov's dog; maybe Newton had a newt called Neville, and it was Neville, and not the apple, via a plummet from his cage that nudged the physician into pronouncing on gravity.

Her head cocks to one side; her eyes roam around my face. She darts forward and grabs my right wrist. Holding it close to her eyes, she turns it over and peers at the veins on the inner side. She sniffs, drops my wrist and crosses her arms. Her eyes twinkle. 'I was right. When have you been then?' she asks. 'Anywhen nice?'

Her voice is rasping and high, rattling up to the top of the lift cage like a torn moth. She hits her ribcage hard with her fist and coughs. 'Beg your pardon,' she says. This time her voice comes out deep brown and resounding, like a parquet floor. 'Can't get rid of this bronchitis.' She blinks at me. 'Are you going to answer my question?'

'What was the question?'

'I asked you when you'd been.'

'*When* I'd been?'

'So you don't know yet.' She takes out a pen from the pocket of her jacket and writes in her notebook, looking up at me occasionally and chuckling.

The lift eases to a stop then, as we move towards the door, gives a lurch. She shuffles out, wheeling her suitcase behind her. Bending down with surprising agility, she unzips her trolley suitcase. It's packed with library books, wrinkled apples and pages of notes, the writing tiny, the lines interlocked by spider-limbed letters. 'It's the only way for books to travel,' she says, lifting volumes up carefully, tutting, blowing on them gently and placing them on the floor.

At the bottom of the case she says, 'A-ha!' She hands a slim book to me. 'You'll need this, at some point. Look after it; don't throw it in the river for God's sake. I should make a waterproof version. Or a buoyant one. That's an idea: the floating edition.' She takes out her notebook and writes it down. 'My address is inside. Return it when you've finished. Don't think I won't remember. If you keep it, I will hunt you down.'

I've got this urge in my chest not to let her

go yet. I walk after her. I know I'm going to say something, I'm just not sure what. 'Is Schrodinger's Cat about cowardice?'

She turns back and her face becomes a big dimple of a grin. 'No. Never think that. It is a thought experiment, not moral philosophy: when does a quantum system stop being a mix of states and become one or the other? Of course you could say it was analogous to indecision and paralysis of the soul, being caught between two paths and you don't want to step on either because then the other one will no longer exist. The question that doesn't involve killing a cat is: when do you make the decision? When you first move your foot? When you make an argument within your mind? Or before the paths are even in front of you, have you laid them out?'

I want to curl up like a cat on her suitcase.

'See you soon,' she says, winking at me. She toddles off, wheeling her suitcase between the book stacks.

The slim book is jacketed by material with the texture of bark. '*Complexities of Time Travel: A Theoretical Look at the Traveller*' is printed on the side in faded gold. Finding a chair, I flick through the pages. Alongside pictures of cones and directions of time travel and other usual physics diagrams, there's a picture of 'a theoretical time traveller', a woman in a red trenchcoat. Her eyebrows are raised, her eyes wide. She's holding on to the wall for support. I touch the smooth paper and goose pimples flare on my arms as if pushing up for a closer look.

'Here you are,' Lana Carver says from behind me as I walk over to the bookshelves.

'You like to creep up on me, don't you?' I say.

She laughs. 'I've got a huge stack of information for you, some of it relevant, most probably not. But we shouldn't stay here. I've been trying to find things out while working and my boss caught me today. He wouldn't be happy to find me showing my discoveries. Not that he's ever happy. He's been less of a bastard recently, actually—I'd say he were in love but I don't think that's possible.' Her eyes shine. I want to kiss her.

'Come on, then,' I say, standing up. 'You can show me your "discoveries" over dinner. It's only fair. So, curry or Chinese?

*　　　*　　　*

Lana's tongue pokes out to the left of her mouth as she positions a sliver of onion on top of a poppadom already anointed with mango chutney, cucumber, mint sauce, lime pickle and a blob of red sauce we can't identify. 'It's poppadom Buckaroo,' she says. 'The trick is to get as much on as you can before it buckles.'

'That sounds like a challenge. Only, to make it a fair competition, how would we quantify the area of the papad and the weight of the chutney gubbins?'

'You mean you don't carry tiny scales around with you?'

'I left them in my tiny trousers.'

She laughs and covers her mouth with her hand.

The waiter walks over to take our order and we haven't even looked at the menu. I scan the lists and realise how hungry I am. Lana orders chicken bhuna and pilau rice; 'Lamb jalfrezi and chicken tikka side, with plain rice and a Peshwari naan,' I say. My tummy grouches. 'Sag aloo. And another Cobra, please. Thanks.'

'How do you eat so much and stay skinny?' she asks, pointing at my chest.

'No idea. It's a curse. So,' I say, leaning forward. '*Star Wars* or *Raiders of the Lost Ark*?'

'*Raiders of the Lost Ark*,' she replies.

'Why?'

'Bullwhips beat light sabres.'

'Fair enough.' My stomach, or thereabouts, flips.

'Dickens or Shakespeare?' she asks.

'Now that's not fair,' I say. She taps her fingers on the tablecloth. 'All right, Shakespeare. For the tragedies.'

'Well, it's your choice,' she says. 'It's the wrong choice, but it's yours.'

I drink more Cobra and smile at her. She smiles down at her hands.

'So do you think it's the same mask?' she asks after a pause, unlocking her phone to show me the picture.

I reach into my satchel and take the mask out of its packing and lay it between us on the table. Lana takes a shallow intake of breath. The mask stares up at us from the white tablecloth with the same partially open lips as the one in her photo, the same accusing lashes that dial out from under the eyes, the same curled hair etched into the edges of the face.

Lana uncurls her fingers and gently strokes the mask's forehead. She could touch *me* like that. No she couldn't. I promised Satnam.

Keeping her eyes on mine, she leans over and takes a box file out of her rucksack. Inside lies a neat stack of meticulously paper-clipped photocopies of newspaper clippings and articles.

'I spent days, I want you to know, researching stone masks in museum catalogues and private collections. Well maybe not days, hours; well maybe not hours, but minutes at least, cross-referencing them where I could with potentially relevant markers like murder, Cambridge, beauty queen *et cetera* and comparing them to your brilliant drawing. And—' She pauses to drum her fingers on the table. 'The Paduan Beauty Masks were four identical stone masks used in a fertility pageant procession in sixteenth-century Italy. All four were stolen from a museum in Padua in 1742 and have not been seen since. It would be a major coup if you, or we, could find even one of them.' She leans back, smiling.

The mask is silent.

'What were they used for in the pageant?'

'This is where it is fascinating,' Lana says, clapping her hands together once, then searching through the box. She glides out a book and opens it at a marked page. '"The masks represented female beauty in a pageant that proceeded through Padua's winding streets accompanied by music, dancing and the suggestion of sexual promise. The masks were worn by men. Attractive ones."' She hands the mask to me. 'Try it. You're a man.'

The almost compliment dawdles over the pickle tray. I finish the bottle of Cobra and gesture for another. She blows at her blunt-cut fringe that sits just above her eyebrows. Her bob sweeps against her neck.

The mask lies on my palm, cool and unhuman. The thought of it so close to me makes me shiver.

'Go on,' she says. 'What's the problem?'

'There isn't a problem.' Only that I don't want it near my face.

'I know what you mean. It's horrible.' She breathes out slowly. 'But I want to try.' She reaches for it but I move it away. The thought of the mask on her face makes me feel sick. I sway as I move it away. I'm such a lightweight these days.

'No, I'll do it,' I say, holding the mask against me. The stone cools my flushing skin.

'It strangely suits you, though it's a bit creepy to carry it around with you.' Lana says.

'I don't,' I say. Not anymore.

Blunt ridges in the underside of the mask force my lips back and clamp against the sides of my nose. All I can see out of the eye holes are swatches of the abrasive blue restaurant lights. This can be all that she saw, the dead girl. I picture her struggling to force it away, her ringed fingers under its cold chin. I jerk away the mask.

'What if the girl was still alive? When the mask was placed over her face?' I say, staring back at the thing. 'If the last thing she knew as she was trying to breathe was this?' I shove it away from me.

'Watch it, that's four hundred years old,' Lana says.

'And that makes it special, does it? Because it's old?'

'Well no, but—'

'You didn't see her. You don't know what he did. The bastard strangled her, left her slumped with this inhuman thing on her face and dragged a tarpaulin over her body, like she were a car or a boat. And nobody is looking for her because nobody believes me.'

Lana's arms fold. She pulls her hands into her

111

lap. 'Maybe that's because it didn't happen.' Her brows contract. She opens her mouth as if to say something else, but doesn't.

The waiter stops the trolley a foot away from the table and shifts from foot to foot, looking from one of us to the other. The chicken tikka gossips in its pan.

I glance away from her, to the book lying face down. There's a picture of a young Robert Sachs in a bow tie on the back, looking smug.

I tear off a piece of naan, jump up and place money on the table. 'I've got to go.'

She hands me the box file and nods without catching my eye. 'And that's it? No "thank you for your help" Lana?'

'I'm sorry. Thank you.' For a moment I think of staying and having dinner. Then the thought of Robert placing that mask on the face of the girl makes the anger and nausea rush back again.

'Please sit down,' she says. 'And tell me what's wrong.' She places her hand on mine.

'Or I could tell you on the way.'

*   *   *

We walk back along Mill Road swinging brown paper bags filled with takeaway containers. 'If you like, we could meet for lunch tomorrow,' she says. 'Curry always tastes better the next day.' She glances up at me and bites her lip.

If I agree, I can't fool myself into thinking this is about research. 'I would like that,' I say. 'Although I promised my best friend, Satnam, that I'd see him. Do you know him? He's in the Reading Room every day, making requests for increasingly obscure

112

physics articles.'

'That describes a lot of people. Sorry. I'd like to meet him though. Why are you smiling?'

'No reason.' Our steps and strides are now in time, echoing in the damp street

By the time we're at the reality lamp-post we're already holding hands. Our kisses taste of guilt and Peshwari nan.

Chapter Nineteen

Death of the Muse

The three paintings wait under pale sheets like cadavers in a laboratory. Charles Witt paces the room, muttering. The other two, Micklesham and Glynd, have gone to collect our subject from her place of employment on Madingley Road and bring her back to their Slaughter Lane rooms. The fourth artist has shown his cowardice and declined to compete: no matter, the number three has a more satisfying symmetry. She has been told to slip out of the house after curfew and meet them by the plague pits on Midsummer Common. The plague pits were my idea, in several ways.

Witt throws his tankard at the wall. 'When will they be here?' he asks.

'You will be no good as any kind of artist if you are not patient,' I tell him.

'If I were not patient,' he says, 'I would have destroyed their paintings so that I could win. I have great patience. I can sit with a subject for hours to know the creases in their palms, the colour their eyes

go in the dark.'

'Very poetic, Mr Witt. I am certain your muses are grateful to you for that.' I pick up a twist of cloth with cadmium red powder inside, tie it with a band and place it in my pocket.

Witt continues to witter. 'I know the whites of their eyes, the way their nipples darken. And there is no need for them to thank me. Or I them. The painting speaks.'

'So it will, Mr Witt.'

The front door opens; the sound of shoes in corridors. The giant one bumps his head as he enters the room.

I laugh and the others turn to me.

The girl's cheekbones protrude. She does not eat enough. 'Do you want me for another portrait?' she asks. 'You have paid me already for the last ones.'

'We are going to view the paintings and judge them against you,' I say, deepening my voice into the voice that makes people relax. 'I cannot imagine that the paintings will aspire to capturing your beauty.' I choose my language carefully. Persuasion is a simple matter: give people the words to make them act.

'Come,' Witt says, stalking the paintings. 'It is time.'

I whip off the first sheet. Lucy Miller the woman gasps as she sees Lucy Miller the portrait, naked but for a ruff around her neck. She walks up to it, and touches her painted face. 'I do not have a mark,' she says. Her other hand goes to the mole on her jawline. She smiles as the woman in the picture smiles.

The next painting has Lucy standing by the window, a small dog at her feet. She looks out at the viewer, challenging them to look at her.

'I like that one,' she says. Her shoulders retract

114

very slightly, her head tilts up. Micklesham shifts his weight; his cheeks flare red.

I reveal the last one, painted by Witt judging from the lack of finish, the petulance of the brushstrokes. He has his muse sitting on the edge of a bed, hands crossed in her lap.

The real Lucy Miller sniffs.

Witt glares at her, drinks more ale.

On the floor the sheets are tangled, like post-coital ghosts. I kick them and stand by the portraits. Now for the fun part.

'You have each achieved much,' I lie. 'Lucy Miller can rest knowing that she has contributed to art, and as artists you must all congratulate yourself for counterfeiting her likeness on the canvas. But,' I say, walking up to each of them and looking him in the eye, 'there can be only one winner.'

Glynd and Micklesham glance at each other and shake hands.

I stride towards Charles Witt's painting and appear to pluck a fistful of coins from the painted vase.

Glynd presents me with a burst of applause.

I present Charles with the money. 'You, Mister Witt, will paint my portrait and be presented to the king when he visits Cambridge.'

Micklesham's shoulders slump. Glynd claps him on the back.

As I look at the paintings, an idea coagulates. 'I would, however, like to amend the rules of my challenge given the scale of your achievements. Misters Micklesham and Glynd, I wish to purchase your paintings of Lucy Miller to add to my own private collection.' I fan new bank notes in front of them. 'How do you respond, sirs?'

They leave with coins and without their portraits.

The muse gathers her items and is about to follow when I grab her by the forearm. 'Tell me, Lucy. Do you like having your portrait painted?'

She shrugs.

'Tell me the truth,' I say.

'I get tired staying in the same place,' she says. 'Sometimes I am to hold an item for hours.'

'And which painting did you prefer? Tell the truth. I will know if you do not.' I shall let her go if she speaks the truth. That would please me.

She sweeps a look at Witt, and away. 'Mister Charles Witt's picture, sir. The one you chose,' she says.

'That is a shame,' I say. I almost mean it. 'Now, Lucy, how do you wish to be rendered unconscious? With a blow to the head or chloroformed like a moth?' I tip the bottle of methyltrichloride onto my handkerchief. The smell of sweet ether mixes with that of artists' sweat.

'What are you doing?' Lucy asks, edging towards Witt as if he could protect her.

I turn to him. 'She is lying. I told her to tell the truth and she did not. She loathes your picture. She considers it ugly. She thinks you can never be a good painter, don't you, Lucy?'

'No,' she says.

Witt shrugs her hand from his shoulder. 'Do you think I have any regard for what a servant thinks of my art?'

'So you think nothing of her?' I say, standing too close to him. My nose is two inches from his.

'Less than nothing.'

Lucy runs for the door and I grip onto her arm, swing her into my chest and pinion her wrists with my hand. I clamp my other hand over her mouth. She

116

struggles and kicks, catching me on the shinbone.

I step closer to Witt. 'Now that you three have painted her, there is no need for her. She is disposable, a still life.'

Witt stares at her. 'Yes.'

Lucy jabs her nails into my chest. Her saliva is hot on my palm.

'In still life, what happens to the flowers?' I ask.

'They die,' he replies.

'What happens to the fruit?'

'It dies.'

'What happens to beauty?'

'It . . . dies.'

'What happens to Lucy?'

'She dies.'

'And are you to do it, or I?'

'I.'

Witt grabs the chloroformed cloth from me and I lift my hand from her lips and mime it being placed over her mouth. He swabs at her, holding it fast to her face as her murmurs fade and she faints.

*　　　*　　　*

Lucy lies on the bed, breathing shallowly. Charles Witt stares down at her.

'Look at me, Charles,' I say, my voice commanding, fatherly. 'Look at me. You have captured her. What happens next?'

Charles Witt turns and slowly lowers his pigment-skinned hands to Lucy's mouth and nose. Pinching her nostrils together, he pushes down so that no oxygen can enter her.

Her ribcage heaves; her legs twitch. Her head moves to the left on the pillow.

Witt clambers over her, knees digging into her hips, keeping his hands clamped down on her mouth.

She reaches up and fumbles but is too drugged, too gone.

*   *   *

When it is over, I place an arm round his shoulder and allow him to heave and cry against me. I give him four minutes of this. His self-pitying sobs cause my shirt to be wet. 'Now we have a still life to get rid of,' I say.

Chapter Twenty

Blue Monday

I walk Lana to her flat and leave after a lifetime on her doorstep. I can still smell her vanilla perfume on my jumper where she leant her head against my shoulder.

Robert Sachs answers his phone on the fourth ring, just as I step through Sepulchre's gates. 'It's a bit late for a phone call, isn't it Stephen?'

'For who?' I ask.

'For whom,' he replies.

'I want to talk to you about the stone masks.'

'At last.'

'Go on then, start wherever you think the beginning is.'

Silence on the other end of the phone.

'Are you there?' I say.

Robert breathes out slowly. I hear him tapping

his pen on the desktop. 'Why don't you come to me? We can talk about the masks and I will have something relevant to show you at the same time. How does that sound?'

'Vague,' I say.

He laughs. 'Meet me at the front of the Shields building. Give me a couple of hours. Half eleven. I'd say midnight but it would sound too romantic.'

'Hardly: that's the medical lab, isn't it?'

'Your candlelit dinner is my graveyard flit, Stephen. Now go and think of some questions for me. I need practice at interrogations.'

Back in my room, I stand in front of Bandit and take his moth-bothered paw. 'Things are moving, old friend,' I say.

New Order's 'Blue Monday' comes out of the speakers on my desk.

Satnam strides in, a large bowl of cornflakes in his hand. 'What is this crap you are listening to? I'll put it down to you being dour and Northern, and we'll say no more about it.'

'*You're* Northern,' I say.

'But I have taste,' Satnam says. 'Just keep the volume low, I don't want to catch suicidal thoughts. What have you been up to this evening?'

'I went to the library,' I say, busying myself with pens on my desk.

'Oh yeah? I went earlier. Saw Lana Carver. I got her to take a book down from a high shelf. I think I'm in there. What were you doing?'

'Finding out about the mask.' I could tell him. Right now. Open my mouth and say it all.

He crouches down and sits rocking on his heels next to me. 'You're a worry to your mother and me, son,' he says in a squeaky old man voice. 'Hey, don't be so sensitive. I'm being serious, for once, mate. I've hardly seen you. You're either out, or I find you silent in your room, staring at that thing.' He swings a finger at the mask. 'You're obsessed.'

I fold my arms. 'Everyone needs a hobby,' I say.

'Couldn't yours be cage-fighting or lion-tickling? I could handle that; it's less dangerous than mooching indoors, mooning over a bird in a mask.' He shakes me by the shoulder then slumps into the sofa, lifts his arse up and digs around underneath. He holds Iris Burton's book. 'And what exactly are you doing with this?' he asks, frowning.

'The author gave it to me. Lent it, I should say.'

Satnam giggles. His fringe shakes.

'What's so funny now?'

'Iris Burton is the biggest joke in the university. And the university is pretty funny as it is.'

'I liked her. She had something interesting in her eyes.'

'Cataracts and glaucoma.'

'Stop it—she was odd, but—'

'But nowt, as you would say. She's an embarrassment to the physics department—she was a great mathematician in the sixties, I admit that, came close to solving the Happy End Problem, which, as I know you've made yourself aware, you being a *meta*-physicist and all, is the problem of determining for $n \geq 3$ the smallest number of points in general position in the plane so that the possible arrangement of points will always contain at least one set of points that are the vertices of a convex polygon. I expect to trounce the problem myself in a few years. Anyway, she had some interesting theories in the seventies that coincided with quantum theory, then went loopydoop, spouting all this time-travel shit. If she didn't have water-tight tenure, she'd've been kicked out way before *this* was published.' He uses his foot to nudge her book across the floor. It gently strikes the feet of Bandit.

'Oi,' I shout, picking the book up.

'It wasn't even properly published—she paid for it herself. The lads will have a right laugh when I tell them she's still giving copies out to strangers. She probably fancied you.'

'I didn't get that impression.'

'You never know when women fancy you; it's your most attractive quality, that and your inability to play darts. All the easier for me to jump in. Come on. Let's go out, take your mind off stuff.'

'Maybe tomorrow,' I say.

*　　　*　　　*

The medical lab is a concrete block bolted onto the back of the Great Hall, funded by a Fellow called Christopher Shields. They've trailed ivy over but it still looks out of place against the stone. I check my watch under the dim lamp-post. 10.58.

Footsteps inside the building, growing louder. And humming, in a low rumble. Robert opens the door and shines a torch at my face. 'Punctuality is a sign of an unimaginative mind, Stephen. Do something about it, before it's too late.'

'You do know you said that to me last time we met, don't you?'

He blinks and, for a moment, his sangfroid slips. 'Some people need telling twice,' he says, stepping back to allow me in. He shuts the door. The torch

121

makes his face pumpkin-coloured.

He starts down a flight of stairs. 'We've got to be quiet. The night porters do a search at eleven and again at one. I've given one of them a bottle but Tim is on tonight. He doesn't like me.' He hands me the torch and rummages in his trousers, pulling out a key; he waves it at me.

Robert switches on the light. We're in a room tiled all over in white. There's a table at one end with a sheet covering something. He whips off the sheet. 'Stephen, this is Mr Blue; Mr Blue, Stephen.' A body lies on the bench. Robert picks up the right hand and extends it towards me. I stay in the doorway.

'Suit yourself.' Robert lets the hand thunk down on the table.

The man on the table is naked and grey. I look away. 'Why have you asked me to meet you here, Robert?'

'That's the first time you've called me Robert. You do pick your moments to be intimate.'

'Don't you need bloody permission for something like this?' I stride forward and point to the man and touch his foot by mistake. It's cold. I want to pull the sheet up to his neck to warm him up, tuck him in.

'What did you think I was going to show you here? A new three-piece suite? A St Bernard? I know—you thought I'd discovered a cure for AIDS.' He scrawls something on a clipboard. 'Are you bothered by being here? Because you could leave.'

I say nothing.

'I didn't take you for someone squeamish, Stephen,' he says, frowning. 'We're not seeing anything more than a young slip of a first-year medic would.'

'I'm not squeamish,' I say.

'Look,' he says, slowly, eyebrows raised as if I were being unreasonable. Maybe I am. 'I thought you might be interested in seeing what Jackamore showed me, before beauty queens got involved. And this.' He bends down by a filing cabinet, opens the third drawer down and rifles through the files. Out of the section marked with an 'M', he pulls out an identical mask to mine.

'Where did you get that?' I ask, walking forward.

'You want the truth?' he says.

'I'm a philosopher. That's all I ever want.' That's not true. I'm being dishonest *now*, angling my body so that I can talk to Robert yet avoid the sight of the dead man in front of me. 'Stop arsing around and tell me, would you?' I say.

He breathes in, then out noisily through his mouth. 'Okay. When I was at Oxford I met Jackamore Grass. He was a medic. A polymath, really. He could pick up a new skill in a matter of days or hours. Charming, attractive, exactly the kind of man you don't want as a best friend—you can never match up to him; he had a gift, among many gifts, for making things happen, for conjuring fun out of an interminable Philosophy of Science seminar; and he had a way of acquiring things that we needed: five Tasmanian devils to release during finals; four renaissance masks for my book—'

'And bodies for an experiment in death,' I say.

Robert tilts his head to one side, neither agreeing nor disagreeing. 'Those are twelve days of Christmas I'd enjoy,' he says.

'And he does this out of kindness, or what?'

I ask.

Robert's laugh bounces off the tiles.

'He's blackmailing you?'

'Not as such.'

'So why are you in contact with him?'

'Now that I really can't tell you,' Robert says. His eyes are softer, direct, his hand on his chest. For the first time I believe him. 'I will tell you this, though, that there is only one reason people do things— love, of themselves or of another.' He steps back, his eyes harden again. 'And I utterly adore Robert Sachs.'

A door slams upstairs. Robert places the mask over the dead man's face, his finger on his lips. We wait, but there is no other sign of someone else in the building.

Removing the mask, I weigh it in my hands. It feels the same as mine.

'He gave this to me as a keepsake of my research. Jackamore acquired the masks, in his own very special way. I believe he borrowed them from a museum. Some time ago.' Robert laughs.

'What's so funny?'

'Oh you'd never believe me. Well, come on, you wanted to know about the masks, so—ask away.'

'I know that they are meant to represent female beauty, and the killer placed it on the face of a beauty queen, but why? Why would anyone want to kill a beauty queen? For all I know, this mysterious Jackamore doesn't exist: you killed Miranda in some weird experiment.' It doesn't stop at pigeons. 'For all I know, you're trying to involve me in order to frame me.'

Robert blinks. 'That's rather paranoid and irrational, don't you think, Stephen? Somewhat

124

extreme? Well I've answered *your* questions; now you can indulge *me* by giving me your thoughts on Mr Blue.'

I make myself look at the man on the bench. It's not as if I've never seen a dead body before. There was Mum. Miranda. And Pops, who was glass-cold when I was taken to see him, laid out in the dining room in a high black coffin. Da had pushed me into the room and kept a hand on my shoulder. Standing on tiptoe, curving my hand round the handle, I could see Pops' big nose jutting up. It was the colour of silly putty. A giggle swam round my chest and I felt guilty, because dead people are serious.

'Get closer; he can't hurt you,' Da said. He swung me up under the armpits, his finger pinching my skin. And it was that that made me want to cry, not seeing Pops there, hands over his tummy, like he'd eaten Christmas dinner and gone to sleep in his chair. Pops' face wasn't all creased up anymore. He looked young, and I wanted to go in and cuddle up but his big tickling moustache seemed darker, and I didn't like it. 'Kiss your grandfather goodbye,' Da said, his voice funny. He leaned over, still holding me, so that my head was close to Pops'. Pops smelled funny, like boot polish, and the stuff Mum used to clean the sink with. I went to kiss his forehead but missed, and got his shut eye instead. It was cool, and round as a ball-bearing.

'Eyeballs are the first to go, you know.' Robert is back, staring at me. I look around. I'm by the dead man's head, touching his eye. I pull my hand away.

'The eyelids are padded out with cotton wool and held shut with spiked caps,' he continues. 'It makes mourners think that all is as was before. The

125

Egyptians used pearl onions.'

Pops could fit four big pickled onions in his mouth at the same time, if he took out his dentures.

The eyes of the man on the table are leaking. I pick up a swab from the tray and dab.

'You should take up nursing,' Robert says, leaning over the body and reaching next to me for another scalpel. There's a small bald spot on Robert's crown, a peeking tonsure. He balances the scalpel on his ring finger.

'What are you going to do with that?' I say.

'You can't understand death without getting close to it,' he replies.

I could tell him how close I've been. It doesn't mean I understand it. He's looking at me as if he knows. And if he doesn't know, and I tell him, then he might pity me. Lead me out of the basement, like throwing back the undersized fish, and I'll never find out what he is up to.

He points the scalpel to the man's genitals. 'Notice anything?'

I look down. The man's balls are huge. Each is the size of my fist, and I resist the urge to place my hand over my own testicles.

Robert reaches into his back pocket and pulls out a magnifying glass. He spins it and it winks reflections off the glass cupboards on the walls. 'What are you doing for your holidays then?' he asks.

I stare at him. 'You're asking me to look at a dead man's balls, and then you want to know what I'm doing for the holidays?'

'Distraction. This is an exercise in perception and one man's idea of beauty against another's. You're here to help me look at things differently.

126

I want to approach death phenomenologically: to disregard any assumptions.'

'You're saying I should amputate my squeamishness in the aim of knowledge? Why?'

'To find new truths. Unclouded truths. Meaning that's been overlooked because of presumption. Do you get it yet, or shall I put it another way?'

'You don't need to patronise me.'

'But can't I anyway?'

I laugh. Can't help it. Robert grins and puts his finger over his lips, then hands me the magnifying glass. 'I know it's a lot to ask, but it would help me if you tried to look at things anew. What are your impressions?'

Breathing deeply, I try and shunt my sympathy for the dead man to one side. It's hard. Feelings put aside are still there, like a box of photos up in the loft. I bend lower and his testicles loom in the glass. Grey hairs stick out of shadowed craters. How would Robert put it? 'You can almost make out the man in the moon,' I say.

Robert claps his big hands together. I touch the man's leg to apologise, and stand up. 'Why are they so large?'

'Gas. Simple as that. Inside you now, your cells use enzymes to break down compounds that prevent them from breaking up the cells themselves. When you die, as you will—Stephen unless you're the world's first immortal, and, let's admit it, were God to exist, and to choose a human to be worthy of that distinction, then he would choose me over you, so when you cark it—shuffle off, pop your clogs or some other euphemism, the enzymes get free rein and start eating you dead.' He makes pincer movements with his hands. 'End

127

result—gas.'

'Lovely, that. Reassuring too.'

Robert wags his finger at me. 'Ah, but there's a problem. You won't be able to expel the gas in your usual fragrant way.'

'Are you saying I fart?'

'Are you saying you don't? Your sphincter will have no working muscles left. So it all builds up. In his balls,' he pats the man's lips, which are pouty, now I look at them properly, 'his lips, his tongue; all gassy. That's what I know. But I'm trying to look beyond or behind that. Look there.'

I move the magnifying glass to the man's leg, peer close. Little white bumps are moving beneath the skin.

'What are you experiencing?'

I watch the slow movement of the lumps. 'I'm hypnotised, to be honest. It's like rice pudding with the skin on top. Or shingle moving under a sheet.'

'Maybe that's exactly what it is.'

'It's not though, is it? It sounds like someone's popping bubble wrap in there.' Conscious that I'm listening to a dead man, I rear up and step back.

'Shhh!' Robert sticks his hand out to shut me up. Heavy steps upstairs again. I move over next to him. Robert switches off the light. The steps stop. I press my hands against the cold tiles. The steps start up again, down the stairs. It's a man, whistling. I feel Robert shaking next to me.

'All clear, Professor Sachs. I've sent Tim off after a student.' The voice of Head Porter Bowles. He sounds smug. Robert switches the light on and grins. He opens the door and whispers to the porter, who nods and stomps back up the stairs.

'I think it's time we left him, don't you?' Robert

128

says. 'We have another subject in need of our attention.' He tugs the sheet back over Mr Blue and takes back the magnifying glass. 'You do know now what those sounds were, don't you? The thing you called bubble wrap, whatever that is. Maggots,' he says.

*   *   *

Robert locks up behind me. I feel sick. The sound of white creatures feasting on tissue crackles on in my head. I don't know why I didn't walk straight out as soon as I saw the body. Yes. I do. The sickness is also excitement.

Robert is staring at me. 'You've got it, haven't you?'

'Got what?'

'The wonderful and worrying euphoria that comes from not being dead yet. Of being in the presence of absence.'

I open my mouth to deny it. Then nod.

'This is how it all starts, you know. I remember when Jackamore first took me into his lab at Oxford. Now *he* had arranged the students' cadavers into a tableau of the Last Supper, complete with bread and salt cellar.' We walk on past the college observatory towards the Cam. 'I felt disgusted but at the same time alive. And yes I did see beauty, both in the sensation and the frailty of the human body.'

'I suppose there could be something beautiful in the process of a body being broken down, recycled, taken away. Maggots are angels for dead flesh.'

Robert smiles. 'I like that. It is a good phrase. I may attribute that to you, my glamorous assistant,

129

in my forthcoming book.'

Holding his hand out, he takes mine and pulls me into a hug. The smell of dead flesh is thick on his hair like wax. 'Thanks, Stephen.' He walks away, whistling down the path. At the back gate he turns and waves, lit from behind by the lights of emergency vehicles. I wave back and feel as if the last hour has sutured us together. I must stop this now. In the morning I'll go to Inspector Horne and tell her about the masks and Robert and Jackamore.

He turns and walks over the Cam, the lights from emergency vehicles lighting his way.

Chapter Twenty-One

Evensong

It's the phone call. Jane can always tell. It's late, and they only call her late if there are 'developments'. And 'developments' always means death.

'Where and who?' she asks.

'Rhys Withins,' the scene of crime officer says. 'In Sepulchre's Fellows Garden. Found by the chaplain when he was walking his dog.'

'Rhys Withins—the boy reported missing yesterday. The chorister.'

There is a hesitation. 'Yes, ma'am.'

'Why the pause?'

'Because the decomposition is, let's just say, advanced, ma'am. He seems to have been buried, then very recently dug up.'

'But he can only *recently* have been buried.'

'That's right, ma'am.' He doesn't sound convinced.

Jane goes through into the kitchen and pours instant coffee granules onto her dinner of cornflakes and milk. 'I'll be there in fifteen minutes,' she says.

*   *   *

'Are you sure? It couldn't be extreme soil conditions or something to do with insects?' Jane asks.

Hana Barinder wipes her hand over her forehead. 'There is no way that boy died yesterday. But he went missing yesterday. I don't know how to explain it. There will be an explanation. I just don't have it, yet.'

Jane's head hurts. She walks back over and forces herself to look at him for another minute: she owes him that.

Behind a mound of just-dug earth, Rhys Withins lies in a deep grave. The remnants of tissue and sinew surround his visible skeleton. His hands crossed over his chest, one ankle over the other. Tucked under his arms is a greying toy rabbit, with one ear missing. Over his little skull is a heavy, stone mask and, beneath the mask, signs of nicks to his neckbone.

Rhys's mother is being held by an officer, refusing tea. Her husband stands watching her, his arms hanging at his side.

Pretending to talk into her phone, Jane strides away, trying not to break into a desperate, blind-footed run.

'Where are you going, ma'am?' Pemberton calls out.

131

She points to her bag, not that he could know what she means but he nods anyway, and she feels a grateful surge towards him.

Outside the garden, a crowd builds up already, peering through gaps in the hedge. Early birds, out for worms. She wants to ram her bag in their faces or grab them by the back of the neck and force their eyes down into the grave. You want to look? Then look.

The wind whips at her face as she legs it across the road. A lorry cranks to a stop next to her, honks its horn. 'Fucker,' she shouts at the windscreen.

As she stumbles up the kerb and through Sepulchre's imposing gate, Stephen Killigan comes into her head. The mask.

The options roll themselves out to her:

a) he found Miranda as he said, and someone took her;
b) he found Miranda and he took her;
c) he murdered Miranda and buried her elsewhere;
d) he murdered Miranda, buried her elsewhere and killed Rhys;
e) he has not had contact with Miranda and killed Rhys;
f) he was lying all along, told someone and they copied his lie into reality.

Jane stops where she is and leans against the willow tree. 'What do I do next?' she says. The willow tree shrugs, and shudders.

Chapter Twenty-Two

The Cam

Sirens again. And flashing lights, coming from over the road and river. One of my students, Melanie, walks towards me, holding hands with a postgrad. Their heads touch. They look like they have a secret.

'Hi, Melanie. Do you know what's going on?' I ask.

She scrunches up her mouth and makes a sucking sound. 'I thought you'd know,' she says.

'What do you mean by that?'

'A little boy has been found, murdered. Wearing a stone mask,' she says, her eyebrows raised in implicit accusation. I know she's putting it on for her older boyfriend, bigging up the moral disapproval. But it goes in anyway.

The postgrad speaks up. 'I expect they'll want to talk to you,' he says. He has ginger curly hair that springs from everywhere apart from on top. He looks like a protest singer who can only protest about getting the wrong coffee in Starbucks as he's never been outside his own head.

They continue walking, heads fused together. At least I've provided them with some currency when they gossip with their friends tomorrow morning. I've been given a stone mask. And minutes ago I was appreciating a dead body.

Inspector Jane Horne stands by the tree outside my building. She is holding its trunk, her forehead resting on its bark.

133

I can't face her. And I can't go back to my room, with that mask on the wall. It is there when I open my eyes and there, imprinted on my retina in reverse monochrome, when I close them.

I can't face anyone. I am a fucking coward.

And then there are the dead bodies. Everywhere.

I can still smell the laboratory. And I can't shift the images. Of Pops in his coffin, and Mum, out of the water, the fisherman thumping at her chest. I can smell the sea water, the formaldehyde, the sick-sweet smells of the dead.

The smell is getting stronger. Maybe it's the city, giving off its odour. Cambridge smells plain ill, and I've heard lots of people say that they never got sick until they came here, never, which can't be true but then I never feel warm here; I feel a pain in my throat and cold to my poky bones as if I've taken a dip in the Cam. Maybe that's what I need. I feel dirty and want to peel off my skin and scrub at it. The idea of leaping in twists and eddies in my mind till I see myself doing it and can feel the sharp wetness on my skin.

Maybe this is what Mum felt, before whatever happened happened and everything changed. The river turns a corner. I stand on the edge of the path and walk out into the air for one warm second before plunging into the Cam.

Chapter Twenty-Three

Expert Witness

Stephen Killigan has walked off the path and into the river. How pathetic. He is shown a dead man and wishes to become one. The boy has no potential to stick around and be interesting. In theory I could move from my bench, lie on the gravel and hold out my hand for the boy to grab. But there is no fun in that. He would be grateful, I am sure, but gratitude is a humdrum emotion.

Ah, but now he is fighting. His hand grabs at the air. The water flinches.

And he is gone.

Not drowning, not waving: gone.

Now I am the one following.

Chapter Twenty-Four

The Granta

The water chokes air out of my lungs, squeezing at my chest with iced hands. The river tastes of spinach and egg and wants to know what I taste like, reaching into my soundless scream and making me gag as I claw at the moss on the walls of the Cam. My feet almost touch the bottom and if I balance on one toe then I can kick against the weeds that cling to my legs. Something, a rock, I don't know, slips beneath me and I'm dragged under the water again, my shoe trapped. I could stop struggling. Just stop. If I let my arms drop, my muscles go slack, my mind not mind that I could die, then I wouldn't have to keep going, struggling, fighting, finding out. Maybe this is what Mum was thinking as her head went under; maybe, like me, all she could see when she opened her eyes was dark and she liked it. I hang like a ragdoll in the water and, though my lungs burn, the feeling that nothing matters at all floods through me. Nothing. It's joy, this feeling. And I thought I'd felt that before but I hadn't. I am going to die here and all that would happen is I wouldn't need to persuade myself to get out of bed in the morning, no need to face any fears or do anything ever again, and there would be a wake at The Black Heart and Satnam would knock pints with my mates Jake and Suzanne, and maybe Lana would be there, crying if I'm lucky. But then I wouldn't be lucky, I'd be dead.

Reaching down, I fumble for my laces and pull till my shoe slips off and, adrenalin coursing, better than the best amphetamine, I launch in the direction I hope is up, towards a light that burns above me.

A hand grabs my arm. I think first of Robert and want to shrink away—the last thing I want is Robert crowing for being my guardian angel—but my body is yanked out of the water. Something crashes against my ribs, then I'm pulled over it, my hip bones bashed, my arm feeling like it's been plucked from its socket the way I did to the limbs of my sister's Ken doll. And then I'm still. I lie, panting, trying out my lungs. I bet Robert is standing above me, smirking, hands in pockets, and Horne is huffing, her hands on her hips. I'm not sure I care any more, all I want to do is sleep.

'What you doin' in there, lad?' That doesn't sound like Robert. Opening my eyes, I see a frowning man sitting cross-legged opposite me on a pile of sacks. He swings a lantern next to my face.

'What?' I reply.

'You should watch yourselves, you scholars,' the man says, searching in a bag at his feet and pulling out a hunk of black bread. He holds it out to me. It's dry and tastes of iron. He throws it at me and shrugs off his coat. It smells of cinnamon and cloves and grains. 'You lost your robes in there?'

'That easy to tell I'm from the university?' I ask, shivering. My head is pounding, my foot throbbing. I look around to see if Robert has noticed me in the water but it is too dark to see anything. I can't even see any houseboats. We're in some kind of punt, deeper and more square than the usual ones.

'Where else you'd be from?' the man says. 'Long hair like that. An' only a scholar, never a day's labour in his life, would have a face smooth as fish belly.' He waggles a fish at me and grins. His face ripples up into lines. He makes a funny kind of angel. 'I'm Bill,' he says, holding out his hand with the fish still in it.

I shake the fish and his hand, and can't help smiling back. 'Stephen. Or you could call me Steve. You could call me anything after pulling me out like that. Thank you.'

'I'll let my daughters name you; they've been after a pet,' Bill says, picking up the flat paddles. The boat moves off.

'I'll get out here if that's all right Bill—I'll wander back to college.'

Bill stares at me, frowning. 'You can't walk from

137

here at this hour, lad, it's miles and miles back. You've been out for a good while. During the day, maybe, but you'd get swallowed up no time. And you got no shoes.'

I look down. He's right. There are my two big feet, stuck onto my skinny legs. But shoes aren't the biggest problem. I can't have travelled under the water that far. I must have hit my head, and lost consciousness?

'Get it out, lad,' Bill says. 'You look like a cat 'bout to cough up a furball.'

'I'm always saying this at the moment, but I don't understand.'

'It's easy enough to lose a day or a couple mile to drink.'

'I didn't think I'd drunk that much.'

He rumbles out a laugh. Above us I hear the sound of a bird that I don't recognise. The sounds are different, and the weir should be coming up by now, sounds of drunk students, tutting locals. But there's only rippling water and birds. And the dark is the darkest dark I've been in. And it's definitely a case of being *in* the dark, like being in the sea, immersed in it, surrounded by it. What if I am dead and Bill is the modern name for Charon, crossing the waters of the Styx with the dead me? I'd wondered if Islam held the key, although I don't like anything that claims itself, and only itself, is the answer. Being dead's all right, if you don't mind being wet. But I do mind being wet. And if I'm sensing damp then either I'm still in a body or my soul is experiencing the kind of phantom limb syndrome that amputees suffer. But that is a problem with neural relays, the brain not the soul, so I must still be in my brain, unless brain and soul are indeed the same. I have to conclude that either I've solved the mind/body/soul problem in one semi-suicidal leap or I'm extremely alive and sitting in an odd-looking punt with an archaic-looking man with no idea of where I am or where I am going.

'Do you often catch people and haul them into your boat, Bill?'

'Only the stupid ones,' Bill says, chewing on the black bread. 'Had another student last year. Delivering fish that time I was, an' all. Reckon fish attracts scholars like worms do fish.' He laughs, a croaky rumble. 'Still, least you don't look as bad as him. He was a sight—hooked him out and his green robe stuck to him. Like rotten weeds, he was. And he complained about Mary's cookin'.'

'Mary's your wife?' I ask, sitting up properly and tugging his coat around me.

He nods. 'You'll meet her soon enough. She won't be pleased to have to share her supper. She's a big girl, my Mary. Huge.' That rumbling laugh again.

I lean back and look up at stars that I've never seen before. I've always wanted to name all the stars, thought that would be a great way to impress: lie back on a judiciously placed picnic rug, pointing up at Ursa Major or whatever, arm sneaked round a girl's cold shoulders.

We should have gone past some kind of civilisation by now, somewhere I can jump out and blag a taxi back to the college. It's one of the dodgy privileges of being a Fellow that you can ring up the porters and they will send a cab for you, as if you were a celebrity. And I'd do that now, only all I can see is Bill's lantern and the reed waving on the river bank. I'm not used to reeds—usually it's all

139

manicured lawn.

The sound of the paddles in the water, punctuating hoots of owls and Bill's comforting silence. makes my eyelids ease down over my eyes. I let myself sleep.

*   *   *

'He's out like Martha,' I hear Bill whisper, though Bill's whisper is more like a foghorn.

'We can't leave him, Bill,' a woman's voice, Mary maybe, says. 'He'll freeze over.'

'I fetched him out the river, Mary, he isn't the river itself.' His voice is soft, full of love, and when I hear them kiss I don't know what to do with myself. Lifting myself up, I stretch out my legs. They feel like they've been rolled up into a taut ball of hamstrings then batted back and forth over a tennis net. The coat that Bill gave me is soaked through—I'll have to find a way to dry it out for him. Bill stands over me on the river bank, beaming down. Next to him stands a pretty woman, very thin, in a grey dress with full skirts, her head covered with a shawl. Bill holds out his hand, again.

Bill and Mary's house smells of peat and weeds and tea-smoked steam and the hot soup that is coating my throat and warming me up as much as the fire. A two-roomed hut not far from the river. Bill's two young daughters, Rachel and Martha, sit opposite me at the wooden table. Martha gazes at me, hardly blinking, with her chin on the table. Rachel tries very hard not to yawn.

'The both of you, back to bed in ten minutes,' Mary says, her tone warning, her hands stroking their messy hair back behind their ears. The girls wear long nightdresses, as if in a re-enactment society. Everything looks as if it were in a museum. Perhaps these are the East Anglian equivalent of Amish people. Martha's fingers curl round a wooden horse; one book, the Bible, lies on the table, open at Job. That's cheery bedtime reading. The writing is old, really old. Leaning over, holding the page open, I turn to the first pages of the book.

'Why is he sniffing the Bible, Ma?' Rachel says.

I sit up straight. The Bible doesn't have that old book smell, more like cotton shirts and sawdust. The paper is uneven. This is unquestionably the oldest book I have ever touched and it seems only a couple of years old. Nothing in the room says this is the twenty-first century. Adrenalin fumes round my body. I stand up, walk around the hut.

'He thinks he can smell God,' Martha replies, nodding, never blinking, like some kind of owl-child.

'And what would God smell like?' Bill asks, lifting Martha up and sitting her on his lap. His pipe smoke curls round his chin like an extra beard.

'That's most like blasphemy, Bill,' Mary says, tapping a loaf of bread on his head.

'Sounds like that bread's done,' Bill replies.

'I think God smells like cheese,' Martha says, licking her lips. Bill laughs into her hair.

'I apologise,' Mary says to me, 'she doesn't know what she's saying.'

'Shows good imagination, I reckon,' I say. She's not the only one. My heart goes fast again. What if I am out of time? In the wrong time as I have woken up in the wrong place. Easier. I didn't even have to change planes, trains, not even a lane on the motorway or get incredibly drunk. Or did I?

Maybe that's it, maybe that's what's going on. I'm dreaming, a new one this time. I've swapped night terrors. Another drunkard's dream. He is welcome to mine.

Bill looks at me and cocks his head to one side. 'Bedtime for you missies,' he says, 'before you get in any more trouble.' Lifting Martha over his shoulder, he carries her through to the other room. Rachel follows, shuffling her feet on the matting.

Mary sits in the rocking chair, lifts a foot up onto her lap and takes off her shoe. The lamps add even sharper angles to her face.

Bill walks in, slumps into a chair. 'So what is it, young scholar? Yer look like you left your smile in the river.'

'Can I ask you something, Bill?'

'You can try, I might'n answer. I'm the fish that swallowed the secret.'

'Secrets catch in the throat, don't they?' I scrape the chair back and breathe in deeply. I'd been holding my breath. 'What year is this?'

'Did you crack your head on the riverbed?' Mary says.

'1635, lad; no earlier, no later.'

'And it's October?'

'You must've been under longer than I thought,' Bill says, his forehead bunching into wrinkles. 'What other month would it be?'

'At least I know that much then.' Bill and Mary look at me, concerned. Bill throws another log on the fire. I can't be in 1635. That's not possible. I stand up and stumble round the room, picking up pots and putting them down, placing my palms against the cottage's cold walls.

Someone is playing a trick. 'Is it you?' I shout

142

at Bill, slamming my hand down on the table to see if I'm really here. My palm smarts as if Da had thwacked it with Mum's Good News Bible.

'Settle,' says Bill, and clicks his tongue as if soothing an animal. 'Breathe. You're not a cod; you won't drown in the air. Remember what your lungs are for.'

Mary reaches up to my shoulders and eases me down into the chair again.

I suck in air, feel my heart beating in my ears.

Mary gives Bill a worried look. 'How did you end up in the river? Were you attacked? Thrown in?' she asks.

I shake my head. My skull feels like it's on the spin cycle in the college laundry.

Bill clears his throat. 'You can tell us, you're safe here.' He nods, places his rough hand over mine.

'I wasn't attacked: I fell in. Or jumped. I'm not sure which. But I wanted to. I've had a few shocks, recently.'

Mary puts one hand on the Bible and a finger to her lips. She nods at the girls who are standing in the doorway, giggling and holding hands. 'What did I tell you? Get back into bed.'

Martha swings on the back of my chair. 'Good night, mister scholar,' she says as her sister pulls her by the sleeve through to the other room. Bill smiles and I know that he is not tricking me. I don't know what's going on, but he is as real as earth and water.

'Why would I have been attacked?' I ask.

Bill lowers his voice and cranes his neck to check that the girls are out of hearing. 'Ther've been some deaths recently. A friend, Luke, another fenman, well he was found face down in shallow water. I saw

143

the boot print on his back meself but no one would listen to me. Said I was making trouble.'

'And the other deaths?'

'Even the overseer said one of them was suspicious,' Mary says, folding up clothes and hanging them over the clothes-horse by the fire.

'What happened?' I ask, leaning forward on my elbows. I want to know more but my eyelids are intent on shuttering my eyes.

'You need sleep, lad,' Bill says. 'More of this talk and you'll get night terrors.'

'I'm used to that,' I say, trying to stand up. My legs feel like they've been replaced with pick 'n' mix red laces.

Bill grabs blankets from a cupboard in the wall and makes up a bed on the woven reed mat by the fire. 'You'll be right in morning. I'll wake you early an' take you back where you belong, with the other head-in-skys.' He places the guard over the fire. 'Don't want you getting yourself burned 's well as drowned, lad. That'd be bad luck indeed.' He pats me on the shoulder and, holding Mary's hand, goes into the back room. I want that: to live a long life with a woman I love. I can still feel Lana's cold hand in mine and remember her face when I blew on the tips of her fingers.

Lying down, I pull the blanket up over my mouth. Above me, fire shadows fight on the ceiling. My pulse is still up, chasing itself. I don't think I have ever been this cold, or this scared. I'm in the seventeenth century. The seventeenth century. Political and religious upheaval. Enlightenment. Witch trials. I could get tried as a witch if I tell anyone about all this. Or sectioned in the present, *my* present, not this present, though this must

144

be my present as I am in it, and that is my future, although I was there in the past and I may never get back. Fuck, I need to go to sleep.

I sit up, blankets sliding down. Maybe this is to do with witches, or something like them—if I can dance from one time to another then someone else can as well. Maybe a witch, maybe someone they would call a witch. Lying back down I feel as if I'm on the brink of my own life.

Chapter Twenty-Five

A Bottle of Red and a Doughnut

Jane checks that the mirror has steamed up, then unbuttons her blouse. She releases the safety pin and, grasping the end, looking anywhere but at her chest, unwinds the Ace bandage till it lies coiled on the bathroom floor. The pain returns, immediately, as if someone is reaching through her back and pinching and pulling at her breast skin from inside. She closes her eyes as she steps into the bath, letting the too-hot water distract her. Sinking down until the bubbles cover her torso entirely like a salt-crusted cod, she opens her eyes. On the tray, straddling the bath, is a notebook; a bottle of Merlot with a ring doughnut round its neck; a novel set in Mary Tudor's court; notes made on Killigan and everyone she has to interview the next day; and a candle that's supposed to smell of crème brûlée but instead makes her think of the stink of condoms.

The day, she hopes, will slope off down the overflow in the bath that she has overfilled again, along with the image of Rhys in his grave with the mask on his little face that keeps coming into her mind. That and Stephen Killigan drawing the mask with the pads of his fingers. What if she called it wrong from the start, and Killigan is guilty? She didn't even search his rooms the night he said he found her. Two cases connected by a stone mask and nothing making sense.

Her forehead feels as if it has been filled with nails and a giant magnet placed against it. She pours wine into 'the glass that holds a bottle' that Sean had given her for Christmas, two days before she found out about Lyndsi. Lyndsi. That's the worst of it—leaving her for a girl who puts an 'i' at the end of her name and draws a heart for a dot. And has two breasts, not one. So that's not the worst of it. She gulps down the wine until she feels it swill around the pain in her head and nudge the nails away.

She throws her notebook over the other side of the bathroom and picks up the novel, letting the words take her somewhere else. Work begins again in four hours' time. She closes her eyes. The pages dip into the water.

Chapter Twenty-Six

The Pillars of Solomon

The fenman is back. He stands over Killigan, rubbing what hair is left on his head. With one hand on his back, he pokes at the embers of the fire and, crouching with some difficulty, tugs the blanket back over Stephen's shoulders, exposed from his turning and struggling in his sleep. The fire rises.

My left hand is hurting from holding so hard to the window. My other is making a fist. I must cut my nails: they are cutting parentheses into my palm. I do not know why I am tense. It must be the weather, and the damp of this fenland hole. But there is also the fact that I feel violated somehow. It feels good, and bad. There are things happening that even I do not understand and it makes me sing. How did Stephen Killigan find my time stream? He does not seem to have any control of it yet. There aren't many others I can talk about this with, and those I could turned their backs on me a long time ago.

I want to get close to him. So I know how best to beat him. Always attack those closest to your enemy, everyone knows that. Killigan has walked into the same year with which I am tinkering. And even I did not know that was possible. It could be coincidence, of course. But it seems unlikely. I do not like admitting ignorance. But it is important to confess the truth to yourself, if only to lie better to others.

I step away from the window and move round to the side of the hut, unwrapping the string tied round the torso of my notebook. The torch has a weakening

147

eye, but it can still glower at the pages. They are stained with ink and tea and blood.

Two sets of handwriting: mine and Robert's. Robert's has changed little since Oxford, though the exuberance of his loops has diminished and he no longer doodles fleur-de-lis in the margins. I recall it. The night after the last experiment. I cross the room to the mullioned windows and stand, arms folded, looking out over the quad to Balliol's library. The windows are dark. Stained glass without light is as a beautiful voice whose throat has been sliced. Robert should be here by now. He should be walking on the flagstones below me, with the swagger that he designed at the same time as his lemon-coloured lounge suits. I commanded him to be here by eleven and he did not give me information otherwise. I have not seen him since last night, not even at Hall this evening where usually he delights in imbibing the college's oldest Margaux, in tipping down the rarest of wines; nor taking his turn in the library overseeing the yawns and covert romances of students until a permanent replacement is found for Peter, the louche librarian, liberated from life by what the police think was an opportunistic thief-turned-murderer caught in the act. We know otherwise.

I read through the contract again. 'The experiments detailed in the accompanying documents are not to be discussed with or disclosed to any other person or persons.'

Footsteps on the staircase. Robert's deliberately slow steps. He is trying to show me that yesterday has not affected him in any way. He is shouting out his denial with every heavy step like a child declaring through sleep-heavy lids that he is not tired.

The door opens.

148

'You're late,' I say.

Robert takes off his coat. He flings it over my dark red wing-back.

'Where have you been?' I ask, using the tines of a fork to scrape last night's dirt out of my nails.

'If I didn't know better, I'd say that you missed me, Jackamore,' he replies. Despite his bluster, his face is pale, his eyes bloodshot and his voice does not have its usual stridency.

'I would miss you, Robert, were you no longer here. If only for the entertainment you provide me. You are the original fool. The follis, the bag of wind. The front you put up is amusing, and fools most people. Not me. I know who you are. You showed me last night.'

Robert holds my gaze. Then he opens his briefcase and flicks through his files for something to do rather than meet my eye again, I surmise.

'You have not answered my question,' I continue.

'I can't remember what it was,' he says, sweeping back his hair. 'Let me guess. You want to know where I get my shoes?'

I tap my foot on the Turkish rug.

'All right, all right. I have been shoring up my alibi.'

'Is that one of your terrible euphemisms? Do not answer that; of course it is. I suppose your sister has stepped forward, again?'

Robert nods.

'You should think yourself lucky to have a sister like her. Pretty and intelligent. A dangerous combination, but a good one. She wouldn't fall to pieces like you. You couldn't even save her when she was drowning in the river. It is fortunate that I was there, was it not?'

Robert rubs his hand across his forehead. 'Jackamore, does this not affect you at all? You

149

disappeared in front of my eyes.' He moves closer to me till we stand inches from my bookcase. 'You weren't always like this,' Robert says, opening his arms to me.

I knock them away. The back of his hand smacks against a hardback book. His shoulders slump.

'It must disappoint you that you cannot follow me,' I say. 'That, try as you might, screw up your eyes and count to a hundred, wish to your God or on a hundred stars and you will still not be able to travel in time.'

Robert's mouth twitches. 'Given what you do with your own ability, I do not want to.'

'Robert, you have an amazing ability to lie to yourself. Another thing you have in common with your sister. Twins are alarming things. You see things in such a black and white way; you will never make an aesthetician that way. Look.'

I reach for my new magician's set on the top shelf, covered in a blue silk shawl. I stole the box from a man who stole it from Dickens, or so he told me, but then who would trust the word of a thief? The box, mid-nineteenth century with red velvet lining and a mirrored back that shows Robert craning forward to peer inside, contains the usual boxwood pieces, a Scotch purse, a Ballanchini's box, a metal kugel hammer, a bonus genus doll and the item I am looking for.

'Your idea of time is based on how it seems. Not how it is. The same can be said for most magic tricks. And the simplest illusions are often the most effective.' Easing two joined wooden pillars from their cushioned nook, I say: 'These are the Pillars of Solomon. Watch.'

Robert stares as I hold aloft the two pillars. A piece

of string emerges an inch from the top of the side of each piece. I tug on one end of the string, and the other shortens; I pull on the other end, and the first shortens.

'The piece of string is drawn through, but what happens if I do this'? Smoothly, out of my sleeve, I glide a knife into my hand.

Robert flinches and grabs the edge of the desk.

I lick the length of the knife and place it between the top of the two pillars. It guillotines, slicing between the wooden sticks. The two columns fall from each other and lie apart on my palm. Two straggles of string stick out from each inner side of the pillar, seemingly severed from each other. 'See how the knife has cut through the string?'

Robert raises an eyebrow, but moves closer.

'So how is it possible,' I say, 'to do this?' I tug gently on the string on the outside of the pillar, and the string on the far side of the other pillar is pulled closer to the wood.

'That's easy,' Robert says, leaning his elbow on the mantelpiece. 'The string never went across the top; it seems that way because they are in proximity. It goes down the length and up the other side.'

'Correct, Robert. Consider yourself given the magician's gold star.'

'Why are you showing me this?'

Taking out my notebook, I draw three diagrams: one of the pillars next to each other, body to body, shoulder to shoulder; the next of the pillars post-'cutting', and then one showing the workings: an X-ray with the string running through the bones of the pillar.

Robert, hands in pocket, ambles over to the spirits on my filing cabinet. 'I'm struggling, Jackamore. What exactly has this to do with time?'

*'Do I really have to explain?' I detach a phalange
from the medical skeleton hung from the hook on my
ceiling and point it at the diagram. 'You think that
time is linear; that history is a series of events pressed
together like the pillars, and that, like the string in
figure one, we are pulled through history until our
length runs out.' I place the finger bone in Robert's
whiskey sour and stir. 'No need to thank me, Robert,'
I say.*

He glares.

*'This is not reality, however. It is because you think
it is that you can be broken.' I place my hand briefly
on his shoulder and he looks up at me. I move away.*

*'It is true that history is held together by those
experiencing it, otherwise it can be compared to
a game of Pick Up Sticks without players, rather
than the Pillars of Solomon, drawing on traditional
Hermetic thoughts that, when you pass through the
pillars, you enter an unknown realm that can lead to
enlightenment. The reality is that humans can adapt,
if they allow themselves, to anything. It is when they
get stuck in any one adaptation that they stop being
able to experience the world. The concept of reality
and personality being fixed is constructed by you, and
believing too strongly in what you have created leads
to fundamentalism and lack of clarity. If you could
accept that life is chaotic, stop holding on to fairytales
of order and know that your string can wind down,
around, through time, however the pillars fall, then
you would be a much wiser man instead of a pathetic
mess.'*

*Robert takes out a photo from his pocket and
gently touches it, tracing an oval shape. A face?
Consoling himself with one of his students, probably.*

This is what he is holding onto. They haven't heard what I'm saying at all. All of the past to play in and they want to hold onto the present.

'You disappoint me. You . . . ' I gesture towards Robert, 'are held back by your attachment and loyalty and ordinariness. You are not worth my time.'

'Leave us alone, Jack,' Robert says.

'You should be on your knees, thanking me for showing you what is real. If you could leave your sister's side and your students' beds long enough then you could have everything you want. What would you do with History if it lay down on the grass before you? That is what defines a man.'

Robert walks over, slowly. 'What you do is not right, Jackamore.'

'There is no right and there are no rights, Robert Sachs. That is exactly my point. I am sad that you are too stupid to see that. Perhaps I should be talking to your sister.'

Grabbing at my shirt, he propels me back against the door. The Pillars of Solomon fall to the floor; cards flee from my sleeves.

Robert clutches my throat. Squeezes. His face contorts.

The borders of my vision are black and blurred like a silent movie. I pull at his wrists, laughing. The sound is strangled and snake-like. 'I told you that you were capable of murder, Robert. Everyone is. It is a question of finding the trigger.'

His grip shifts and I take the opportunity to peel one of his fingers off and snap it backwards. He howls. I imagine handing it to him in a cocktail glass. I shove him and reach into my magic set. I swing the kugel hammer in a looping motion and hit him hard on the side of the neck.

Robert's mouth drops open; his eyes close. He sways once, then topples like a stout tree, his arm knocking books off the shelf.

I stand over Robert's unconscious body. There will always be fall-out when you reach the limits of experience. This is of course regrettable. Though not for long: there is so much to do. It is a delicious irony that the only way to tightrope through time is to know there is no rope, no safety net, no circus. There are those who know to avoid the cracks in the pavement and it is these people that I wish to talk to. I am being most eloquent on this subject. I should write all this down.

I take out my notebook again and write, my handwriting as joined, smooth and elegant as it has ever been.

*   *   *

My torch closes its eyes to what is on the page. I shake it but it gives up as easily as Robert. Those events took place thirty years ago. I did not see him again for twenty-nine of those, when he came and begged for my help. He does not deserve my assistance, but then no one does. I am cold now, standing in seventeenth-century mists. Thinking about that time of experimentation has caused the warmth of nostalgia to Benylin my chest, but that is, as is so often the case, trailed by the cold-fingered poke in the ribs of reality, which is much like the comfort of urinating oneself, and the chill and chafe that follows.

I walk back round to the window. The fenman has gone, leaving his lantern to cast ghosts on the walls around Stephen.

He stretches an arm above his head like a cat.

154

His breathing is as slow as a sigh. He *has not fallen to pieces—he is adapting, even in his sleep. I don't know how he got here, if he is following me, but I shall reward him. I will give him more of a chance to untether himself and find wisdom.*

I whistle as I walk along the marshy bank of the river. I need the fourth victim, to complete the set. And he must be the one to choose her. This one I will kill myself. I deserve that, after all I have done for others.

Back to the city, where I have a muse to exhume, and rebury.

Chapter Twenty-Seven

Scio me nihil scire

Hana Barinder hands over her initial report. She has the decency to look embarrassed at least.

'You don't know. That is your conclusion after a night of tests. That you don't know.'

Hana doesn't look up. She rearranges her scissors, scalpels and hammer, for no good reason as far as Jane can see. Hana then picks up a piece of paper and starts folding each corner. Pathologists are a strange set. Not that she can talk, dealing in bodies and death.

'Look at me, Hana. I need to take something away with me. Anything. A whisper; a snippet; a pale hint of a pale hint that we've got something to get on with so I can sit with Rhys's parents and not feel like a cunt.'

Hana holds up the rib shears.

'I hope you're not thinking of using those on me.'

'Not until you're dead,' Hana says.

'And when will that be?'

'Any time in the next half hour if you keep going around being rude. Sorry, Jane, but I've done everything I can. These are the facts: Rhys's body was buried no less than a year ago, in the spot where he was found. The decomposition patterns all support it: the tissues have nearly broken down so that he is not far off from skeleton; the chemicals released from his body during autolysis have affected the fauna in the area; given the average temperature in the area and the fact that being buried in soil increases the time it takes to decompose. It's all there. Even if his body were laid out under the sun in the hottest desert it would still take twenty-plus days to become skeletonised. There is no way he could have been alive yesterday.'

'But he was.'

'So it seems.'

'And the DNA results confirm it is Rhys.'

Hana nods slowly.

'And there is no method of stripping the body down that can fast-track the process? No, I don't know, acid or something?'

'Nothing that I know of. No animal or chemical or biological process that I am aware of can cause the body to still have the remnants of ligaments and tissue and have the beginnings of decomposition of bone consistent with being buried for a year. The only thing I know of is time.' She rubs her eyes and splashes cold water from the sink onto her face. 'But I'll keep looking.' She yawns, becoming all jaw and mouth. She's been in here all

156

night already.

Jane feels herself relenting. It's not Hana's fault that this doesn't make sense.

'What about the mask, anything?'

'We have picked up DNA from around the eye area, as if someone were holding it by the holes. No match as yet. But it's the same with the teddy, around the ear. The one interesting thing is that this DNA has turned up before, on the music box for one, but in other cases in Cambridge and in other cities and towns. Never identified, but always there in the form of one fingerprint, one strand of hair, one careful dot of blood.'

'Like someone intends to be found out.'

'Or wants us to acknowledge him.'

'Him?'

'From running DNA from previous examples, we believe it to come from a man who prefers night to day.'

'Any more genetic wizardry and stone casting?'

'You know . . . '

'That it can be controversial. Yes. Carry on.'

Hana picks up a printout. 'Okay. The PER3 gene is present, associated with people who are night owls. And the profile shows a gene on the X chromosome that codes for monoamine oxidase enzyme that is associated with sensation and thrill-seeking. But research in this area is limited, has only just started.'

'So we don't know who it is, why they are present at crimes, or whether any of this genetic stuff is any cop.'

'And we have no idea how Rhys ended up the way he did.'

Jane shivers and sticks her hands into her

pockets. 'Cold in here, isn't it?'

Hana hands Jane an origami flower. 'Nope,' she says.

Chapter Twenty-Eight

The Great Level

I open my eyes expecting to see the damp walls of my college room. Instead, inches from my face, a fire crackles and spits under a pot. A headache gnaws at my temples; my stomach cramps. I have no idea where I am. Sitting up, I see a small girl in a linen nightgown sits cross-legged a metre away, staring at me. She prods at my tattooed shoulder with a cold fire iron. And now I remember. I'm somewhen else. I've woken up in foreign time.

I retch, bile attacking my throat. A man sits at the table, smoking a pipe. Memories fix in place: he fished me out of the river. How did I get in the river? I wanted to be in the river.

I hold onto the flames that lick at my elbow. The fire tattoo reminds me to be like fire, to use the fuel that's around me, to blaze and not be benign. Now, again, things are happening around me, and to me and I am drowning.

I jump up from the bed. The man walks over. Bill. He throws a bundle of clothes at me. 'Get yeself dressed, lad, in some respectable clothes; yours are still sopping.' He puffs smoke up into my face. I cough and he grins at me, showing his dead front tooth. 'You're alive then. Mary was worried you'd perish of river plague overnight. I said you were strong as five rope.'

Mary hands me a tankard of beer and a bowl of off-white gloop. 'Bet you've never been up this early. You should see the fens when the sun comes up,' she says. 'Is better than any fancy building.'

The porridge soothes my sore throat and starts a sweat in my armpits.

'You ready then?' he asks.

'What for?'

'I'm takin' you home. You're goin' back where you belong.'

'I doubt that,' I say, pulling on his rough tunic. The sleeves stop five inches short of my wrist.

*   *   *

The sun is barely up when we climb into the boat. I take the paddles and start rowing.

'All right then, boy. Tell me if you want me to take over.'

'As you can probably see, I'm thirty-five. And not a boy.'

'Well, I'm forty, right? And you look like a boy to me.' He laughs, his weather-whipped skin raw. He breaks up the bread Mary stowed in the boat before we left. 'She gave you an egg as well. You're lucky.'

'You have it,' I say, then regret it as he looks like I've punched him.

Drawing us through the water, I look round at the fenlands, trying to find something solid to hold onto. The water covers everything, cloaking the earth. 'I never realised how stunning the fens were.'

'Stunning is good, is it?'

'More than good. Look at it. It takes the light

159

and turns it back on the sky.'

'It won't for much longer if the king has his way.' He looks around him as if worried that someone will stomp out of the reeds and arrest him for treason.

'What do you mean?' About a week ago I'd read an article on the draining of the fens in the *Evening News*. The Environment Agency is planning on flooding the fens again and farmers are objecting. The accusation was that farmers never like change.

'You bein' stupid again, lad? Do they not talk 'bout anything other than clouds where you come from? Can't blame your sort, suppose; raised with paper in your mouth, not milk.'

'Sorry, I know they are draining the fens to make more money.' Ahead, another boat bobs towards us.

'Make money out of us, more like. They're commons; we rely on 'em. They say we'll make more, that crops'll grow and money will fall and that the fen water is diseased, makes us, and the rest of the city, ill. But they spill lies as easy as pissin'.'

'Who's "they"?'

His jaw juts out; the bristles of his beard glint white. 'The king's pups, Killigrew and his friends. They'll make a penny out of it.'

I stare into the water. Reeds move like slim green limbs. Solid shadows glide and dart. There's a parallel, vivid world under the skin. 'Will all this go?' I ask, waving a paddle across the water.

'If it works.' Bill chews on more bread. His eyes look so wet that they could be drained as well.

'In centuries to come the authorities will want to

flood the fens again.'

'You know that, do you?'

'As sure as I am sitting here right now.'

'You're a strange one all right.'

The man on the other boat waves. I wave back and Bill turns, raises his hand and gestures for it to come closer. 'Don't know who that is,' he says. 'I normally know everyone out here.'

Our boat rocks gently as the other approaches.

In the boat, a man rows in a black cloak, scrunched up like a bin bag.

Bill nods his acknowledgement, his arms cross his chest and his chin tilts up. 'Haven't seen you before round here. Are you all right? You look pastry pasty.'

'I'm okay. Shocked, I would say.' His voice, low and sonorous, shakes. He holds up his hand; it is quivering. 'I've been at the draining,' he says.

Bill clears his throat.

'I was handing over the food when the machine stopped.' His fingers weave together. 'They found a girl. Dead. I saw her. She had a stone face.'

No, no, no, no, no.

The man and Bill stare at me. Bill places his hand on my shoulder. 'What is it? No what?'

I'm losing it. I've lost it. I drop an oar and Bill has to scrabble to grab it.

'Is it far?' I ask.

'The drainage site?' Bill bites his lip, looks in my eyes. 'Too far for us. I've got to get you back to where you belong, not out here.'

'This is something to do with me,' I say, quietly.

Bill sighs. 'It'll take about twenty minutes if I row.'

The man nods. 'If that.' His eyes do not seem

161

shocked and tired, they gleam as if the sun were in them, but that's probably because I am so far beyond those states of being that I don't recognise them.

'We'll have to keep low,' Bill says. 'The drainers aren't keen on me. I say what I am thinking.' He takes back the other oar and turns the shallow boat to face east.

The man waves us goodbye, sitting up tall now. I sit watching him watching us as Bill rows us away.

'What were that man's name?' he asks. 'Did he tell us?'

I play back the conversation. 'He didn't, no. But then we didn't tell him ours.'

Bill shrugs. 'True enough. Onwards then.'

He glances at me occasionally, and talks so I don't have to.

'I was part of the riot couple month back. Standin' up for fenmen, our access to commons for fishin', grazin' and fowlin'. And for the land, if you get my meaning, for the water. It belongs here. Chase it away and it'll come back in the end. Made us feel better, knocking shit out of the Flemish boys they've got doin' the drainin'. The Flems, they're called in our house. But we didn't stop 'em. The king's folk have made up their minds.'

Bill stares out at the sky behind me, his eyes grey and still. He belongs here as much as the water, moves as smoothly over the earth.

I see the appeal of rowing across water all day, rootless thoughts sinking, horizons wherever you look. It's a form of yoga. I did a whole week of yoga with a girlfriend once and it was the nearest I've come to Zen, hitting the monkey mind on the head with a monkey wrench. But you can't

162

stop it chattering, not really; the brain is made for making connections and I like it. I thrive on the flying mind. Right now I am turning over anything that could help make sense of whatever weirdness is happening to me. Events are converging and I am at the centre, the calliope in the carousel, and dead girls surround me like fairground horses. I am collecting coincidences like butterflies. Coincidence. Cause and effect are based on linear progression, and I am in the past. If I can go back, someone else can too, and cause a seemingly impossible future.

We hear the noise first. The whirring, the shrieking of a machine. It sounds like a monster deep under the water. As we get nearer it changes pitch to a dark thrum, a purr. When we're about 500 metres away and the water has become a river once more, we see the cluster of people standing on land. They are facing the other way, looking down. Bill puts his finger to his lips and, leaping onto the bank, pulls the boat into the side. The boat bobs and each time it rises up I can see the group of drainers in the distance, huddled together.

Bill holds the boat while I climb onto the bank. A small hut is to our left and I motion for Bill to follow me. Putting the boots that Bill lent me down one after the other, I walk the makeshift path that winds behind the hut. Each time a stone shifts, I wince and want to freeze but if any of them look behind them it will appear more suspicious. At the back of the hut, out of sight, our clothing camouflaging with the faded grey stone, Bill turns to me and frowns.

I move down the side of the hut until I can see the cluster of drainers. Staying close to the wall, the ridges of the stone pressing through the coat into my sore ribs, I watch the men carry a body towards us.

'What is it, lad?' Bill says.

'Ssh. Looks like they're coming this way.'

'Come on lad, we shouldn't be here.'

I don't move. The men get closer. One of them, a tall man in a tall hat, is carrying a limp young woman, her muddy hair clinging to his neck and shoulder. There is no sign of the mask. Bill yanks the back of my coat and we run back down to his boat. Clambering in, lying flat to the hull, I lie down next to Bill, trying to catch my breath. Bill coughs and covers his mouth. His chest stutters in and out.

The men sound close, twenty metres away. Their boats are further along the bank but if they come any closer they will see us. How can this be explained—a saboteur taking a nap with his friend? That probably doesn't look good in any century.

I raise my head, just enough to see the girl carried across a man's chest, her head thrown back, arm trailing. The man stops and I raise myself up further. The boat rocks and Bill hisses at me. 'Stay yeself still.'

The man places the girl's body on the ground. 'Who brought a woman out here?' he shouts. His voice has the clear bark of someone used to being obeyed. The men around him reel back, muttering in Flemish. One of them takes off his cap and looks around. Leaning forwards, I steady the boat by grabbing onto the bank. The brown heads of the bulrushes weave in front of me like a crowd at an execution trying to grab a better view.

'Does anyone know how she got here?' the overseer barks. The men stare down to their feet.

Some shake their heads. 'There are rules to follow. Women are forbidden from the works.'

'Who should we take her to, sir?' one of the workers says in accented English.

The overseer stares at the body, his hands on his head. He kicks at a clod of earth, which skims across the ground, landing near us. 'If this is known it will hold up our progress. The Level will be stopped.' He looks around him, stamps on the ground with his boot. 'We have no choice. We will have to bury her here. No one will miss her.'

The man who took his cap off runs over to the hut and comes out with a muddy spade. The overseer points to the earth. I can see the top of the woman's head, her clagged hair. No one will ever know her name. One of them holds up the mask.

Lurching forward, I climb out of the boat. Bill grabs my foot and hisses at me. 'What you doin'? Come back, lad.'

Shaking him off , I grab onto reed heads and pull myself over the edge of the boat and onto the bank. I stand up. A worker points to me. Blood pulses in my ears.

The overseer turns, his hands on his hips. He takes the spade from the worker. The ground is firm beneath my feet but soft enough that I will sink if I do not move. I walk over in what I hope is an authoritative manner. I hold my hands behind my back so they cannot see my tattoos. 'You cannot bury anyone in fen ground,' I shout to them.

The overseer stalks towards me. He is covered in mud from carrying the dead body. 'And why not?' he asks, holding the spade so the blade is aimed at my chest.

Work brain, work. 'I'm from the university.

Undergoing a study on the soil. If you bury a body in there without proper precautions, it will leak poisonous chemicals that would corrode any foundations. I'm sure the king wouldn't like to hear that.' Standing up, I hold my hands behind my back so he can't see them shaking.

'I have not been told of any such work on the soil,' the overseer says, moving towards me. 'And I would know.'

'Maybe there are some things you don't know,' I say. We stand inches apart, jaws jutting, There's doubt in his eyes now, a flinch in the corner of his mouth that suggests that he doesn't want to jeopardise cash flow.

'How did you get here?' he says. 'For all I know you were the one buried the girl.'

I point to the boat; there's no sign of Bill. 'I came by boat to see how trade routes to the college will be affected and to take samples.'

The overseer thrusts the spade into the earth. 'You don't look like you're from the university,' he says, looking at my clothes. Bill's trousers only reach my shins; his boots have worn to his feet. There is no right or left, only a box for feet that takes on the impression of a person.

'I like to blend in,' I say, pulling at the oversized coat and grinning.

His eyebrows shoot up and his lip twitches, breaking the tension. The workers shuffle now, shifting weight and talking to each other. One of them translates for the non-English speakers. Even the natural world around us seems more relaxed, the reeds bending at the knee, birds joyriding on thermals.

'I am Arthur Renwick,' he says, holding out his

hand.

'Pleased to meet you, Arthur,' I say, trying, and failing, to remember the name from the front of that book in the University Library. 'I am from the Natural Sciences, Sepulchre College.'

'You're a strange sort. I've heard that about the university men—in a globe of their own. Who do you answer to?' Renwick asks.

'I am to take my findings to Mr Reed only,' I say. 'Once they have been verified. I will also have to report the death of that girl. She could have been murdered.'

'You take her, then. She's nothing to do with me,' he says quickly, gesturing towards the body but not actually looking at her. A muscle twitches in his jaw.

'I'll need the mask as well,' I say.

'How did you hear of that?' he asks.

I don't reply.

'It's gone. It must have slipped into the mud when we pulled her out.' Renwick's eyes go to the man who held it aloft, standing to one side, his hands behind him.

I stride over. The man stumbles backwards and the mask spears the mud with a *thuck* sound. 'I am sorry to take your souvenir but this does not belong to you. It shouldn't be here at all.'

Renwick shrugs then looks at the girl properly for the first time since I arrive. His forehead wrinkles up, the sides of his mouth turning down for a moment then his lips move but no sound comes out. It looks as if he is saying sorry. Then he twists his head back to me. 'She's your responsibility now. Do what you must.'

I tuck the mask into the back of my trousers

167

and take the girl in my arms. She is heavy, her mud-covered arm slipping over my shoulder. I look over towards the boat. Bill's not going to like this.

*   *   *

Bill doesn't like it. Sitting with his back to the body and me, he hasn't spoken since I carried her into the boat and wrapped her in the spice sacks. We're approaching the centre of Cambridge, which looks tiny compared to the city I'm used to. Fields run right up to the colleges, no sign of the swathes of housing which have surrounded them since Victorian times. Spires reach up over the flatlands like students raising ink-stained hands in class.

Bill clears his throat, spits into the Cam. 'What you think you were doing, jumpin' up like that? They coulda killed me,' he says, craning round. He frowns and glances at the girl's body on the floor of the boat. He begins to cross himself then stuffs his hands under his arse.

'You don't have to censor yourself with me,' I say. 'I don't care what you believe.'

'Tha's grand of you.'

'And as for those drainers killing you or me, they wouldn't have dared. Not with so many people watching.'

'Mebbe you haven't heard in the university but there's been some suspicious deaths since the last riot. People disappearin'.'

'Don't the police get involved?'

'What're police? They university types?'

'Sorry, I don't know what I'm saying. I'm confused.'

168

Bill stares at me. 'You are that. You make as much sense as a green moon.'

I reach down and pull the sack up so that it covers the woman's shoulders. I smooth the woman's hair off her forehead. Long strands reach round her throat like ivy round Sleeping Beauty's tower. I peel them away. She's cold, her skin clammy.

'What you doin'?' Bill says, snatching my hands away. 'Show some respect.'

'I'm trying to find out how she died,' I reply. There is no sign of strangulation this time. The skin on her face and neck has small red blotches. I gently pull back one of her eyelids. There is red in the whites of her eyes but her eyeball is still intact. She can't have been dead long.

Bill's normally red face turns pale. Closing his eyes, he rocks back and, before I can reach him, hits his head on the back of the boat. One of the oars clatters over the side and the boat rocks as I plunge my hand into the water to grab it.

'Bill,' I say, flicking water onto his sweaty forehead.

Bill moans and grabs for my sleeve.

'Put your head between your legs,' I say, patting his knee.

He lurches forward and is sick onto his lap. Bile and partially digested bread dribbles onto the floor of the boat.

'That wasn't what I meant,' I say, rowing the boat in what I hope is the right direction. The sun is higher in the sky, giving the water the look of white fabric. Every time I do anything other than stare straight ahead, I see the body and Bill and the questions glaring at me in neon or gaslight or tallow

169

candlelight or whatever they use for illumination in this time, in this place. So I stare straight ahead.

Bill turns his head to me. Thread veins glare out against his drained cheeks. 'You do too much thinking,' he says. 'I don't know who you are, Stephen, but heard your nightmare and it seems to me that whatever you're involved in you should row away from and not look back.'

'I wish I'd met you a few months ago,' I say. If I had wandered out of time when I first arrived at Cambridge then none of this would have happened. Not found the girl, nothing.

'You're a daft lad. But being confused is natural as water. That gets through somehow an' so will you.' Bill holds out his rough hands and I give him the oars.

'Thank you, Bill,' I say. 'For everything.'

'Don't go jumpin' in the Granta again, will you? And leave the dead be.'

'I couldn't let her be forgotten.'

'I didn't mean this one,' he says.

*   *   *

I'm exhausted. My calf is sore, my thighs ache; I want to be held and have hands, Lana's hands, on the places that hurt.

I recognise places now, at the wide part of the river where The Mill pub will arrive in time. A boat comes towards us, rowed by a fisherman. He nods to Bill, stares at me. I cover the girl's hand with sacking.

We pass Queens' College, but there isn't a mathematical bridge to go under. It was nothing to do with Newton, despite the rumours. He won't be here for another thirty years but there are the philosophers of this age, walking round Cambridge streets, having a think and a drink, sitting on the edge of rationalism, backing away from theism as if it were a child throwing a tantrum.

People walk alongside the river, heads down against the wind, wrapped up and carrying packages as they have done for years and will for years to come. The sky has the grey promise of snow. As we pass the back lawn of Sepulchre, I crane to see my room. It glints at us behind the younger version of the oak that knocks at my window. I don't exist yet; my parents don't exist yet; somewhere in Ireland my ancestors are doing what they need to do to make sure the Killigans exist.

'You can stop here, Bill,' I say as we approach Sepulchre's dock. Bill stands up in the boat and wraps the rope round his hand. Legs in a wide stance for balance, he hoops the wooden bollard on the dock and yanks the boat into the deck.

'I'll be round most weeks,' he says, clumping me on the back. 'If you need any help.'

A rush of sadness hits my chest and I pull Bill into a hug. He pushes me gently away and points to the dead girl. 'Go on, lad,' he says.

He waves as he rows away but I can't stand here watching him till he disappears round the bend. I have a dead woman in my arms.

Chapter Twenty-Nine

Mrs Withins

Katie Withins rocks in the chair, her sobs creasing her in half. 'Tell me what happened. Tell me how my baby ended up like that.' She scrunches her eyes shut.

Jane touches her hand. She goes to the same gym as Katie and has seen her, pretty and confident, striding on the cross-trainer, chatting in her soft Welsh accent, drying her hair upside down under the hand-drier, smiling at the fitness instructors; now she will not smile for some time, and every spontaneous beam will feel like a betrayal. Jane has seen it and known it. Knows it. She lowers her voice. 'Mrs Withins. This is awful for you, but I have to ask these questions. Monica, your Family Liaison Officer, is on her way and she'll be keeping you up to date with everything that happens as well as helping to find the person or people responsible for Rhys's death but we need to get started now. Do you understand?'

Katie nods and takes a cup of tea from Pemberton, her hands shaking. Sitting up taller, she wipes her face with the tissue, redistributing mascara from under her eyes to across her cheeks. 'Are you interviewing that lecturer?' she says. 'The one who said he saw the beauty queen in the mask?'

Jane glances at Pemberton. Stephen Killigan can't be found. He hasn't been seen since last night and has not returned to his room all day. 'Don't

172

worry, Katie, we're taking care of everything. Take a long, deep breath, a swig of tea,' Jane says, 'and tell me what happened yesterday afternoon.'

Katie pulls at the corner of her tissue. 'Same thing as every day. Rhys is at choir till five and walks home with the others.' Her face crumples like the tissue in her hand. 'Walked home.'

Jane steps in, quickly. 'The others?'

'Adam, Barty and Simon. They're all in our road or the next one. Simon lives with his Dad next door. We all work until five so we've arranged it so that they wouldn't ever be on their own.' Her nostrils flare. A sob tears through her.

Pemberton reaches into his top pocket and takes out a linen handkerchief, folded and pressed into four. Katie takes it and places it on her lap. She continues pulling the wet tissue apart. Her solicitor, Mr Cardman, moves his hand closer to hers, then pulls it away and crosses his crane-like legs for the twentieth time. Jane can smell his garlic breath from over the table.

'We understand that Rhys didn't walk home with his friends yesterday as usual but instead stayed behind to talk with John Creda, his choirmaster.'

Katie's eyebrows jolt upward. 'Is that why he was killed, because he was on his own?'

'We don't know yet, Mrs Withins,' Pemberton says.

'If he hadn't done then Rhys would still be alive. He'd be home, with me.'

'You can't live on ifs, Katie,' Jane says, gently. 'Can you think why Rhys would be asked to stay behind?'

'Well—' Katie pauses. She drinks her tea in three long gulps. 'Rhys had been asked to do the solo at the college carol concert; it was probably about that.'

'Did he really need to be separated from his friends? Couldn't they have talked about that during practice?'

'Mr Creda is very good at making sure the other boys don't get jealous. The solo is a big honour at his school. Rhys was so excited. And now it will go to someone else.'

The tissue piles up in a sodden drift.

DC Pemberton glances at his notes. 'Rhys was seen running out of the chapel, crying.'

'What?' Katie grabs at the arms of the chair. 'Why was he crying?'

'The choirmaster told him off for not practising enough.'

'That's rubbish,' she says. 'He practises all the time. Practised.' Her mouth twitches. 'Why didn't they go after him if he was crying? And where did he go? Someone must have seen?' Her face contorts with further unsaid thoughts.

Jane shakes her head and catches Pemberton's eye. The last known sighting of Rhys is on security camera footage from the college gates at five o'clock the previous day. He walks, head down, his little shoulders shaking. He then stops, a tiny figure in black and white, and waves at someone behind him out of sight of the lens. He moves towards them, into Sepulchre's Fellows Garden, and is not picked up again, even though there is working CCTV covering most areas. Whoever killed him knew the range of the cameras and kept out of it. 'We are trying to find out,' is all she says.

Pemberton takes over. 'Did Rhys regularly spend time on his own with Mr Creda?'

174

'No.'

'Are you completely certain? You didn't know that he'd talked with him yesterday,' he says, tapping his pen on the table.

'What are you saying? That I didn't know what my own son was doing?' Her grip tightens round the mug. 'That I'm to blame?'

'There are no implications in here, only questions,' Jane says, quickly. There are also lies. 'Did Rhys get on with Mr Creda?'

'All the kids do.'

'And why is that?' she asks.

Katie sighs. 'He makes practice fun.'

'In what way?' Jane can't think of any way singing in a church could be fun.

'One day Rhys came back saying he got them to run round the chapel throwing balls at each other while singing to help their lung capacity. Last winter, when they were all complaining about an upcoming concert, he took them to the top of Great St Mary's tower at dusk to sing the sun to bed. Rhys said he looked over the edge when they'd finished and saw a crowd of a hundred, which probably means ten, all staring up with their mouths open, amazed at the sound. People cried.' The faintest sign of a smile flickers on Katie's face. Then fades.

'Did Rhys have any problems with friends, teachers or anyone else?' Pemberton asks.

Katie shakes her head. 'I can't think of anything. He's a very happy boy. Perfect.' She takes her purse out of her handbag and opens it, showing Jane a photo of Rhys sitting on the beach. He is wrapped up in a parka, blond hair whipped by wind, squinting at the camera and grinning. 'That's the last photo I took. It was a week ago; we took

175

him on a pre-birthday trip to Great Yarmouth. I should have been taking photos all the time. Every moment.'

'"Should haves" and "would haves" need to be thrown out with the "if"s—they don't help at all,' Jane says, knowing full well that she does not take her own advice. She often gets lost in the would-haves.

Katie points to his smile. 'You can still see his last milk tooth there. He lost it the next day. Oh God,' she says, her hand snapping to her chest. 'Where did I put it? He left it on his bedside table for the Tooth Fairy; he didn't like to leave it under his pillow in case it was lost when he slept. He never kept still. I can still see the tooth in the palm of my hand, tiny and shiny.' She looks up at the ceiling and shakes her head. 'I don't know what I did with it. I can't remember putting it in the box with the others. What if I didn't? That was his last one.'

Jane waits for the sob to shake through Katie. 'Do you remember when Rhys's toy rabbit went missing?'

Katie breathes out. 'He hasn't had Bunny for weeks, since his birthday party. That's when he first mentioned it. He said: "Bunny's disappeared—the magician took him".'

Jane places her elbows on the table and cups her chin. 'What did you think of that?'

'Bunny wasn't in his room but Rhys is always losing things. It was either that or one of his friends had gone up to his bedroom and taken it but Rhys refused to ask any of them—he didn't want them to know he still had cuddly toys. We got him an identical one but he wouldn't touch it.'

176

Rhys's skeleton hands holding the rabbit's paw. Jane blinks the image away. 'Why did he say the magician took it?'

Katie shrugs. 'I don't know. We did phone to check, but couldn't get an answer. Rhys went on about things disappearing for days. He was so impressed with the magician's tricks and said he'd decided to be a magician when he grew up.' She looks down to her hands and picks at her cuticles. 'Anyway. The magician took him to one side and taught him a trick while the others had tea. Wait a sec,' she says. 'It should still be on my phone.'

Katie scrolls through the videos, pausing over every thumbnail to touch Rhys's face, moving her fingertip as if brushing his hair behind his ears. She hands the phone to Jane and presses play:

The screen shows a comfortable, mainly beige living room, sofas pushed back, silver balloons bobbing at the coving. Kids sit cross-legged on the carpet; adults stand at the sides and a woman is at the piano. The door opens and the chatter subsides as Rhys strides in wearing a Superman cloak and waving a child's fishing rod. Katie cheers behind the camera. 'I am the Magic Withins,' he says, swishing off his baseball cap and bowing. A hand reaches in from off-camera and places a top hat on his head. The hat slips down over the boy's ears, covering his face. Katie laughs and the image shakes. A hand removes the hat.

The magician steps into the frame. He stares straight at the camera. 'I have taught the Magic Withins my signature trick; he will make the item that you prize most vanish before your eyes.' He winks once. Slowly. A chill chases another chill down Jane's back. He is tall and thin, with pale blue

177

eyes under dark eyebrows. He looks to be in his late fifties, handsome still, lines engraved on his face. Nodding at Rhys, he steps aside to lean against the wall. He swipes a finger over the dado rail.

Rhys holds out his cap to the adults. 'Your wallets, if you would, gentlemen; your purses please, ladies.' The adults drop their possessions in his cap, smiling patronising smiles. 'And now for the magic,' Rhys says. He taps the cap with the fishing rod and closes his eyes.

The woman at the piano plays a dramatic chord.

'Say the word,' he tells the children at his feet. He frowns and places his fingers against his temples. His eyes dart across to the magician.

'Abracadabra,' some shout.

'Expelliarmus,' shout others.

'Let's see if it's worked,' he says, holding out the cap to a small boy in the front. 'Little boy, look in here and tell me what is within.'

The boy reaches into the cap and his hand comes out empty. The microphone doesn't pick up what he says but Rhys turns the cap inside out and shows the lining. 'That's right,' he says. 'Everything has disappeared.'

Everyone claps and he jumps up and down and turns to his mum with a huge smile.

The footage stops. Katie crumples onto the table.

*   *   *

Jane prises open her office shutters with thumb and forefinger and watches Katie walk away from the station, five paces behind her husband. They get into their car, not looking at or talking to each

178

other. 'Monica said they wouldn't even be in the same room together for more than five minutes when she was taking them through the next steps. I don't blame her; I didn't like him at all.'

'You'd never have known, Inspector.'

Jane studies his face. 'Are you being sarcastic, Pemberton?'

'No, ma'am, of course not.' Pemberton's eyebrows lift: *I don't even know how you could ask*, they seem to say. Oh, he's good. 'Do you think the breakdown of their relationship has anything to do with the murder?' he asks, heaping sugar into Jane's coffee.

'Instinctively? I don't think so, apart from both being wrapped up in whatever's wrong between them, rather than paying attention to what Rhys was up to. And they both have alibis that are checking out so far; so does that choirmaster. But Monica will winkle it out if there is anything there: she has that innocent, sympathetic look that means people open up. But let's face it: I doubt either of them is capable of making a body decompose overnight. That,' she says, holding up a still of the magician's face, 'sounds more like magic.'

Chapter Thirty

Discovery

People are staring. I tug the sacking down so her toes are covered. She seems to be getting heavier and I heave her up in my arms and walk faster through Sepulchre's gate.

'Come back here—what are you doing?' a man booms. I could run and make it to Great St Mary's and claim sanctuary, or I could stay here and see what happens. I stop walking and slowly turn. A tall man in a black gown strides towards me like an unmasked Darth Vader on the dying Death Star. 'Where do you think you're going with her?' he asks.

'Taking her to church,' I say.

'Don't get cocksure with me, boy. Are you unaware of the decree by the vice chancellor, and heads of colleges including myself, in regard to females in the company of students?'

'I'm not, sir.' He thinks I'm smuggling a live girl out of the college.

He narrows his eyes. Lifts his chin. 'I quote from the edict: "No woman of whatever age or condition, dare either by herself, or being sent for, be permitted by others, in any College, to make any one's bed in private chambers; or go to the hall, or kitchen, or buttery, to carry any one's commons, bread or beer to any scholar's chamber, within the limits of the college; unless she were sent for to nurse some infirm sick person."' He stops and glares at me. 'Are you sick?'

'I may be.' My chest is heaving under the weight, my biceps burning.

'You do not look ill.'

'I am not feeling myself exactly.' I cough, careful not to shake the girl too much.

'Even if you were in poor health, "The nurses,"' he continues quoting, rolling 'r's like an actor, '"of sick persons, and all laundresses, should be of mature age, good fame, and wives or widows, who themselves should take the scholars' linen to wash, and bring the same back again when washed. That young maids should not be permitted, upon any pretence whatsoever, to go to students' chambers—"'

'I promise you, this woman has never been in my chambers,' I say.

'What is your name? I don't remember having seen you on disciplinary matters before. Which, judged on your current behaviour, now seems improbable.' He makes a noise between a snort and a 'humph'. 'You must realise that a woman convicted of contumacy will be expelled to beyond four miles of the city. And what do you have to say about that, young woman?' he says, squinting at the girl's body beneath the sack. His eyes ooze down to the curve of her breasts. He reaches out for her with his thick fingers.

I step away from him. If my hands were free I would smash his cheekbone. And then fracture the other one.

Catching hold of the sack, he tugs, a greedy look in his eyes. I clamp my arm against my ribs to try and stop the material slipping away. He pulls harder, his face bunching up into a gurn. The sack comes away from her body and he stands there, his mouth open. Behind him, a short, sweating man waddles over to us and a crowd forms.

The Master shouts for a porter, starts marching towards me. 'He's got a body,' he screams.

The sweating man stares at the girl. 'I know her,' he says. 'Lucy Miller. Our housemaid—she went missing last month.'

I run, holding Lucy as tight as I can. Her bones bite into my chest and the cold air slices through my lungs as I run over the cobbles. A man selling chestnuts sticks his legs out trying to trip me up and I jump over, landing awkwardly in the ill-fitting shoes. Stumbling, I right myself and sprint. The tower of the church is visible against the sky and if I keep running then maybe my heart won't burst till it gets me to the steps.

Barging through the gates, I hurdle a rock on the path and push at the front door of Great St Mary's. It's locked. I kick the door hard three times. My toe burns and the pain makes me feel alive. I kick again. Footsteps echo inside the church and then the sound of a metal latch lifting. The Master is at the gate; others push through, faces twisting. A hand on my shoulder, another on my coat. The door opens. A bearded clergyman yawns, his fingers wrapped round the door. 'Can I—' He looks down and sees the girl.

'This man is a killer and a heathen,' the Master of Sepulchre says, jumping up, his head bobbing up and down among the crowd. 'He is carrying a woman as if she were a bundle of wood.'

'I need your help,' I say to the clergyman, struggling to grab at the words. Everything is going blurry.

182

He sighs. 'Come in, quickly,' he says, putting his arm round me, careful to stay away from the girl.

My heart hurts, like it's going to lurch out of my chest and fall, pulsing, onto the steps of the church. Hands yank at my clothes, my skin, my hair. Her body lies, heavier by the second, in my arms. The clergyman's voice dilates as he tries to restore order; his shouts morph in my ears till they sound like a bell donging over my head with me as the clapper. I clamp my palms over my ears but the scrape of the metal screeches through my skin, tunnelling through my bones and out of my toes into stone.

My arms sag and I stumble. Dizzy, I fold down, slumping onto my knees, holding onto Lucy's body like she's a life raft. Her arm thumps onto an engraved stone. I look up. A large man raises his fist and I lower my head, my face hot, vision slipping. The shouts of the crowd fade to the sound of the sea in a conch shell, their grabbing arms tighten as my eyes close, waiting for the blow to land

and my brain shuts
down.

Chapter Thirty-One

Examination

Jane leans over Pemberton and hammers the horn with her fist. 'Can't we do something about this?' she asks. 'Declare that everyone must stop where they are and get out of my way?'

'I don't remember any provision specific to you in Butterworths Police Law, ma'am.'

'Then that is an error that should be remedied immediately, don't you think? Or maybe you should have arrived when I asked you to.' Jane feels the familiar tightness in her chest. She's being a cow, she knows it. She had only remembered her appointment at eight that morning and put off phoning Pemberton until nine, demanding that he pick her up five minutes ago.

Pemberton says nothing, and guilt soaks through her like milk into the Weetabix she had left untouched and soggy in the sink. 'Don't be so infuriatingly reasonable, Pemberton. You're fucking me off.'

'Sorry. We don't need to be at the magician's house until eleven, do we?' he asks.

'I need to be at the hospital,' Jane says, looking at her watch. 'Now.'

*   *   *

Jane sits alone in the consulting room. Her knee jogs up and down, the green gown rustling over her legs. Dr Pindar's room is just about big enough for an examination bed and a desk with a computer, files at right angles to each other and equidistant pens on its surface. His order is reassuring. Jane leans forward and picks up one of the three freebie pens from drugs companies and, not having a pocket to pop it in, tucks it into her bag. Well, he told her that she had cancer; at least she could get a ballpoint.

Dr Pindar walks in. He's holding her file, looking at whatever is inside.

Jane's heart is huge and unruly in her ribcage.

He smiles, but that means nothing. Cancer specialists give the same benign smile to the malignant.

'So,' Dr Pindar says, sitting down opposite. 'How are we doing?'

'Can we get on with it, Dr P? I've got something important to get on with. What are the results?'

He moves the mouse and clicks on his email. A large file is being downloaded. 'We will have to get a new biopsy, of course—that will go off today. But I couldn't see anything on the scan.'

'So why does it hurt so much then?'

'I am afraid that post-mastectomy pain syndrome is common. Many women undergoing mastectomies end up with some injury to the brachial plexus nerve that results in a faulty feedback loop between injured sensory nerves and emotional pain centres in the brain, making the pain seem worse than it is.'

'I'm imagining it. That's what you're saying?'

'We can give you strong pain relief. It may improve over time.'

'Nothing that gets in the way of my concentrating on my job. I can't risk it. I'll stick to the bandage.' Jane touches her side and feels the edges of the

185

binding that she now sees as her skin.

'Have you discussed your pain with your employer?'

Jane laughs.

'Not that it must be easy at the moment, with the murders. We saw the press conference with the boy's parents. My wife couldn't sleep she was so upset.' He stares at Jane as if it were her fault. 'With so much on, it could help to keep painkillers to hand. You must be having a stressful time, trying to work out how he got into that state so quickly. Any ideas?'

'Are you fishing, Dr Pindar?'

Dr Pindar grins. 'I believe I am. Well it's up to you.' He stands and moves over to the tiny sink. 'How about taking our follow-up counselling?'

'The Cancer Consoler? The Post-Breast-Removal Soother? No thanks.'

He soaps up his hands and dries them. 'Let's see how we're getting on then, shall we? Before the biopsy?'

We? Jane lets that go. She pulls herself onto the bed, peels down the gown and turns her head to look out of the window. Trees stick their fingers up in the distance.

'Lift your arms, please.' Dr Pindar rubs his palms together. Jane flinches as Dr Pindar reaches into her armpits and checks under both her arms. Her nipple stiffens and she hopes he knows it's not him.

'My hands are a bit cold,' he says, 'I'm afraid. Terrible weather.'

'Terrible.'

He touches the scarred skin over the area where her left breast used to be, now as flat as the fens. 'It's healing well,' he says. He palpates the sides

186

of her right breast then moves away to the lymph nodes below her collarbones. Then moves back to her remaining breast. He pauses.

'What?' Jane asks, goose bumps rising and not from the cold.

*   *   *

'Is everything all right, guv?' Pemberton asks as they pull out of Addenbrooke's car park.

'Everything is the very best it has ever been, or is ever likely to be. At least it will be once we have obtained a bacon sandwich. A bacon sandwich smothered in maple syrup. A bacon sandwich smothered in maple syrup topped with a dollop of ice-cream. Then the day will be complete.'

He looks over to her, head inclined, forehead scrunched in a decent facsimile of being concerned. 'You can trust me, you know, guv.'

'Of course I trust you, Pemberton. I'm just not going to tell you much. Any news?'

Pemberton fills her in as they drive out to Arbury. The mask is exactly as Stephen Killigan tried to tell her on the phone: a Renaissance mask that represented beauty. One of four made by the sculptor Signior Marcus Lorelli for the parade through the streets of Venice in 1580. It was stolen in 1742 from a museum in Padua. 'There is an interesting document in the museum's archives,' Pemberton says. 'It's being scanned over now but it describes a tall man ambling into the museum, breaking into the cabinet displaying the masks and, doffing his shiny black hat to the museum's gentleman curator, walking away as a fire broke out that destroyed the rest of the collection.'

187

They stop at the greasy spoon on Milton Road. Maple syrup and ice-cream, being unavailable, the owner hands over bacon sandwiches in paper bags. 'The *new* news,' Pemberton continues as they walk back to the car, 'is that the fingerprints found on the underside of the mask match those on the tarot card in the music box.'

'The magician,' Jane replies.

'The magician.'

*   *   *

Roy Fielding's 1970s semi in Arbury is not the house you'd expect a magician to live in: no turrets, no black cat twitching its tail on the front step, not even a swagged velvet curtain in the window; only brown netting, pebble-dashing and a terracotta pot with the last trumpet of a frail geranium. Belinda pulls up in a car with two other officers.

'Not much magic about this place,' Pemberton says.

'What did you expect?' Jane asks, pressing the doorbell. She snorts.

There is no answer. Jane presses the bell again. Still no response. Jane holds the letterbox open. There's a pile of unopened letters on the mat. 'Mr Fielding, are you there? It's the police, Mr Fielding and if you do not answer then we shall be undertaking a forced entry. No? Here we go then.' She rams the enforcer at the door.

They walk through the house, calling out, the sound muffled by swirly taupe carpet. Still no answer.

Jane turns to Belinda. 'You three check out the house; Pemberton's coming with me into the back garden,' Jane says. 'Apparently he had what he called his "magic shack" out there. That's a line to hook the ladies with.'

The windows of the summerhouse are painted black; the door padlocked. Pemberton picks up a spade leant against the fence and smashes open the lock. A strong smell of urine and putrefaction hits Jane's nose as she steps inside. She pats down the walls for a light switch. The shed is full of magicians' equipment. In the centre, lying on a workbench, is a long black box topped with hats and wands and dice and cards and what looks like a stuffed dove. Catching a glimpse of a figure in the corner, she jerks her head around. Hanging from a hook on the ceiling is a black suit complete with white tie and gloves, limp from lack of magician.

The ammonia emanates from a cage in the corner. Hay is tumbled together into one mound; the food tray is empty, turned on its side, and the water bottle, run dry, has green stuff growing inside. Jane undoes the latch and reaches into the bank of hay, expecting to touch the cold, stiff body of an animal.

'Ow,' she says, whipping her hand away. Blood drips from her forefinger. 'Little bastard bit me.'

'At least it's alive,' Pemberton says as a black dwarf rabbit hops out. It sniffs the air and its whiskers twitch.

'Yeah. Brilliant. I'm so glad.' Jane pulls on a pair of gloves and looks through all the paraphernalia. 'This is the saddest shed I've ever seen. What's wrong with a stash of soft porn, a wind-up radio and a camping chair?' she asks. 'Boxes in sheds should be for turning over and putting your feet up on: not for poking swords into.' She points to the tall black

189

box leaning against the wall, symbols painted in white on the side, knives thrust into it like a lifesize game of Kerplunk.

'Have you checked it?' Pemberton asks, pointing to one of the swords plunged halfway into the prop. A red substance has dried on the blade.

'Go ahead.'

Pemberton grasps the handle of the sword. 'There's resistance,' he says as he pulls. There is a wet, sucking sound from inside the cabinet. He bags up the sword and, with a glance at Jane, opens the door. Inside is a just-off joint of meat, skewer marks all the way through it. 'That's one way to practise,' he says.

Belinda gives a shout from the house.

Jane runs down the pink paved path to the back door. Belinda greets her, as pale as weak tea. 'We found this on the lounge table and a key.' She holds out a wand.

'Did you find what the key was for?'

'Yes ma'am.' Belinda swallows.

'And?'

'It opened a chest freezer in the utility room. And in it, laid out on frozen packets of food and that, was what looked like his body, but it was actually his red suit and frilly shirt, stuffed full with frozen peas and sweetcorn and mini carrots like a beanbag. And a face had been drawn on the back of a Cornflakes packet and placed on top of the collar, and a toupee on top.' Belinda gulped.

'It's all right, you don't have to gabble. Take your time,' Jane says. She places a hand on Belinda's shoulder.

'Only it wasn't a toupee, ma'am.' Belinda blinks. 'It was proper hair, in Mr Magic's style, I mean Roy

Fielding's style. He's had it since I was a girl. And there was something else. A playing card, a Jack of Hearts, was in Mr Magic's hand, I mean, glove.'

'But *he* wasn't there?'

'No.'

'Go back in, I'll be with you in a minute.'

Belinda nods and hurries inside.

Jane calls out to Pemberton, but there's no reply. She walks back up the path to the summerhouse. 'Can you please pay attention when I'm—'

Pemberton stands by the horizontal box. It is now split in two, swung open. Magic tricks lie scattered on the floor. He opens the lid of one half of the box and steps back for Jane to see. Roy Fielding is inside: knees to his chest, folded like a handkerchief. One of his hands is missing, hacked off above the wrist. His eyes are blown with flies and in his mouth is a gag. Pemberton pulls from between the magician's teeth a six-foot-long pennant, flag after union flag.

Chapter Thirty-Two

Lucy Miller

A door slams behind me; a bolt slides over. Someone is speaking, like the teacher in Peanuts: mnnnow mah maow, mlah ma mao. I recognise the voice. The clergyman? Maybe he's speaking in tongues. Glossolalia. That's a nice word. If I think of words then I don't have to think of what's going on outside of my eyelids. Gloss-o-la-li-a. La-li-a. Aaaaaa.

The sounds coagulate into words, meaning pumping under them again. 'It is all right, do not worry, breathe in, breathe out.' His voice is deeper, rinsed of its shrillness. 'No one will come in for a while. 'Don't open your eyes yet. Come through, sit down. That's it.'

Behind the screen, a choir soars; strings cry. My legs buckle and I'm supported under the armpits. Hands push me down and I feel the edge of a pew against the inside of my knees. I test out my eyes. My eyelids are gummed shut, as if I've had three days' sleep. Something wet is thrust into my face and I duck away.

'Stop that,' I shout, ripping open my eyes. Opposite me, sitting cross-legged on a chair, is a man, a vicar or chaplain, in a dog collar. That's not very seventeenth century. What is he doing here? Has he travelled back as well? Then I see the lyrics screen suspended over the font and the overhead projector set up by the lectern. I'm back.

'You fainted,' he says, smoothing his hands

through his hair. 'I wouldn't worry about it. Happens all the time. Something about this place.'

I'm alive, and in the same century as Lana and Satnam and my life. I stretch out. There is something digging into my back. I reach round and take the mask out of my waistband. Its eyes are filled with mud. My arms feel like they are missing something. I feel a punch in my stomach, like when bread is beaten down for getting above its station. Lucy. My dead girl. What happened to her? I crane my head so I can see the entrance to the church. No sign of anyone else, alive or dead.

The choir gets louder, insistent, mourning.

Maybe I am dreaming these girls up. Or I am dreaming all the time. Trying to stay awake could be causing a rift between my mind and body that cannot be bridged by reason.

'Say that again,' the vicar says. 'I didn't catch it.'

'I didn't say anything,' I say.

'You did, something to do with spinning.' He looks at me closely. 'You're still pale. Wait there.' He walks up the aisle and opens a drawer beneath the altar, moves a candlestick so that it is slightly out of symmetry with the other one, then returns with a goblet and cardboard box. Holding the box out towards me, he takes a communion cube of bread for himself and sits down, sucking it.

I chew on a cube of bread. It tastes sugary.

'What day is it?' I ask him.

He laughs. 'You weren't unconscious for that long,' he says. 'It's still the fifteenth of October.'

The day after. I sit up straight.

He hands me the goblet. 'You'd better get that down you,' he says, tipping the cup up. Cold, blackcurrant-rich wine slides down my throat.

'I don't suppose you've seen a dead body, have you?' I ask.

'Of course I have. Sometimes it feels like I see more dead than live ones. And I'm surrounded by their bones all day.' He indicates the plaques and inscriptions on the walls and tombstones that make up the floor of the church.

'Any dead body in particular?' he asks. There is something familiar about him. But then there is about all clergy: they all have that way of looking through you as if your sins were fluttering on a washing line with the labels showing.

Standing up slowly, I move over to the door. My feet feel strange—staring down I see that I'm still wearing Bill's shoes and clothes. His boots clump against the floor. I'm surprised the windows don't rattle. 'It won't mean anything to you. But her name was Lucy Miller.'

'Lucy Miller?' the vicar asks. 'I believe I have. She should be in the parish records, considering.'

'Considering what?' I ask.

He walks up behind me. He points to my feet. I think he's commenting on the old strange shoes and then I see what is written on the stone beneath my feet:

Lucy Miller
Beloved of God,
the eye
and the artist

Chapter Thirty-Three

Stalker Talk

Stephen staggers out of the door and I close it behind him. I have not danced in a very long time and now I am waltzing myself down the aisle, ripping off the dog collar. The choir is practising something wonderfully contrary, Mozart's 'Requiem', as I turn between the pews, one two three, one two three, everything comes to me.

This is more fun than I've had in centuries. I've stalked before, of course: a knife thrower in the nineteenth century; a nurse in the sixteenth; triplets in the twentieth. My excitement comes from the subject's ignorance. They have no idea, then when they find out and look back at the string you laid like Ariadne: the times you turned the calendar two months on and circled a day and they shrugged it off; the doors left open, the gas on, the mail left on the table and not on the porch floor. And that is before I really start work. That is the beauty of time travel. Much is possible. So much harm can be done when you've mastered the skill. The time-travelling art is not being taught in schools and it should be. I should become secretary of state for education. That would certainly be enlightening for many.

The confusion on his face is almost better than seeing the life leach out of eyes like water from the fens. And the longer he is unaware that I have him tied to so many strings, ready to pluck and tweak at any time, the more fun it is.

The side door is being unlocked. I whip off the dog

collar and place it in my pocket. Disguises are too easy. Time to go.

Chapter Thirty-Four

No Return

I sit down on Great St Mary's steps, closing my eyes till the tipping sensation subsides. I open one eye and look back. A white-haired woman walks towards me, an orange plastic bag looped over her wrist and biting into the flesh. Still the twenty-first century. Her arms are full of roses and lilies, carnations and chrysanthemums; ivy feather-boas over her shoulders. She looks down at my trailing laces and up to my face. 'You all right, duck?'

It's the 'duck' that does it. My stomach crimps and I want to go home. No, I'm not all right. Something is very wrong with me.

'Where have you been?' Satnam says, peering round his door. 'And what the fuck are you wearing?' I shake my head and follow him into his room. 'That bad, eh? They found you, then. You haven't been chucked out, have you?'

'What are you talking about?' That comes out gruffer than I intended. I sit down in his desk chair. I can't even be bothered to make it spin around. 'Who found me?'

'The police came round requesting your presence at the station for another friendly chat. And Frank Utter puffed up the stairs. He was furious. From your face I thought you'd seen him— you could be on a disciplinary.'

196

'But why did the police come? What the fuck is going on?' Did they find out about Lucy Miller? But how can they? It was another time, wasn't it? Did the last few days happen? Oh god, I want to stop all this and sleep.

'Rhys Withins, a lost boy,' Satnam says slowly. 'He was found dead, wearing a mask like yours. And a magician has been killed. The killer took his place at Rhys's party. Grim stuff .'

I grab his arm. 'He was wearing the mask? The police will have to listen to me now. Have they questioned Robert Sachs?'

'The poncey philosopher who loves himself?'

I saw him that night and then bumped into a student who told me about Rhys. That's it. I remember something about that.'

'Remember something about it?' he says. 'It was only two days ago. You're talking like it was the seventies.'

'I am, you're right. It was a long time ago.'

'You are making as much sense as the boy's death.'

'What do you mean?'

'He was reported missing days ago, has been in the company of over a hundred people in the last week and been seen singing by five times that, yet his body has decomposed to such an extent that they believe there is no explanation other than he was killed and buried one year ago.' He holds up his hands. 'It is a mystery.'

'It *can* be explained,' I say, jumping up. 'Mysteries are simplicities with the lights off.' I run out of his study and up the stairs, my hand trailing against the cool stone to remind me that I *am* in my body and this is happening. Satnam follows me up, slowly.

I dash around my room, picking up books, searching through drawers, throwing clothes around.

'Whoah, you were messy enough before,' Satnam says. 'Look, Stephen, I'm going to be serious for once. Are you okay? Because you seem a little manic. Or a lot manic.' He tries to tidy books back into piles, then gives up. 'What are you looking for? Maybe I can help.'

'There it is!' I shout, retrieving the book Iris Burton gave me. I hand it to Satnam.

He laughs. 'Why have you given me a crappy book on time travel?'

'That's how you could do it. Let's assume that time travel were possible—'

'It's not.'

'If we say that Rhys Withins was killed on, what, Wednesday, taken one year back in time and buried, then he is found one year later. His chronology would be in place, wouldn't it?'

'The assumption is too great to progress to that point. Occam's Razor, boy, that's what I use.'

'But you're a physicist. Last I heard there is nothing in the laws of physics to stop time travel.'

'The equations in Einstein's General Theory of Relativity don't forbid time travel, no, but they don't forbid self-cleaning underpants either. This is a work of fiction. It's creative writing for the mathematically minded and myopic.'

I breathe in and out. 'What if I told you that I knew it could happen?'

'Are you giving me the "there are more things in heaven and earth, Horatio, than are dreamt of in your philosophy" shit? Because that's one of the most patronising lines in literature.'

'Listen—'

'So tell me, what is this really about?'

If he shoots down I will have to go back and breathe life into them. This is real and I won't let it be otherwise.

'It's nothing, I'm thinking out loud. A thought experiment.'

'*Thought* experiment? You know what happens in those, don't you? Cats die. You like cats.'

'Or don't die. Or both.'

Satnam holds up his hands and leaves, shaking his head. I am keeping it all from him. And a part of me likes it.

I lie on the bed and close my eyes; waves of grey sleep come for me but still the last few days flicker in my head. The images, the smells. Although my rational mind says otherwise, my senses say I travelled in time. *I* travelled in time? What could I do if I managed to time travel again? What could I see, do, change?

I scramble off the bed and sit cross-legged on the floor in front of the mask. If I could be there again I would stay with her, remove her mask and see her properly for the first time. And this time I won't move till the police arrive.

I grab Professor Burton's book from the sofa.

'Initial instructions,' says the first page. 'You will need an old towel, some warm clothing, an ability to let go and a body of water.'

Then that's tomorrow sorted.

Chapter Thirty-Five

Simultaneous Equations

Climbing down to the banks by the Mathematical Bridge, I watch punts pass, each carrying a gullibility of tourists.

'Here,' one guide says, pointing at me. 'Here we have a hardworking student by Newton's mathematical bridge, studying its mystical construction, which, local legend has it, once solved will reveal Newton's last revelation.'

The huddled puntees coo and ooh.

'Don't listen to him,' I shout to them. 'Local legend has it that if you believe him, your head will fall off.'

'Shut up, mate,' the punter said, pulling up the punt and pointing it at me, wobbling.

'I'd watch out for Newton's more famous revelation if I were you,' I reply as he loses balance and stumbles backwards. The boat see-saws, he waves his arms, sticks out a leg, then tips into the river. The tourists take pictures of him bobbing up, camera flashes snapping off the walled flanks of the Cam.

He doesn't disappear.

Standing on the edge, I bend and hold out my arm to help him.

When he has punted them away, ducking under the bridge and turning the corner back to The Mill, I check no other punts are coming

and jump.

The Cam gulps me down.

And belches me back up. I look round. The same walls, cars beeping, my rucksack still there on the bank.

I try again, hauling myself out and leaping back in. It's warmer this time, but no more willing to take me anywhere other than to the surface of the twenty-first century.

Sitting on the ledge, feet dangling, I dry my hands and rub at my hair, then skim through the book.

> There is no need for a time machine: a human being *is* a time machine. The only machinery required for time travel is the human brain— that is not to say that the brain of any other animal cannot achieve time travel; they certainly can. The human brain has only the very loosest attachment to the present but as a species we do all we can to strengthen the attachment. Of course in this case I mean the present to mean the moment that came just before you thought about it, as by the time you think about it, the present is past. A fly sees time differently. If you have ever attempted to kill a fly with a *Financial Times* you'll know they are formidable prey that can see you coming several presents before the present you decide to kill it. The only flies you catch are the suicidal flies. A surprisingly existential insect, the fly.

I skip a few pages, but sentences stick out:

> Time travel is a mind-body problem. Those who have had crises in their pasts may be more

201

susceptible. For this and many other reasons: never fall in love with a time traveller. Or let them fall in love with you.

Time is a flexible fabric: it stretches, folds, kinks—if you try to use it as a table cloth to cover up the stains, it will slip off eventually.

Certain towns and cities are more conducive to time travel, more than you would realise, certainly more than can provide good coffee and buns to their citizens. Buns, it should be said, are one of the better restoratives after travelling, particularly in time, but there are few occasions that are not better met with a bun. I follow with this horrendously simplified equation:

Instability + History = Time Travel

Those who have time travelled can be identified by a translucence and a faint smell of cocoa to their skin, a sensitivity to sense data and improved taste in music. I made the last one up. There are other signs that I have yet to verify with a significant sample. It is not easy to find travellers. The percentile of travellers in the United Kingdom is approximately 0.1%

I sniff my arm. It smells like it's been dipped in liquid Milky Bar. I need to find Iris Burton.

Chapter Thirty-Six

Interviews

'Who the fuck sent this?' Jane says. The email has been blown up on her screen to the point of pixellation. The photo is of Rhys, recently dead, with a backwards 'S' cut into his wrist.

'It is a very clean cut. Must be someone who knows what they are doing.' Pemberton inclines his head. His face shows no emotion. 'We're checking on the source, guv. The ISP shows up in the Cook Islands. There are a number of blocks and swerves in place; we are trying to locate a starting point.'

'Well hurry up. We're getting nowhere.' She closes her eyes in remembering walking through the gathered press this morning, microphones up her nose, questions buzzing round her face that make her want to freeze like when being circled by a bee.

'Is it time to get someone else in, Detective Inspector Horne?' the reporter had said. 'Would you say you had outserved your usefulness, inspector?' said a man with hair swung over one eye like an eyepatch.

'Would you say you were an ugly bastard who—' She stopped herself there but it was too late; he was writing it down. He looked up and waved the tape recorder at her. It had not been a good morning so far, but few were at the moment.

Pemberton sits down in the chair, whistling. Sometimes she worries that she's being assisted by a robot. A robot that can't make tea. You'd think that robots would make better tea by now. And police officers definitely should be able to: it's the fuel that runs the station.

'So let's have a rundown: we have interviewed fifteen people and there is fuck all in the way of leads. Connections between Rhys and Miranda are limited: they shared a choirmaster, though not at the same time; a music teacher who has, at some point, taught most of Cambridge to plonk out Chopsticks; a primary school teacher with chronic eczema; and a love of Harry Potter.'

'We still can't get hold of Stephen Killigan, ma'am. The college are tight-lipped as you'd expect but nonetheless, no one's seen him.'

'Since the body was found.'

'Yes. Interesting, isn't it?' He jerks his head like a blinking bird picking up seeds and dropping them.

She wants to grab him and shake him. 'Doesn't anything move you, Paul?'

Something between a smirk and a grimace flashes round his mouth.

Holding onto her right fist to stop herself slamming it into Pemberton's birdcage chest, she forces herself to look at the picture. 'Okay,' she says, breathing in and out slowly, trying to bring down her heartbeat. But using anger management techniques makes her angry as she's admitting that she is angry.

'Who have we got then?' she asks.

*　　　*　　　*

Robert Sachs sits by himself in the interview room, smiling.

'What has he got to be so cheerful about?' Jane

asks. 'People only smile at the police when they've got something to hide.'

'But he's not grinning *at us*, guv; he doesn't know we can see him.'

'Of course he does. He's not stupid.'

'I'd hope not, otherwise there's not much hope for us,' Pemberton replies.

'At least you've got a degree. You'll be fast-tracked up the tree like a particularly tall squirrel.' She takes a sip of the coffee she is bringing for Sachs. 'Why do you think he's volunteered his services when we were about to call him in?'

'Maybe *because* we were going to bring him down.'

'Well why are we standing here talking then, Pemberton? Honestly, get in there.'

Robert Sachs takes the mug of coffee and turns it around in his hands. 'How delightful,' he says, pointing to the slogan. *40–Love: New Balls Please.* 'Whose balls are we referring to here? Surely not yours,' he addresses Pemberton. 'You can't be a day over thirty.'

'Why did you want to come and see us, Professor Sachs?' Pemberton asks. He's actually blushing.

Robert Sachs's face drops into seriousness as easily as it slides into smiles. 'I saw the terrible news about the young boy. He's a choirboy at my college, Sepulchre, and when I found out about the mask I had to tell you about a young lecturer.'

Jane tightens her hold on her pen. 'Oh yes?'

'Yes. Dr Stephen Killigan. He is very new. I believe you have already encountered him. He claimed to have discovered the body of Miranda Pilkington, who he says was also wearing a mask.'

205

He waits as if for confirmation.

'Go on, Professor Sachs.'

'Well he is a very keen young man, I cannot fault his enthusiasm, so when he came to me asking to know more about the masks that I studied for my second doctorate, in Bologna, I was only too happy, and flattered. Yes I will admit that, I was flattered—he is an attractive, intelligent and intriguing young man. So I was only too happy to show him the one mask that I had in my possession. There are four of them in the world, you may already know. Three of which haven't been seen in centuries.' He turns to Pemberton and winks. 'I'm a bit of an expert.'

'*Had* in your possession?' Pemberton says, ignoring the flirting.

'That's right. It was stolen from my rooms shortly after I showed it to Stephen.'

'How did you get hold of the mask, Professor Sachs?' Pemberton asks. 'Shouldn't there be a record of ownership?'

'If only there were: it would make it much more valuable. I found it in the back of an antiques centre in London. More of a junk shop, really.' Professor Sachs blinks.

'That's a bit of a coincidence, don't you think?' Jane replies. 'You are studying the masks and happen upon one of them.'

'I've been looking for years. I'm surprised I haven't found one before.'

'When was your mask taken?'

'Days ago, when Stephen left my rooms with a dead pigeon.'

Jane and Pemberton stare at Sachs. 'A dead pigeon,' Jane says.

He nods. 'That's right,' he replies, as if that were the most ordinary thing in the world.

Chapter Thirty-Seven

Iris Burton

The doorbell rings on my second try. From this angle I can see through the window—*Countdown* is on the television. A lucky Chinese cat waves its paw on the sill. The letterbox opens and Iris Burton's voice comes out: 'Who is it?'

'Sorry to disturb you—'

'Don't say that unless you mean it.'

'Er, right. I'm Stephen Killigan; we met in the University Library the other day.' No reply. I crouch down. The letterbox has a black brush over the opening. 'We talked in the lift?' Nothing. 'You lent me a book?'

Small dirty fingers emerge from the bristles, parting it. Seeing a pair of wispy eyebrows, I hold the book out.

There's a clanking and clinking and rattling and the door opens, sticking on the mat. Iris Burton stands in the doorway holding a plate of Bourbon biscuits. She cocks her head, looks at my hair, dripping sleeves, river-dark jeans then scuttles back down a hallway that smells of cigarillos, tea and old roses. On the wallpaper, a shoal of brown Mobius strips swims up the stairs.

The lounge is lit by a single lightbulb. Iris Burton places a plastic bag on the seat of one of two deckchairs and gestures for me to sit down on it.

She sits in the other one and squints at the big box of a telly with sticky tape over the buttons. Swinging her legs above the beige carpet, she nibbles round the edges of one biscuit and places it back on the plate. She takes another one, prises off one cocoa side and gnaws the chocolate cream off with her teeth. 'Did you read it then?' she asks.

'I did. I've got a few questions for you. If you don't mind.'

'Of course I mind. I'm in the middle of something.' She stares at the *Countdown* clock and scribbles something on the back of an Indian takeaway menu. 'Only "numinous". That's terrible. Anyone can get that.'

'I didn't.'

'No?'

'No.'

'Well, maybe it's not so bad. But I got a fifteen last week. Biscuit?' she says, passing me the plate.

I take the only one that hasn't been nibbled or dismembered. The dusty sweetness makes my fillings itch. 'You can't get more than nine.'

Grinning at me, showing her very tiny teeth, she leans over and pulls out a stack of laminated letters from under the deckchair. 'I like to make it challenging,' she says.

'Your book, Professor. It reads as if you are speaking from experience.' I breathe in and words come out in a blast: 'Have you ever time travelled?'

'At no point do I say I have,' she replies.

'You haven't answered the question.'

'The most pertinent question at this point, notice I say at this point, the most pertinent question at this point, is whether this tea tastes of fish.' She turns down the volume on the television and takes off her glasses. Her eyes get bigger.

I stare at her. 'What?'

She passes me the plastic mug and speaks very slowly: 'Does this taste of fishywigs?'

I take a sip. It seems the only thing to do. My mouth fills with the taste and sensation of fish scales. 'Urgh. Yes. Tuna.'

She nods and claps her hands. 'Goodgoodgoodgoodgoodgoodgood,' she says, wriggling out of the deckchair to standing, her eyes shining. This is good. 'Something to do; I've missed having something to do.'

I stand up and watch as she busies around the lounge, muttering and filling a satchel with books and biscuits.

'Why is it good that it tastes horrible?'

'You're brighter than that, I think. You don't have to hide it here.'

'You're making my head hurt, Professor Burton.'

'I like the way you roll your "r"s when you say Professor Burton.' She wiggles her hips. 'And it's not me that's making your head hurt. Bang it when you fell in the river, did you?'

'How did you know that?'

Iris Burton makes a swatting gesture. 'We're not talking about me.' She stops and peers at me. 'You're here to find out how to do it again. From the look of you you've been in and out of the river all afternoon.'

I nod.

'And you got back the same way?'

'No, through Great St Mary's church.'

'Really? How interesting.' She tugs on a chin hair. When she lets go, it curls up into a delicate spiral like a butterfly's proboscis. 'Never heard of that. Some buildings I have, of course, of course, stands to reason, but not that.'

'What other buildings? Can't we go now?'

She laughs and tickles herself on the waist. 'You're like Doppler, a Labrador pup I had—she liked to lick my hand and to run into the road when the dustmen were coming. I won't tell you what happened to her. Only that I was glad they stayed behind long enough to scoop her up. Oh don't look like that, I'm only joking.' Sulking now, hunched into her bony chest, she wrestles on a cagoule and glares at me. 'Right then,' she says. 'Let's get going. I want to be back in time for Krishnan Guru-Murthy. He's got a lovely smile.' Tugging me by the jeans pocket, she leads me out of the door.

Chapter Thirty-Eight

The Portrait of Jackamore Grass

Charles Witt pulls a loose animal hair out of the brush and flicks it from his fingers onto the floor. 'Be calmed, would you?' he says to me. 'I would like some separation between your shoulders and your ears.'

'This portrait is for me, not you,' I reply. 'I want to preserve myself, as I am at this time.' It also amuses me to leave these indicators of my existence. I like to toy with detectives: leave a footprint here; a forged postcard there. If they can get me from a painting or a strand of hair then they deserve great acclaim.

'Could you show an expression on your face? You resemble a man who never feels.'

'Then the painting may have verisimilitude after all.'

Witt stares at me, scratches his beard. 'I haven't painted in weeks. I am experiencing some disturbance in my mind after . . . after . . . what happened to Lucy.'

His hand shakes as he smears black on the palate and jabs the brush into the thick paint. He is starting with shadows.

'You do not need to thank me. It is polite, but I don't require politeness.'

Witt strides over to me, waves the brush in my face. A globule of paint lands wet on my cheek. I place my head on one side. His countenance has turned an interesting colour. If there was a mirror in this house then he might like to look in it, paint his own face.

Storming past, he opens the door to a cupboard in

the wall. On the shelf lies a shoe, the muse's shoe. The assonance of 'the muse's shoe' amuses me.

'Why do you laugh?' Witt says, holding the shoe in his hand, stroking the dirty ribbons. 'How can you laugh?' His face has crumpled like a woman's empty stocking.

'Laughing is how I know I am alive. That and killing.'

He places the shoe back on the shelf, wipes under his eye. 'I am having dreams,' he says.

'Sentimentality leads to mistakes,' I tell him. 'I said the same thing to my other associate. It is love that will betray you, and sentimentality is all love is— missing the presence of someone at Christmas. It is only ever about you.'

He is not listening. 'Of a woman haunting me.'

He is scratching hard at his beard now; his black-clogged nails tear at the epidermis.

'Do you have a skin complaint?' I ask.

His face contorts. He twists back to the easel and begins.

Chapter Thirty-Nine

Rolling Back the Year

His killer has done a thorough job. I will tell them it is good. The boy is wrapped in the old carpet, his head emerging from the top. His eyes are closed, as if ready for a bedtime story. His skull is cracked open but not enough to spoil his looks. He has been dead for at least two hours. There will not be too much mess when I carve into his skin as I did the beauty queen's.

It is my turn now. I carry him into the garage. I can be tender, and decide to be as I lay him on the back seat under a blanket, the bunny tucked into his pocket.

There are some difficulties involved in holding onto something heavy when travelling, but it can be done in the same way. We pass through one layer of the text into the year before. One precise year. The accuracy of my work pleases me greatly and I sing as I place him in the earth, holding his head till the last and laying it down on a small pillow. He lies there, plump hand holding tight to his bunny. He would not let it go, right to the end. His murderer took no account of that, showed no mercy, did not see the humanity. I respect that.

I take a shovel-full of earth and shake it over Rhys's body. This feels right, a ritual. I would prefer that his murderer took part but they could not come with me as well. This way they will be protected. I do the dirty work, the real work. I sometimes wonder if I am really appreciated.

The earth looks only slightly disturbed when I finish. The rolls of turf are stacked by the shed, ready for tomorrow when the ground will be pressed down and Rhys with it, ready for the lawn that will grow above his bones.

I stretch backwards. My back is as knotted as that tree.

He will be safe there, under the skin of the grass. I lie down next to him.

Chapter Forty

Tutorial in Time Travel

Iris Burton clambers over the stile. 'I thought you young people were sprightly.'

I run and catch up. 'I'm thirty-five, hardly young,' I reply.

'When I was your age I was dancing the can-can on a Paris stage with half a swan on my head. Compared to me you are a zygote.'

We walk across the fields; three of her quick, tiny steps matching one of mine. Beyond us the sun is giving up on the day and squishing itself into the horizon. Behind us, a cow bellows. In the field beyond, a huge spider sticks its metal legs into the ground.

Iris sees me staring. 'That's a draining machine. Jeanie and Martin are still removing the water even though this whole area is part of the project to return the fens to floodland. I admire their persistence.'

'What about your house?'

Iris shrugs. 'I shall be relocated. Probably into college accommodation.'

We walk down towards a stream. In the field beyond, Martin—presumably—walks out from beneath the limbs of the draining machine. He plucks a yellow jumper from the fence and walks wearily away. 'Don't you mind that this whole area will disappear?'

'Just because you can't see it, doesn't mean it's not there. Like your murdered girl. It still lies beneath.'

'What do you mean?'

'Water is patient; it bides its time. I admire *its* persistence too.'

'There are *two* murdered girls,' I say, quietly. 'One in this century, another in the seventeenth.'

'That's a bit of a coincidence don't you think?' she asks.

'I do,' I reply.

'And do you believe in coincidence?'

'I don't believe in ghosts, astrology, coincidence or trifle.'

'So what do you conclude? That you attract dead women?'

'More than alive ones. But I have no idea. I think there may be someone playing with me. Or that could be paranoia. Or narcissism. I mean, why would anyone want to toy with me?'

Iris nods, distracted.

'You don't have to agree with me.'

'I agree. I don't have to agree with you.'

'There is a name that has come up in connection with what's happening.' Can I trust her? She blinks. 'Jackamore Grass,' I say.

She stops, turns to me with an abrupt shift of her shoulders. Blinking several times, She takes off her glasses and cleans them with a pink-spotted cloth. 'Never heard of him,' she says.

'Are you sure? He could have gone under another name, Robert said—'

'Would you shut up? My mind likes to work without chatter. That's why I live out here. At least I can't understand the birds if they are chuntering on about celebrities and cellulite and celebrities with cellulite. Honestly, you'd think people didn't have brains anymore.' She glances suspiciously up at the roosting birds in the trees. 'Now what were we talking about? Time travel, that's right.'

We stop by the stream. 'Here we are,' Iris says. She takes off her sandals and edges down the bank.

I've only just got dry from the last try.

'Stop your humphing: you came to me, remember.' Iris slaps the ground next to her. 'Come on, you. I'll give you a humbug.' She digs in her pockets, pulls out a nude, fluffy sweet and picks at it.

'Get in, then,' she says, sucking on the sweet.

The bank is fringed by whispering reeds. The shallow water stumbles over stones. 'You sure it's deep enough?' I say.

She folds her arms tight across her body. 'Do you trust me or not?'

I take off my coat, throw it at her and push my jeans up my calves.

'Off you go, then,' she says. I wade in and she claps her hands. The water nips at my ankles like my aunt's angry spaniel. 'Throw yourself down.'

I hold my arms over my head. Close my eyes.

A moment falls,

then my face and chest thwack at water; my hands and knees graze against shifting stones. The stream creeps into my jeans. Peeling myself up, I look around: the sky is the same sky, lit with orange and purple stripes like an indie-girl's thighs. The same land spools out into the distance. Professor Burton laughs. 'Again!' she says. She pops another humbug in her mouth and dabs her toes into the water.

I fold my arms against my chest and fall backwards. My spine smacks through to the river bed. I lift my head.

'There must be another way. I've already tried all this, earlier.' I stand and face her with my hands on my hips.

'Not with me, you haven't. Do it again, and this time recite the Fibonacci series before and during your fall.'

'Why?'

'Would you ask a yoga teacher why you have to get into The Camel? No, you wouldn't, because he or she is the expert. Would you ask a mechanic, while they were fixing your car, "Why are you singing the national anthem while wearing a balaclava?"'

'I would. Yes.'

'Okay, bad example. And you *should* question that yoga teacher: camels are irascible and irrational and their position should not be assumed unless you wish to resemble one when you're eighty.' Iris stands up, brushing her hands. 'My point is: I know what I'm doing. And you don't. Get over it. This is beginner's stuff, you know. Using water the way of the amateur traveller. But you have to get the hang of it first, young man.'

Breathe in, breathe out. 'Okay. I'm sorry. The Fibonacci series: every number is the sum of the previous two.'

'No need to look cocky. My dead cat knows that.' She flicks her hand back and forth. 'Go on then.'

I say the numbers in my head: 0, 1, 1, 2, 3, 5, 8, 13, 21, 34, 55, 89, now I can't add up quick enough, 144, 233, is that right? What am I doing? I don't know—

'Tell me whom you lost, Stephen.'

'What?'

217

'Whom have you lost? You wouldn't be so keen to find the girl unless you lost someone else. Who was it? Your father? A sibling? A friend? A lover? No? Your mother?

Numbers tumble out of my head.

A shove between the shoulder-blades.

Water punches me in the nose.

Iris's laughter skims across the river. Satnam was right. She's a lunatic.

'If you think I'm going to keep making an arse of myself for your entertainment, you can—' I turn.

Iris is not there.

The bank is not there.

A wall *is*. A stone wall, to my chest, flanking the river on one side. The fields beyond are shin-deep in water. The stream hugs my knees.

'Professor Burton!' I shout. 'Iris!'

Disturbed birds rise up from beyond the wall and twist into a sky that is stained the dark blue of a new cagoule. Not the same sky I was under two minutes ago.

Reaching down, I scoop two palms full of water and drink from the heel of my hand. The water smells of the bottom of a bin. Heraclitus may be right: you can't step into the same river twice.

Another sound behind the birds. Professor Burton's giggle. And behind that, a cow's guffaw.

The wall backs away from me, fading away as if losing consciousness. I reach out. I can see my hand, and I can see the wall but all I feel is a sensation of cold, not the sensation of wall.

'Lower!' Iris's voice.

The bank shimmies forward and Iris waves through the transparent bricks of another century's wall. Two slices of time lie on a slide, vying for

218

attention. Opticians ask: 'Two lenses, both blurry, which is clearer?' and I never know which is. If both are blurry, then how can you tell? *Really* tell? You can't. Can't I have both? Like choosing between beans and peas, or chips and mash. I want all four.

Iris's voice scissors through. 'Concentrate. Centre on me, Stephen. Bring me in. It's like calling in a pedalo when its time is up.'

I fix all my attention onto the bobble on her hat. It shies away and becomes see-through but I hold my eyes wide and concentrate on its form. The bobble hat is becoming less of a phantom; below it, Iris is scrabbling down the bank towards me. The wall fades away to let her through.

'That's it, Stephen.'

Iris wades into the water and holds out her arms.

*   *   *

Sitting in her deckchair, covered in towels, I take the cup from the tray.

'Now, no tea after travelling,' Iris says. 'Unless you want to drink something that tastes like liquidised fish. Stick to cocoa. As much sugar as you can stand before your teeth itch.' She pours in another stick of sugar. 'I take these from college,' she says, waggling another tube.

My head feels as if it could roll off onto her carpet and under the curtains. 'Why does reciting the Fibonacci series work?' I ask. 'No, don't tell me, something to do with the Golden Mean? Nature allows time travel at a point that matches the ratio of a sunflower? Something to do with symmetry where the past and future are balanced and you can walk a board between them? It's something like

219

that, isn't it?'

'No,' says Iris. She turns on the television and watches the *Channel Four News*.

'You can be annoying, you know,' I say.

She giggles. 'Thank you. There are few better compliments.' She grabs my head and looks in each of my eyes. 'Okay. I think you're settled enough now.' She picks up her book and flicks through it. 'The reason I got you to recite the series was to stop you thinking too much about where you wanted to go. That can fix you to the spot and not let you move. The times when people can time travel are when they are not anchored to the world they think they exist in. That can be trauma, extreme emotion, inebriation, anything where perceived stability is disrupted. The funny thing is,' she says, pushing my T-shirt up my arm and wrapping a blood pressure cuff around it, 'for you, it was when I made you jump from the process of thinking of the next number in the series to feeling the emotions associated with loss, and the trauma that connects you to that point in the past.'

'My mum.'

'Your mum.'

I can still feel that pain, from the day she went beneath the sea. I can still touch the edges of it. The centre is the white heat of a length of hot thin pipe placed against the flesh of my inner arm and the edges are the blue heat at the base of a candle flame.

'I don't see how they can make me able to jump from one time to another,' I say.

'It is when we are at our most alive, honest and vulnerable that we can locate the place between constructed realities and step through the gaps.'

220

She bustles out of the door and I hear her in the kitchen, humming and rummaging. I can't help thinking of the wombats I saw in a wildlife park in Australia, bumbling and twitching. Instructions are beeped into a microwave.

I stand, fold up the towels and place them over the clothes horse next to the television. My legs are steadier now, less like sticks of rock before they are set. The mirror over the wall is crooked. Fuck me, I look bloody awful. My skin is pale, my eyes bracketed underneath by dark blue. Lana is not going to want me now.

I pick up a snowglobe from the mantelpiece and shake it. Dessicated plastic falls over Cambridge. I could see Cambridge in the snow in another time. The possibilities of time travel, when not searching for dead girls, are incredible. Imagine what I could do, the people I could meet, the stories and smells and all that I could bring back. The things to change. Or not. And there must be others like me.

The microwave declares itself finished.

Iris comes in and hands me a plate of food. 'Curry,' she says. 'It's not good, but it's right. And I don't have naan bread, so you'll have to use this.' She passes me a stale croissant. 'I was going to give it to the birds so think yourself lucky.'

The last smudge of madras swiped up, I take my plate out to the kitchen and fill the sink ready to wash up. There are stacks of teetering mugs everywhere. Iris follows me in.

'Who else can time travel?' I ask. 'In your book you say it is only point something per cent.'

'Feeling lonely already?'

'Just wondering.'

221

She picks up a tea cloth and starts drying up the cups. 'Everyone, I think, has the potential to time travel. It happens often. Those times when people see something out of the corners of their eyes, then when they concentrate on it, it disappears: for that moment when the mind is not focused, they see into another time. Some put it down as illusion, others to ghosts. While that isn't physically being in the past it is a sign that time is not as linear and distinct as people like to think. And God knows where most of us are when we are sleeping. This skill is inherent, but is present in all and can be amplified, controlled and used to your advantage. Anyone can do it; they simply have not had access to that part of them for a very long time. Either that or they are doing it all the time and not noticing. Here are some rules for you. A few things you should know.'

Chalk squeaks against the board. Her writing rises up and down the board in peaks and is so tiny it is like watching a distant flock of migrating birds. She stands back so I can read:

1. Always carry your Time Travel Kitbag which should include
    i.   Medical kit including water purifiers, arnica tablets, electrolyte powders, antiseptic wipes, antibiotics, iodine, Kendal mint cake, painkillers, kaolin and morphine and a lemon
    ii.   Notebook containing hand-copied maps of the area in different time periods
    iii.   Smartphone and app ascertaining year and day from the position of the stars without recourse to internet

iv. Money from different periods. Investment documents. Gold.

v. Disguise: an academic gown if male. Obtain appropriate clothing as soon as possible. Money and guile are required

vi. Documents to support an alternate identity

vii. List of likely friends

viii. Pen knife

ix. Key

2. When you arrive

i. Consume mint cake and take arnica for shock, aspirin for headaches etc.

ii. Discover when you are: from your surroundings if during the day, from your smartphone or by subtle methods of enquiry. I said subtle

iii. Locate funds

iv. Dress and act in way appropriate to the time

v. Find shelter

3. Avoid:

a. Paradoxes. The Paradox roams the past, waiting with its many limbs and hands outstretched to keep you tied in its grasp. There are three main species to avoid: the Ontological, the Grandfather and the Predestination. Look them up. And for God's sake, avoid smartphone getting into other hands. We don't want it discovered and invented before it was invented. I have no wish for Twitter to exist sooner than it has to

b. Messing with time: you are an observer of, not a participant in, the past

'I would also have said avoid a man called Jackamore Grass, but it seems to be too late for that.'

I feel my face freeze. 'But you said earlier that you had never heard of him.'

'I did. Oops.'

'Why?'

'Because I didn't want to talk about him then. And I'm not keen to now. Just stay out of his way, okay?'

'And why should I do that?'

'He is the most dangerous man I have ever met. He can turn his hand to any skill and charm the pages from a book, the fur from a cat, the life from a man without once feeling remorse. And if he is involved in this then you should be very careful about what you do next.'

'You've met him?' I ask.

She looks down at her tiny feet. 'I have. I encountered him several times in my active travelling years. An intelligent man with very different ideas about time travel: I like to meet people throughout history; he likes to murder them.'

'And I should stay away from him, and Robert Sachs, even if that means that a missing woman he possibly murdered isn't found?'

'You think a lot of yourself, don't you; thinking that you could make a difference?'

'I *should* stay away then.'

'That is your choice. It is up to you what you do with the ability you have. And then you tell me about it so I can write a second edition.'

She places the chalk back on top of the board

and rubs her hands against her sides. 'Now,' she says. 'I'm thinking of doing something which my head tells me not to and my instinct insists on. You'll get that a lot. I should have written down "trust your instincts". But that's not just a rule for time travellers.'

She studies my face for what seems like ten minutes, then scuttles out of the kitchen. 'Well come on then.'

Up the first set of stairs, and a second. Iris goes on ahead, closing doors and glaring at me as if I had considered peeking inside. Holding up a stick with a hook on the end, she pulls down a hatch. A rope ladder tumbles down.

Up in the attic, she sits on top of a large, dusty trunk. 'In here is something I haven't shared with anyone else. Not my late husband, nor my early one.' She jumps up, hefts up the lid and lugs out a silver box. She pushes it along the paint-spattered floorboards.

*　　　*　　　*

I get as far as Waterbeach before I peek. Inside is a brown knapsack, a folder full of documents, two old gold bars and a key with a brown luggage tag.

The taxi driver glances in his mirror. 'What's in the box?'

'A time-travel survival kit,' I say.

He sticks a thumb up his nose and scrapes out a skein of snot. 'All right, if you don't want to tell me, just say so.'

*　　　*　　　*

The taxi stops at the side door. I run through the college, as best as I can with a metal box poking at my ribcage. I don't want to see any porters or students or anyone if I can help it, no one judging me, asking me questions. I want to be on my own and read through Iris's documents.

The smell of Satnam's favourite hangover cure—burned toast and egg-fried rice—fills the hallways. I go to knock on his door. Then stop. I couldn't explain this to him, let alone about me and Lana. Lana. I must phone her.

Relief hits me as I walk up to my rooms, and tiredness so thick I feel as if my eyes are being dragged down to the ground. I open the door and collapse onto the sofa.

'Would you care to come through, Dr Killigan?'

Inspector Horne is in my bedroom, on my bed, the masks in her gloved hands.

Chapter Forty-One

Forces of Attraction and Repulsion

Inspector Jane Horne looks up to me from the masks' eyes. 'Would you mind telling me where you've been these last few days, Dr Killigan? And where you got those masks?'

'Are you allowed to search without a warrant?'

'Your college Mistress is breaking with Cambridge tradition and being very helpful. This is their property, not yours.'

Now I can go either way here. Keep it in or let it out. Or ignore the problem altogether.

'Okay,' I say. 'I'm done with secrets.' I jump up and shine a light at the window. A 0 now fills the top right corner of the noughts and crosses grid. He's been back. 'I believe that a man called Jackamore Grass is behind the murders of Miranda, Rhys and a woman in the seventeenth century called Lucy Miller. I believe that he has killed many, many times before.'

Jane rubs her eyes. 'You are making no sense, Dr Killigan. How can someone kill a woman in both the seventeenth century and the twentieth? If a Cambridge egghead has discovered something useful for once, such as the secret of eternal life or, better still, eternal youth, then I want to know about it. Now.'

I take a long slow breath. 'He travels in time. And so do I.'

Jane stares for a moment, then bursts out laughing. She winces and presses her palm against her breastbone.

'Are you okay?' I ask.

She nods. 'Can we please get back to an explanation of how you are in possession of two masks identical to one found on the face of a dead boy?'

'Two masks? I only had one.' Inspector Horne breathes out slowly.

'I know I'm not making sense, but then Rhys's murder doesn't make sense. Nor does Miranda's disappearance. Give me ten minutes and I'll try to explain.'

'Okay. I'm listening,' Inspector Horne says. 'For a maximum of four minutes. No, three. Then I shall arrest you. Your time starts now.'

Sweat covers my back. How can I get out of this? I could lose my job if I'm taken in again, and I will have brought it on myself. They warned me. And I didn't listen. My mouth fills with the taste of a rusty cog that has cut my tongue. The only option is the truth. I start talking, pacing the room, tipping out everything I can remember, rushing out a weir of seeming nonsense: from Sachs's letter; to falling into the seventeenth century; to all the bodies and masks that haunt my dreams and days.

Jane shakes her head.

'You have no reason to believe me, I know that. I have to convince myself sometimes. But the masks help. They are tangible. You could have them examined.'

'Thanks for telling me my job, Dr Killigan.' Jane carefully places the masks inside evidence bags. 'Let me get all this right. You have two of only four masks made yet they have not been seen since a fire in the Museum of Padua in 1742. There are reports of a tall man wandering from the blaze, smoke rising from his jacket, swinging what sounds like a bowling bag. Are you suggesting that this man—'

'Was Jackamore Grass, and that he stole them? I am,' I reply.

'Oh really.'

'Imagine that time travel is possible, for certain individuals at least, and is definitely possible by Jackamore Grass, the man the press calls The Killer Magician, and by me, then what is to stop him travelling to Italy in 1742, nicking the masks and using them when he gets the chance?'

'He then places one on the beauty queen, wherever she is,' she says. 'Another on Rhys. Another on this Lucy Miller of yours. This is what you're suggesting.' She puts away her notebook and rubs at her head. Her eyes seem darker than before. 'Then this is my suggestion: seek help. Immediately. Do not pass Go or any other sign unless accompanied by a responsible adult. You. Are. Not. Well. You're amenable, and you make me laugh, and you have an interesting brand of interior design but know that you are utterly insane. And from what I've heard, you'll be lucky to keep your job.'

'I know you don't believe me,' I say. 'But I have told you the truth. I don't know what else to do. At some point you are going to have to start trusting me.' I lean forward, fear chasing my heart into a corner. 'I'm worried that the four masks means that there will be four victims, who will each die with the mask as their face; that there will be another. We've got to stop it from happening.'

'I think that's entirely possible,' she says, 'unlike time travel.' She stands up and stretches. 'I'm

229

taking you to the station, before that fourth murder can take place.'

*   *   *

My solicitor, a curly-haired woman who never smiles, reaches into her briefcase. A copy of the *National Enquirer* peeks out from behind a Law Society magazine. 'I don't know why you didn't call me the first time.' She scowls and runs her tongue across her teeth. 'There is no evidence linking you to the mask found on Rhys Withins; in fact there is the DNA of another man, not you. Don't say anything other than give a reasonable explanation for how you obtained the masks.'

'I already have.'

'It is suggested that you stole them from Professor Sachs.'

'I didn't.'

She leans on her elbows; her eyes have no warmth in them. 'I can get you bail as they don't have enough to hold you. But you aren't helping me. Or yourself.'

'Are you telling me to lie?'

The interrogation room clock crosses its arms.

Chapter Forty-Two

Police Informant

'Why have you summoned me, Jackamore?' Robert asks. His voice is trembling and he stands hunched over, looking behind him down the corridor to check

230

that no one is watching us.

People pass. The carpet snuffs out their shoes. I nod to one of them. Robert turns his head.

'My informant has been in touch. Dr Killigan is in custody. Not for long, most likely, but enough to rattle him. They want to know where he got the masks.'

'Aren't you worried that he'll lead them to you?'

I laugh. Loudly. 'That would be an adventure,' I say. 'I have been told that Dr Killigan is in danger of losing his job. I don't want that, not yet anyway. Put in a word for him, several long admiring words. Get him a reprieve.'

'I don't know if I'll be able—'

'You will,' I say. Robert shrinks back against the wall.

He holds on to the banister as he walks down the stairs but still stumbles as he looks back at me. It's a pity. He was promising, once.

I walk back to my desk, looking up at the rain on the high windows. All is going well in the game. My informant has told me where they are keeping the masks and I will retrieve them again. I will need them, soon.

A colleague flinches when I turn to her. It seems they don't like to see me smiling.

Chapter Forty-Three

The Tea Leaves Paradox

Frank Utter is fussing, leaning over the kitchen staff as they lay the tables for Formal Hall, straightening napkins and picking up wine glasses to hold them to the light. Anwar the butler stands in the doorway and links his fingers, presumably so he doesn't point at Utter and tell him to keep to what he is paid to do.

Utter glances up. 'Thank you for deigning to come and see me, Stephen, what with your terribly time-consuming schedule with the police.'

Don't bite.

I nod. The thought that Utter is in charge of what happens to my career makes me feel sick.

'I thought that we agreed that you would not pursue this matter. Instead you get yourself arrested and once again bring the college into disrepute.'

Don't bite. Don't bite.

His eyes bulge at me, waiting for a response. He turns his back and gazes at the paintings of former Masters of the college that glare from the walls. Above me, a Lord Mortimer stares scornfully down.

'Sepulchre is an old, highly respected institution and we have a duty to continue the good name established by our predecessors. The great and the good have passed through this Hall and you are letting them down.' He strokes a panel in the wall.

'I'm really not.' Now that I've bitten, I might as well chew. 'Would you like me to leave you alone with that wall?' I ask.

He stares at me. His fingers jolt away from the panelled wood. 'It is fortunate that you have made a good impression in the short time you have been here,' he says, spitting out the words. 'A number of students and staff have spoken up for you. As a result you will not be suspended, not yet.' He reaches into his jacket and hands me a letter. 'Your formal warning.'

I look back up at the old Masters of the college. 'You would look good up there,' I tell him.

'Really?' he asks; his face changes from sneering to eager.

'Oh yes,' I say, 'you'd fit right in.'

*   *   *

Lana's phone rings and rings. Perhaps she is ignoring me. I was away for days and said we'd meet for lunch and I didn't even call when I got back. Perhaps she is getting me back. Perhaps she's found someone else—

'What's going on?' she asks. She sounds the kind of pissed off people get when they've been worried.

'You wouldn't believe me.'

'I would,' she says. 'You've been in the news again.'

'I know.'

'You sound exhausted.'

'I am. I'm really sorry about missing lunch. Would you like to—'

Satnam's broom knocks urgently at the ceiling.

'—to meet up for coffee?' I say. 'I have a supervision, but after that?'

*   *   *

The Red Shoes Cafe is almost empty when I arrive three hours later. Two dons sit at opposite ends of the room with books and notebooks next to their teapots, crumbs scattered, pens uncapped and ready to be picked up and pointed at the other to elucidate their arguments like academic duelling pistols, doilies to hand to mop up the spilled ink

233

of a palpable hit. I'm early. Lana isn't due for ten minutes so I can plan my next lecture. I'm behind on everything. But at least I still have a job, for now. From downstairs comes the spiced fug of tomorrow's cakes. I stir my tea. Stray tea leaves dance in the centre of the cup like Lowry stick figures. You'd think they'd cling to the sides due to centrifugal force. The Tea Leaves Paradox.

There's a knock at the window. Satnam waves his hand. Please don't come in. Please don't come in.

He comes in. I check my watch. 'You off somewhere?' I ask.

'I'm off to see the stars at the observatory. I'm setting up the telescope. We're hoping to see something pretty special happening in this nebula.'

'And you insist that physics is boring.'

'You can't bring me down with your petty sarcasm. Not today: I'm buzzing, mate. My lecture on classical mechanics was so bloody brilliant that a girl came up afterwards wanting me to sign a copy of my thesis. She's printed it out on pink paper.'

'You lucky bastard. There are usually only five people attending mine, and one of them is only there to get some decent sleep. I got things sorted with Utter, by the way. He was sitting in the Senior Common Room, crossing and uncrossing his legs like a grasshopper. I reassured him that the police wanted my help with their enquiries into the mask. He's still suspicious though.'

'You'll win him round eventually. You usually do.' He pats me on the shoulder and I feel terrible.

'By the way, what were you doing talking with Takola outside the lecture theatre?'

I laugh. 'Jealous, are you?' Takola Beckford is a maths postgraduate who talks with the speed and pitch of a cricket clicking its wings. She is Satnam's main rival in the 'Chief Geek and Genius' genus and is rarely on her own, always surrounded by a group of men and women who would be happy to sit with their heads on their hands just staring at her. She never notices. She's building me an app today that will take a picture of the night sky from any point in the last two thousand years, and, as long as you input your longitude and latitude, compare it with data stored in the memory to tell you precisely when you are. She didn't ask why, and won't care if it keeps her brain from standing still.

'You won't believe me,' I say. 'Well I don't want to keep you from your nebulae; see you mate.'

The door tinkles open. Lana comes in and drops her umbrella in the teapot-shaped stand. She smiles at me and comes over. She bends and kisses me. I freeze. Satnam stares at us, mouth open.

'It's good to meet you,' she says, holding out her hand. 'Stephen's talked about you.'

'We've met before,' he says.

'Have we?' she says, her brow wrinkling.

'Well I think I'll leave you two to it,' he says. He smiles too widely. 'Don't do anything I wouldn't do. Oh, you already have,' he says to me as he leaves.

'He seems a bit, well, wired,' Lana says. She orders earl grey tea and lavender chocolate layer cake.

'Someone's going out with the girl he fancies,' I say.

'Poor bastard,' she says. 'Unrequited love is shite.'

'Were you trying to do my accent?' I ask, laughing. 'Because that was rubbish.'

Our shoulders touch as we stop talking for the

ritual of tea: the pouring of just enough milk; the arc of the liquid as it pours from the pot.

'I have a favour to ask you,' I say.

'Shouldn't you be making it up to me for our lost lunch rather than asking for favours?'

'I'm not one for shoulds,' I reply. I turn on my impossibly-cheeky-and-charming eyes.

'You don't have to switch on the charm,' she says. 'Just ask.'

'I need your research skills to find out about a woman called Lucy Miller. I need to know where and how she lived in 1635. There is a stone dedicated to her in Great St Mary's. We could go there after tea, if you like.'

'Oh, the romance,' Lana says, then bends and licks the topping from her cake.

*   *   *

The town hall clock ticks half past three.

'Get a room,' someone shouts, but we don't break away.

Lana finally places her hand on my chest and pulls away. 'I really need to go to work,' she says, smiling as I lean in again. 'My boss has got me working late nights.'

I watch her walk off until she turns the corner, and stay still for a while in case she turns back.

Stallholders are packing away boxes of bruised fruit and knock-off hoodies back into vans. The market square is emptying, everyone off home for the football results and a pint.

The Eagle is a proper pub—I can picture the student Wordsworth and the student Byron chatting girls up against its smoked walls, dipping under the beams and lining up the laudanum on the tables. In the back room the vidi-printer etches last-minute goals and results onto the television screen. Men thump pints on the tables in celebration or anger, either way losing a third of their pints to the carpet as some kind of offering to soccer gods. I should do it: maybe then we wouldn't lose.

The volume on the television is turned up. 'In a press conference today, Katie Withins spoke again of her distress at her son's death.' The bald man next to me turns to watch. Katie scrapes her hair back with her fingertips. She looks young, in her twenties. There'll be experts analysing her stutter, her eye movements, the way she keeps covering up her yellow fingers in one hand with the other. They'll assume she's lying. She might be, but I don't think so. Her bottom lip is crimping, doing what people do when they're trying not to cry. 'Please,' she says, 'if anyone knows what happened to Rhys, contact the police. I need to know what happened to my little boy. I'll do anything; there must be someone who knows something.'

Inspector Horne places her hand over Katie's. Katie edges her hand out and moves it under the table. 'Information from the public will be vital in solving this case,' says Horne. 'If you saw anything suspicious on the evening and night, then we must know about it. Now, are there any questions?'

A reporter in the front row raises her hand. 'Have you identified how Rhys died?'

'A blow to the head. That's all we have at the moment.'

'Has the weapon been found?' a blonde reporter asks.

'My team are still searching for the murder weapon, although it is likely that Rhys was placed there in the middle of the night, and murdered elsewhere.'

Horne glances across to her right to a man standing behind her. I recognise him from the college. 'That's all for today. A further statement will be released later.'

The reporter in the front row puts up her hand again. 'Would it be fair to say that the college is obstructing the police? And would it also be fair to say that the police are without any clue as to how Rhys's body could have decomposed so quickly?'

Horne stares at the reporter, her mouth opening, but nothing coming out.

The reporter continues, jumping in. 'Are you happy with the way the police are conducting the case, Mrs Withins?

Katie glances quickly at Inspector Horne and down at her hands. 'I'm sure they are doing their best,' she says, 'but—'

The woman next to her puts her hand over Katie's. A warning dressed up as support.

'Do you have a statement to make about your husband moving out of the home, Mrs Withins?'

Katie Withins's head lowers, her shoulders shaking.

The news report switches to images of the Withinses' home. Overhead views of white suits in their garden. The reporter is one of many outside in the road under an umbrella. He has that revelling in tragedy look: serious glee. Neighbours are appalled, but not enough to have not had their hair done.

Big hush in the pub. Even the men playing

darts are still, the flights poking out of their fists like funeral flowers. The man next to me digs into his back pocket. 'My daughter,' he says, holding a torn-off photobooth picture. It's of him and a girl of about four with a gappy smile. I nod, not knowing what else to do, but he nods back, so it seems to be okay. He kisses the photo and slides it back in his pocket.

*   *   *

There is already a bundle of handwritten notes from Lana in my pigeonhole when I return, and a note stuck to my door with a dart. Maybe Satnam has come round—maybe he has forgiven me and wants to make up, or at least drink beer, which is much the same. I unfold the note, grinning.

Allow me to introduce myself, formally, at last. My name is Jackamore Grass. The police know me as The Magician Killer, and by other pseudonyms that they have yet to connect with me. I, too, am a doctor, although my doctorate is in the legitimate field of medicine. I know of no one healed by philosophy. Killed, yes. Healed? I think not.

I know that you have travelled in time. I know you desire more. I know that you are in appreciation of all the work I have done to make the murders a work of beauty. I know how you are interested in beauties.

Allow me to give you some advice, Dr Killigan; give up love. Give up love and you can stride between times with the same ease as emerging from the house into the day. Love ties you tightly to time. Love will pass anyway—you know this more than

239

most: so why not pick off the limpets that stick to you? Believe me, be rid of love and you will fly. You will free up more of yourself than you know.

I could give you more handy tips. I could show you everything, and maybe I will, in time. I can show you more than that shrew Iris Burton, that is for certain. But be warned, Dr Killigan: pursue me in order to bring me to the police and I will do you the service of liberating you from this tie.

One more piece of information. You'll be glad to hear the beauty queen put up quite a fight; as did Lucy Miller. You remember Lucy, the girl in the mud that I made sure you saw? She was the very picture of bravery. Rhys has little idea what happened to him but the same will not be said for the last victim. She will know exactly what is happening to her. It is so much more interesting to watch.

You should know now that I never lose. Never. So do not attempt to win.

Yours most sincerely
Jackamore Grass

Evidence: at last. I check the noughts and crosses grid on the window. He has blocked my next move and set up a possible three in a row on his next turn. I place a cross in his way and am so absorbed I don't hear Satnam till he is through the door.

'I can't believe you went behind my back,' he says, storming into my room. 'When did all this happen with Lana?'

'There's lot going on you don't know about—'

'You're telling me.' He stomps across to the dartboard and starts throwing at the bull.

240

'I am sorry for going back on my word,' I say, 'but you are being melodramatic, Sat. We're thirty-five not fifteen. It's not as if you were going out with her, or had even known her. You just fancied her. We both did, and I was stupid to agree that neither of us would be with her. That was my mistake. I won't make it again.'

'You're different,' he says. 'Something's happened.'

'You're one to talk,' I reply. 'Since you've been to Cambridge you've crisped up your consonants in the icebox. You'd never know you were a Northerner.' That's low. I know it even as I say it.

He stares at me, throws another dart without looking at the board and walks out.

Chapter Forty-Four

Of The Magician

Parkside Street is quiet. The shocked neighbours are probably in their houses watching themselves on television. There's the house: in the middle of a cul-de-sac there's a house with a pile of flowers against the wall. A police constable stands outside, his head at the height of a hanging basket. I'm not going to get in there.

The nearest newsagent is up an alley of steep steps between a Chinese and a chippy. I sit on the wall, waiting for Katie Withins, a packet of fat chips going cold in my pocket. I could tell by the way that her liaison officer touched her hand that she was breaking with the police line when she said that she'd do anything, talk to anyone to find Rhys's killer.

Hurried steps snap up the alley. Katie Withins has a man's coat wrapped round her, so she nearly trips as she walks head down into the newsagent. I follow her. The door tinkles shut behind us.

'Ten, please,' she says, voice muffled by a scarf.

The newsagent glances at the papers, her face on all of them. He hands her a packet of cigarettes and pushes back the money she fumbles onto the counter. A pound coin rolls off onto the lino and I crouch to catch it before it runs under the magazine shelf.

'Thanks,' she mutters, as I stand and hold it out to her.

'I'm really sorry,' I say, 'about your son. And your husband.'

She flinches and makes for the door. She's heading for the steps, trying to open the packet.

'I really am sorry,' I say. 'I'd like to help.'

She stops. 'How could you possibly help?' Her hands are trembling as she puts a fag to her lips and drags on it. It's not lit.

I want to put my arm round her. 'I'm a tutor at Sepulchre College. I can find out things the police can't. The college make it difficult for anyone to interfere.'

'This isn't college business. It's my business, my son.' Her face contorts. She steps back till her calves find the wall, then sits. 'Just how could you help?'

'I was the one who found the beauty queen. I saw the first mask on her face. The police wouldn't believe me. I'm investigating on my own.'

'Why should I believe you, then?'

242

'There's no reason to. But you should.'

She stands up and crosses her arms, glancing around as if looking for someone to help in case I turn out to be mad. 'Did you follow me here?'

'This is the stalkery bit, I'm afraid: I saw your home on the television. And your fingers.'

She lifts up her hands in the fingerless gloves and looks at them.

I point to the suede-yellow patches around two of her fingers on her right hand. 'I thought you'd need more fags at the moment, and this is your nearest store. I know it seems heartless.' It *is* heartless.

She stuffs her hands into her pockets. 'Think you're Sherlock Holmes, do you?' she asks.

'Not for a minute. I'm rubbish on the violin.'

She she sits back down on the wall. 'Rhys played beautifully. You should hear him. And his voice, it—' She stops, her own voice splintering. 'You couldn't do worse than the police. I know less than I did the day he died.' Her hand moves to the pocket of her coat. Two grey flannel ears appear. She rubs them between her fingers like sage leaves.

'Is that Rhys's?' I ask.

Her mouth tugs down at the edges. 'He wouldn't cuddle it, after Binky disappeared, even though it was exactly the same. He said it didn't smell like Binky.' Her eyes are red and sore. 'If I had found out where Binky went, not just giving him a new one, letting his dad make it all okay by buying things, then—'

'Then what? This was not your fault, you know,' I say. 'None of this is your fault.'

'I paid his killer. That's all I can think of.'

'You trusted a human being, and he turned out

243

to be a monster. The problem doesn't lie with you.'

'If me and his father hadn't been—' Her hand covers her mouth. The sob sneaks through her fingers.

'Can you describe him? Did he say anything to you that now seems important?'

She closes her eyes. 'He was tall, slim, between craggy and handsome. I've been trying to remember everything that happened, but I can't.' She stares at the wall.

'Are you okay?' I ask.

'I'll tell you one funny thing,' she says. 'The magician said when he left that I couldn't see what was playing away under my nose in my own house. He was right.' She crosses her arms and clenches her jaw.

I've seen that hard, will-never-be-the-same-again face on aunts and female friends. And one girlfriend.

'On the night that Rhys was found my husband told me that he's been fucking our son's French teacher. And he always told me he couldn't stand the French. He wouldn't even take me to Paris!' She laughs and keeps on laughing.

I hand her my card. 'Please let me know if you remember anything important. I'm going after this man. And if I find out anything, I promise I will let you know.'

I can still hear her laughing as I walk away.

Chapter Forty-Five

Secrets and Underwire

Jane runs out of the station, coat pulled over her head against paparazzi and rain. Both find the easiest way in and the quickest route down to the dirt.

At least the rain seems to be keeping away the press, for a while. She'll be late for her appointment again if Belinda doesn't hurry up with the car. She's not the most urgent of creatures is Belinda, but she can be trusted: last time they went out for a drink, which turned into twelve drinks and a four a.m kebab, they gulped down secrets like shots.

'Inspector Horne,' says Stephen Killigan, emerging from under the canopy of the next-door delicatessen. 'I've got to talk with you,' he says, grasping a box of mixed olives. He holds them out. 'I don't even like olives. I only bought the buggers so that the deli wouldn't object to me lurking.'

'You are extremely annoying, Dr Killigan. Don't you have some students to seduce or piss off or, I don't know, educate?' Jane says.

'Please, you have to look into Jackamore Grass. He is here, in Cambridge, somewhere. He sent me this.' I hand over the letter from Jackamore.

Jane reads through it. Then reads through it again.

'Take it,' I say. 'I've made a copy. Test the writing, whatever you do. I need to say it again: both he and Robert Sachs are carrying out an experiment into the aesthetics of murder, up to

245

and, I think, including killing. I can't do this all on my own. Please help. Please trust me.'

Trust me. Pemberton said that, and now Killigan. Two men in whom she could never place her trust. She watches him walk quickly away, with what looks like a Dick Whittington knapsack over his shoulders.

*   *   *

'So there you are. It is entirely your decision.' Dr Pindar takes off his glasses and rubs his eyes.

'But what do you recommend?'

'*My* job is to make you aware of your options and lay out the consequences for you. I will then see you through every aspect of your treatment.'

'A preventative mastectomy on my remaining tit will reduce the risk of tumour by ninety per cent.'

'That is correct.'

'Then again I might never get cancer again and I would have taken off my breast for nothing. And I'll never know if it was in vain or not.'

'On the other hand, if you don't, you'll go through never knowing when the cancer could return.'

'But that could happen anyway, and I would still need further surgery. At least keeping it means I have my original breast. What kind of woman would I be without any breasts?' Cells of panic and self-pity metastasise and stick to her chest wall. Does it really matter whether she's got no boobs or two if no man ever wants to touch her again?

Dr Pindar passes her the box of tissues.

She pushes it away. 'I don't cry,' she says. A tear drops just to fuck her off.

246

'Are you happy with the situation now, though?' Dr Pindar says.

'Don't be a clever arse. But what about my reaction to the anaesthetic last time? That's got to be a factor.'

'Any operation is a risk. But there is most likely a bigger risk if you ignore it and play a game of chance.'

'I could pick a card from a pack.'

'You could. Do you want to?'

'No.' She looks out of the tiny window. The trees have lost all of their clobber. Winter is nearly here.

'I don't want to rush you,' Dr Pindar says, 'so if you want to go away and—'

'I'll do it. I'll have the operation,' she says.

*　　　*　　　*

Jane walks out of the consulting room with a stridency that she thought she'd lost. Just making the decision has lifted her; whatever happens she will cope. And what was it anyway? A few pounds of maybe/not malignant flesh. And there was another decision. Ignoring the signs on the walls, she takes out her phone and calls Pemberton. 'I want you to find everything there is throughout history on Mr Jackamore Grass.'

Chapter Forty-Six

Strings

The alarm kicks off, jolting me out of sleep. Books slide off my chest onto the floor. I could press 'Snooze', again, in fact I could easily just sleep right through All Hallows' Eve and wake up on a day when ghosts won't bother me, but Robert texted to say that if I accompanied him to the concert, the drinks would be on him all evening. Lana is away in Oxford on a research trip and Satnam is not talking to me. And I most definitely need to drink.

Witches and demons in very short skirts totter past me into the town where they'll bare plastic fangs and sup frothing cocktails coloured with cochineal. I would have loved this last year. Or even a month ago.

Robert is at the bar, semi-circled by six students dressed as zombies. One of them peels a skin flap from his cheek and lobs it at an undead undertaker who laughs and pretends to eat it. Robert tops up their glasses from a bottle that doesn't look like the usual Shiraz or Merlot. He's been at the cellars again.

'Ah! There you are, Dr Killigan. How wonderful to see you, and looking so handsome. Don't you think he is looking handsome, Sandy? Even if he's not in the culturally acceptable attire for the evening.'

I'm her personal tutor and she's called Maria, not Sandy. Maria nods and smiles and says nothing.

Robert stares at the top of my head. 'You could

have done something with your hair. Smarten yourself up a touch.' He spreads his fingers and pretends to rake a hand through my hair. 'Or maybe you couldn't. Some elements in nature cannot be tamed.' He goes to fill up a glass.

I tap one of the pumps behind the bar. 'Pint for me. Stout.'

Robert shrugs. 'You do know that drinking stout or ale or pale-piss-water lager does not make you more of a man?'

'I like beer.' I watch the dark liquid vein and striate in the glass. I dunk a finger in the bubble-topped beige head. 'It's Friday, Robert. You can stop critiquing everything. Give your brain a break.'

'For me to disengage from hermeneutics would be as a dog to stop licking its cock.' The students titter as if they've never heard someone say cock before. I suppose there is something taboo-breaking about a lecturer saying it. Like teachers, we aren't supposed to be human, with lives and people to return to.

'You've got a gift for the charming example, Robert, I'll give you that.'

'Whereas you have a gift for dressing like a charity-shop donation.'

'You *wish* you could carry off this look.' I point to his clothing. 'Corrugated britches might be very Brideshead but I bet you've been wearing them since the twenties. Have you considered the twenty-first century at all?'

'You are one to talk about inhabiting another century, Stephen.' Robert takes a sip of his drink and smiles at me over the rim. I freeze, not knowing what to say next. Say something, do something,

Stephen.

'And what do you mean by that, Dr Sachs?' I ask, opening my hands, palm up in innocence. 'I have no idea what you are talking about.'

The students turn from me to Robert, waiting for his reply.

'I think you do, Dr Killigan. I suspect our friends here would be very interested to hear what you have to say on the subject, particularly relating to the renaissance masks that the police think you stole. And how little Rhys's body could have decomposed so impossibly swiftly?' One of them, a lad I've seen chatting up the waitresses at Formal Hall, trains his phone on my face. He's filming all this.

'Cut it out, would you? I don't fancy my conversations available to anyone who fancies a listen.'

'It's absolutely my right to use my phone,' he says.

'Aye, you have,' I say, grabbing the top of the phone from him and lowering it into my pint glass.

He lunges at me and I hold the pint glass up. The phone sinks to the bottom and only the light at the top can be seen, winking through the dark beer before it goes out.

'I could report you for that,' he says. 'You've destroyed evidence that could be used against you in a court of law.'

'Have you been watching television police dramas again, Samuel?' Robert asks. 'Because I've told you about that. Television is the best way to demote a perfectly good brain from top of the Premier League to the arse end of the North Premier League Division One North.'

More titters. I hope they choke on their dry roasted peanuts.

Robert puts his hand to the side of his mouth and says to me in a stage whisper aside, 'Notice how I am using an analogy from the parlance of the audience: that's a rhetorical trick you'll learn as you improve your teaching, Stephen. I wouldn't expect you to know such things at your level.'

'Well when I get to your level of being a patronising bastard, I'll know I've made it,' I reply.

His acolytes wait again for his reply. He simply raises his glass to me and bows his head. He drains his wine and empties a packet of pistachios into his mouth. Checking his watch, he says, 'Now we must hurry, or we'll be the last ones in and my sister will have my knackers for snackers.'

I finish the rest of my pint in one. The phone slides and pats me on the nose.

*   *   *

'Your knackers for snackers?' I say as we stride out the back of Wemlow Court and under the arch. 'That must be a southern thing. Do you serve up testicles as canapés at your posh dinners I've heard about?'

'Maybe one day you'll find out, Stephen,' Robert says. Something in his voice makes me look at him. He is smirking like a man holding in his hand a suitcase full of secrets. I can't help picturing him carrying it round with him like an encyclopedia salesman.

'This enigmatic act is getting boring, Robert. You said that if I came with you, you would get me drunk, which you are not even close to achieving,

251

and tell me about Jackamore Grass. What do you know about him and time travel?'

Robert sighs. 'I don't think we should be talking about this so openly.'

'I do.'

Robert sighs. 'Jackamore has certain abilities. He was experimenting with time travel at Oxford. I tried to do the same, and failed miserably. If it hadn't been for my sister jumping into the Cherwell and rescuing me I would have drowned; and Jackamore did the same for her. So everyone is the hero apart from me.'

'Self-pity doesn't really suit you, Robert,' I say.

He smiles, but his eyes look sad.

'What was he exploring?'

'He was seeing what they could get away with. What would you do if there were no consequences for you? If you could slip away without anyone knowing you'd done anything wrong?'

I am about to argue that there are always consequences for others, but I can't claim any moral high ground on that.

We step under the gate. Angela doesn't smile at me as she opens the door for us.

'All right, Angela?' I say. 'Bad evening?'

'What?' she says, glancing up.

'You seem distracted and not a little grumpy.'

Robert taps with his nail on the face of his watch.

Angela mumbles and looks away. It keeps happening, people ignoring me, whether it is students or others here. They don't trust me. I've been connected with these murders; I'm not sure I would trust me. They turn away, pretend they were talking about something else as I walk down corridors that let me know through the echoes of rumours that slither against stone and twist round corners that they were speculating about me. Either that or my paranoia is returning.

'That was somewhat extreme, don't you think, Stephen?' Robert says as we step out.

'Asking Angela if she was okay?'

'Oh is that her name? I wasn't even listening. No—dumping that poor boy's phone in your drink. Though your pint couldn't taste any worse even if it did have a mobile bobbing in it. I don't know how you can drink the stuff. That will corrode your insides more quickly than any poison.'

A swagger of vampires passes. Robert laughs.

'What is the concert again?' I ask as we approach Great St Mary's.

'Fauré, amongst others. My sister is a cellist and teacher, starring in a string quartet season. I go to every third one, less if I can get away with it, to show support, willing and face. It stops her pouting.'

At the Senate House gates we wait for a taxi to pass then cross the road. A crowd waits at the doors of Great St Mary's. I try not to look over to the bushes as we pass. It doesn't work.

'Isn't she any cop, then?' I say, swallowing as if to drown the rising fear in my stomach.

'She is actually very good, not that I would tell her so.' His eyes soften. 'It was because of her that I became interested in aesthetics. She played in the room above and I sat for hours, cross-legged on the bed, listening and trying to dissect and analyse the ache that I was feeling.'

Ma playing guitar on my bed;

Ma playing painted keys on the dining room table after the piano was smashed during one of

Da's nights, me attempting the bass notes, my sister the top 'uns and Ma coming in to make up the chords;

Ma digging out stones buried in the sand on the beach and banging them on Tupperware lids.

The memories slide in and out of my head projector, the sounds merging into one melody. Robert is still talking but all I want to hear is the music.

And I can smell something different, cooking: smoking sage sausages. Someone is having a barbecue.

'What are you doing, Stephen?' Robert asks.

I open my eyes. He is staring at me.

'Why are you holding onto that door,' he continues, peering round at the line of people behind us, 'as if it were going to wrench itself from its hinges and hop away?'

I'm gripping the fittings of the huge door that opens into Great St Mary's. I let go and try to hide what is going on inside me, a shifting of the ground, a fairground tilt.

'I told you not to drink stout,' says Robert.

He leads me to our reserved seats in the second row. The pews are hard and it gives me something solid to concentrate on even if phenomenology is losing its appeal—*that which appears* is confounding me, because it keeps disappearing.

Now that I've read up on Great St Mary's, the place holds a different significance. For over 800 years there has been a church on the site; Rasmus and Cranmer preached here; Bucer and another reformer were buried here then their remains, judged still blasphemous by Mary Queen of Scots, were dug up and burned in the market square; it

254

held the first University Library in the tower and Queen Mary, fond of a bonfire, ordered heretical books to be blazed by the door.

The quartet are on the raised part of the church, waiting. The lead violinist is beautiful; I can't stop staring at her. At least I'll have someone to look at if the music is awful. She is wearing a strapless evening dress and, every few minutes as she pushes her hair behind her right ear with the bow, I can see her smooth, very slightly reddened armpit. Her hair hangs down her back, the same colour and shine as the violin in her hand. She teases the bow across the strings and a rich, low note sounds into the stone.

The others in the quartet follow her, playing the same note, adjusting the little knobs, till the notes stop weaving in and out of each other and become one and the same. The viola player is a small, young woman whose eyebrows meet in concentration; the other violinist is a middle-aged man with a moustache that has movement independent of his mouth, it seems from here, twitching and straining towards his ear as if making a break away from his face. His skin hangs around him like it is two sizes too big for his bones. He is tall, as tall as me probably. He dips his head once and a pale tonsure peeks out under carefully placed strands of hair.

Robert's sister sits with the cello resting between her knees like a child sitting at a parent's feet. I'd forgotten we'd met briefly, outside his study. She cajoles the cello into producing a moan. She does look a little like him. She has the same intensity of blue, her eyes standing out even from this distance; they have the same cheekbones and crossword boxes of lines on their foreheads.

The Sachs twins have a look of linen that needs hanging up in a steamy room, of faded curtains and one-time glamour like the grand hotels on seafronts that can no longer command the attention, apart from on days when the sun hits them just right and you stand and your mouth becomes an O.

Robert nudges me. The members of the quartet have their eyes on each other. Great St Mary's now holds the quality of silence where you can hear dust motes shuffle. The lead violinist nods.

Ravel first, his string quartet in F Major. The lead violin pleads. The programme rustles as I open it. Sarah Randall-Clark, that's her name. A bit posh, but I'll forgive her. The conductor, SimonAtherstone, is from Bridlington, so he can't be all bad.

Robert's hands sway as he listens, his fi ngers curling.

'Stop it,' Robert hisses, hitting me in the arm.

'What?'

'You're talking to yourself.'

Someone pokes my shoulder. I turn around. The man behind me is smiling at us, putting a long finger to dry lips. It's the vicar who was kind to me. He's off -duty, dog collar gone. He grins wider at Robert, showing very white, wide teeth. Robert grips my arm.

The last movement, the *Vif et Agite*, starts with battling swarms of wasps. Sarah Randall-Clark leans forward and back in her chair, the muscles in her lean arms flexing.

Julia Sachs waits, then strikes at the strings. Again and again, then the cello underpins a shift in mood. It is uplifting but I can't trust it. Two forces are dancing and duelling in the one movement: one

256

is a romantic melody; the other, stabbing arpeggios that stiffen my spine.

The time signature of the movement keeps changing. I tap out the beats on my knee to keep hold of them but they duck and feint from 5/8 to 5/4 to 3/4.

My heart is running too quickly, catching on beats like a coat on thorns.

I stand up

I stand up, the beats repeating in my temples.

Disapproving murmurs sound like moos from the pews behind me.

The quartet continues reaching its rapid, rabid conclusion but on top of that, like the layers in rock, is another sound, an organ, blasting out, when there is no organ. My eyes are blurry.

It's happening. I've got to get out. I slip Iris's knapsack over my shoulders and grip one of the straps in my hand. I can feel the gold bars shifting.

'Is there a problem?' A man moves and stands next to me. I try and focus on his face, call him in as Iris said. His features swim. His blue eyes quadruple. 'Can I be of assistance?'

He blocks my way up the aisle so I turn, programme falling from my hand, and run past the quartet, past the altar, gasps from the audience, like sprays from a congregation of opening Coke cans, I leap through a door and start up a turret
of medieval steps
so very many
there is an echo behind me
and I am tumbling
with no idea of the time.

257

Chapter Forty-Seven

Kiss Chase

'Whoah,' he says, falling forward. He thwacks his knee on the stone step. He is a time-travelling toddler. A laugh builds in my chest cavity and splits my lips. I want to let the laugh out and listen to the sound resounding up the turret to the tower, but I do not want him to know I am here, ten steps behind, not yet anyway.

I am glad he ran. I could not stand being there anymore, with those careful players and their musical approximation of chaos and order. These people do not know darkness. Not really. They think they do. And that audience, so polite, sitting in rows with their hands in their laps, following the rules, with their applause at the correct time and the correct place. I can fit in to these situations, I can fit in anywhere given access to money and disguises which, as a time traveller with an interest in simple, compound and interesting interest, is no problem for me, but I do not want to be part of anything. I have not been part of anyone or anything for a long time.

One hundred steps stepped out of 123. Again, he misses a step, and cries out, and he has gone.

The chaplain shouts up to me. 'Do you need help?'

'I have everything under control,' I shout down to him.

Stephen will have emerged into the tower by now, looking out over the Cambridge of another age. I should think about writing a chronicle of his experiences. This new traveller: getting his time legs, his water wings. I would write it well. It is very amusing to watch him unable to comprehend events.

I walk back down the steps. He has made me happy. Let him play, let him do as he wishes. I am interested to see what his instinct is with his new-found skill. I will reward him with another gift: freedom, for now. I think it's time the beauty queen made her last appearance.

Chapter Forty-Eight

The Search for the Muse

I peer over the walls of the tower and feel the need to leap. This Cambridge is dark: no street lights, bright-lit offices or trendy blue restaurant signs, only faint candle light in windows and flames licking at the faces of college gates. Beyond the tiny winking city, the fens wait. I can feel them, and smell them, holding the town to siege until the waters return..

After all that jumping in rivers, all it took was going to see a concert. My stomach surges upwards. I fish the anti-nausea pills out of the medical kit and nibble at the corners of a slab of Kendal mint cake. Closing my eyes, I wait for my body to stop feeling as if I'm a purse being turned inside out and tipped onto the ground.

I take out Iris's notes and flick through them. First: find out when you are; get a back story; clothe yourself properly. I open Takola's app and hold up the phone to the sky. I take a picture—thank fuck it's a clear night. I plug in the longitude and latitude for the city centre. Three stars are selected and triangulated. Star charts scroll across the screen, going backwards in time from the 1700s, the dates ticking down:

1688

1687

1686 . . .

1659

1658

1657

It stops, finally, at 1635. October 31. The same year as before. Maybe I can only move back and forth between these two times: but why then? And what has Jackamore got to do with it?

'Twit-twoo, twit-twoo . . . ' Three young men in academic robes weave across the road below me, bellowing out a drinking song. They slap each other's backs in time with the chorus. They stop at a grave in the churchyard at the front and point and laugh. Students: not giving a shit in any century.

I lift my head slowly. The world moves at normal speed now and I'm not going to be sick. What to do now? Last time I was here I had a dead girl in my arms. I take the file out of my bag and flick through Lana's pages of research. Her vowels are round, looping. Lucy Miller worked at Sepulchre as a maid. She's there in the employment records, which also detail years of service (six) and remittance (5d, more than any other maid). She was also the youngest maid by over twenty years. Lana has written a note: 'Colleges rarely employed women under fifty as they were likely to tempt the students. Strange that she should be paid so well, comparatively, and that she was there at all. There is precedent for very young maids in that period, but only one at a time, and for a maximum of six years.'

She lived with her family in a small house near Christ's. I think it's time to pay her family an evening visit.

'Good afternoon,' I say to the man standing in the doorway. He has a stiff thatch of hair. His skin is blotched and pocked.

'What do you want?' he asks.

'I'm here from Sepulchre College, to enquire about the funeral arrangements of your poor daughter.' My mind chases itself. How long has it been since I was here? Maybe she's already been buried. 'We would like to contribute to the cost, if we may.' That works whether she's buried already or not.

'I'll be taking nothing from you. And neither will any of the family. I don't know what happened to my daughter but that college of yours did nothing to help. You paid her so little she was forced to get another job, just to keep the household going.'

'I thought she was well paid for her position.'

He points down to a bound leg. The bandaging is brown and crisp and there's a smell of decay and disease. 'Not for a family. On one maid's wage. I couldn't help and now she's gone, Mary, her sister, will have to take her place. Lucy would never've wanted that.'

A small girl, Mary perhaps, inclines her head out from behind his back. She puts her finger over her lips and smiles at me without guile. Her eyes are bright and playful, her skin clear at a time when people wear the plague on their faces.

'You should be in your bed, Mary,' Mr Miller says.

She smiles and ducks behind him again.

'It is customary for the college to provide a servant's family with five years' wages when they die and,' I search my head for a suitably obscure college tradition—the more ridiculous it is, the more believable here, 'and half a wild boar at Christmas.'

'Which half?' Mary says from behind her father. She giggles and he turns to ruffle her hair. For a moment he looks young and happy, before age bakes into his face again.

'Where else did Lucy work, Mr Miller?' I ask. 'That way I could find out what the shortfall was and make it up to you.' There is enough gold in my knapsack to buy the family all of St Andrew's Street.

He narrows his yellowed eyes. 'I don't understand. Why are you saying this? One of you lot, from the college, came here looking for her, month or so ago, saying she was neglecting her duties for her other job. That they suspected it weren't respectable. And that if she continued she would be got rid of.' He places his hand against the door frame. 'She worked there since she was ten, and this is how they treat her. She weren't doing anything wrong.'

Mary steps out and sneaks her hand into his. She looks up at him.

'There is no suggestion that she was, Mr Miller,' I reply.

He breathes in and releases his breath slowly. He smells of egg. 'I can't tell you where she worked other than the college. I don't know. I wish I did as I would go round there and use whatever strength is left in this useless body to find out what happened to her.'

262

'Do you remember which of my colleagues visited from the college?'

'Short man, with a bumpy nose. His face got red easily.' Mr Miller's jaw moves side to side. 'I can't remember his name, but it makes me think of death.'

'I will find out how Lucy died, sir. And make sure she is remembered.' I think of the stone on the floor of the church. Do I get that made? If so then that would be an ontological paradox, giving myself my own clues without which I wouldn't be able to give myself a clue.

'Leave us alone,' he says.

*   *   *

I feel strange walking up Smoke Lane, and not just because I'm carrying a side of pig, its carcass opened up to the world. I bought it from a butcher named Nathaniel along with his blood-caked coat, in the hope I can pass for a pork purveyor. Hopefully I'll appear to anyone not looking that hard to be a pork purveyor.

The lane is only a dirt track at this point, with a ditch on either

side in which rubbish is chucked and people loot, but I still feel as if I'm walking into *my* college. The one from my time. The grey stone of the gatehouse is yet to get smoked by the industrial age, but otherwise it looks the same. I know it's dark, which will hide some of the difference, but the same gargoyles spout down water; the same statue looks down at her subjects.

The porter gives me the appraising stare he will pass on to his post-bears. His tongue tips at his lips as he looks down at the pig.

'Cook's ordered this in specially,' I say, spatchcocking my vowels even more than usual. 'Said I should hurry straight there when it came in. But I don't usually deliver here.'

'What's it making?' he asks. He's salivating now, swallowing hard. His belly already curves outwards like a sail in the wind.

'I heard it's going on the spit,' I say. 'Then stripped for Hall tomorrow night. I can make sure some comes your way though,' I say, winking.

He steps back.

I've gone too far.

'Go round the back,' he says. 'Kitchen's on your left. Tell him I'll be down this evening with ales from the cellar.'

*   *   *

A ginger cat sits on the top of the steps down into the kitchen. It flicks its tail and follows me down, rubbing its head against my shin and nearly tripping up me and the pig. The smell of baking bread makes my tummy rumble.

'Leave it there,' a man with a knife the size of a forearm says, pointing to the far side of the kitchen. He goes back to chopping; the sound of bones splintering fills the room.

I lean the pig against the wall. It looks oddly louche, as if waiting for a date with a maid, trotter cocked to conceal a fag. 'You new?' he asks. 'I haven't seen you before.'

'Haven't been here in a long year. I used to deliver years ago when my father was busy. He passed last year and I've come back from the north

264

to take over. I can't find a delivery boy I can trust—do you know anyone?'

He stops chopping up bones. 'My brother is in need of something to stop him running about and finding himself trouble.'

'Send him up to the meat market,' I tell him. 'Ask for Nathaniel.' And I had better remember to put some more money in Nathaniel's hands. 'What was your name?' I ask.

He comes around the long wooden table covered in carcasses and root vegetables and stirs the pot of broth belching in the corner.

'Simon Turner,' he says.

'Good to meet you, Simon,' I say, shaking his hand. 'Do you know where Lucy is? I was going to give this to her while I was here.' I pull a package out of my butcher's coat pocket, trying to act coy. 'She says she likes chicken oysters.'

He raises a fist and swings it at me. I duck, and he glances my cheekbone and temple. 'You're the one, he says,' running at me. His eyes are mad wide, nostrils flared. I turn, push the pig at him and he wrestles with it in a grotesque waltz as he stumbles and throws it to the ground.

I hold up my hands and back away, the table between us. 'I didn't hurt her; I want to find out who killed her.'

He edges round, his eyes flicking around the room as he tries to find a means of attack. 'If you didn't then someone you knew did. She was fine until she started working for you. She loved *me*,' he says, 'and I lost her.'

'I never met her, honestly.'

He picks up the packet of chicken oysters and throws it at me. It hits the wall with a thuck and slides to the floor. 'Then why are you bringing a dead girl gifts?'

'I told you: I want to find her murderer. He has killed before, and will after. I need to find him and stop him.'

'You are exactly as she described him. Her artist. That is what she called him, her "artist". She said he was handsome, of a kind, and fond of pretence and artifice. Dressing as a butcher would be exactly what he would do.'

'I am not a painter. I am a philosopher.'

His jaw clenches. 'A philosopher? You have dissembled all along. If you aren't the artist who killed my Lucy, then you are of the kind of liar who did.' Hands reaching for my neck, he propels himself at me; I turn my shoulder and side into him and he gasps out, winded.

I pick up a ham hock and hold it out as a club. 'This is not the fight to have, Simon; we should find this artist and—'

Lurching forward, he barges into me and slams my head against the wall.

Silence. Then the fizz like a missing television station and blood running down the back of my throat like an iron drip. I hear strained voices and mumbling but I can't make out words, only the smell of meat and days-dead fish. There is nothing to hold onto and it is wonderful. I am washing into the world and merging with the sounds and smells of now and then. It is as if I am flying and there is no need to do anything except feel.

Something is scratching at my hand: something wet and rough. I open one eye. The ginger cat is next to me, licking the back of my hand and purring. Simon sits by the hearth. I can see the glint

266

of the knife in his trembling hand.

'What category of witchcraft is that?' he asks. His voice is shaky and high.

'There is no witchcraft,' I say. I'm on the stone floor, curled into a ball. My body feels like it has been flayed. 'I'm not a witch or any kind of supernatural being, I promise you.' My voice feels strange in my throat, as if it has been put back in a smaller box.

'That is exactly what a witch would say.'

'What would you like me to do to prove it to you? Dunk me? I believe that always worked. My mouth keeps working, but I am not thinking. I'm not sure even if the sounds coming out of my face are actual words or whether he hears what I hear: murmurs and mumbles.

I drag myself over to the table and, grasping one of its legs, pull myself up to standing.

'I could call someone now,' he says, leaping up, holding out the knife. 'I saw it. I saw you fade and return, grow faint and return again.

Fear grabs, starting low and cold and lapping its way up me as if I'm being lowered into the North Sea and I check on the sensations: nausea; headache; stiff muscles; strong sense of smell: I time travelled, or nearly did, and Simon saw me. 'I can explain,' I say. That is probably the phrase most closely associated with guilt. My mind ticks through things to say but the boxes are empty. Say what is in some way true. 'I am not a witch; I am a ghost,' I say.

'A ghost,' he replies, sitting back down, staring at me. 'What do you want with me?'

'Your help,' I say. 'The finding of Lucy's murderer will be my last act of cleansing. I can then pass into paradise. She too can then pass from purgatory. I have only a short time, which is why you saw me fade from this world into the next, and back again.'

He nods, slowly. 'It is the only explanation. And Lucy's cat likes you.'

I don't contradict him. Never contradict a man with a cleaver. And I *am* a ghost, in a way. I should not be walking on the earth: I was not born at this time, yet I do. I am the ante-ghost of me. 'This is Lucy's cat?' I say as it butts its head into the crook of my arm.

He nods and looks away. I don't think he can bear the memories.

'Tell me more about the painter, anything you know.'

He edges around the room, keeping his eye on me at all times. 'Could you disappear at any moment?' he asks.

'I could. So we have to be quick.'

'She started out as a maid when her mother fell to the Death, and her father could no longer work,' he says, hanging the ham back up. He never turns his back on me. 'She was happy enough. Then he was painting her. Her portrait. That's what he called it, anyway. Sometimes she came in crying, a bruise spreading on her cheek because she had moved. But she would not stop, she needed the money and—' He swallows and rubs his lips together. 'She said he made her feel beautiful.'

'What about where she went? Did you ever accompany her there?'

He shakes his head. 'She worked there very early in the morning before coming to the kitchens. I am always here baking bread at that time.' He gestures

268

to a sideboard and a row of loaves under towels.

'Her father said that a man visited him complaining about her work here, that he knew about the other work and it was getting in the way.'

'That would be Lord Mortimer,' Simon says. He picks up a knife and sharpens it against a strap. 'The Master. He came in here with a frown like a trout and shouted at me for allowing her to work elsewhere. She brought his meals to the lodge on time every day for years, without fail. He had no reason to complain: she was courteous and demure and pleasant. He came in here when she died, too, wanting to collect her belongings and take them to her father. Do I have your word that you will return to tell me about Lucy?' he asks. He lightly touches my shoulder as if checking I still have a body.

'I promise,' I reply and hold out my hand.

He shakes it. 'Are there more ghosts?' Simon asks as I leave.

'More than I thought,' I reply.

'And can they be any animal too, or just cats?'

'What? I don't know what—'

The cat jumps onto the table and rubs its big soft head against my hand. It flops onto its back, purring, and fades in and out again, like an optician's chart under different glasses. Cats can time travel too.

Chapter Forty-Nine

Trauma

Charles Witt jerks back when I arrive at the door. A tic winks around his eye-lines and slips to the speechmarks that have deepened around his mouth.

He shows me through to his studio, talking quickfire nonsense about how he is coming on well with the painting.

'Let me see,' I say.

Reluctantly, he takes off the sheet. I am in an austere chair, the one in the corner of the room, staring out of the canvas with eyes that he has not caught the blue of. It is a likeness but no more. There is an element of me that is relieved.

'Please, would you mind sitting for me? I need to refine the details,' he says.

'So I see,' I say, sitting down in a grand chair, my hands on the arms in a replication of the painting.

I am an excellent sitter. I keep my eyes on the fruit bowl on the sideboard that includes oranges that have collapsed in upon themselves like dwarf stars and plums that are shrunken and spore-frosted. My head and hands and spine are as still as the dead, more so. Corpses, when you look close, never stay still. Decay is moving.

'I am not here solely to sit for you. Or to enjoy your company. Unless I have underestimated him, which would mean I had overestimated myself; and that is not possible, a man will appear at your door. His name is Stephen Killigan and you will welcome him and give him anything he requires. Within reason.'

'Who is he?'

'He was the one who carried away the body of your muse. And he is here to find out who killed her, and, I suspect, locate me. He is dark haired and dishevelled.'

Witt stares at me, his tic twitching faster. 'Is he a Justice? Or in a guild? How does he know I was involved?'

'You have nothing to fear. I gave the paintings to Lord Mortimer, the Master of Sepulchre College, in return for his not pursuing the circumstances of her death. He was, I believe, highly fond of your muse for some time.'

'Then why would he not set out to discover her murderer?'

I laugh. 'It is also in his interests not to draw attention to himself.'

'I don't want to know about all this. And I do not have time to play host to one of your friends. I must finish your portrait and I cannot be rushed,' he says, mixing the tone of my flesh on his palate. There is more grey in there than I would like. 'My work takes the time it takes.'

'That is an absurd argument,' I reply. 'And one used by the lazy. Art and pressure are connected intimately. There are few times when one does not cause the other.' My knee is moving up and down. Irritation burns in my chest.

He stares at my patella. 'Please do not move. I need you to remain absolutely still.'

I sprint off the chair, dipping my head under the bowed parts of the ceiling, and pin him back against the panelled wall. He struggles: his muscles bulge and strain yet they are cossetted and weak due to never having been required to fight. I slick my hand across

271

the palate and, removing the other from his windpipe and shoving at his chest, wrap it around his soft throat.

'You know what I can do,' I say. 'I have the ability to make you kill and think nothing of it. One squeeze and your brain would fire out warnings and a confusion of images and pulses as oxygen was stopped and your last thoughts would be of my face . . . '

He gasps for air. Petechiae bloom in his eyes like red carnations. It is the beautiful moment. I have not caused it myself in too long. He grabs at my jacket. I could continue. But then the game would be over. 'You will complete the painting, and befriend Killigan. I need him to come back here; I need to know how he can follow me. I want to meet him, but not yet and you will play host whenever he is here. Is that clear?'

He nods, as much as he can with his throat in my hand.

I let go. He stumbles, holding his neck.

I stride out into the street and walk through the back streets of the city. Rage fires through my veins and I can feel time flexing. I do not know when I am. That is the best, when I have no connection and no consequences. I am bored with being careful. Considered. Cautious. This construction of a beautiful, century-stretching murder that places time on a rack is making me organised and boring, and too dependent on an opponent who has yet to prove himself. I miss the chaos I used to sail in.

A woman stands at the end of an alley, a shawl across her shoulders and a hand on her hip. She smiles at me and there are still teeth in her mouth. Prostitutes are so easy to kill. Killing is about intimacy, being close enough: they bypass the boundaries for

expedient cash; I bypass them for expedient death.
    She rests her hand against my crotch.
    I rest my knife in her stomach.

Chapter Fifty

Lord Mortimer

Lord Mortimer's study is in the centre of college, in what is now the Senior Common Room. An ornate mirror over the fireplace doubles the candles in the room and those in the looking-glass opposite so that I cannot keep track of where the walls are.

If Mortimer is Jackamore, hiding in another time in a position of power, then I will know him at last. My hands are shaking. I shove them in the pockets of the stiff trousers that Simon found for me, along with an academic robe.

I pace the room, looking at the books, trying to slow my breathing. The Senior Common Room has a concealed door that is used by the butler to go to his pantry to serve port. I walk over, keeping an eye on the main door. Servants pass with slow strides along the public halls and then scurry down the back stairs.

I feel for the edges of the door within the panelling and, finding it, frisk it for an opening. My hand closes on a key made out of the same stained oak as the lock. I turn it.

The back room is small and unlit. I open the inner door wide, pick up a candelabra and walk around a pair of armchairs, a low-lying chaise longue and a table readied with a glass and a decanter. One wall is covered with paintings. They are of a young woman, in states of undress, posing in different ways. I know that face. Lucy. I peer closer. The signatures are hard to read in this light but I can make out: Glynd, Mickle-something, and Charles James Witt the Second.

'I do not usually allow people into my private study,' Lord Mortimer says from the doorway. I've seen his painted face on the wall at Hall. His portrait sneers down at the long tables, as if he is wondering why there is so little wine compared to his time, and why there are so many strumpets sitting with the students. Could this be Jackamore Grass? The reports about the man who stole the mask described a tall, thin man whereas Mortimer is small-boned and bird-like, his nose lumpy. He has the extra skin of someone who has lost a lot of weight. In the light of the flames, his loose-fleshed face looks like dripping tallow.

'I apologise for the intrusion,' I say. I hope the quicktime of my heart is not obvious in my voice. 'I was sent to discuss an endowment from the king and this must be conducted with the utmost privacy and discretion. I am sure a man of your tastes can appreciate that.'

He walks slowly around the room, lighting more candles. He does it with care and solemnity, whispering as he goes, as if conducting mass.

'I apologise once more: I did not introduce myself. I am Sir Henry Edwards, the king's private emissary in these matters. You may have heard that he is expecting trouble from certain quarters?' Even as I say the words I am amazed by how easily they come now. The lies are coming easier and easier. But this is deceit for a reason.

Mortimer raises his eyebrows. He is not about to agree or disagree.

'His Majesty King Charles is requesting that Cambridge colleges faithful to the Crown hold a portion of his wealth in store,' I say, strolling around the room and looking at objects on the mantel. 'Unlike the politicians of the city, who will be punished for their disloyalty when the time comes, the colleges which keep the king's funds in trust, and offer it up should he need it, will receive endowments that will set up the college long into the future.' I pick up an open box at the end of the mantel. Inside is a lock of hair wrapped around a ring and a woman's shoe. Lucy's shoe. The pristine twin to the mud-covered one. Either he murdered her and kept it as a trophy, or obtained it from her killer. I clench my fist.

He pecks the slipper from me and holds it to his heart like a bizarre Prince Charming. His tiny eyes glance quickly to the portraits of Lucy. In the portrait by Witt she is lying on a bed wearing the slippers, and nothing else.

Mortimer bows. 'We are loyal to the king, as we were to his father and his hallowed mother, the queen, our gracious founder. It would be a privilege to store anything the king desires.'

'His Majesty, of course, is a lover of art and has several works from the Italian masters that he would appreciate being stored. Alongside these, maybe?'

Mortimer licks his lips.

I examine the paintings of Lucy, nodding my head as if I know what I am looking at. 'These are fine works, but I do not recognise the artists. Did you discover them yourself?'

He settles into one of the armchairs and pours the fortified wine. 'I discovered the muse,' he says. His arm drapes over the back of the chair, now in boastful mood.

'You are a lucky man,' I say, taking a glass from him and sitting in the other chair. The wine is sour and thick.

'A servant here from when she was a child.' He flicks his tongue at the rim of the glass. 'She was beautiful.'

'I'd like to meet her.'

'Her beauty is all mine.' He stares at the paintings as if it is not enough that she is caged in a frame for his benefit.

'Where did you acquire them?'

Mortimer blinks. 'A gentleman gave them to me. He too said he was a representative of the king.'

'What did he look like?' I ask.

'Why do you wish to know?' Mortimer says, sitting down in his chair. He looks up at me, eyes narrowed, tapping his cane against the floor. 'I do not wish to hold anything back from the king, but I also must protect my suppliers. This particular supplier provided me with portraits of my favourite maid. And certain other material.' His eyebrows lift.

'All I can provide you with,' I say, 'is gold. Or rather the king can.' I open my bag, take out a gold bar and lay it on the mantelpiece. 'Tell me of the muse, the artists, the man who sold you the paintings and this other material and there will be more gold. Much more.'

His pupils widen like ink dropped onto blotting paper.

He writes down a name and address as I gaze at

the pictures of Lucy. One shows the panic in her eyes and I want to rip her from the wall.

'I can see you are a fellow admirer,' he says, moving his chair closer to mine.

I do not contradict him.

'And imagine when she was younger.' He leers, leans forward and grabs my knee.

I wish to peel his fingers back until they break; instead, I nod.

'I cannot share with you the material others have composed—that is a private pursuit—but I will show you my own work.' Standing and turning his back on me, he slides a panel on the wall and retrieves an item. He moves to stand behind my chair, and, leaning over so close I can smell his stale sweat and see his pores, he drops a small, leatherbound book in my lap.

I don't want to look.

I look.

It's his diary, beginning five years ago. There are pencil sketches of thirteen-year-old Lucy cleaning and dusting, of her standing in the corner of a room, of her sewing. The first few pages are filled with accounts of Mortimer gaining Lucy's trust, learning what she likes to eat and to talk about.

'Today Lucy sat on the bed and told me of her journey home yesterday. She found a mewing sack by the river and, on venturing to look inside, saw, nestled among five unbreathing siblings, a red-coated Cat. The tender-hearted Child took it home and has taken to carrying it around the College. I have not the feelings to reprimand her nor order its destruction. She kissed my cheek today in thanks. I explained to her that more extravagant thanks were necessary and customary.

Love is such a perfect gift .'

The passages continue, accompanied by sketches signed by Mortimer. I have to stop myself crying out. All I can think of is what I would do to someone who did this to my sister, or someone else I loved.

'As you can see, I, too, am an artist,' Mortimer says. 'And as such I can appreciate beauty. The man sold me the paintings of Lucy on the condition that I desist my search for her murderer. I agreed, but not because I was not fond of her; you have the evidence in front of you that I loved her . . .'

'Evidence. Yes, it's that all ri—'

'But due to the fact that she was killed in her capacity as muse, he would say no more and I did not press him. I can, in many ways, see that it is the ultimate sacrifice for art.'

'About this man . . .'

'You asked me what he looked like. I would not have remembered his appearance, other than for his height—I had to crane back my neck to talk with him; however, he included this portrait among the others.'

'Portrait?' I say.

He opens a tall, thin cupboard in the wall and takes out a gold-framed painting. 'I do not want him on my wall,' he says.

'I do not blame you,' I say, staring into the face of Jackamore Grass. His face is gaunt but handsome and he stands straight and tall and thin with a skeletal athleticism. He stares at me with a smile on his lips and eyes colder than the winter city. I've seen him before somewhere. Some time.

Mortimer walks to the door. 'Would you care for refreshment?'

278

'Thank you but no,' I reply, quickly. I have to get out of here. I can't keep up the deceit. I want to wash some of that sin-slick room from my skin. 'I need to collect the king's goods and your further reward. I will return.'

'Good night.'

Even before I leave, I regret not hitting him in the face.

As it's too late to go calling, even on artists, Simon makes me up a bed in a servant's rooms down the corridor. The ginger cat sits on the stiff pillow, licking its paw. I bend to stroke it and it leans over so much that it falls onto its back. *Her* back.

'Budge up,' I say. I want warmth and affection. Lying on the lumpy mattress, Lucy's cat on top of me, I picture Lana with her books, her tongue poking out of the side of her mouth. I couldn't do this without her. Warmth spreads through me, and not just on account of the cat pouring its purrs into my chest. I will tell Lana how fantastic she is when I return. I miss her and long to hold her and talk about the people I've met, the progress or not, the smells and sights of the seventeenth century, or about whatever has been on television this evening.

I don't know where we're going from here, but I know I want us to be together. But then there is nothing like having all your previous assumptions blow up in your face to realise that anything is possible, and that the walls of perception can be brought down with nothing more than a whisper, or a whisker.

Chapter Fifty-One

The Cracking of Charles Witt

He answers on my eighth knock. He has a painted handprint around his neck. There is a painted handprint around his neck. 'Are you Charles Witt?' I ask.

He looks up at me, then down to the cat sitting by my feet. She followed me all the way from college. I didn't think cats did that. He places his hand to his neck, a nervous reaction perhaps, and holds his paintbrush out as you would a lantern. 'Who are you?' he asks.

'I am a teacher at Sepulchre College,' I reply. It is good to tell a truth. 'Lord Mortimer showed me your painting of Lucy Miller and directed me here, and I wondered if you had any more, or any drawings. I was Lucy's cousin, you see. I want to find out how she died. Nobody else seems to be concerned.' I stare at my feet in what I hope is a gesture of mourning. And now I am back to lies in order to bait the truth.

'How did you know how to find me?' he asks, peering behind me. Three boys kick a stone to each other in the narrow street. 'Lord Mortimer told me where to find you. Your name was on the paintings in his study.'

'The king does not have my paintings?' He seems surprised, and disappointed, then remembers who I am supposed to be. 'Come in, come in. You must be very upset at her loss.' He ushers me through into a dark hallway. The cat does not follow.

Charles Witt is welcoming. Too welcoming. He pours ale and lays out a meal. You don't just invite a stranger in from the street, slap them on the back with a rictus smile and say that they can help themselves to whatever they want, just because I'm related to a girl that he painted. When I press him on his hospitality, he says that's just what they do around here, that obviously that is not the case wherever in Scania I am from.

I let that pass as it may be to my advantage to be Scandinavian rather than Northern.

'Was Lucy happy when she died?' I ask.

'I was not there when she died,' he replies, quickly.

'That wasn't what I meant.' I pretend to ignore the too-swift admission. 'I meant, was there anything she was concerned about? I've heard that she was scared of Lord Mortimer, the Master of Sepulchre. I've met him, and I wouldn't be surprised.'

'She would go to Lord Mortimer after working here. Even at night. She said she had done so since she joined the college.'

'But she was only young at the time.'

Witt shrugs but cannot look me in the eye.

'He has some of your paintings, I believe.'

He stares at his feet. 'My portraits were given to the college.'

'And what did you get for them, Charles?' I ask.

He doesn't answer.

'She was my cousin.'

'And she was my muse.' He looks me in the eyes and in them I recognise the pain of someone blocking out death. Charles finishes his ale. 'I need to drink,' he says.

281

Charles leads me through Cambridge's ginnels and gunnels or whatever they call them here. The smells of damp and meat and sweet disease are so thick they make the streets seem skinnier and give me the sense-impression of wading.

'We're nearing the plague pits,' Charles says, handing me his handkerchief. He points over to a meadow, soil fresh, where the bus station is now. The bodies of plague victims are still there, under the fumes of farewells.

Holding my breath, I stumble after him. I splutter when I can't hold my breath anymore. My lungs burn at the ribs and when I take a breath it is like inhaling yellow gauze. I imagine platelets of plague forming, sliding down.

The taverns of Cambridge are smoky and full of robed students. Both students and robes are saturated with alcohol. We join them in drinking games that seem to have no rules other than to laugh at each other and drink more. I should be staying sober, pouring the beer over my shoulder or something, pretending to join in so I can find out more, but

I want to drink.

I want to forget.

I want to not be responsible for young girls's deaths.

I don't see why I should be the one to find all this out; it's not as if I'm being paid for this.

No one else seems to care.

Why can't they leave me alone?

'That is exactly right,' a drunk boy says, slinging

his arm around my shoulders. 'They shhhhould leave you alone. You deserve moooore.'

'He does, he deserves more,' Charles agrees.

I've been talking out loud.

'You know what you should do? Drink more,' one of them says, crashing his tankard into another. Beer spills on top of the beer-washed floor.

'I love you,' his mate says to him. They embrace.

'I loathe students,' Charles says.

*   *   *

The ginger cat is still there when, swaying, we return just as dawn kicks the night out for the day. A dead rat lies at the cat's feet. 'You better not have brought me the plague,' I say, picking her up and tickling her.

While he finds glasses, I open the cupboards in his studio and search sideboards for anything that connects him to Lucy's murder. I find paints that are probably poisonous, dried into dust in forgotten pots, but no more than that.

He comes in, swearing at having misjudged the position of the door.

'Is this what you're working on?' I say, pointing to the painting on the easel.

He nods and blushes.

'Can I see?' I ask.

He shakes his head, goes pale.

'What are you hiding, Charles?'

'Nothing!' he replies. He turns round the painting.

I step back, not wanting to be close to the flesh of the painting. It is not like his other one. The background is dark red, the paint rough-textured.

Lucy lies on a bed, naked, eyes closed, neck twisted, red marks on her throat and a grey stone mask on her face.

'This is Lucy dead,' I say quietly.

'It is not,' he replies, his eyes wild. 'I painted her on the bed, asleep.' He cannot stand still, and paces the room.

'This is a woman whose life has been seized from her throat.'

'It is not true,' he says, grabbing at my arms as if he could shake the words out of me like apples from a tree.

'Denying it will not relieve your conscience. I don't believe you are a bad man, Charles; merely weak and malleable.'

Charles sinks to the paint-covered floor and weeps, muttering words I can't catch.

'Charles. Let's speak plainly. I am not Lucy's cousin. I need to find the man who sold the paintings to Lord Mortimer.'

His hand strays to his neck. His handprint is smaller than the one spanning his throat. 'Leave me alone.'

'I know that he threatened you. You must be very frightened of him, but you do not have to let him control you. I can help you. I know some of what this man is capable of. Don't be a coward: face him with me.'

'I cannot,' he says, his hands over his face. 'I cannot.'

*   *   *

Charles Witt's snores come at ten-second intervals. I ease myself off the blanket on the floor in the next room, having refused the bed that Lucy had lain on, dead and alive.

I am becoming accustomed to lamplight and the magic-lantern flickering that causes the world to move when it's still. The house is tidy, for an artist, tidier than any house I've owned. There are paintings stacked against the walls in every room. I go through each portrait. Some are better than others, but none are exceptional. I go upstairs to the rooms that are scattered with men's clothes and stiff brushes, treading lightly on the creaky boards, but there is nothing other than the painting to connect Witt with her death.

Thirsty, hungry and still drunk, I go downstairs. In the small kitchen I find a mouthful of water at the bottom of a jug, a bottle of sour cider, rotten vegetables and, in a basket of wood, a parcel. I open it up and a painting the size of a book falls out.

It is of a face—Lucy's face—but not a life drawing like the others, or even a drawing of her when dead; it's a depiction of her death mask, white and ghostly against a black background, features weighed down by plaster, her eyes shut, her lips tight together as if forever holding her breath. A painting of her death mask.

I turn the canvas over. Attached to the back is an invitation to a masked ball in five weeks' time, signed by Jackamore Grass. 'I think we should meet,' it says.

Chapter Fifty-Two

Gingerbread

I can't stand to be in this time anymore. It sits on my skin and makes me want to do things that I don't consider to be me. I close the front door carefully so as not to wake Charles and wait for the little tap of the ginger cat on the cobbles but all I can hear is shouting from the house next door. A bucket of water is poured out onto the street, missing me by inches.

The death mask portrait is in my rucksack. If I could appeal to Inspector Horne's vanity, to solve a 300-year-old crime—but that would mean her believing everything else.

The ginger cat trots up alongside me. I stop; she stops. I look down; she stares up at me, and blinks. Crouching down, I tickle her and find I'm swaying. The insides of my eyelids feel raw and demand that I close them, just for a second. In fact, my body says, why not lie down here, by the towpath, yes, of course by the towpath, it's as comfortable as any bed and even if it isn't, it's nearer, there, that's it, get yourself lying down, don't worry about policemen, they'll get you a blanket. Just as I slide into sleep, the wet Velcro of the cat's tongue rasps at my stubble. I open my eyes and look into her amber ones. They are lit up by artificial streetlights. 'I'm home,' I say, 'I'm back.' I unsteadily stand and look down at her. 'Go back; this isn't where you should be.' I move off and she follows me, all the way back to the college gates.

'They won't let you in,' I tell her.

The cat blinks again, her tail swishing.

Mark, one of the nicer night porters, walks over. It's a good sign that, when a cat likes yer. Or is it a bad sign, means you're a bad person? Or some kind of portent? I can't remember. It's important, anyway.'

I bow to the cat as I open the door within the gate. The cat leaps through.

'Cats go where they please, that's the rule of cats,' says Mark, nodding his head as if that is all there is to say. Staying up all night does funny things to other people too.

The air is sharp in my lungs as I walk into the court. The trees look like a line of naked Fagins bending over the river. Cambridge is so cold that I can't imagine a time when it will be hot and they will be fully clothed. The cat is still following me, her ears fl icked back. The door to my staircase is open and she nips in before I can stop her, then runs up the stairs. I hurry after her, thinking she'll go and take cover under one of the beds in the empty rooms but when I get to my floor she is sitting in front of my door, looking round at me.

I tickle her in the dent between her shoulder blades. Her eyes close, tongue partly out, dribble on her furry lower lip.

'Mao,' she says, when I stop.

'You're not coming in,' I say.

'Mao,' she says, following me in. She sniffs the fringe of the sofa, sticks a paw under, flicks out a fountain pen and chases it around the room. 'Don't let it get away, the fiend.' I am talking to a strange cat. The pen shoots under the sofa again, back into its hiding place where I like it—I know that,

287

if ever without a pen, a five-pound note, a loaf of gingerbread or a condom, I will always find one under the sofa.

'Mao,' the cat says.

'Either you're a devotee of a dead communist or you're hungry.' There's a tin of salmon in my cupboard. I shouldn't do this—feed a cat and they'll never go away—but her ribs show through her coat. She reminds me of Elsie, my next-door neighbour's cat when I was growing up. Da never let us have pets, not even a goldfish, so I used to sit on the wall between our back yards and wait for her to jump up and rub her big head against my arm, then I'd tell her everything; that I had a crush the size of Scarborough on Jennie Mason from over the road and that my trousers had got too short but I didn't want to tell Mum and that the bruise on my arm wasn't from falling off my BMX at the top of Crikes Hill.

The ginger cat leans into my leg as I open the tin onto a plate and place it on the floor. The cat juts her tongue at the salmon.

Switching on the gas fire, I sit down on the rug in front of it, wrapping a blanket around my shoulders. I don't think I can make it into bed. The sheets will be damp from the cold anyway. The cat steps into my lap, turns around twice, then flops down. Her paws rest on my thighs like she is propping up a bar. 'I could call you Chairman Mao. Or Chairwoman. Or Chairperson. She jumps onto the sofa and next to half a cake of parkin.'

'Gingerbread. I'll call you Gingerbread.'

She half closes her eyes, the inner lids at diagonals, silver and opaque like a Sybil's trance. My eyes close and the text of the Greek myth scrolls down in my mind and, as sleep sticks a black pillowcase over my head, all I can see are empty eyes.

Chapter Fifty-Three

I Love You

'You bastard.' Lana sits at the edge of my bed. I must have got into bed at some point last night. She's holding a dripping mop. 'Whoah—what you doing with that?'

'It's the best way to wake people up,' she says, jabbing the mop. It flops towards me, one strand sloppy on my face.

I reach for the heater cord. It spatters out an orange glow. 'You couldn't just give me a kiss and slide into bed?'

Lana laughs. 'I could have. But you stood me up. I waited outside Heffers' for,' she checks her watch-less wrist, 'four hours.'

'You didn't, did you?'

'Course I didn't. Turned up at ten—When. You. Said. I came here, couldn't get an answer, huffed and puffed for a while, then came back. A woman let me in. She asked when you were going to let her change your sheets. That they must be filthy.'

I feel my face get hot. 'That's Sue, my bedder.'

'Bedder?'

'Bedmaker. Employed by the college to clean the rooms and kitchens and do the laundry. Another of those Cambridge traditions. I'm not keen. She shouldn't have to change my sheets—I'm a grown

289

man.'

Lana's eyes dive to the slightly tented duvet. Her mouth twitches. So does my cock. She places the mop against the wall but it falls, like a drunken Andy Warhol.

She moves close to me and kisses the nape of my neck and around to my throat. 'I missed you,' she says, and my heart goes funny. 'So where were you?' she asks. 'And who is this!'

Gingerbread is tarting around her ankles, her purr loud and victorious.

'Her name is Gingerbread, and she followed me home.'

'Gingerbread, I like that. So she's a stray? Has she been tagged?'

'I doubt it. She used to keep the college rats away.'

'But not anymore?'

'Not for three hundred and seventy years.'

'That's a very old feline.'

'She's only five.'

'You'll have to explain the joke,' she says. 'In fact, fuck that. Can you tell me what is going on? I deserve that much. And no more half-truths. Whatever you're involved in involves me too.' She sits down next to me and holds my hand.

'You sure?'

'Go on,' she says.

'I have been travelling back and forth between now and one year in the seventeenth century, before the Civil War,' I say, staring at my kneecaps. I hold my breath, waiting for her to laugh or snort or reject me.

'Don't stop,' she says.

And so I tell her: from the tea that tastes of

sardines to the time I knew I wanted to be there with her, the fear that I'll never come back, the strange smells, the lost bodies, the paintings, the feeling that I am in a game and I don't know the rules or the board that I'm standing on.

She's silent.

Here it comes: the bittersweet retreat of 'it's not you, it's me' when what they mean is 'it's all you, freak'.

'That's quite a story,' she says. She can't look me in the eye. I knew it.

'If you're not going to trust me or believe what I tell you then I don't think we have any kind of relationship,' I say.

'I never said I didn't believe you.'

'You don't though.'

Lana stands up and walks into the middle of the room. 'You told me that you are a time traveller yet you don't even give me five minutes to think and take it in.'

That's fair. 'Do you want tea?' I say, in its stead.

We sit in armchairs, fire radiating and mediating between us. 'Can you go into the future?' she asks, at last.

'What?'

She repeats her question.

'No,' I reply, 'although Iris Burton assures me it's possible, and that Jackamore can.'

Lana turns to me. 'Iris Burton the mathematician?'

I nod.

'Her book is popular with the mathmos. They borrow it either to laugh at her or try it out.'

I dig into my rucksack and take out Iris's lists and the copy of Jackamore's letters. She reads through, scratching her head: 'Well that's some hobby you've got there. My previous boyfriends stuck to gaming, scuba diving and gambling.'

'You believe me?'

'I want to. Do you have the picture?'

I go back into the bedroom and she follows me. I drag the picture out from underneath the mattress.

Lana shivers. 'I wouldn't keep that under my bed,' she says. 'I'd imagine her lying there.' She places the painting face down on the bedside table. Then turns it the right way round. 'I want her to be able to breathe,' she says. 'Stupid I know.'

I kiss her temple. 'It's not stupid,' I reply. 'It's why I love you.'

'You love me?' she says, grinning. 'That's good. I think I love you too.' She pulls her T-shirt over her head.

*   *   *

'Where did Gingerbread go?' I say, sitting up at last.

Gingerbread stirs from the pile of my clothes, jumps on the bed and whiskers us.

Lana's make-up is smudged, her cheeks blotchy. She looks wonderful. 'It's hard to get my head around. Both you and Gingerbread were interacting in the past at the same time as I was staring at my phone, hoping for a message.'

'I still haven't come to terms with it,' I say, nuzzling Gingerbread's soft head. 'Do you think she'll stay with me?' I ask.

'Do you think it's possible that we talk too much about *you*,' she says, poking me in the stomach. I tense my muscles so that she'll find some semblance of a six-pack.

'How could it be possible to talk *too* much about me? I'm fascinating.' I try to ignore the pointedly loud music from Satnam's room.

She laughs and the sound of it makes me laugh too.

'You've got to admit, though—have you ever been out with a man who can travel in time?'

'Well,' she says, 'there was this bloke from Oldham, he seemed stuck in 1984—his hair was, anyway. Can you be serious for once, though?'

'I don't know. Can I?'

'Stephen . . .' She strokes my neck and curls the back of my hand into her palm.

'You're right,' I say, stroking her hair and wrapping a lock of it around my forefinger. I turn over and lean on my elbows. 'Tell me what it is you love about being an archivist which, as far as I can tell, seems to be about wearing kinky little gloves and sticking books into storage.'

She spoons herself into me. 'I love finding rare objects, old objects,' she says. 'I've always wanted to work in a copyright library. All published knowledge in one place. Of course the University Library is not like the British Library, but it still has up to eighty per cent of all books. I'm overseeing the acquisition of new repositories for books that are low or nil use. I block up whole rooms full of books in the recesses of the library, so we need warehouses just for books that no one will read. We can't get rid of anything; it has to be stored.'

'But that could just go on and on.'

'I know!'

Lana nods, her eyes shining. She sits up in bed, her arms wild and gesturing. 'Imagine a city of books, walls made out of books and—' I kiss her, breathing

293

in her breath till I'm dizzy.

Chapter Fifty-Four

Beauty

Jane sits in the front of the car on the journey, looking straight ahead, but the fens still roll themselves out in her peripheral vision and she holds onto the sides of the seat. 'You can go a little slower, Pemberton,' she says. 'We can be of more use to her if I don't lose my breakfast all over the dashboard.'

'Yes, guv,' he says. Jane notes the pushing forward of his jaw, the force with which he said 'guv'. She needs to get some respect back.

The car stops outside The Fenland Arms. She was a teenager the last time she was here: she threw up a bottle of Merlot and two packets of crisps in the men's toilets. The thought does nothing to settle her stomach.

Mud sucking at her boots, Jane walks over to the cordoned-off mound at the top of the field. The wait is over. This is the time she feels alive, these few moments where it's all her, before the body and the sadness and the reality of violence tugs her back down; this is her stage moment, the striding onto the scene with her protective police jacket, not minding the hard rain slicing at her face.

Hana Barinder looks up as Jane approaches, raises a white-gloved hand. 'This isn't pretty. Again,' Hana says, frowning. She points into the ditch.

Jane stares at the body lying face-up in a ditch.

The woman is wearing a stone mask. It covers her face and stares out at the onlookers in grey silence. Bare legs, bare feet, in a man's shirt, dirt on her feet as if she's been made to walk over the field to her death, a sash around her, hands across her chest. Jane crouches. 'Can you remove the mask?' Jane asks Pemberton. He kneels down and takes it away. Jane grabs onto Pemberton's calf and leans in. 'Shine that torch down here, would you?' Mud oozes through the skin of her tights, making shivers run up her leg. The light picks out Miranda's slashed cheeks and neck. The sash gleams in the torchlight.

Standing up and pressing her heels into the ground so that she doesn't take a step backwards in front of her team, Jane forces herself to take in every aspect of the body and the makeshift grave: the reeds were trampled down before the body was placed and no attempt was made to cover her; the ditch runs next to a path used by farmers and dog walkers; any footprints in the mud or ditch have been washed away by the rain; Miranda's long shirt clings to her stiff legs; six of her pink-painted nails are broken and underneath the others lies dirt; she has been killed in the last twenty-four hours if her rigor is any indication; the sash has been re-tied so that only the word 'BEAUTY' can be seen. Jane swallows down bile.

Hana touches Jane's elbow. 'If you're all right for her to be moved then I'll take her back to the office. You can come and watch later if you like.'

Jane nods. Two men in jumpsuits climb into the ditch and cover Miranda with tarpaulin. She turns back and walks towards the car. 'The office'

295

was a weird way to describe the laboratory off Lensfield Road. 'Office' to her meant umbrella plants and water coolers and the regional manager accidentally-on-purpose prodding your breasts while easing past you by the copier; not stainless steel and white tiles, corpses and sluice gates.

'Guv,' Pemberton calls out, sharply.

Jane looks back.

'There's something under her body,' he says, waving something at her. Pemberton jogs over, a smug look on his face that she doesn't like at all. 'You know that man you keep interviewing, the "harmless" one?'

'What about him?'

'She's got his library card,' he says.

Chapter Fifty-Five

Handcuffs

BEAUTY QUEEN'S BODY FOUND, the scrolling tickertape on the telly says, MYSTERY SURROUNDING TIME OF DEATH.

Shaky helicopter pictures of a mound of marshland bordered by yellow tape. Figures in jumpsuits. Flashing lights. I turn up the volume on the set. Two graduates playing poker glare at me. 'He's got a flush,' I say to one and to the other, 'he's bluffing, a two of hearts, five of clubs.' The bluffer pulls his hat further down over his ears.

I lean back and watch the screen. 'Police are baffled by the circumstances. She went missing almost a year ago but her body has barely decomposed at all. There are thought to be further complications but the police have not yet released details. A link to the murder of eight-year-old Rhys Withins is yet to be confirmed although there are reports that Miranda was wearing a stone mask identical to the one found on his body.'

'Someone's kept 'er alive,' a male voice says behind me. 'Then they did 'er in when they'd finished with 'er.'

'That's gross,' another voice chips in.

'Nah, it'll be the mud,' a girl says next to me. 'Like they get in mud packs. She'd be glad she looks young. If she were still alive. She'll never get older now. She's the chav Marilyn or Princess Di.'

Her friend laughs and punches her shoulder. 'You can't say that.'

'Can,' the first one says. She manages to look vaguely guilty though and offers to buy the next round of Baileys.

'Creepy though, isn't it?' her friend says, her eyes sparkling as she scans the room. 'Somewhere in Cambridge there's a murderer,' the girl continues. 'Maybe he's going after pretty girls.'

'You won't have to worry then,' one of the boys replies.

The girls sitting opposite stare at the door; behind the bar, Colin the barman shoves a box of cigarettes under the counter. Twisting round, I see two policemen walking over to us.

'Stephen Killigan?' the taller one says, looking at my hair.

'Do you want me to do an "I'm Spartacus", Dr Killigan?' one of the boys asks, looking at me.

'I think you've just ruined that option,' I reply. 'But thanks anyway.'

The short policeman stares around the bar while

reciting: 'Stephen Killigan, I am arresting you on suspicion of murder. You do not have to say anything, but it may harm your defence if you do not mention when questioned something which you later rely on in court. Anything you do say may be given in evidence.'

The handcuffs bite into my wrists. A wave of helplessness crashes in me. There is so much evidence pointing to my involvement. Maybe that was Robert's aim all this time. And all I have done is make it worse. I could be convicted on this; who would believe me? As the shorter policeman leads me out into the court, I look up at Robert's study room. A squat shadow stands in the window.

Chapter Fifty-Six

Lying in States

'Miranda was stabbed over and over with a metal stick or spike of about ten inches.'

'Like a stake? Or a skewer?' Jane forces herself to look at Miranda's cadaver. She failed her. She was alive until yesterday, well-nourished and beautiful, ready to be found and returned to her family: instead she lies stiff on the metal table.

'Not a skewer,' Hana continues, walking around the body and taking notes and measurements. She very gently pulls at the side of one of the wounds. The flesh gapes open. 'You can see that the trauma is at its widest nearer the skin. Therefore the blade or stick most likely gets thicker toward the hilt or top. It's not a weapon I can match with anything

I've seen and I've seen a lot. We can tell, though, from the force used, and the length of the weapon, that it is likely that she was lying down for most of the attack. The down force would have made it hard for her to get up again. She fought: there are wounds to her hands consistent with her defending the initial stabs.' Hana gets down on the floor of the lab and holds her hands out to deflect an attack, her head turned away.

Jane feels a sense of pride that Miranda fought her killer, and she never even met her. How does that work? Maybe we all take pride in humans doing things we hope to do ourselves given the circumstance being right. 'What about the mask?'

'The prints match a suspect on the books. Stephen Killigan. I've got you something you *will* like, I hope,' Hana says. Opening up a cupboard full of sterilising equipment and surgical instruments, she takes out a box wrapped in plain paper and a red ribbon. Jane opens it while Hana tugs on her earlobes and hovers, trying to find something to do.

Inside is a box with a handwritten sign on top: 'Jane's Mastectomy Survival Kit'.

'Pemberton told you?' Jane asks, not looking up. 'Or a doctor at the hospital?'

Hana pulls both earlobes at the same time. 'Pemberton thought you should have some support.'

Jane snorts. 'That's black humour even for you, Hana.'

Hana looks confused for a moment, then realises. 'I didn't mean—'

'It's okay,' Jane says. Inside the box is a pile of goodies including chocolate, the new Hilary Mantel, a Cindy doll with her tits strapped down, a written voucher to call three times and moan, and a water pistol.

'I thought you could shoot it at children,' Hana says, 'or anyone with breasts. Or use it to self-administer morphine.'

'Thanks,' Jane says, and means it.

Chapter Fifty-Seven

Coffee

The smells of a police station: the slap of sweat as a sergeant walks past; the yellow scent of sick and the bleach that doesn't quite smother it; machine coffee; the curdled rose perfume of a girl in ragged tights rocking backwards and forwards in the chair opposite. I smile at her, but she just flinches and rocks harder.

The officer gestures for me to follow him into the interview room. He leaves me sitting on a cracked plastic chair behind a desk. I sit on my hands and wrench round to look through the slit of a window.

Outside, the wind winds itself up, shaking the fist of the tree that leans in towards the station like a criminal trying to strike a deal. A leaf flings itself at the window and sticks.

The door clangs open. Inspector Horne walks in with my solicitor. Her face looks different; the space under her cheekbones has been gauged out. Her sergeant, Pemberton I think, stands by the door with his arms crossed.

'I am fed up with seeing you, Dr Killigan,' she says. But I don't believe her somehow. Then again,

I don't know what to know anymore. I am in a mixed state of believing everything and nothing at once.

'Can you explain to me how your library card was found in proximity to the body of Miranda Pilkington?'

'I can't at all. I still have all of my library cards—for the university, faculty, college and local libraries—in my wallet. Which one was found?'

'Your University Library card.' 'I've only got one UL card: they took my picture to go on the front the day I joined. I used it this morning.'

'It comes up on the system when they enter, ma'am,' Sergeant Pemberton says.

'It must have been a copy that was found on Miranda. And why would I put that there? I can be a fool sometimes, but I'm not stupid.'

'Some murderers, the ones who are really bad at it, leave obvious clues in order to achieve recognition for what they have done, and let's face it, Dr Killigan, you do like the attention of the media,' Inspector Horne says.

'I did not leave my library card near Miranda's body. And you cannot prove that a copy wasn't made. There, can I go now?' My solicitor shuffles his feet. That might be his attempt to shut me up.

'You seem very familiar with using her first name. And yet you say you never met her.'

'I didn't. I feel as if I know her from having found her body the first time.'

'And what about the prints on the mask?'

'You know that I had two of the masks in my room until you took them. I have told you of the circumstances in which I obtained them; and I touched the one that was on her face when I found her. Either it was from that occasion or when one of the masks was placed in my room. Look, it confuses me too. I've lost track.' This sounds ridiculous, even to me. Maybe I should do as my solicitor suggests—ask for psychiatric assessment. I can't breathe; my hands are shaking. 'What about the letter from Jackamore Grass?' I say. 'There must be something there?'

Inspector Horne does not seem to be listening. She wipes a hand over her forehead. Her face is yellow-grey. She gestures for Sergeant Pemberton to follow her into the corridor but as she stands her knees buckle, and she crashes onto the floor.

Chapter Fifty-Eight

The Hospice

'Wake up, Mrs, it's the pigs,' Jane says, whispering into the sleeping policewoman's ear.

Former Detective Chief Inspector Marion Eckhart smiles before she opens her eyes. 'You'd better have brought chocolate, D.I. Horne, or I'm getting one of the nurses to turf you out.' She eases herself up into a sitting position.

Jane hands over a small red Christmas stocking packed with chocolate. 'I haven't had one of these since I was a kid,' Marion says. She takes out a Twirl and offers half to Jane. Pemberton arranges pillows behind her. 'Oh I can do it,' she says, her face creasing into the crossness that Jane recognises her showing when tired.

Jane brings her chair nearer. She looks down at her skirt, not wanting Marion to see the concern and, yup, pity on her face. Marion has become small. The white sheets overwhelm her hollowed face.

'So, what's for dinner round here?' Jane asks. 'I haven't eaten all day.' She won't say that she can't face eating. That she has been given the day off for fainting and being weak.

'You never do, apart from junk. It's not going to help, you know,' Marion replies. 'Vegetables can be your friends.'

'I don't want any friends.'

Pemberton stands and stretches. He can almost reach the ceiling. 'Do you want a cuppa, guv?' he asks. He gazes at the door. I'd probably want out too if I were in the company of two cantankerous, cancer-struck women, but he should be able to hack these things—he's an officer.

'God, sorry.' Marion opens the drawer in the bedside cabinet and shoves things away until she finds a mirror. She holds it in front of her face and grimaces. Her eyes are shiny. The drugs can make your eyes water constantly, although Jane had the opposite problem, eyes so tight and itchy she wanted to pop them out and soak them overnight in Steradent. Marion sticks her tongue out at her reflection and tucks the mirror under her pillow. 'Jo came to see me.'

'You're joking.' Jo is Marion's daughter. She hasn't seen her in ten years, not since Marion left her dad for Tania. Tania then left *her* for a life in the army but Jo still refused to take Marion's calls.

Marion shakes her head and the gold veins in her headscarf snatch at the light. 'I suppose she wanted to see me before I died.'

It's the first time she's said it. That she is going to

die. To Jane at least. It is not fair. Cancer kills and she is a detective: she should be able to apprehend it, lock it up and prevent it from murdering again.

'Get that look off your face, Amanda Jane Horne. So suck it up or get out.' The old fire is still there, burning in her charcoal voice. 'Now tell me about the case. I need something to take my mind elsewhere.'

Jane fills her in, then stops.

'What is it?' Marion asks, wincing as she leans forward.

'That lecturer, Stephen Killigan, came to me with a letter he says was written by The Magician Killer. Killigan claims that—' She breaks off. She waits while the tea trolley is wheeled past to another patient.

'Hurry up, I'm dying here.'

Jane looks around at the other patients.

'Don't worry: we're all bald, bored or batshit on morphine. Nothing you could say could possibly matter.'

'Batshit-on-morphine sounds like a seaside town.'

'Get on with it, Horne.'

'Fine. He says that he can travel in time, and so can the murderer; he says this murderer is responsible for murders and other crimes across time. It sounds ridiculous, I know.'

'But you're still telling me: you must think there's *something* in it.'

Jane blushes. 'I'm not sure why I'm telling you.'

'Have you told your boss?'

'You've met him, haven't you? His main interest is in how many photos he can get of himself in the press. It also seems like a sure way to get myself fired for believing a mad man.'

'So you *do* believe him.'

'I don't know what to think. His prints are on the mask we found with Miranda, his library card tucked beneath her. He's in custody, asking for me, saying he knows how to solve a seventeenth-century murder.' Jane sighs. 'The thing is, the DNA we have from the letter and the knife and the music box matches evidence found in various different times around the world. It sounds stupid.'

'Who cares about stupid? Your instinct was always good; you'll winkle out the facts. The only reason you haven't yet is that you're not asking the right questions.' She swallows with difficulty.

'You're tired; I'll go.' Jane doesn't move.

Marion opens her hands wide. 'Come on, then. What aren't you telling me but are desperate to?'

'Dr Pindar talked to me again about a preventative mastectomy. He says that with my family history I should at least consider removing the other tissue.'

'Your other breast.'

'Yes, that. I'd rather stick to reducing alcohol, a low-fat diet, vegetables, yes, regular exercise and avoiding menopausal hormones. I'm doing well on the last one at least, but then I'm not menopausal.'

'And you're not likely to be if you don't take his advice. They don't suggest these things for a laugh, you know. You want my advice? Remove it. Otherwise you're keeping asbestos in your asthma inhaler.'

'But I already look disgusting.'

'So be a pretty, one-breasted corpse or lop it off, love your flat chest and live well for a long time.' Marion taps Jane's hand and lies down, slowly.

'Now go away and let that philosopher out. See where he goes.'

Jane picks up her bag, touches Marion's damp forehead and walks towards the door.

'Oh, and Inspector Horne?'

Jane turns around.

Marion opens one eye. 'Did I ever tell you what a silly name you have?'

*   *   *

Jane unlocks the door to Stephen's cell. She tucks the letter from forensics into her bag, her heart pounding.

He sits cross-legged on the thin blue mattress, stretching his long arms above his head.

'Getting comfortable, are we?' she asks.

'I'll miss this place if I ever leave. It could do with a touch up though, but then again, who couldn't?'

'If that was an invitation, it failed.'

'I was just thinking a nice fresco on the walls would work. A mural of someone being wrongfully arrested, perhaps?'

Jane sits down next to him. 'This is probably the most stupid thing I have ever done,' she says. 'And if anyone asks, I'll deny everything and say you are mad.'

'Fair enough. Most of my friendships work in the same way.'

Jane pinches her knee to distract herself from the pain across her breast. It doesn't work. She stands up and marches across the cell to the door. 'Right then, you're free to go. But only as far as Frank's Cafe. First on the left past the bookies. I'll meet you there in an hour.'

It is more like two hours until Jane is able to join him. The cafe is quiet, only a couple of tables occupied. She sidles into the booth and picks up the plastic menu before throwing it down again. 'Why do I always look at the menu, when I know what I want?'

The waitress slinks over in a top tied above her belly button. Jane glances at Stephen to see if he is looking. He is. Her name is Simone, according to the laminated badge attached to her pushed-up breasts.

'Bacon and banana sandwich with maple syrup, please. And tea,' Jane says, crossing her arms.

The waitress flashes a waxed eyebrow.

Stephen scans the menu. 'Large full fry-up, please. With two slices of toast, a banana and maple syrup.' He turns to Jane. 'I thought you might know something I don't.'

Jane waits for Simone to sashay back in with the drinks and wiggle away before speaking. 'Now none of this is strictly official, but I asked my friend in forensics for a favour and sent that letter you received to be tested. The one from The Magician.'

Stephen leans back against the red pleather, folding his arms. 'What made you decide to trust me?'

'I don't trust you, Dr Killigan. That would be stupid and there are already sufficient people in the press and police accusing me of stupidity for me to confirm it by being calamitously stupid in trusting you. The sensible approach to life is to trust nobody: they either betray you, die on you or sleep with your sister in your grandma's caravan.'

'You should come to my next party, inspector. Your winning optimism and cheery disposition will go down a storm.'

A crash from the kitchen. Simone bends behind the counter and reappears with an armful of smashed plates. The chef shakes his head and swabs his forehead with a tea towel. Jane smirks. Opening her bag, she takes out a report from Hana's team and pushes it over the Formica table.

He slips it out of the envelope and begins to read. His eyes widen. He looks up to Jane. Looks down. Looks up again. 'I can see why you don't want this getting out.' Stephen stands and paces the space between the door and their table in the corner. 'Imagine what the press would make of that. DNA found connecting the Beauty Queen Killer with murders from the eighteenth, nineteenth and twentieth centuries. It would be Jack the Ripper fever times a hundred. Maybe he *is* Jack the Ripper. After all, he can travel to any point in the past and then disappear again into the present. That's how he can get away with it always,' Stephen says, scratching at the left side of his face as he paces. His skin is raked with red streaks.

The man on the nearest table, a Labrador sleeping on his feet, is so gripped by watching Stephen that he forgets to stop squeezing the sauce bottle and swamps his chop with ketchup.

Stephen sits back down. His eyes seem more blue, as if the sun has come out over the sea. 'I think there's a reason why the beauty queen disappeared that day when I found her by the church. I stumbled into the future. Jack travelled into the future with her.'

'Now that must be one of the most implausible stories I've heard from you yet.'

'He must be able to: I can't see any other way that he disposed of her body.'

'It's simple as far as we're concerned. He has kept her somewhere for a year, and then killed her.'

'Okay, and maybe he did. But can't you see that time travel is the perfect method for disposing of bodies and hiding your tracks. So simple, and impossible to those who consider it impossible. He could then orchestrate when she would be found.'

Jane leans forward, exasperation rising. 'But Miranda wasn't found by Great St Mary's—she was in the fens. Like this other girl you say you found.'

'I don't know all the answers. But there are always more options; I'm learning that all the time. Either Jackamore, realising I was onto him, moved her body to confuse us, as if we need any more of that, or just to play with us. Or . . .' he paused, 'it wasn't her.'

'Then who was it?'

'Another victim who hasn't been found yet. A victim who hasn't been a victim yet. Who could be still alive.'

Jane shivers. 'It's too tangled up,' she says.

'There's a chance we could prevent the last victim's death.' He frowns. 'Or has he already done it, and we have no option at all? How does this all work? And how the fuck can we stop someone like that?' Stephen's voice has been increasing in volume and now rivals the radio hiss.

'Can you at least tell me that you are willing to entertain this as a possibility?' he asks.

'All right. But that's all.'

'That's enough for me,' Stephen says, grinning

now. 'Right. I have to be as good at travelling in time as him, otherwise he'll always be one step ahead. 'Maybe then I can stop him.' He slices the toast down the middle then traces a finger over the spidery tattoo that circles his wrist. *I was much too far out all my life* it says.

'I will continue following Robert's fetish with the dead and the beautiful in order, to get information on Jackamore, or evidence against Robert, and you will get me any information that can help. Agreed?'

Jane shrugs. How could it hurt? If it was all nonsense then Killigan was kept busy; if it led her nearer to the enigmatic man then all was well. 'Agreed.'

Jane holds out her hand then freezes. What if the prospect of cancer is affecting her judgement and her willingness to take risks? Especially with other people's lives. She blows those thoughts away. They shake hands. 'What did he mean in the letter,' she says, 'that you will only travel by letting go of love?'

'From what I've learnt, it happens when the brain is in the present, in fear, when drunk, when inhibitions have gone, when happy, in pleasure. Maybe love is a connection to chronology; maybe to travel in time you can't think about a future and the future is always implicit in love.'

'Are you in love?'

Stephen smiles and touches the St Christopher between his collarbones. 'Yes. I am. She's called Lana Carver and I love her. She gave me this today.'

Jealousy scratches at her, leaving a papercut. 'And will you drop her to stop him?'

He smiles even wider. 'I can do both, no

problem. He's not going to tell me what to do.'

Simone swings over with their order. 'We've got no maple,' she says. 'Will golden syrup do?'

Chapter Fifty-Nine

Lana and the Fireworks

The fireworks have already started, lighting up buildings that stand spiky against the smoke-purple night. Head down, I move through the crowd, away from the expanses of grass where people are gathering.

Lana is on the University Library steps when I arrive. 'I only just managed to escape,' she says. 'Mr Findley has only been back a week from sick leave and now he's off again,' she whispers. 'So I've got to pick up the slack. It's why I can't do as much research for you as I'd like.'

The city barks and spits and whistles into the sky behind us like an army sergeant. 'Are we going to Midsummer Common?' she asks, pushing back her fringe with her mitten.

'Not telling,' I reply. 'You'll have to wait.'

My rucksack clanks against my back as we walk over the river. People hurry past, swaddled in scarves. Kids waddle between adults, togged up in extra layers.

'If you're cold, tell me. I've got two pairs of gloves on,' I say, holding up thickened fingers in white gloves like an alarming mime artist. 'On Bonfire Night Mum made us wear two pairs of pants, two pairs of socks, two T-shirts under two jumpers, and pyjamas under our trousers. We toddled out with our parka buttons busting like little Incredible Hulks.'

'Who's "us"?' she asks.

'What?'

'You said your mum "made us wear two pairs of everything".'

'Oh. My sister and me. Shiv. Short for Siobhan. She's in the US now.' I pause.

'Are you close?'

My last memory of Shiv rolls into my head, causing a penny-falls of images. Change the subject. 'Have you got brothers? Sisters?'

'No, I'm an only child,' she says.

'I refused to go unless we all carried neepy candles—lanterns that we hacked out of turnips.'

'I thought they were for Halloween,' Lana says.

'I got Halloween and Bonfire Night mixed up. I thought Guy Fawkes came back from the dead on November the fifth and came looking for naughty boys.'

'And a neepy candle would ward him off?'

'I was a very imaginative little boy. Shows initiative. Or insanity. Or both. What were your Fireworks Night traditions? Don't tell me. I'll guess.' I place my hands on my temples and close my eyes, psychic-style. 'You dressed up as a Catherine wheel and cartwheeled with sparklers stuck to your wellies?'

'Not even close. This is my first.'

'What?'

'My parents are Jehovah's Witnesses. No birthdays, no Christmas, no Halloween, no Bonfire Night. And I've been busy since I left home.'

No pressure then.

'How was Oxford?' I ask.

'Friendly,' she replies. 'And round.'

'Round?'

'It's in this big ring of roads, with the colleges cuddling around the edges. Cambridge feels cold and isolated by comparison. The buildings here are cool and grey, whereas Oxford stone is cream and golden and beige and—'

'Boring,' I say. A bolt of jealousy burns in me. I could lose her to Oxford. I move slightly further away from her. I shouldn't be at this stage so soon.

'Then there's the Bodleian, which—'

'Is round as a Tunnock's tea cake, I know.' I want to do away with the small talk. 'Get to the point, lass. What did you find?'

'I was about to tell you,' she says, reproachful. 'I went down into the stores at the Ashmolean. They took out documents from the time of the 1742 fire at the Padua Museum.' Her eyes are bright and focused. I want to touch her. 'It was brilliant. I got to put on my special archivist gloves. Only one pair, though. It wasn't Bonfire Night.'

I laugh and the tension breaks and disperses like a willow firework. Funny how they're named after natural things, these man-made fireworks, beautiful parts of nature: chrysanthemums, flying fish, waterfalls, palm trees, peonies. And war: barrage, shells, artillery, mine, missile. You could argue that war *is* natural. Killing is part of survival after all. It is when killing becomes murder that it is considered unnatural.

'Where have you gone?' Lana asks, stopping me.

'What?'

'You wandered off somewhere in your head.'

'I did?' I did. 'Sorry. And sorry 'bout being short

with you just now. I got impatient and—'

She flaps her hand; my words fade. 'Shut up, Stephen. So I had on my special gloves.' She waggles her fingers. 'I've got the photocopies of documents including the report of a man emerging from the museum's flames. And he also signed in on that day in 1742.' She unzips her canvas bag and drags out a folded piece of paper. 'There.' She points at the name halfway down the page.

This is his handwriting. The one on the note that came with the mask.

'But it doesn't stop there,' she says. 'The museum was restored and is still thriving. In the visitor's book for that year, where people such as Mr and Mrs Arbroath wrote platitudes like 'lovely museum, we'll be back!', there is Jackamore Grass's name, written in the same handwriting, and next to it the letter 'S' and the message: 'hold up a mirror'.

'"Hold up a mirror"'—from *Hamlet?* '"To hold, as 'twere, a mirror up to nature?"'

'I don't know. But do you want to know what was really weird?'

'This isn't weird enough?' I kiss her on the tip of her nose.

'The *really* weird and spooky thing is that, according to two Italian newspapers, the 1742 fire kept going through the night and, when it was eventually safe to go back inside, they found paintings blackened and twisted, display cases shattered, statues scorched, the walls heat-blistered, yet at the back of one of the galleries, the only thing that survived intact was the glass cabinet that the masks were kept in, and in that cabinet, still locked, where the masks had been, were the silhouettes of five heads, like the Victorian daguerreotypes.'

'Completely untouched by fire?'

'Utterly. This mysterious Mr Grass likes to intrigue. And publicly. Whoever is using the name at least wanted it known that he stole the masks, and lit the fire.'

'Wanted *me* to know. *Wants* me to know.'

'That's a bit grandiose, even for you,' Lana says, then grins.

'Maybe. I'm not sure.' Four masks, five outlines of faces. Does that mean four or five victims?

'Anyway, after that I got on with the training that I wangled myself onto,' she says.

'Thank you, Lana,' I say.

We walk in silence up Hills Road. Occasionally, a firework wheezes up and one of us jumps. Usually me. I lead us down an alleyway and stand in front of the door in the wall at the back of the Botanic Garden. The door is warped.

I take a key out of my pocket. 'I stole this,' I say. That's not entirely true. It's not true at all: Stuart Lennard, Sepulchre's senior botanist, lent it to me in exchange for the loan of one of my ancient, but still working, computers. But she *doesn't* need to know that. Stealing is dangerous; dangerous is sexy and that's that.

The door sounds out a belch as I push it open. 'Ta da,' I say. I hold back the branches of trees, creating a path for her.

Even in the dark, in November, the Botanic Garden makes me breathe more slowly. Forty acres of awayness from a city that never stops thinking. I lead her down the Main Walk, between the cedars and pines, passing the fountain.

'It smells like Christmas,' she says.

I stop us at the lake, by the stepping stones

315

and shine my torch up at the nearest tree. The still-clinging leaves glow. I pull one of them from a resistant branch and hand it to her. She holds it under the torch. It sits like an amber tear in her hand.

'I hope you're hungry,' I say, and smooth the checked blanket out on the damp grass. Kneeling on one of the cushions, I take each item out from my rucksack with the solemnity of a sportsman picking the teams for the FA Cup.

Bowing, I place the silver Thermos flask of hot chocolate into her hands.

'I can't believe you're laughing,' I say, giving her the mock-seriousness of a butler. 'How could you possibly giggle at a can-dle-lit picnic of home-made toffee apples (I'll have you know that I took the skin off three fingers and the roof of my mouth, not to mention ruined a perfectly good milk pan just so you could enjoy the crunchy delights of a caramelised *pomme-de-terre* on a lolly stick and possibly lose a tooth or two in the process; come to think of it, I must get you to sign an indemnity form, waiving your right to sue should you happen to suffer dental displacement or oral discomfort of any kind) old olives; cheese and grapefruit on sticks, which as everyone knows is very now and not seventies at all and isn't one iota to do with not having any pineapple chunks in the cupboard; marmite sandwiches; and cake made by a student who is either trying to ingratiate himself or poison me. How could you possibly guff aw at *that*?'

'You're right,' she says. I chase the smothered smile from her mouth to her cheeks to her eyes. 'Shall we start?' Lana picks up a toffee apple and, looking me straight in the eye, opens her mouth

316

and takes a huge bite. The toffee skin cracks like a mirror. I lean in and kiss her, taking the piece of apple into my mouth.

*   *   *

After, I clear away the remnants and plates and hold out a packet of sparklers. She takes one and I light it. The sparkler bursts into conversation, crackling. She pauses, then draws, her wrist twisting:

S

The letter fades as if wiped from a blackboard. 'S' for Stephen.

An idea fizzes. I hand her another sparkler. 'Quick,' I say, 'do the same again.

Forehead creased, she sketches another 'S' at the same time as I copy her movements as if they were reflected:

SƧ

'What does that look like to you?' I say as the echoing images fade.

She shrugs. 'A heart?'

'Could be. Maybe that's it. Half of a broken heart on each wrist: the loss of love he talks about

317

in the letter.' I turn the key and let us out onto the busy road. Sound crashes in on us; cars pass, taking families home from Guy Fawkes, sleepy kids slumped against windows.

As we walk, straggling fireworks still put on a show. I put her arm round my waist and for the first time in this city, I'm home.

Chapter Sixty

Great Yarmouth

I promised her a daytrip, and here it is: Great Yarmouth. Why? It is only a couple of hours away by train; the seaside is always romantic in a Kiss-Me-Quick kind of way; and then there's yesterday's phone call with Harry Zappa:

'I've been asking around, after what you said, and I heard via a mate via a mate and probably via another mate that a tattooist in Great Yarmouth was coerced into showing a man the technique for incision. The bloke sat practising the same sign, over and over again. The one you showed me. The tattooist was so freaked he closed the shop for six months.'

'Can I talk with him?'

'You can do whatever you want, mate. He may not want to talk with you though. He's reclusive.'

'He'll talk with me,' I said. Harry Zappa's laugh rumbles down the phone.

*　　　*　　　*

'Let's not talk about the murders. Or dead women. Or masks,' Lana says, rolling up candy floss into a ball and popping it into my mouth. 'Agreed?'

'Not even in passing?' I reply. Stray hairs of sugar melt on my tongue.

'Not even in passing. I want to see what we have without all that.'

'Then that's what will happen.' I take her hand, turn it over and kiss her palm. 'Do you promise, though? Because it keeps creeping in.' 'I won't talk about it, I promise you that. Now shut up and snog me.'

The rain freezes into sleet and strikes our faces. 'Come on,' I say, pulling her into the nearest pub. 'I challenge you to a game of shove ha'penny.'

The Flying Moon has a dartboard, two pool tables, a wide selection of board games, but no shove ha'penny. 'Now you'll never know how badly I would have beaten you,' I say, taking our drinks back to the table by the window.

Seagulls squawk outside, turning up their wings to the wind and flicking it the V. I miss seagulls. They are belligerent, bellicose, balls-out bastards.

I take the darts that Satnam gave me out of my pocket. 'Let's play darts,' I say.

'I warn you,' she says, taking off her coat. 'I grew up in Frimley Green. I know my darts.'

'Then it will be a match worth watching.' I look around the pub. A Labrador snores in the corner. 'Or it would be if anyone were here.'

'They'll never know what they're missing,' she says, opening the doors to the dartboard. She walks up to the bar and asks the barmaid for the darts.

'They keep on getting nicked,' the barmaid says. 'So we stopped buying them.'

I offer her my flights. 'There you go,' I say.

'You're going to get beaten with your own darts,' she says. 'Are you sure you can take the humiliation?'

'I'll take any humiliation you want to dole out,' I say, waggling my eyebrows. She punches me lightly on the shoulder.

*   *   *

We play five games. I manage to win a grand total of one. 'Best of two hundred and thirty,' I say. 'And you have to sit out the last hundred.'

She hands me back the darts but I only take one. 'Keep the other two,' I say. 'A memento of the day.'

We play on the penny arcade on the pier, calling on the teetering coins to take the jump.

'What we need is one suicidal five pence to leap first,' I say. 'The rest will follow like lemmings.'

'It's rigged so that you cannot win,' Lana says, pulling me away to play another game.

'I don't believe that for a minute,' I say.

We wander back over the road to eat chips and kiss with salted lips. She tells me that her boss is sending her back to Oxford on another research trip and I realise how much I will miss her.

'Do you have to go?' I ask.

She smiles and nods. 'I'll be back before you know it.'

'That isn't true. Never lie to me, Lana Carver. Tell you what,' I say, looking over the road as if seeing the tattooist for the first time, 'I'm going to have a tattoo done as a surprise for you. Give me an hour or so. I'll meet you at the tea shop on the corner.' I take out two pocketfuls of copper change.

'Go and push them over the edge.'

It is more of a booth than a shop. The old-fashioned and wonderful kind of tattoo parlour white-tiled up to the ceiling, enough room for a chair, a table of works and Johnny Swindon, the tiniest tattooist in the world.

'What would you like?' Johnny Swindon says. He doesn't look me in the eye; he twangs the elastic bands onto his machines.

'I'd like you to write "The Great Lana Carver" around the flames on my inner arm,' I say. 'That won't take more than an hour, would it?' I have never had a girl's name tattooed on me before. I've always thought it a bad omen but all my previous relationships ended badly, coolly or with tears so I don't think it makes a difference. And I feel guilty for bringing her here under false pretences.

Johnny Swindon shuts the door again. 'Bloody wind,' he says.

He has Radio 3 on loudly and dips his head to concentrate on the tattoo.

'I was wondering if you could help me,' I say.

He doesn't reply.

'I heard that you had an encounter with a man who wanted to know how to carve this symbol.' I take the symbol out of the bag.

He jumps up; the tattoo stops at The Great L. 'I can't say anything,' he says. 'I shouldn't have said anything. Please leave, please leave, please leave—'

'I'm sorry,' I say, holding up my hands, 'I didn't mean—'

He starts rocking, screaming at the radio and the concerto playing. I leave the money on the table, apologise again and leave. I never should have come.

Lana is quiet. I show her the tattoo but she won't look at it; I make jokes but she either nods or shakes her head or stares out of the window at the waves. Next to her, the pink elephant won on the knock-tin alley sits in the plastic seat, its trunk lowered.

'What is it?' I ask her for the fourth time.

She pours out the last of the tea. 'You promised,' she says.

'What?'

'You promised that you wouldn't talk about the murders and the mask or anything to do with it.'

'And I haven't. We've had a lovely day.'

'I came into the shop to surprise you,' she says. 'I've never seen a tattoo being done and they mean a lot to you, so I wanted to know more. About you.' She takes a deep breath. 'Only you were there interrogating a poor old man about a traumatic experience, just so you could find out more about this Jackamore Grass.' She spits his name out. 'It's the reason we came here, isn't it?' she says.

I consider lying. And then nod.

'I think you're fantastic, Stephen, I really do. You are the best company and I love you but—'

'Oh, here we go,' I say. My ears are hot and I feel anger build up.

'I can't be with someone obsessed with another girl. Even if she is dead. In fact, that might be worse. How can I beat that?'

'I'm not obsessed. I'm trying to find out what happened.'

'Say it how you like, it's not for me. I'm sorry,' she says. She kisses the top of my head as she

322

leaves.

I stir my sugar into my tea.

There is no point staying here. Everything is tacky and dull and the high strung-up lights can hang themselves. I get the train back and all the time I am thinking: she left me there and I am glad it's like this because I am better alone. Thank God we were only this much in because I really loved her and wanted to be with her for . . . And so my brain loops into a Möbius strip and I have endless pairs of scissors.

*   *   *

Cindy's is full of bodies, sweating and waiting and sizing up and I need one of them, need to be one of them, need to be one with the writhing mass and forget, drown out it all and make it none. I shimmer in and out of time as my heart beats to the 140 beats per minute and a girl smiles at me, smiles at me with teeth blue in the UV and I try to block the images of Lana that come into my head as she does not want me. But this girl does, with her long hair and low top and high boots.

I don't ask her name as I don't want to know but, she's coming home.

Chapter Sixty-One

Dawn

She's half an hour late and counting, but I can't be angry seeing as I don't even know her name. 'Pizza Express on Thursday at 8' is all the information I left myself. We were up all night. That's a long time not to ask someone's name. I needed not to think for a while. That's my excuse.

I'm not sure I even want to be here, but I need to do something normal. Meet a nice girl. Have a nice meal. Get away from death.

The door opens and a blast of cold air enters with a couple holding hands. Being stood up smarts—it's happened once before and I deserved it. I probably do now. Still. I've got a book in front of me and can convey the impression that I'm a lecturer out for a quiet pizza by myself thank you very much, catching up on my *Tractatus Logico-Philosophicus* over a Sloppy Giuseppe. I've started on the red wine already, to numb the jazz trio in the corner. The double bass player grabs the neck of the poor instrument as if he wants to strangle it.

Pummelling a dough ball in garlic butter, I'm about to pop it in my mouth when she walks in wearing a short dress, tights and no coat. I can see her goose pimples from here.

'Decided to come, then?' I say.

'I told you I might be late,' she says, slipping her coat over the back of her chair.

'You told me you'd be here at eight,' I reply.

'But you forgive me, don't you?' She does this

cute crumpled grumpy face.

I pluck the red gerbera out of the vase. 'All is forgiven.'

She takes the flower and lays it on her lap. 'Are you okay?' she asks, looking at me with her head on one side. 'You look like you haven't slept since I last saw you.'

'I'll have you know I've slept at least twice since then.' She slips her hand over mine. Her fingers are red from the cold, the nails nibbled down. 'It's okay,' I continue. 'I just don't like sleeping much. Tends to make me dream.'

'I like dreaming,' she says. 'I've been dreaming a lot about that boy in *High School Musical*.'

'Isn't he a bit young for you?'

She sits up straight, looks affronted. 'I'm twenty-one. I told you in Cindy's.'

'In which case you're too young for me and should leave immediately.'

She laughs. The waiter comes over with a menu for her and, doing the flirty eyes thing, takes her drink order.

'You can't be more than, what, forty?' she says when he's gone.

I feel a surge in confidence when her eyes don't follow him into the kitchen. 'Fuck me,' I reply. 'I really should sleep. And eat. I'm thirty-five,' I say.

'Then I've been out with men years older than you.'

'You're very forward.' And straightforward. I'm not sure I like things to be this easy. Romance should have overtones of the forbidden, and ultimately, sadness.

'No point in being otherwise, is there?' she says. 'Anyway, you're hot.'

325

Not sure I've ever been called hot before. Maybe this is the way to go. None of that dancing around the point, heart beating so fast whenever I see Lana that I think I will cough it up like a furball in front of her, trying to interpret signals so mixed I can't pick out any one in particular to focus on. 'What you having then?' I ask, leaning towards her, my elbows on the marble.

Her tongue sticks out just a little as she reads the menu. It is pink and makes me think of Gingerbread as she drinks water.

'I don't like mushrooms; the texture is all wrong. Like seaweed. I got my foot trapped in seaweed once.'

The waiter stands close as he takes her order and only moves away when he catches my stare. She takes the last dough ball and squashes it with her fingers. I can't believe how wide she can open her mouth. Stop it: this is dinner. Subtlety required. This is why they have muted lighting, shit jazz, umbrella plants in the corners and all the while the promise of sex is spun in the air like pizza dough. I can't even remember her name. Deviousness is required. I can do that.

'You've got your bag on you, haven't you?' I say. 'I've got this gift. I can tell everything about someone by what's in their pocket or wallet.'

She heaves her handbag onto her lap and digs around. There's a packet of those moist pocket tissues, a cold black stone, two lip balms, folded A4 sheets, pens from the bowling lane where she works, broken-up pieces of tissue that she stuffs to the bottom of the bag, the hopeful glint of a condom wrapper, her face flushing up to the red of her mock-croc diary that I flick through, finding out what's she's been up to this week and also gleaning that her name is Dawn Burley. Dawn. In her Velcro-wrapped purse is a crumpled bus ticket, a return to Arbury, and a folded piece of squared paper with To Dawn on it, a kiss under her name. Male writing, spiky. Other than that, stamps, credit cards, Sainsbury's loyalty card, a receipt for milk, thick-sliced bread, chickpeas and a Double Decker. No library card.

Our pizzas arrive and I cut into the egg that stares up at me from the centre of mine. 'I'm particularly interested in this, Ms Burley,' I say, holding up the note. 'Would you describe yourself as single at this point in time?'

Her pupils flare.

*   *   *

After dinner, I walk her to the bus stop down the road. Prickles of something, instinct, hover around my neck. Looking back, I see two men standing under a lamp-post on the other side of the road. One eases a fisherman's hat over his bald head like a black condom. They start walking towards us. Dawn's boots stamp on the pavement. I put my arm round her and bring her under my coat.

'You don't really want to go home, do you?' I ask.

She looks up at me, grins.

*   *   *

She's asleep, her head on my chest. Every now and then she quivers, or kicks. Gingerbread does that. I always hope that she doesn't have to dream like

I do, that it's just the central nerve centre of a cat testing out the equipment—claws: present; front paw: present and correct; hind legs: able to run away at any moment. Gingerbread isn't in yet. I've got to stop comparing Dawn to Gingerbread; that's just weird.

Dawn sighs and turns over, freeing my arm. It tingles. I pick up Dawn's wrist and trace the shape of the girl's tattoo with my finger. Sleep tries to drag me under.

*   *   *

Stuck. As if my legs have been potted, my arms wrapped in twine by my side. Mum stands in the sea. She's with someone. A man. He's tall and not Da and his hand is on her shoulder like I've seen priests do in Mum's church before dunking them. His hand is still on her but her shoulder is now under the water. Now her head. The man has his back to me and holds out his hand.

*   *   *

A cold hand on my forehead. It must be Lana; she's let herself in. My heart starts booming so loudly she'll think she's got tinnitus. I grab her hand and kiss it up and up the arm.

I open my eyes.

Dawn. Stroking my hair, tucking it behind my ears. It feels like insects and I brush her hand away. She looks down at her knees and stretches my T-shirt that she's wearing over them.

'Don't do that,' I snap. She did that.

She steps back and crosses her arms over her

328

chest.

'Sorry,' I say. 'I'm not good in the mornings.'

'I can leave if you want,' she says. Which means she doesn't want to leave.

Gingerbread jumps in through the window and winds round Dawn's legs. Gingerbread's more of a tart than I am. Last night scrolls through my head. Clothes struggled off under covers, hot breath condensing into ghosts, tights on one of her ankles, legs up in the air. My cock responds with a half-hearted twitch, like the sticking hand of a clock. Dawn is smiling again. And I have lost myself.

Chapter Sixty-Two

Dinner

A note in my pigeonhole from Robert: 'Dinner at mine tonight? Don't bring wine: it won't be nearly good enough. Shall we say eight?'

Maybe I can find proof of his friendship with Grass, anything that links him to the deaths or the masks. I turn over the postcard. It's a picture of the Cam in summer, river boats alongside ducks. A smudged arrow points to one of the boats.

Half an hour of wandering up and down the towpath in the rain and I find his boat—red, with painted vines twisting up the sides. It sways against its restraints as I walk up the gangplank—do they call them gangplanks on houseboats, or is that just pirate ships? Everyone wants to be a pirate these days so it doesn't matter. Unless you've been got by an actual pirate leaping on a cruise ship. Old-style pirates would never do that.

The door is down three uneven steps and features a knocker that I've seen in Hammer Horror films, ones accompanied by a brick-headed butler, a power cut and a comely hostess with uncommonly pointed incisors. I knock and the door is nudged open, on the latch. Robert appears through a bead curtain at the end of a narrow corridor, holding a white sauce-coated wooden spoon. He hurries up to meet me, thumps me on the back with his spare hand and steps back for me to enter. We squeeze through the hall where Robert points out two small bedrooms and bathroom, and down a few steps into a living room with a sofa, an armchair and bookcases built into the walls. The smell of cooking comes from the tiny kitchen at the other end behind saloon doors.

Robert retreats into the kitchen. 'Sit down, would you?' he calls through. 'I need to clear things away. Help yourself to wine,' he says.

A bottle and two glasses have been placed on a small round table. I pour myself a large glass of blackberry-dark red wine, my hand shaking. I peek through the heavy curtains over the portholes. The walls of the Cam bob up and down. There is a pile of papers on a small desk next to me, and more in a magazine rack on the floor next to a large present wrapped in red ribbon. I check that Robert is occupied then flick through printouts of articles; student essays with his looping handwriting all over them; pairs of old tickets to concerts and the theatre but nothing more personal. There aren't even any pictures of family.

Robert comes through wiping his hands on a

dishcloth. 'I thought it was time I shared a secret with you,' he says. He looks tired and resigned. He waves towards the tiny gallery kitchen: 'After you,' he says.

I lean against the work surface, my pulse rising like the water level in a lock. 'Well?' I say.

'Patience,' he says, 'that's what's needed in all things.' He clatters in cupboards, pulling down mixing bowls and whisks, oil and vinegar and mustard. Reaching into a wicker bowl, he collects four eggs in one hand.

'This is it. Your big secret.'

'I told you in that first lecture that it is one of the things that men should achieve. And I am determined to help you achieve it. There won't be a woman alive who can resist you once you can whip up home-made chips and fresh mayonnaise for a movie night at home.'

'And how would you know?'

'What do you mean?' he says, frowning. I can't tell whether he's joking.

I press on. 'Robert, I thought we were trying to find a way to catch Jackamore.'

'I thought you were trying to find a way to catch me,' he says, lightly. 'You've told the police everything I've told you in confidence.'

'And have you been absolutely honourable in your dealings with me?' I ask him.

We each hold the other's gaze for a moment, then let go.

'Well then,' I say.

'The secret of the best mayonnaise,' he says, 'is getting the emulsion right. It is the right balance between the oil and the water, egg yolks being half water. There is a symbiosis, a pairing of twin

331

pillars, a joining that takes two allied ingredients and transforms them. It goes from a sickly hue to pure and white, from the texture of semen to soft whipped peaks.'

This is ridiculous. 'Robert, I don't want to know about your mayonnaise and emulsions. I want to know who the last victim is going to be and whether I can save her; I want to find Jackamore Grass and not murder him because then I will know I am a better man than he, though he deserves it.'

Robert stops pouring oil into the bowl. 'So you see now, how a murder could take place? The righteous anger on one side or both, the justifications and excuses for not stepping out. Isn't that stunning?'

'Doesn't that tell you that death isn't beautiful at all, that all this theorising is a load of bollocks?'

'Stephen, I am disappointed in you. Look, can't you think of this from a professional point of view, a paper on the metaphysics of suicide and murder, being and non-being, all that nonsense? It's so unusual, and people already know your face and voice.'

'You think it's all nonsense.'

'Listen, imagine how proud your parents will be to see you head up a groundbreaking study.'

'There is no one here to mind. My mother is dead,' I say. 'She died when I was seven and I have no idea what would make my father proud.'

'I didn't know that about your mother,' Robert says. His voice is low, floor level, slinking over the rug towards me. 'It is interesting, the parallels between us, Stephen. My mother was killed in Krakow when I was small, smaller than you were. Julia, my sister, and I were handed over to my

332

great-aunt and we shared a room in her house in Sidcup. My aunt had been just about blonde enough to survive, that and shagging an SS officer for a pass out of the country.' He shrugs. 'Well you would, wouldn't you? She was the one who taught us about the importance of aesthetics: it can save your life. While others lose theirs.' His face puckers like the skin on top of cooling milk as he frowns, looking past me as if into memory.

Something feels wrong, staged, twisted. There's an undercurrent and my skin rises into pimples as the familiar sensation of the past presses up against the present, trying to force its way through. I close my eyes. Something turns inside me, an instinct to run. I know that I've been drawn into something that will cost me more if I don't get out now, even if I never find out where Miranda went.

Opening my eyes, I stare at Robert. 'I'm sorry about your family, Robert, that's terrible. But you aren't studying the beauty of death. I don't know what you *are* doing, but it is not something that I want to be involved in. Find someone else to experiment with. Or on.' I swipe aside the strings of clacking beads and storm. The door slams; the houseboat shifts in the river.

Halfway across Jesus Green, dew soaking into the hole in my trainers, I stop. What am I doing? I've let him goad me away from finding anything out. I'm leaving with nothing other than his family history and a partial recipe for mayonnaise.

I turn back towards the boat, forming words of apology. I push open the front door and am about to call out when I hear him.

'No! I couldn't stop him,' he shouts. 'I can't exactly wrestle him to the ground and tell him to do my bidding.' He's in the lounge, his back to me, holding the mobile between his ear and shoulder, nodding as he listens to whoever is on the phone. His hand strokes his own hair. 'I'm so sorry, I shouldn't yell at you.' His voice is now as soft as Yorkshire water. 'It's not your fault, I know that. And I know that we need him. I want a perfect murder as much as you do.' Silence. 'Please don't think I'm not doing everything I can. It hurts that you would think that.' He walks out of my sight and hearing toward the kitchen and I slip back out of the door, feeling more alone than ever before.

Chapter Sixty-Three

Christmas Eve

'When have you said you'll return to work?' Dr Pindar says after taking Jane through the procedure for what feels like the hundredth time. She has a form to fill in, recording what she is feeling and doing at various times of the day. That can go straight into the recycling bin.

'I've got leave till day after Boxing Day,' she says. She hasn't told anyone apart from Pemberton. It will only cause those looks of pity and fear, and people crossing the corridor to stay away from you. And her boss would send her home with a smirk at the same time as calling in one of his favourites from Ely. It happened before. She's not going to let it happen in Cambridge. Her tit would have to lump it. She giggled. Lump it. She laughs more and it shakes the tears out.

*   *   *

The choir in the corridor sing *O Holy Night* and, although she'd never tell anyone, it soothes her and makes her want to curl up with *A Christmas Carol* and mulled wine.

*   *   *

The anaesthetist's mask sucks in and out as he fiddles with knobs and equipment that beep and breathe. 'Now soon you will be feeling very tired, Jane,' he says, placing the black mask over her face. Panic rises above Jane's Plimsoll line: she's going under and may not come out again. She counts the people she can see in the operating theatre. When she wakes up she won't have any breasts. Like the upside down calculator trick that she did in school to spell 55378008: there was a girl who was 13, had size 84 breasts and wanted size—

Chapter Sixty-Four

Christmas Eve

Faith did not leach out of me, slowly draining until one day I woke up and found myself parched. It was flushed out and didn't refill. I tried; after all I'd wavered before, faith tugging back and forth, a tide that came right up to me then ebbed away on a daily basis. It's like a lock where two levels, rationality and the higher level, are made to move into one place so that you can sail across and now it's like I can't make the lock-keeper appear anymore. What does it matter? Life without God is very much life with God, only there's no reason to follow the rules. No reason not to kill.

Chapter Sixty-Five

Christmas Eve

I was lucky to get a seat. All of the carriages are full. Overhead storage space is spilling over with gifts and poinsettias and coming-home luggage. As the train travels north and the day gets darker, a measure of seasonal spirit is passed round: a spotty boy plays carols out of his phone, a woman shares a bag of homemade peppermint creams and people ask each other where they are going. The young woman in the seat opposite is from Robin Hood's Bay. At least I think that's what she said: her voice is muffled by the bulging bag of presents in her lap that reaches up to her nose. She wraps her arms around it with a small smile on her face. I wish I were the one she, or someone like her, was coming home to. Or that I was coming home to Lana.

I stayed away from North Yorkshire for years, partly because of Da, but also because of the hallucinations I had there. But what if I had been time-travelling and not dreaming? I could have been travelling for years. One Easter, I passed two men in Edwardian dress arguing about a dog. It had bitten the leg of the taller man and now sat, hunched over, licking itself. And then a baseball-capped child rode her bicycle through all three of them. I put it down to bad beer and too many horror movies. But both Iris and I think I was two-timing, and now I want to bring it on. I want control.

*   *   *

Da switches on the telly. A blond boy pours out a thin stream of voice: 'Once in Royal David's City'. Carols from King's. The shots of Cambridge make me think of Robert and how Lana is and how she has probably found someone else and is having festive sex under a fir tree.

But I'm leaving all that behind. I flick at a bauble on our plastic tree. It hits the window and rolls back near my foot. There's a crack in its silver seam.

'That was your mother's,' Da says, not looking up from the *News of the World*. He thumps down an empty can of Special Brew to the collection surrounding the untouched pile of last year's mince pies. You can't get more Christmas than that. 'You going to Midnight Mass,' he says. It isn't a question.

'Thought I'd go down the Black Heart, see if Schoony's around.' Most of all, I hope Satnam will be there as usual, winning at pool and chatting up barmaids. Surely, pissed, on Christmas Eve, he will forgive me.

'Saw Schoony's dad other day. Says Simon's off travellin'. Won't be back till May. Least he's done sumthin' afore pissin' off, worked with his da this last six year. Takin' over when he gets back.'

'I'll have a pint anyway.'

'Father O'Malley's after you. He confirmed you—and after your mother wasn't.'

'Mum didn't need to be confirmed; she didn't believe. It's your religion.'

'Not that it would've made a difference, seeing as, you know.'

'I know, Da.'

On the telly, the camera swoops up to the ceiling of King's Chapel. Wordsworth called it something like a branching roof, scooped into ten thousand cells and I'm thinking it's a line-up of sliced lungs.

'We'll go round eleven, get in front row—it's quicker up to get the Host.'

All the words that are pooling in my head and the one that rises to the surface—'okay,'—lies there dead, all the flesh stripped off.

*   *   *

Outside the church, sitting on a gravestone, I dab a red lollipop into a sherbet dip. It's what I used to do all the time as a teenager—sit on the Whitby clifftop watching the castle go from ruin to pristine and back again. That was not daydreaming, and speed could be the reason. And old places. The common denominator. This church is sixteenth century, and there was a Saxon church here before that. I rattle the lollipop over my teeth so the sugar eats into my gums and digs into my bloodstream. My head is fuggy from the three quick beers in the pub. I would have stayed longer, but Satnam came in, saw me and walked straight back out again. Goodwill to all.

*   *   *

My bum is numb by the time the Eucharist is announced. Father O'Malley's manicured hands rest on the golden eagle on the lectern. The murmur of the congregation drops to an expectant hush. Da squeezes past me; he wants to be the first to receive Christ.

I tip the packet into my mouth. It fizzes against my tongue strings. Kneeling next to Da at the rail, I stick my tongue out and O'Malley rests a round wafer on it, a hand on my head. The goblet of cheap red appears in my eyeline and I swill it round my mouth, washing down the rest of the powder. It's bitter, drying my throat out like Yorkshire tea.

'Bless you,' O'Malley says and I immediately feel time flicking its pages around me. The same ritual, the same incense, the singing that soars into the rafters for centuries, and I feel pulsing in my fingers and neck and groin and wrists and know if I simply reached and focused without focusing I could get to another time.

I don't go back to my seat; instead I take one of the hanging censers from the wall and, feeling Da's stare between my shoulder-blades, I open the door and, step out into the cold.

On the steps outside I close my eyes and swing the censer by my face. The cold and memories are making my heart race, the incense slowing it and I am freewheeling but consciously. All is now. I feel a lurch and an icepick pain pins the centre of my forehead.

'Would you move out of the way, please,' a man says, nudging me with his cane.

He stares down at me, as does a woman holding her cloaks tightly around her. They are looking at me as if I could jump up and rob them.

I jump up.

They jump back.

I could do this all night. 'I am sorry to inconvenience you,' I say, leaning against the wall. 'But I seem to find myself inebriated. I blame the Eucharist wine. Very potent tonight. Be sure to partake. As a result of this intoxication,' I say, 'I seem to have forgotten the year, as well as any appropriate clothes.'

The man stands between the woman and me. 'It is 1635,' he says. 'As you are aware.' They step inside and a great big laugh escapes me. I can do it at will now. I jump into shadows as if they were puddles. I am a traveller. But only to the same year. At the moment. But I know I've done it before and just have to get something back I never knew I had. All those times I thought I was losing my mind, instead I was losing time, and gaining it. I will go back to Cambridge; I couldn't hand my notice in till next month anyway, but I will be in charge now, less running about without a head, not knowing what to do; more running about without a head in control of time and Grass.

340

Back home and back in my own time, from my bedroom window I watch the sea that Mum died in. I remember the dress she died in but it's the colour of the sea that stays with me. That day was the kind of Mediterranean blue that says holidays and ice-cream and that nothing can go wrong. That kind of blue makes me suspicious.

Tonight the sea is rough, snatched up and dropped by the wind. The waves, picked out by streetlights, are white and frothy as if a plane-load of Santa beards cracked overhead and they are now crashing onto the shore. The shore. And I am there again, seeing Mum in the sea, and there is the man holding out his hand as if to press down on her head and she is gone and she is dead.

I turn away from the window and fetch the stocking down from the top of my cupboard. It hasn't been filled since Mum died, which gave the game away, but I put it out anyway, hanging it from the mantel of the whistling fireplace. Some of the felt letters that spelt out my name have fallen off over the years so now there's only STEP. I'm missing my hen. I also remember the night that I found out that Father Christmas didn't exist. It was a few months after Mum died, Christmas time. They'd taken ages to release her body, 'give her back' as Da said. Eventually she was cremated as she wasn't allowed to be buried in St Michael's graveyard.

'She's not in heaven, then?' I say.

'I've told you. No, she is not in heaven.' He spits out 'heaven' like it was a bad almond.

'What 'bout man in sea with her?'

341

'There was no man in the sea with her. Just her, on her own.'

'I saw him, Daddy.'

The slap comes from across the table. My cheek burns. I push my peas into the holes of the burnt potato waffle on my plate. It looks like a wooden portcullis in my toy castle. I remember how proud I was when I learned the word portcullis and how that doesn't matter now. Da stares out the window at the sea. I don't like doing that much.

'Does heaven not exist then?'

'Don't be blasphemous, Stephen Killigan.'

'What 'bout ghosts?'

'Ghosts are real enough.'

'What 'bout fairies?'

'I won't hear about fairies in this house.'

'What 'bout—'

'Why can't you accept what you've been told? Heaven exists, ghosts exist, God exists—fairies don't and neither does fucking Father Christmas so don't ask me 'bout him neither.'

I wait up though, in case Da is wrong and Father Christmas plummets down the chimney. It's not as if I want to sleep as that is where dreams live. Dreams exist, that's for sure.

*   *   *

The walls of my room billow and I feel the same reeling feeling as when I went into the past and I stare and stare and try and hold on to the nail in the wall and in my head are the faces of the dead. Cambridge is calling me back, a grey ghost in my peripheral vision.

My nose is bleeding. In the stained mirror above

the mantel I see dried red lines running down my chin from the corners of my mouth like I'm a vampiric ventriloquist's dummy. Happy Christmas.

Chapter Sixty-Six

The Homeless Man

Someone has scratched 'YOU ARE DEAD' on the train window. Charming. Is that a threat? Or a statement? I trace my finger over the rough edges in the glass, put my feet up on the seat opposite, pick at the yellow innards of the seat tufting up through the faded blue fabric. The fens spool past, flat as green dough running through a pasta machine. I'm used to the Yorkshire moors: ground that ducks and rears and dives away, heather-pubed and full of bodies, holes and secrets. On the fens you can see for miles but that just means the secrets are deeper, hidden beneath the grasses, beneath the ground, swirling in water that could be drained at any moment. I can feel them now, the secrets of the fens and this part of the east country, pulsing under the skin of the present. That skin has got thinner for me. I can't ignore things anymore. I have to finish with Dawn, properly, and find the truth, as all philosophers try, and fail, to do.

*   *   *

Somewhere near Doncaster, it starts to snow. The flakes at first are small and light and whipped all ways by the wind, then they swell and fall and

343

dust-sheet the ground.

By the time I'm back in Cambridge, the streets and pavements are all one and the same, all white, with any tracks from cars or feet or cold-toed birds covered over in minutes. Snow makes me feel lonely.

I try Satnam: his phone rings twice then goes through to his voicemail. He's still rejecting my calls.

And then I do what you're not supposed to do around New Year: I phone Lana and feel my heart step up to hard house tempo when it rings, but it keeps ringing. And ringing. Till I make it stop.

Iris does at least answer her phone. 'What are you doing calling me at this time in the morning?' she asks.

'It's three in the afternoon, Iris.'

'Are you sure?'

'According to my watch.'

'Do you think I trust those things?' I can hear her shuffling across the room in her slippers. Her voice is clipped and terse.

'Do you mind if I come round?' I ask. I have an urge to hug her.

There is one of those pauses that no one wants to give or receive.

'Don't worry,' I say, stepping in quickly. 'It was only a thought. I wanted to see if you were okay, that's all.'

'Oh I'm fine,' she says. 'Nothing like spending Christmas on your own, doing exactly what you want, to remind you that you're better off that way. I spent all of yesterday beating myself at board games. It was all very good-tempered till it got to Monopoly. And the charades, well, that turned very nasty. But Twister was fun. I'm having a lazy day today to compensate for all the festivities. How was your Christmas?'

'Interesting,' I say. 'I realised that I've been travelling in and out of times since I was a child.'

'But of course you have. What else would you be doing? Well, I must go. I promised myself a bowl of brandy butter. Good morning, Stephen.' She puts the phone down.

I get off by the taxi rank and stand up to my calves in snow. The city is crystalised and the sky is grey and gravid with more to come. I don't want to be alone.

*   *   *

Robert slams a drawer shut in his desk. 'I'm glad you phoned, Stephen. I think we should celebrate your return with a pre-New Year celebration. How do you fancy a volta?'

'I doubt it,' I reply. Being near Robert makes my skin itch. But I did agree with Jane that this could be a way to catch him.

'As you well know,' he says, 'a volta in a sonnet is the point at which the poem switches and becomes personal.'

'Or universal.'

'Yes. Or both. And in modern Greek, as you may equally well know, it is to take a turn, by car or perambulation, in which you let instinct dictate where you go. In short, an adventure.'

'I like adventures. Enid Blyton is a big favourite of mine.'

'Ah yes, George the tomboy. Anyway, this will be *Two Go to the Town Centre*.'

345

'You know how to live, Robert.'

He stands up and smoothes back his hair showing a deep 'V' shape in his hairline that I'm sure wasn't there before.

*   *   *

The fast food queues curl around the market. Robert steps back from the van with a Styrofoam container of eased-off meat and chips that remind me of the night I found Miranda. Chilli sauce has been lobbed on the top. He passes me the box but I shake my head.

'You don't know what you're missing,' he says. 'This is the best enema known to man. If the Romans had had kebabs, they would have their own altar in the corner of the Colosseum.'

*   *   *

I should have brought a hat and some gloves. I wrap my coat around me. It still smells of Dawn's perfume. Dawn. I didn't even think to phone her when the lonelies came.

A firework coughs up over the marketplace. It hangs over us before fading into the sky. Another rocket wheezes up. Three men point at it. I recognise them; they were the ones who set on Lana. Now they are smiling with childlike delight. I wish there weren't fireworks.

I don't know why we all go 'ooh' and 'aah' at them when we are en masse, sighing over man-made stars that die before us, building up into a fizzing finale of pops and shouts and then, when we believe it over, a resuscitated spark shoots out zigzagging on the blank screen above before flatlining and the sky is dark, the air full of smoke and then there's the long walk home in two pairs of socks that bite at the ankles.

Robert shoves the container into the too-full bin and we walk off past the parade of shops with their posh signs swinging, past 'Cindy's' and I think of leaving Robert and going inside to dance, my feet sticking to the floor, knocking glasses off tables with arms that flail too wildly, being recognised by a student and that being the most complicated situation of the evening.

Robert keeps walking, his head down. 'Stop dawdling, Stephen,' he calls back.

'I thought we were volta-ing,' I shout to him.

'Don't be facetious. And don't turn a noun into a verb without apologising first. You're worse than my students.'

I follow him into the small bandstand opposite the entrance to Lion Yard. The nearest lamp-post is out bar the occasional flicker and there are no lights in the bandstand. Which is probably good for the old man curled up on copies of *Varsity* on the bench. Robert reaches into his jacket pocket and pulls out a long thin packet.

Ripping off the top of the packet, he hands me a sparkler, and a lighter. I light mine, then his and stand with the sparkler spitting in my hand.

'Hold this for me,' he says, passing me the sparkler. They giggle in my fists and I stroke the sparks against the air, drawing circles, squares then a name in the air. It is lucky that 'Lana' is short.

The last letter of her name ebbs. Paper rustles on the other side of the bandstand. Robert stands over the old man, a paring knife in one hand, the

347

other pressed down on the man's neck. He looks at me, blinking. The sparklers burn down to my fingers and Robert jabs the knife at the man's ribs. I try to shout, but it comes out as a strangled scream. I drop the sticks. Robert tuts, slinks over to me and bends to pick them up. I walk over to the old man. His eyes are still, his blood slowing with no heart to pump it round. Unable to feel my fingers and toes, I place my hands on his chest and close his eyes. They feel like crepe paper. I shouldn't be relieved to see no wedding ring, as if that was all right. I try and feel for his pockets, and finger inside for a wallet, anything that will tell me his name, where he had come from, why he was there on the bench on New Year's Eve, unable to see the tie-dyed sky above him.

A hand pulls at my shoulder. The man on the bench recedes as I am yanked away.

'Did you see it?' Robert asks as we walk slowly down Trinity Street. 'The beauty of murder?'

The whole event lasted a minute, maybe less, maybe more, but the images chargrilled. There are lines scored right through me now. I lean and vomit over the railings. I don't feel cold anymore. I don't feel anything. We pass The Curry King. The river is now at our feet, flowing over stones as if there is no trouble at all in the world. Rushing down into the weir. We stroll—how could we be strolling, how could I be walking next to him and where did the sparklers go and how can I be thinking of that and what do I do now and how many questions can fit inside a head before it implodes?

The police, that's what happens now. That is what happens when someone is murdered in front of you and you are holding sparklers like you are a stupid cocktail. There's a cocktail called a Zombie and that's what I was and what I am, a fucking zombie, with nothing in my mind apart from a man dying in my eyes.

I lurch forward, bend over and release more sick into the Cam. It fans out, some of my dinner sinking, most going the way of the water into the weir.

We stop at his houseboat. I force my mind to work, chewing round what happened like a brown bit in an apple. I have to get away, but not anger him. I'm an eyewitness now, that he is a murderer, the murderer.

Chapter Sixty-Seven

The Homeless Man Illusion

One day, when my book is published, people will know of my performance last night. They will not believe that I got away with it. Perhaps I have not. Judging from the way Stephen has filled in the noughts and crosses so that he is about to make himself lose, I think I have won.

All it took was some stage make-up, clothes matured in a bag of old flannels for four days and an ability to relax so entirely even in stressful situations that a panicking man would not detect the slight heartbeat.

Chapter Sixty-Eight

Conscience

I wake up with my hands over my face. It's five in the morning, the fire is still on and I'm sweating cobs, the drips cooling as they run down my back.

I'm lying curled up on the floor.

My heart is going too fast.

I can't see the cat. What if she got too close to the fire? I try to get up but my legs have gone numb and turned a shade of blue-grey.

And then I remember last night in reverse: the sleeping on the floor; the thinking that lying on the floor was a good idea; the taxi back as I could barely speak; the spasms in my stomach whenever I thought of blood.

Reality is being shaken and shaken so that nothing ever settles. Every time I begin to make sense of what's going on, the snowflakes melt.

'Mao.' Gingerbread stalks through from my bedroom. She's all warm, so she did the sensible thing and actually got into bed last night.

'What would you do, Gingerbread?' I ask. She stretches out a paw and snags herself in my jumper.

I stare down at my clothes and panic seizes me. What if there's the homeless man's blood on my clothes? I didn't think to check after last night. I think I'm okay though. Robert hadn't been covered in blood. He had been surprisingly bloodless. Bile rises but my stomach doesn't have anything to be sick with. It rumbles its objections, asks for more ammunition.

I get out of bed, a mechanical man, and walk over to the mirror. I do look terrible. At least I can scrape the hair off my face. I breathe in, breathe out. Amazing how lungs keep on working, heart keeps on churning.

Satnam's snores float through the floor. They used to reassure, now they say that he doesn't care, that anything could be happening to me and it wouldn't matter because his pride has been hurt. I stamp on the ceiling just to show him. The snores stop—he might come up—we could talk, and I could tell him everything and he would laugh at it or say that it could be worse, I could be dead and I wouldn't be so lonely—

The snoring starts again.

I spin through the names in my phone for *someone* I could call. My finger pauses over Lana, and then I scroll up again.

Chapter Sixty-Nine

Not Again

'Jane Horne,' she says, her voice strained and muffled. Every time she moves, pain like a red marker pen is scraped across her skin and digs into her ribs. She holds her chest.

'I think I was an accomplice in a murder last night.'

'Who is this?' she says.

'I'm sorry, this is a bad time. I'll phone back tomorrow.'

351

'Is this Stephen?'

'It is.'

She eases herself out of bed, avoiding looking at herself in the wardrobe mirror. 'Well I'm sorry, Stephen,' she says, going through into the kitchen. 'But confessing to murder is not something that you can do and then say you'll fill me in later. Thanks to you I now have to get out of bed. Now if I heard correctly you said that *you think* you committed murder.'

'No, I think I was an *accomplice* in a murder.'

'How can you think that? Wouldn't that be something you know?' She turns on the tap and fills the kettle, the phone on hands-free as she needs both to hold the kettle. The muscles in her armpit scream.

'I'm not sure I know anything anymore.'

'Well that's great. You'll be as much use as a pot of yogurt in court if I have to use you as a witness, unless you are indeed a murderer in which case you can be declared insane and put away. Which would suit me as I wouldn't have to be woken up at all hours to hear your confessions. Don't you have a church or something?'

'Can we meet somewhere?' His voice sounds urgent, desperate. Pleading.

'I don't think that would be appropriate.' But it would be nice, someone to take her mind off things. She wraps a robe around her and sits down cross-legged on the sofa. 'Tell me a bedtime story then: whom did you help to kill?'

'Please don't be so flippant,' Stephen says. 'I was with Robert. He wanted to show me more in his experiments. We agreed, didn't we, that I would go along with it, to see if he incriminated

352

himself? Well he did. He knifed a homeless man. It happened before I could do anything about it.' He lets out a huge sigh.

'Feel better now?' she asks over the rumblings of the kettle.

'Like someone has undone a band that has been wrapped round my chest,' he says.

She freezes for a moment. Then shakes her head. He can't know. 'Well I'm glad you feel like that, Dr Killigan. Where did this happen?'

She picks up a pen and writes down the address. 'I'll meet you there.'

*   *   *

Pemberton says nothing when he picks her up, just sighs several times and changes the radio station back to Lovelorn FM or whatever it is he and a million melancholic taxi drivers like to listen to.

Stephen is already there by the bandstand when they pull up next to it. He is crouching down, staring under the seating. His hand is rubbing at his head. He turns. 'I don't know what to say,' he says. 'He's gone.'

'The homeless man,' Jane says.

'Yes.'

'The one you thought was dead.'

'Yes.'

Pemberton breathes in noisily. He can show disdain in so very many different ways.

'I would have to say, then, that he was not really dead.'

'But you said that could have been a possibility with Miranda,' he says, nodding as if trying to convince both them and himself.

Chapter Seventy

Temple of Doom

The lecture hall is full. I feel like Indiana Jones standing in front of students with love notes written on their fluttering lashes. And I keep on losing my place.

'So, how can we know what reality is?' I ask.

Richard, one of my students, slams his hand on the table. 'I know the table is real because I hit it and my hand hurts as a consequence and my eyes saw it.'

'Your eyes *perceived* it,' I say. 'There is a difference.'

'I perceived it too,' Samaria, another student, says, leaning forward so I can see her cleavage.

'But did you experience pain?' I ask.

She shakes her head and her chest follows. 'It wasn't *my* hand that smacked the table.'

'Are you sure?' I ask. I bend down into the cupboard under my lectern. I pull out a rubber arm. 'I was going to demonstrate this later in the lecture series but I think this is an ideal opportunity. Samaria, would you come up here please?'

I move the table from the back of the stage forward and ask her to sit facing the side of the room, her right hand behind her back and a mirror stood up in front of it. I then place the rubber arm where you would expect her right one to be.

She stares down at her arm. 'Urgh,' she says. 'That's gross.'

'How dare you,' I say. 'That arm was modelled

354

on my great Uncle Bertie's. He was very good with his hand.'

The lecture hall laughs. I've turned into Robert.

'Now keep on looking in the mirror,' I say. I direct her head to the mirror so she can't play up to the audience—that's my job.

After a short time of her staring into the mirror, I reach out and touch the rubber arm.

She screams. 'I felt that!' she says.

'Did you?'

'Yes, well, no, well—'

'Did she?' I ask the audience.

'No', 'Yes', 'Depends', 'Can I have a go?', 'Fix', 'Trick', 'Bonkers', 'Freaky'—the replies tumble on top of each other.

'Right. Back to reality,' I say.

'How can you talk to us about reality, sir?' a boy in the back row asks. The 'sir' is heavily sarcastic. He looks familiar but I can't place him. One of the students I supervise from another college maybe.

'Good question. I stand up here and open my mouth and something called sound in the form of—'

'I mean, how can you talk about reality when you don't know what it is?' He holds up the local paper. There I am again, same picture, but a different headline. I step down from the stage and run up to the back. Snatching the paper from him, I read: LECTURER LIES AGAIN.

My knees are shaking and I feel myself grow faint, the edges of my sight clouding in and I can't tell whether I'm going to faint or travel in time.

*   *   *

I push open the door to Great St Mary's, sweating from the run from the Sidgwick site. I ran because I didn't want anyone following me, asking me what was wrong. After all, I might tell them. The actual vicar is restocking the books in the church shop. I turn to sit in the pews, hiding my face.

'Something wrong?' he says, his brow contracting. 'You look like death.'

He pats the stepladder for me to sit down. 'I'll put the kettle on, shall I?'

'There's really no need—I'm fine,' I say.

'Don't be so British about it,' he says. 'You're clearly not fine. A brew will sort you out.'

'I thought you said don't be so British.'

He laughs and putters off to a back room behind the shop.

I put my head in my hands, try and slow my breathing, tell myself it will be okay. My hair is so oily, it feels like I've rubbed fat on it instead of gel. Taking my hands away, I see a dash of blood on my fingers where I cut myself shaving. I'm in a mess.

'Tea. And a spoonful of sugar for shock.' The vicar places the mug gently between my hands. The tea is the orange of an ancient Greek pot in the archaeology and anthropology museum.

'I haven't had a shock,' I say.

He ducks his head so he can see my eyes.

'You're lying again,' he says.

I wince. 'Okay, maybe I have. I'm not sure. What would you say to someone who is hallucinating, on a regular basis? Seeing bad things on a regular basis?'

'I would say "Be glad they aren't real, and try and cling to what is".'

I laugh and the sound echoes in the church,

356

sounding wrong. 'That's never been one of my strengths. I study metaphysics because it aims to find out what really is, not what is perceived.'

'I studied theology for much the same reason. My name's Roger, by the way.'

'And did you find what you were looking for, Roger?'

'And more,' he says, smiling at me. 'One thing I've found useful is the power of the seeming non-sequitur. Always keep people guessing, I say.'

'This place certainly does that.'

'Which do you mean?' Roger says. 'Great St Mary's or Cambridge?'

'Both, so Cambridge overall.'

'Yes, Cambridge does that. It keeps you hooked by giving a little sugar then turning away.'

'Are you saying that the city plays hard to get?'

Roger laughs. 'More like she's an Ice Queen, beautiful and cold and luring you in with promises while slipping a sliver of ice in your heart.'

'Why are you here then?' I ask.

The church door opens and the vicar slips off the desk. A a man walks down the aisle and, looking around as if doing something wrong, lights a candle with a shaking hand. I haven't done that in a long time. I had almost forgotten I was in a church but suddenly the heavy hush is loud and clear in my ears. It is twilight now, and blue light streams through the windows, placing a filter over the stone. It feels safe in here, like when I built a sandcastle on the beach out of reach of the sea. I don't know what's wrong with me—all these childhood and adolescent memories. I feel trapped in an old school scrapbook.

'There have been legends about this church since

the tower was built in 1608. The usual ghost stories that any old place attracts—'

'Don't tell me: an old monk and a grey lady. There's always a grey lady.'

He laughs. 'The main ones are Erasmus, who was a Professor of Divinity at Cambridge and lectured in here—people claim they see him reading in his robes, mouthing words, in a corner of the church—and Martin Bucer. He was buried here but when Queen Mary ascended to the throne she had him tried for heresy and insisted that his remains and books be burned. His ghost is said to stand where he was originally buried, clutching his books and looking sweaty. People have seen him who don't even know the story.'

'You don't expect to see a sweaty ghost, do you? Clanking in chains, going whoo, pointing obscurely, but not sweating. Spectres are not supposed to perspire.'

Roger shrugs. 'I have not seen either of them here. But I have seen other things.'

Maybe it's happened to him; maybe he knows what is happening to me. 'What have you seen?'

'Things moving in the corner of my eye. Incense smoke when I haven't burned any. And I keep on experiencing déjà vu, as if I've been here in another time.'

'Maybe you have.'

He smiles. 'Maybe I have.'

Chapter Seventy-One

The Masquerade

I tuck the invitation from Jackamore to the masquerade ball in the pocket of the seventeenth-century suit that Iris helped me pick out a from a tailor who looked like he was from the nineteenth century, all twirling fingers, shuffling eyebrows and obsequious 'sirs'. I kept asking Iris whether we had travelled back in time and she hit me on the back in denial. But I'm still not sure.

It is January dark, the kind of dark that seems to have swallowed up the living world, perfect for lurking round corners of a college that has changed very little in this part of the layout and walking into another century. I pass the huge oak tree in the small court and think of its smaller self waving to me. I wish I could see it grow, skip years and stroll back from the first wave to the time its roots spread so deep into the college it threatens to expose its foundations and is cut down.

I need Jackamore. I need his brain, his experience. He is the one who holds all the information on how I can travel properly in time, pinpoint a date and reach it as easily as a letter in a dictionary. I need him to be able to stop him.

My heart has jumped up to pound at my ears as if screaming *run away*. Iris asked me earlier if I was scared and I bluffed at first and said no, but I am. I am more scared than I have ever been. My body is sweating and sending blood to my legs and telling them to run, run, run away and most of my brain says the same but the part I am listening to says 'Do it, who cares, he challenged me—besides, there is no one to give a fuck whether I live or die or live my life in another time'. I walk into the shadowed passage that connects the small court to the even smaller one . . .

. . . and slam into a wall.

'What are you doing?' a tall dog shouts.

The feathered woman with him rearranges her skirts.

'I'm very sorry,' I say, backing away.

My brain is firing with dissonance—dog—legs—feathers—

Masks—wall—masquerade ball. I've travelled without trying.

Jackamore was right. It is easier to travel when you have no connections. I have to be more careful and keep to areas I know are clear passageways otherwise I might end up inside a wall next time, with no way of getting out.

At the entrance to the Great Hall, I hear Charles's voice behind me. 'I thought you might be here!' he says. He winks at me behind a lion's empty eye.

'Did you?' I say. 'And who would have told you about that?' I put on my fox mask.

The huge door opens and a page, long-haired and wigless, trots down the hall in front of us, our names in his hand.

The hall is lit by candles winking at mirrors, blinking at more mirrors, in a selective, reflexive, unending trompe l'oeil: hundreds of men and women swirl as masked ghosts in the walls, their skirts taking up the floor. A girl in a fox mask bobs at me, and I bob back. She laughs, and the fox face

360

is friendlier.

A cat curtsies to a grinning bear then slips off into the forest of animal faces. The trumpet blasts and I turn with the menagerie to see who is being announced, hoping for the king. It'd be something to see a dead king living; the last of the kings with real power.

Everyone else turns back, disappointed—it's not the king—and I keep staring. I don't catch the name, but I know it. He is holding the mask against his face, the pale stone catching the candlelight. I turn to Charles, but he is bowing to a woman and opening his arms.

Jackamore is dressed in dark brown and moves with a dancer's grace through the crowd, twisting, raising arms high, showing thin white wrists. My fox face smashing on the floor, I jostle after him through the whirling tufty ears and bared teeth and eyes who glare at my bare face as he moves towards the far end of the hall. I lose him for a moment, then catch a flash of white mask as he ducks behind a large tapestry.

It seems like an age of armpits before I reach it, and lift the edge of the wall hanging, expecting to find him hiding, but there is only a door and beyond the door, a low-ceilinged corridor, and the sound of running footsteps. My lungs are lit from the inside as I sprint after him. Turning a corner, I see him, mask facing me, a tall man in a cracked moon, then he twists, and his cloak flares down stairs into the wine cellar.

Reaching the top, I can't see the bottom of the stairs, but can hear breathing, and dripping, and smell vinegar. Shoes slipping on the steps, I reach for walls that feel as if they are covered in seaweed and slowly walk down.

Something slams against my shoulder-blades, and I career forward into darkness, my shins smashing against stone steps; white pain explodes in my head and I fall, tumbling, to the bottom and lurch face down into water. I panic, turning over, but it's not deep, only to my knees. Licking my lips to stop the blood, I taste something acidic, and sweet. I'm ankle-deep in wine. I take my phone out of my jacket pocket. It doesn't look too wet. I place it on a barrel to dry.

'It is a pleasure to meet you at last, Stephen,' Jackamore says. He stands at the top of the stairs. 'To meet you properly, I mean. I believe you have seen me before. I, of course, have seen you many times, which puts me at an advantage and you in a position of being greatly flattered.' His voice is deep and banister-smooth. I try to make out his face in the dark but I can't. He still holds up the mask.

'I can't say I feel flattered,' I reply. I try and move and shout out in pain.

'You seem to be having some trouble. Can I assist you?' he asks. 'I'm trained in medicine. It comes in extremely useful in my current line of work.'

'You are a sick bastard.'

'No, Stephen. I am in the peak of physical fitness. If you are referring to my mental health then consider this: I do what everybody else would love to. Somewhere. Deep down. Beneath the morals is mischief and murder.'

'Most people choose not to,' I say, grimacing as I pull myself forward on my hands and knees. The wine enters my mouth and I lift my chin. It seems to be getting higher, or maybe I'm slinking lower.

Jackamore sits on the top step. 'I am not most people.' He takes off the mask and I can make out his face. Just.

'The funny thing is that most people think that. But they have a voice in their head that persuades them that they can't be.' I edge onto the first step. The pain in my leg and one elbow is heat and I want to scream. I lift my arm and it is stained; I can't tell if it's wine or blood.

'I feel sorry for them, then.'

'You don't, though, do you?' I reply.

He laughs. 'No! I don't. If they cannot look after themselves then why should I? For example, why leave a wine cellar full of wine? You must know that at some point someone will feed the voice that says: "Go on, empty it, destroy it, see what happens and why stop there? Do them all!"'

'You did this?' I ask, looking around the cellar. I can now see bits of barrel floating on the surface.

'I was bored,' he says. I see him shrug.

Concentrate. You need him. 'How do you find the right time?' I ask.

'Good question. You seem to be floating from 2012 to 1635 and back again. Is that correct?'

I don't answer. Do not give him anything more than he has already; that's what Iris said.

'And this was the year *I* chose and found, and you followed me into it like a little puppy, and have been chasing me around ever since. With me leaving you the odd scrap of a body or tin of new friends. How do you find Charles Witt? It is unfortunate, do you not think, that he falls so short of his name? Humiliating really. I must

363

decide where I shall go next. I've never been to the eighth century, the dark ages. I doubt they are as dark as popularly thought, but I can always make things darker. The human heart does not change: the desire to murder is always there, ready to be formed. For example, should we need an example, it wouldn't take much to convince you to murder right now.'

'Yes, it would.' I turn away.

'Really? Do you think we are so different? That is arrogance for you, which I have in abundance. Just ask yourself how you are following me so precisely to this year. Do you think we are connected in some way?'

'No,' I say.

I am at the mid-point on the stairs. If I can only travel back to 2012, I may be stuck in the cellar but at least I will be away from him. I stare down into the wine, peeling back the skin of periphery thoughts into what is now, the smells, the pain that has my nerves and is twisting them in its pincered fist—

'What are you doing?' he says, coming closer. He shines a torch at me. 'You are trying to travel, aren't you! Oh it will be such fun when we learn to fly, little fledgling. You'll be able to visit any time that you choose when you have mastered the art. What kind of traveller are you, I wonder? A gentleman observer, a flaneur, content to be passive and watch?'

—the greyness is edging in to take over my eyes and—

'You remember what I said, don't you, Stephen?'

—wine, beer, mead, honey spice cloying sweetness that is marinating my skin and I can almost make out the future with my fingers and part the tissue that makes up the layers and step—

'I told you, did I not, that if you came after me you would give me no choice but to cause you to lose the one you love.'

'I do not have a love,' I say, slipping through. 'Sorry to disappoint—'

'No,' Jackamore Grass replies. 'You have two.'

'What?' I jolt back.

Goose bumps rally on my arms.

'Yes, two. Lana Carver, bright girl, would have had an interesting future, and Dawn Burley, somewhat dimmer but a life worth taking, all the same.'

'I am not with either of them anymore.'

'No, but unfortunately for them you love at least one of them and, I suspect, feel guilty about both. But you'll have the choice, if you can get back in time. I'll let you know where and when they are. If you have managed to master isolating time then you'll be able to save them.'

Jackamore Grass starts singing, a lilting parody of an Irish ballad that my mum used to sing.

The beautiful girls are dying so,
The beautiful girl is dead
The beautiful girls are dying
in their ticking beds
One will die
The chances are even
They made their choice
and so must Stephen
The beautiful girls are dying so,
The beautiful girl is dead
The beautiful girls are dying

in their ticking beds ...

'But they aren't yet,' I say. 'That's in the future.'

'They will be, however. They will be. You have a choice, Stephen,' Jackamore says, shuffling a pack of cards. 'And I don't envy your choice.'

'No,' I say.

'What?' Jackamore twists to face me.

'I won't choose. I do not have to choose.'

'You are the product of a time that thinks it can have everything. And this will be a valuable lesson for you. You'll have to choose. You are equidistant between the two. Both of them cannot live.'

'That is no choice or opportunity at all.'

'I know,' says Jackamore.

I charge up the steps. I don't know how I am moving but the anger fuels me and I reach out for him. I grip his arms and they are wiry as a tree and metal hard. He kicks at my leg and pushes me back again. 'Fuck you, you bastard.'

'Try getting back now,' he says, 'while thinking about Lana and Dawn being tortured. You will find it very difficult. I said I would help you travel and this is how I am doing it—removing the obstacles. Let yourself go: when there is no one to worry about, you are free to be wherever and whenever you choose. Believe me. Good luck, Stephen. I'll be back soon. Have fun down there.' The door heaves closed, and there is no light.

My right leg gives way as I try and get back up and I fall back and back into the cellar.

Chapter Seventy-Two

Strike

Stale fries in baskets; clanking braces and spit-ball machinery; strike celebrations from birthday parties: pins knocked down like outsized teeth. Every lane of the bowling alley is busy. The throwers are buzzing with the feeling that, while not quite Friday, it is close enough to sniff the feet of the weekend.

I have a lane to myself. The computer has been programmed to recognise four bowlers and I shall be playing all of them. Picking up the heaviest ball, I feed it my fingers and cradle it like an infant's head to my chest. With my eyes singling out the slender neck of the centre pin, I run to the line and release the ball, my hand outstretched as if a modern god on a secular frescoed ceiling.

I do not need to watch. The green ball will roll smoothly and swiftly with the slightest of arcs and the pins will lie down, defeated. I turn back to the plastic seats and shake my coat back on.

The pins make a clean crash as they fall. This is expected. My years as a surgeon honed my hand-eye co-ordination but I have always been exemplary in that area. I can shoot the hoot from an owl at 500 metres.

There is no sound of a strike. And there is no strike on the screen. Spinning back, I catch the automated clearance mechanism sweep a solitary remaining pin into the gulley. The green ball is vomited back up. I pick it up and, covering over its holes with the palm of my hand, walk over to the counter.

Dawn stands behind, her jaw ruminating on chewing gum. 'What size?' she asks every customer, never looking up to see whose feet she is shodding. She plucks the clown shoes from shabby cubes and sprays them with air freshener when returned. From what I have gleaned from the lavatory walls, Dawn will fuck you every which way as long as you bring her a top-up card for her mobile. This is perhaps not true. There are men who lie because they have been slighted.

I watch Ryan, the bowling alley manager, go out the back door for his break with Poppy. Poppy really should not go for her break for another half an hour but they would not be able to exchange intimacies with such satisfaction on their own. 'One of the balls is stuck in the clearing point,' I say to Dawn and point to the lane where the pin setter chamber has stopped with the pins in its teeth like a deranged dressmaker.

She looks around for Ryan, or Poppy. 'Is there anything that can be done?' I ask. 'I don't want to cause any trouble only I have to get back in twenty minutes.' I look suitably troubled by this scenario, and even more so at causing her aggravation.

'I'll have to go down to sort it out,' she says. She calls over the loudspeaker system. 'Would Poppy or Nadine come to the reception centre please.'

Nadine shuffles up to the counter. Her sparrow-brown hair is the sort that looks greasy even thirty minutes after washing.

'Look after the desk, would you?' Dawn says to her. 'Don't worry. It's really not that hard.'

Nadine stares at the shoes. Their tongues loll. She flips up the lid and stands behind the desk with her hands on top as if daring the whole building to a quickdraw gunfight.

'I'll come with you, if you like. It's my own bowling ball stuck down there,' I say. I lower my voice: you are not supposed to bring your own balls to this alley, presumably for this very reason. 'I don't want it confiscated if your boss sees it clogged up the setter.'

She winks. 'No problem. Come on.'

She leads me down the corridor and down into the basement to reset the machine. We are only halfway down when I stop. 'It's this way,' she says.

I reach into my bag and pull out the green bowling ball that hit all but one of the pins.

'I thought you didn't have your ball?' she says.

'You're not the brighter of the two, are you?' I say. 'Whatever did he see in you, other than oblivion?'

She steps back as I raise the ball above my head, but not far enough. Strike one.

Chapter Seventy-Three

Lana and Jane

Belinda pops her head round the door. Her hair has been sliced short and teased into points around her ears, making her look like a police pixie. 'There's a young woman in reception, ma'am, who says she needs to see you about Stephen Killigan. Name of,' Belinda checks on her notepad, 'Lana Carver.'

'Lana Carver. Lana Carver,' Jane says out loud. 'That's familiar for some reason. Sounds like an Edgar Allan Poe poem.'

Where does she know that name from?

The image in her head is of Stephen sitting opposite her in the cafe.

Jane is scored by jealousy all over again.

Lana was the girl he said he was in love with. It's completely irrational to feel like this about him. She doesn't even like him.

She should see her, just to have seen her. 'Send her up, would you?'

*   *   *

Jane taps her pen against the table's edge. 'Sit down, please, Ms Carver.'

'I won't, thanks, I've got to get going.' She stands instead in the doorway. 'Do you know where Stephen Killigan is? I've been trying to find him. I heard he was with you at the police station. Is he in custody? How much is bail? I can get it for him if he can't get the money.' She rubs at the necklace that hangs on her collarbone—a grey stone with a hole through it.

'You can wear stone down, you know,' Jane says. She tries but can't keep a barb out of her voice.

'But not for a very long time,' Lana replies. She is fierce, staring Jane out.

This is stupid. 'Please sit, down, Lana. Is there something you want to tell Stephen that I can help you with?'

'Do you know what is happening to him?' Lana asks. 'No one has seen him at his college. His friend won't talk about him; Robert Sachs won't reply to my emails or phone calls. I don't know what to do.'

Jane could tell her what she knew, of course she could. But if Stephen wanted Lana to know, wouldn't he have contacted her? He could be protecting her; she was threatened by Jackamore, after all. 'I'm afraid I have nothing to tell you, Ms

370

Carver.'

Lana stares at Jane as if trying to trust her, then takes a large book from her briefcase. It is the size of a dictionary and bound in leather. She touches it as if the binding is poisoned and she could expire from a flick of its pages. 'I found this,' she says. 'In an archive in the University Library. I have been helping Stephen research the identity of a magician called Jackamore Grass and last traced him as a museum curator in Oxford. I have never seen an image of him, but I have read every word in this book. It was, and is, being written by him, and details every one of his crimes, and how he did them. Stephen needs to see it. It will tell him how to get where he needs to.'

'I don't think we need the euphemisms, Ms Carver. We both know where and when Dr Killigan has been. May I see the book?'

Lana pulls it back towards her. 'Tell Stephen that I've hidden it in one of the strangest and messiest collections in the world.' She laughs. 'He will probably find it.' She stands up to go and walks towards the door. 'And tell him I was wrong to go,' she says.

Jane tries to be magnanimous. 'I believe the magician told him that to be successful he must lose connections from this world. Such as love. I can understand that. I am sorry.'

Lana covers her mouth and her eyes fill up. 'I want this to be over.'

Chapter Seventy-Four

The Librarian

Lana Carver is working late. The library closed at midnight but it is surprising how easy it is to get someone to stay beyond their time. She is searching through a pile of papers I have not given her. She packages a thin yellow book into an envelope and drops it into the postal system. Productive and conscientious to the last. I watch from the stacks as she teases off the archivist gloves and yawns, covering her mouth with her newly nude hand. She is smiling.

'Would you come over here, please, Miss Carver.'

'Yes, Mr Saunders,' she says.

'You look pleased with yourself,' I say.

'I've found something very interesting,' she says.

'And that is of course why we work in a library.'

'Yes, Mr Saunders,' she says, slinking out of the door.

'I need to locate a collection in the basement of the north-west corner and need some help wielding the trolley back up. Would you mind assisting?'

She has no choice. She is paid to assist me and it has been no small pleasure to sit writing my masterpiece, my mighty tome, knowing all this time that she would be the last victim in this crime.

'Do you know, Miss Carver,' I say as we walk into the lift, 'I think I have made a mistake in not talking to you much. We work together every day yet I know nothing of you other than what I have gleaned from others.'

She inclines her head at the last sentence, puzzled.

I continue. 'You are very much a librarian. A library contains more secrets than any other place. Think of how many labyrinthine secrets a librarian can store away. No brain, no matter how degenerate, can compete with even a shelf-full of literature for its portion of secrets. And then there's the library itself, with its corridors and sealed off rooms. I wager we could murder and hide more than a dozen people down here in the University Library and it would take years for people to realise.' I laugh as if joking.

She laughs, nervously, steps back and strokes a book on top of the trolley. She is as easy to unnerve as a library card is to copy.

The lift jolts to a stop. We push the trolley out of the service lift and down the cold corridor.

'I thought we'd closed this one off?' she says, frowning, when I stop and look for a key among the dozen in my hand. This is one of the archive rooms where the volume of duplicated, foxed or unpopular books has grown so great that its contents are fully recorded and then closed. We declared this one completed last month.

'I thought we could get just one or two more redundant texts in there,' I reply.

She pushes the trolley into the room. I lock the door, very quietly. The trolley stops. I know what she has seen. I came down here earlier and cleared enough space for two chairs and a table. And on the table is the mask. I move so I can see her reaction. It is the only way I am alive, when I see the fear of me in another's eyes.

I stand in front of the table. Her hands grip the trolley. She is keeping her face admirably still, as if trying to make a mask of it. She is trying to trick me into thinking she is not aware of what is going on.

373

My laughter scales the book-lined walls.

Her stillness smashes like a mirror. She drops her bag from her shoulder, leans back slightly then drives the trolley at me with a low roar. I'm forced back between it and the table, still laughing.

Her face twists and she slams the trolley into my chest and legs, using her other hand to throw books at me. The books glance off my arms but one hits my shoulder and I feel the sharp sting of the edge of a hardback at my temple.

I am bored of this. I push the trolley back. There is a moment where the forces between us are equal and I feel a surge of excitement at not knowing what will happen next. It shifts, as these moments always do, and she edges backwards, her soft shoes sliding. Books tumble from the trolley and I have the momentum. She screams in frustration and calls for help but few come down here and only if sent by me. Swinging round, I grab the mask from the table and, reaching for her, twist her hair round my hand and pull her to me.

I hold the mask over her face, my arm looped and tightening round her neck. She kicks back but her shoes are soft and pathetic. 'This is how you're going to die,' I say. 'With the mask that I saw you researching held down on your face. And he will find one of you and he will be as broken when he knows, as you are.'

Her hands slip from my shoulder as she slumps out of consciousness. I remove the chloroformed cotton wool from the inside of the mask and strap her into one of the chairs.

*   *   *

374

I am drinking mint tea and flicking through a gardening magazine when Lana wakes. The magazine was in the room I had been storing the other girl in. I think I will start to garden again, when all this is done.

She blinks as she begins to focus. And then she sees Dawn tied in the chair next to her, slumped over. She groans and her head jerks forward as she vomits onto her lap. There are chloroform sores between her nose and mouth.

'I hope you had a pleasant sleep, Lana,' I say.

'I have had better,' she says, swallowing with difficulty.

'You should consider yourself fortunate: there are few that I have rendered unconscious that do not stay that way. The side effects of heavy chloroform, other than cardiac arrest which you avoided, congratulations, include brain damage. But do not worry; that will not be an issue for long.'

'You're Jackamore Grass,' she says.

'That's just one of the surprises I have for you,' I reply.

'I'm only surprised because my encounters with Jackamore Grass on the page suggested that he was a genius,' she says.

She is braving it out, blustering.

'I saw your annotations in the Hippocratic Corpus. I've seen your manuscript. The Jackamore Grass I read had a way with simile that lit up my brain. You are prosaic and charmless. The ultimate dull librarian. One among a silence of librarians.'

That is not true. She is attempting to goad me. Prick me.

Dawn murmurs and lolls her head. Sensations will be returning, her brain attempting to make sense of the flood of data coming from the snapped ulna in her

*left arm; the fractured scapula; the cranium cracked
like an abandoned china doll. She sees me and
flinches. She sees Lana but the gag absorbs her words.*

'Have you two met?' I ask.

They do not move or speak.

*'Allow me to introduce you to each other. This,' I
say, pointing to Lana, 'is Miss Carver, archivist, with
an interest in graphic novels and stationery; this is
Dawn Burley, a bowling alley attendant and collector
of plastic-cast trolls. One of you will be dying over the
next few days. I hope you enjoy your stay.'*

I check around the room and move for the door.

*'How are you planning to keep us here? Hundreds
of people come here every day.'*

*'As I said in the lift, Miss Carver, I could keep you
alive down here for years. Or I could simply book it up
for good. Nobody would find you, or until someone
millennia from now wants to research the mating
call of the fire lizard and needs to get down here. Of
course that all depends on how well the archive is
managed. And look where I've put the archivist!'*

She turns her head away.

*'You should be grateful. You told me once that you
could spend your life in the company of books. Well
here is your chance.' I unlock the door then turn back
to the women. I can smell the adrenaline salting up
their skin. 'Enjoy yourselves, you two: you have so
much in common. I cannot wait until you work it
out.'*

Chapter Seventy-Five

The Experiment

I wake with wine lapping at my mouth. A sound coming from the back wall of the cellar, a scraping sound. And someone swearing.

I raise myself onto my arms and use the buoyancy of the wine to take the weight of my legs, moving forwards, occasionally dipping to stop the pain with wine.

There is a door in the back wall, bending at the top and prevented from opening by the wine leaning against it.

'I don't know what is wrong here,' a man says. He kicks against the door. I can see part of it give and a hole appear just above the level of wine.

'Can I go home now?' A young girl's voice.

I freeze. No, no, no.

'Soon, darling. You can go back with your father in an hour or so. He is working until then. Don't you want to see where I work?' It's Lord Mortimer, but not as I remember his voice. It's as if he's covered it in honey. 'I'll try again; you help me this time, okay?' As gentle and wheedling and deceptive as mead.

I raise myself up using the struts on the walls and grab the handle to pull at the door as they push. It bends more, winesoaked and softened.

Wine charges through the gaps. Mortimer gasps and I hear him scuffling to avoid his feet being soaked. 'This way, Mary,' he says. 'There are other ways up. This is an adventure, isn't it? Come on, hold

377

my hand.' His loud, and her soft, footsteps retreat down the passage.

*   *   *

The wine continues to escape and I wish I could flow out of here with it, just atoms within atoms. I wrench at the door as much as possible but don't have the strength to hold it for long and collapse onto the floor, my skin punctured by broken pieces of glass. I pick up a sharp piece of clay from one of the bottles and gouge at the hole, widening it, deepening it until the liquid flows through.

The level of wine is going down. I pocket my phone and wish I could call someone. My mind keeps slipping back to Lana, and the danger she is in, right now, in the future, because of me. And I am doing nothing to help.

Voices at the door, discussing which of them has a key in their possession. No one. I could tell them who does.

I drag myself to the bottom of the stairs and stand as straight as I can, my hands out of my pockets.

Running footsteps.

The door opens. Three men stand in the doorway. 'Who are you and what have you done?'

Chapter Seventy-Six

Dart

I take the masks out of my bag as I go down in the lift. They were too easy to steal from the station; I must have a word with my informant to tighten up security otherwise the fun is lost.

This is when I am most alive, when I can hear their cries before I unlock the door. I can smell her urine, soaking the fabric of the chair. I could mock her for that but I do not. That is gracious of me. It was also gracious to separate the girls after a few hours together; to keep them separate so as not to raise each other's adrenaline in panic or oxytocin in bonding. One would make things harder for me, the other easier for them, and I don't want either.

Lana is hunched over the table, her right arm moving in front of her. She freezes when I walk into the room but does not turn.

The ropes that she was tied up in are still round her wrists, the length of it still snaked on the flagstones but she has managed, over the hours, to loosen the bonds and she is scratching at her arm and screaming. Does the tattoo cause her such pain? A pity. She is less strong than I thought. There is beauty in strength. I should know. I stand alone. I have the strength of knowing that nothing matters. And that is truly beautiful. I stand at her shoulder.

Flinching, she turns. And lunges at me, twisting, shouting. Her fist is at my chest, and there is pain in my chest. Her eyes are wide on mine.

Her fingers slip.

Something is sticking out of my chest. Where her hand was, the flight of a dart blooms. The dart itself is inside me.

She lurches to one side, rocking over so both her and the chair are on their sides on the floor. Using her elbows, she tries to drag herself towards the open door.

'Lana Carver,' I say, kneeling next to her. 'Your brave attempts to get away are duly noted, and by that I mean I shall write of them in my manuscript so in time everyone shall know of your resistance. Now, tell me, why were you screaming?'

I grab her arm, the one she was shielding from me when I entered. There is red on her white shirt. She yelps as I peel back her sleeve. Blood covers her inner arm, and scratches. I pour a glass of water from the jug on the shelf and tip it over her arm.

She has written something on it with the dart: THIS IS NOT YOUR FAULT.

'Ah. As final words go, they are a little weak, would you not say? Are you sure that you wish this to be your last statement?' I am so very close to her now.

She spits at me. The sputum lands on my cheek.

I feint a red scarf out of her other sleeve and position it doubled over her eyes. 'Now you stay here,' I say, pulling the dart from its place to the right of my heart. 'I have work to do on your friend next door, and then I will be back for you.'

Chapter Seventy-Seven

The Little Yellow Book of Witt

Jane opens her post at her desk while attempting to eat a muffin. Pemberton is on tea duty. She brushes crumbs onto the carpet; blueberries stain the pages of her credit card bills. The next envelope is from the University Library. She has no idea what that could be—she doesn't have any books out and is not expecting any research.

She slices open the envelope and tips out a pamphlet of frail, yellow pages. The title page states it contains *The Last Confession of Charles Witt*.

> I hereby confess to loving Beauty with all of my soul, to loving Beauty more than God as God also creates the imperfect. I confess to seeking out Beauty's symmetry and shape and to wishing to give it Life on a flat page. I confess to the murder of my muse when she had expended her use, and to taking my life when it is God's.

The next pages could be from a novel. They set out in rich language the series of events that led to Lucy Miller's death, from the role of a benefactor who encouraged Witt's painting and set up a prestigious competition, comprehensively won by Witt, and the violent but stylish way that Lucy surrendered herself to death following the sad abuse of her beauty by a college don.

Pemberton comes in with the tea tray. 'What

have you got there, guv?'

Jane laughs. 'One of Killigan's attempts to prove he is not barking, and presumably, that I am,' she says.

Pemberton picks up the pamphlet and smells it. 'I don't know, guv, this seems very old to me.'

Jane slices open the letter that came with it. It's from Lana Carver, Stephen Killigan's ex. The one with the message Jane will not deliver, what with her not being a carrier pigeon or telegraph service. She scans it, her eyebrows lifting. *It's all true*, Lana Carver writes.

Chapter Seventy-Eight

The Experiment Continues

They take me the long way round to the Master's formal study, not the inner room that I met him in before. 'We will wait here,' says a man in a black mask that covers the right side of his face. 'The Master will see you when he is ready.'

I breathe out slowly. I don't want to think about what is happening to the girl I heard him with, but the images come and I want to kill him. I want to kill him.

'You had better be telling the truth, about knowing the Master,' the man says. The visible side of his mouth twitches. He strokes his hand across the gun under his arm.

I have used a gun only a few times, at shooting centres in San Francisco. This one is over a metre long and heavy. He keeps switching it from one arm to another: he's not used to it either.

'Is that for keeping peace at the ball tonight?' I ask, trying to squeeze sympathy into my voice. 'With the rumour of the king arriving?'

He nods.

'That is an honourable responsibility indeed. There must be many out to hurt him.'

'With the Fenlanders rioting and the protests, it is only right to ensure his protection.'

'You have my admiration,' I say, bowing. Sweat is easing down my face and neck. In the candlelight my wine-matured skin glows. I could almost disappear into the red-painted walls.

He lowers the gun, slightly.

'Do you think I could sit down?' I ask. 'I think my leg is broken. And I feel sick.'

'Sir Henry,' Lord Mortimer arrives, holding out his hand. I shake it and the stain of red grape finds out his fingerprints. He stares up and down. 'You look as if you have come to the masquerade as the Devil. What will you ask me to trade my soul for? Do you have another one of those gold bars, or more, that I can buy your exit from the college with? Three would go some way to repair the damage to the wine cellar. Although where I will find replacement wines I do not know. The Flemish are unwilling to trade at this time. I do not know why.'

The man in the half-mask looks from one to the other of us. 'You *do* know him then, sir?'

'Oh yes,' he says, clapping me on the back. I stagger forward. 'Sir Henry is a great benefactor of the college. I am sure he has nothing to do with the unfortunate incident in the cellars.'

'I apologise, sir,' the man says to me, bowing low.

'You can go now,' Lord Mortimer says to him.

383

He retreats, nodding his head at me, still holding his gun.

'Is the king here?' Lord Mortimer whispers, drawing further into the room. 'Do you have more gold? Is that why you have returned?' The gold bar is still on the mantel, next to the box of Lucy's effects.

'You have many questions, Lord Mortimer,' I say, sinking down into an armchair. I feel faint. 'I have talked to the artist. He murdered her. His muse, your Lucy.'

'*My* Lucy?'

'Don't dissemble, Lord Mortimer. I've seen your book, remember. We both know you were intimate with Lucy since she was a child. But you don't seem surprised by what I say. Don't say you know that it was Charles Witt that killed her?'

Lord Mortimer takes a roll of tobacco and fills his pipe. 'I suspected as much. As I said before, it seems almost fitting. It does not trouble me.'

'Why is that?' I ask as if curious and not filled with rage.

'I shall keep the pictures and Witt will paint my portrait. And another.' He goes to the box on the mantel and picks out another ring, this time with brown hair around it. 'Mary,' he says, stroking the hair.

I walk over, as if intending to admire it.

He looks at the hair with such fondness.

I pick up the gold bar and slam it against his head, he cries out and falls forward and I slam it again

and again

and raise it again high above his head. I *could* see death flooding his eyes or open his skull and make him gone. It would be easy. So easy to do.

But I don't.

'Why did you stop?' Robert's voice says behind me, 'when it feels so good to kill?'

Chapter Seventy-Nine

Lana Carver

Dawn is already in place. She is conscious, her wrists scored with the symbol and tied together behind her back. She is in the fenman's hut, as it stands now in 2012 and has little time before she dies: the waters are rising up to her face. She has a small straw she must hold erect in her mouth or she will not survive even five hours.

The symmetry is beautiful: one girl exposed by the draining of the fens, another hidden by the flooding. If I can simply find my manuscript then I will be able to publish and tell the world of the beauty I have created.

*   *   *

Lana Carver is the one I am truly interested in. I force her hands into the beauty queen's dress, wrench her round. It does not fit, does not hang perfectly on the shoulders, and that niggles at me; it grates. At least she knows now she is going to die. I've told her. But I've given her a choice: the knife for gutting fish; the rope; the spade; or poison.

I peel off the blindfold. She stares at me, refusing to blink. I like that. Her chin is trembling. 'Please, let me go. Now.'

He has chosen well: she is beautiful. Her hair, of course, is plastered to her head, her eyeliner smeared by tears but you cannot dispute the cheekbones. It will make a change to do the killing of a central character myself rather than franchising it out. She focuses on my instruments, laid out on the cloth in alphabetical order. Her eyes widen, her hands flare against the gaffer tape like the last spasm of someone in an electric chair.

I hold each weapon to her left nostril, and then to her right. She twists her head away and I squeeze her jaw so that her mouth pops open like a purse. Moaning, she slams down her palms, scrapes her remaining nails against the arms of the chair.

'Please do not vandalise the furniture,' I say. 'If you struggle you will hurt yourself. Stick out your tongue.'

She glares up at me. I squeeze her jaw so hard I feel something break. The tip of her tongue pokes out.

'You will taste each method, experience it. And then choose your weapon.' I pick up the knife and rest the curved blade on her red tongue, then twist it downwards gently to let run a thin stream of blood. She only begins to struggle when the knife runs down her neck.

'Not that one? Maybe you are right. The rope tastes much better. No? Well you must choose somehow. I'll make it easier for you. Wait there.' I shuffle in my pockets, bring out the new pack. The cards fly in my fingers, sighing. 'Choose Hearts and we take out your heart; Spades, we bury you alive; Diamonds, we hang you with a noose in the shape of that stone; Clubs, we poison you with clover. Now this is a game show people should watch,' I say, then spin round and hold out the fanned cards to her shaking fingers. 'It's your Way of Death. Take your pick.'

She closes her eyes and takes a card between her thumb and forefinger.

'Show the people at home, but don't let me see,' I tell her, turning my back. I know what she chose, of course. It's easy when you know that magic is simply the illusion of choice. Like Stephen, running through time to find me and save her and save himself. As if anyone could be saved.

She twists the card over and can't help looking. The Jack of Diamonds. Her throat tightens before the noose hits her neck.

*   *   *

I carry her through the streets. She is still breathing; I have not done enough yet, but the poison will take over within the hour. He has till then, as does Dawn.

'Is she all right?' a girl asks. She is walking arm in arm with another girl. Her speech is slurred and her skirt is short.

'We've been at a party,' I reply, shaking my head. I throw in a laugh for good measure. 'Too much free champagne too soon.'

'Lucky cow,' she says.

I laugh for real this time.

I place her in the bushes, against the wall. A gasp, a gurgle comes out of her mouth. A bubble forms on her lips. She is trying to speak.

'Say it,' I say. 'He may not get to you: I am giving you your last chance. You are indeed a lucky cow.'

'F—f—uc—k

y—ou,' she whispers. Her voice is cracked porcelain. Her blood-riven eyes shine with hate. She is the most beautiful she will ever be.

I place the last mask over her face.

Chapter Eighty

Robert

Robert stands with his hands on the mantelpiece of the Senior Common Room. He doesn't look at me. His shoulders shake. But he is not laughing.

'What are you doing here?' I ask him. I look around; I don't know when I am at all. I've just catapulted from one time to another: the world is merry-go-rounding and I am on it and off it at the same time.

'I'm seeing the last part of my experiment through. You nearly killed someone, did you not?'

My mouth gapes open. 'I did,' I say.

He nods. 'And would you have felt justified in doing it?'

I search myself for any mixed feelings. Nothing. 'I would.'

'And what did you experiencing when considering the kill? Would you say that it was a sexual thrill?'

'I would say that was a ridiculous question.' I take my phone out of my pocket and, turning it to silent, press Jane Horne's number and hope she answers. 'How did you know all of this?'

'I'm not the person to ask. Jackamore knows you, he said you would be tempted but would be too scared to murder.'

'I wasn't scared.'

Robert shrugs, as if he doesn't care either way. He glances at his watch.

'The whole thing was a set up, wasn't it, an illusion, so that I would fulfil the experiment and you

388

could prove by a methodology that would never be approved of, that death and murder were beautiful and noble?'

'There was sleight of hand and misdirection, yes. Red herrings, if you like. But you made your own decisions. I never suggested that you even consider killing someone. But you did, just as he said that you would.'

'How come you are here, waiting for me?'

'He knew you were here, in another time, and said the violence would shock you back into our present'

'And if it hadn't?'

Robert smirks. 'He always has a contingency plan.'

I approach him with my hands spread, dragging my leg. 'Maybe he thought I would kill you for putting me in this position. Perhaps he wanted that.'

'Perhaps he did.' Robert drops his head. He twists the ring on his finger.

'You were trying to frame me,' I say. 'Why?' My voice sounds like I'm in the bottom of a well.

'I told you early on, Stephen, that you should stay away, that you could not cope with this and that it did not stop at pigeons.'

'I thought that was from Jackamore.'

'We work together.'

'He did all this for you?'

'Not just for me. Nothing Jackamore does is ever for anyone but himself.' Robert's mouth twists into a sneer. 'He is entirely responsible for his own actions. As you are responsible for yours, and I for mine.'

'And what's your responsibility now?' I ask.

'I'm here to slow you down,' Robert says. 'These are from Jackamore.' He holds out an envelope. I look inside and three cards fall onto the floor. The Joker; the Queen of Hearts and the Jack of Hearts.

Robert reads out a message. He looks grey and old. 'One of the girls is by Great St Mary's, another in the hut by the fens. You cannot save them both; or I dare you to come after me instead. I promise I will be waiting for you in the seventeenth century, ready to give myself in to the Watch or the Guilds. The choice is yours but you cannot do them all. Till next time, Stephen.'

'I'm not going to play any of his games,' I say.

Robert laughs. 'We all say that,' he says.

*　　*　　*

I run out of the building, shouting down the phone. They've got to have enough time to get there. My mind fractures, in and out, and the world changes around me, sometimes I sprint on cobbles, others on a dirt track, but the seconds are the same whichever century I'm in, working against me, building up around me like sand.

The church bell—I can hear it. And I know I'm there, bending over her, freaking out, stumbling, a fool. There are sirens in the distance. I must get there first.

Chapter Eighty-One

Sure and Certain Knowledge

Jane runs down King's Parade, muttering with every punch of her boots on the cobbles: 'Please. Please. Please.'

'Wait,' Pemberton shouts from behind.

Jane keeps running: past girls in ballgowns holding high heels in their hands, past shuttered shops and black lamp-posts till she reaches St Mary's Church. She hears him before she sees him.

Stephen keens a dissecting bellow that echoes around the stone city.

Jane covers her mouth with her hand and bites at the flap of flesh between her thumb and index finger. Stephen is crouching on the path, rocking backwards and forwards. The last mask lies face up, grinning.

Forcing her feet to move, she walks up to Stephen, slowly, and bends down. The girl is in his arms, covered in a long coat, her legs stiff, her head held in his outstretched palm.

His breath comes in short stabs. 'I couldn't,' he says. 'I couldn't.'

It takes three officers to move him away from the body. She watches, wincing, as his arms are forced behind his back, his legs clamped together. And he still twists, his eyes fixing on lifeless Lana lying on the path, his coat around her.

'What about Dawn?' Jane says. 'Where's Dawn?'

'Fuck Dawn,' Stephen replies. 'I don't care about Dawn.' He is pushed into the back of the police car and lifts up his hands. He breathes in, and out. 'He said she was in the fens—a hut south of Waterbeach. The map is in my pocket—they're flooding the area. You'll have to run.'

*　　　*　　　*

Jane grips the side of her seat with one hand, the map in the other, as Pemberton speeds down the narrow lanes. There are few signposts or lamp-posts

391

but he is calm; his face doesn't even flicker as a badger stops, frozen, before them and he doesn't swerve—she knows he shouldn't but still—and a hedge turns into a blind curve. He knows this area, has lived here since he was a boy.

'Not far now, ma'am,' Pemberton says.

They stop by a ditch at the side of the road, water lapping up the tyres. 'We can't get any further in the car,' Pemberton says. 'The hut is in the far field, behind the farm. The whole area is being swamped.'

Jane scrambles out of the car. Pemberton opens his door into the hedge, calls out to her to wait for him but she can't. She's needed. The night screams with sirens. If Dawn hears it, she may hold on. *Hold on, hold on.*

She clambers over the stile, but loses her footing, slipping into water that comes up to her calf. She gasps. Doors slam behind her: back up.

Lungs burning, she wades across the first field. The dark is thick around her; only a half-empty moon to hang a hope on. The water soaks through her trousers, and it is rising. Looking back, Jane sees a line of officers, with more adding to each end. Arm-lengths apart, heads down. Her legs feel like hams she can't lift from the freezer. 'Where am I fucking going?' she yells down her phone. 'I've lost the fucking map.'

'Where's Paul?' the chief's voice says.

'He's somewhere, I expect.' She looks over her shoulder.

Beams laser the field, picking out the spider legs of Pemberton scissoring the water towards her. 'Wait,' he's shouting.

'Can you not be more exact?'

The chief's puffs of exasperation are clear, even over the shouts and calls of the searchers.

'Have they stopped flooding the area yet?' she says, shining the torch at the surface of the water. *Don't think about it, don't think about water. Of it moving up your body, not able to breathe as it . . .* the panic punches her stomach and grips her ribs, clamps a hand round her throat. Jane's foot slams into something solid; she stumbles, drops the receiver, reaches out to stop herself but water cannot stop her. *Water cannot stop me. Water cannot stop me.* She struggles up, her coat hanging heavier.

The sound of wading comes from behind. She turns and yellow light fills her eyes—someone near with a torch. It turns off.

Jane wades on. There is a darker area ahead, somewhere to hide. Stretching her hand out, she grasps slippery leaves and a twig that jabs into her palm. A hedge. Nowhere to go.

Squelching sounds alongside her. Pemberton. 'Through here,' he says, ducking low and pushing his back into the hedge. 'I think the hut is the other side. I know these fields like the back of my hand.' He shines the torch on his hand: a fenland of blue waterways branch and rise to the surface of his skin. The hedge rustles and strains as he bends his body into a makeshift arch, creating a small space for her to squeeze through. Turning her face into his chest, Jane inches past Paul. The hedge tugs at her hair, pulls at exposed skin on her wrists and blocks her. She sinks to her hands and knees, water just below her jutting chin as she lowers her head under the branch of a tree that is trapped in the hedge.

The hut is at the far side of the field, water lapping at the door. Her lungs burn, Pemberton

393

holding her up, her holding up Pemberton as they run. The door resists her foot then shudders and gives way. A bowl of porridge floats past. And then she sees the low bed and the lying body of a woman in a stone mask.

Jane knees aside bobbing saucepans and reaches for Dawn's hand, paint-covered nails trailing in the water. She is cool, but not cold. Pemberton leans over to place a mirror over her mouth. Jane pushes him aside and presses her fingers into the indentation in Dawn's wrists. The beat is slow, faint, sluggish, but there. 'Don't move, love,' Jane says, stroking Dawn's swollen, bruised, alive, beautiful face. Placing her fingers in her mouth, Jane sends a whistle screaming out across the flat land.

Chapter Eighty-Two

There Will Always Be a Dawn, Until There Isn't

Dawn is carried out on a stretcher, her hand moving on top of the blanket. The screen is small but I can make out the apple I gave her, gripped in her fist. So they found her. That is good. One girl dies, the other lives, for however long she will. I won't bother looking her up. Stories should end in hope for some. It leaves doors open that can be slammed. They will have checked her pulse and felt her will to hold on counting down the minutes she has left, which now is, most likely, many. I take my own resting pulse rate: 52. A little high.

The presenter turns back to the camera to gabble

394

and I switch off my phone, wipe it, bag it and place it in the strong box. On top I lay copies of The Times *from the day that the victims died. I will go to the bank, before moving on, keeping it safe here with my certain items for when I return or returned.*

They will scrape DNA from the skin of that apple and find the saliva of a child who hasn't been born. Yet. I'm sure there will be traces of me: I would not want it any other way. I have nearly packed my bag. As always: two pairs of trousers, an ironed shirt, one packet of lemon bon bons, a new pack of cards and five Cox's Orange Pippins. My stomach groans. I cut out the mould from the corner of the crust and place the bread in the toaster.

Chapter Eighty-Three

Tea

They keep offering me tea. Bringing it to me in my cell in plastic cups. I drink it, for them, though it tastes of sweetened fish broth. They've loaded in the sugar—for the shock. The Americans have therapy; we still have hot sweet tea. Tea persists where the stiff upper lip got soft. How can my brain just carry on with thoughts like this, throw up banalities? It stops the images and I don't want to stop the images. I want to remember what she looked like, what she felt like, what he has done to her and keeps doing to her in that pocket of time. Because I need to be angry. Soon I need to be angry and I must not forget what I saw.

'Do you need anything else?' DC Millins asks.

There is a mix of pity and fear on her face.

'I need to find him,' I say.

Chapter Eighty-Four

Pemberton

Jane stands in the hallway. In interview rooms at opposite ends of the corridor, Drs Robert Sachs and Stephen Killigan wait. The burning sensation in her ribcage won't go away, hot indigestion, even though she hasn't eaten since last night. Everything depends on how the next few hours goes. And she has no idea if she can do it.

She looks through the window at Stephen. He's slumped in the chair, all urgency gone, and shivering—his coat bagged up, ready to be scraped for emissions and tissues, steamed and, eventually, if he wants to forever be reminded of what happened, returned. This job is like that. She has her dry-cleaning tricks that get rid of the worst but beneath the fabric the memory of the memories remains.

Someone taps her on the shoulder.

Jane jolts back from the door. 'Paul, one day you are going to have to tell me how you manage to emerge out of nowhere to scare the shit out of me. Not that there's much of that left.'

Pemberton's lip twitches, once.

'What's that face for? Not used to women talking like that? You think that the ladies should be covered in foundation and feathers.'

Pemberton's face stays still. He's the teapot

that doesn't spill, even when the magician whips out the tablecloth. 'I don't, ma'am,' he says. 'I was wondering what your plan was for interviewing Sachs and Killigan. Would you like me to take one of them? Killigan, say?'

'That won't be necessary, thank you: I'll be moving between them. Right then, can't put it off any longer.' She opens the interview room door.

*   *   *

Robert Sachs sits with his hands in his lap, looking straight ahead at the wall. His lips tip up a little at the sides, more Mona Lisa than murderer. He reminds Jane of someone but she can't dredge up who it is.

'You look pretty happy with yourself, Dr Sachs,' she says.

'In this case, appearances have some basis in reality.'

'Why is that?'

'Inspector Horne, may I call you Inspector? How lovely it is to see a young—let's say youngish, for accuracy's sake—a youngish woman like yourself in an office of such power. I'm all for it. Really, it's a joy. There has been such a lack of balance, historically, pastorally, tragically, and now look at us. But I can see you don't want to hear about that. I shall answer your question: I am happy because I have done what I set out to do, with some improvisation along the way thanks to the intervention of our young friend Stephen. But that just improved the art: spontaneity breathes life into clay.'

'And you set out to . . .'

'To prove that there is beauty in the act of murder, in the murdered and in the murderer.' Sachs speaks slowly, rolling out the words with equal weight. 'I was hoping to frame Stephen, pretty boy that he is. I should say right now that I murdered Miranda and I murdered Rhys and I murdered Lana and the only other person involved was a Mr Jackamore Grass, or "Grass" as Stephen would say, who murdered one of his fellow magicians and helped me with my experiment.' Sachs rhymes the second grass with 'ass', shortening the word. 'Have you perhaps found Mr Grass?' He steeples his fingers and rests his chin on his deeply ridged nails.

'We cannot tell you that, Dr Sachs.'

'Of course you haven't found him. He doesn't mean to be found. I could give you a little tiny hint, but that wouldn't be much fun, would it? I've got time to fill in prison: veiled revelations in the press, pillow talk to jail-bird botherers, murmurs in my memoirs. I could spin this out for years like Hindley. She's the Penelope of the murdering world.' Sachs has a benign, Buddha-like air about him and a glow to his cheeks.

'You are making everything very clear for us, Dr Sachs.'

For the first time, a crease of concern appears on Sachs's face.

'Apart from, of course,' Jane continues, 'the details. How you managed to decompose Rhys's body for example, and what happened to Dawn after she disappeared and before she died?'

'Aah,' Sachs says. 'That's where you have to talk to Grass. He was my go-to guy for the tricky bits. He was a medical wizard at Oxford when I was there. Not bad at chemistry either, which is how I gather he managed it all. Jackamore Grass: very good at making things disappear, for a time.' And there's that half-smile again.

*   *   *

'I know this will be difficult for you,' she says to Stephen, 'but can you take me through what happened?' She leans back in her chair then stops: she's in the chair with the cracked seat. She resists the urge to rub her arse where the seat pinched it.

Stephen's forehead flexes, contracts. He flares his palms, holds them open.

'Go backwards if that helps,' Jane says. 'Tell me about finding Lana.'

Stephen shakes his head.

'All right then, what led you to the church?'

Taking a dragging breath that looks like it hurts, Stephen starts talking. Slowly at first, then faster. Words tip out like broken biscuits from a smashed packet. He tells them of Robert's experiment, how he was trapped him in the cellar, Robert's confession, only breaking off when DC Millins brings in tea and lays a piece of paper in front of Jane.

Pemberton leans towards her so he can read it. 'There is no evidence that the man that the library thought they were employing ever existed,' he reads out loud. 'Papers and references: all faked, very well indeed; his bank account was wiped after last month's pay, the rooms he was staying in have been left completely empty. And yet there is no footage, or sighting, of him leaving the library. How do you explain this, or the way that the bodies were found

399

out of synch with when they were killed?'

'I can't, and don't have to, explain anything,' Stephen says. He looks at Jane, not blinking. Jane can explain. Shifting in her chair, she winces as the plastic snaps at her legs. 'Swap with me,' she whispers to Pemberton, standing up and glaring down at the seat. 'I'm sorry about this, Dr Killigan,' she says.

'Can I talk to you outside, ma'am?' Pemberton asks.

Jane pushes down her irritation. 'What is it?' she says when they get into the corridor.

'You're treating him like a victim, ma'am. We still don't know if the three of them were involved,' he says. 'I don't know how they could have achieved this between two people.'

Jane snaps up, standing taller. 'I think you're right, Pemberton,' she says, 'but what if it wasn't Killigan?'

*   *   *

Slipping back into Stephen's interview room, Jane turns off the recorder. He looks up. His eyes are the grey of fresh concrete. 'What else do you know?' Jane asks.

Stephen tugs his sling higher. He looks older. Jane resists the urge to reach over and touch the bump in the middle of his nose.

She crouches next to him, holding onto the table leg for support. 'I think I'm a bit more prepared to accept the far-fetched now. Tell me what happened.'

Stephen turns his chair to face the wall.

*   *   *

The chief congratulates her on the way out, slapping her shoulder and shaking her hand off. 'I'll be making a statement later. It'll be a relief to be putting an end to this. Well done, Jane.'

'We haven't found Grass yet, sir,' she says, peeling away from him and edging towards the door. She imagines the water rising up, washing away evidence—if any exists.

The chief puts his hand against the wall, blocking her. 'We have a confession to all three murders, physical evidence, motivation, details that only the murderer would know. CPS, the press and the families will be more than happy with that.'

'I don't think you could say that the families will be happy,' she says as she ducks under his arm, catching a whiff of pine deodorant on top of sweat.

'You know what I mean, Horne. Where are you off to?'

Jane turns in the doorway. 'I've got a lead on another case, sir,' she lies.

'Make sure you're back to give me everything I need before the press conference. We wouldn't want me to look uninformed, would we?'

Jane lets the door close before she replies.

Chapter Eighty-Five

Bathtime

Jane presses play on her iPod and eases herself into the bath. The water is too hot, so she hangs her leg off the side.

Something about Sachs's testimony doesn't make sense.

Sachs is either at peace because he has been caught—and many murderers *really* want to be caught—or he believes what he has done to be noble, or he thinks he has been someone's saviour. And if that is the case, then someone else may be at risk.

Jane soaps around her scars by feel not sight. She can't look, not yet.

She grabs the chain between her toes and yanks out the plug. Having a bath is no fun now she's less afraid of water. She really *is* contrary. Marion would love to know that she'd agreed with her—she'd laugh and splutter into her morning coffee. Jane must go and see her. After she's worked out what Sachs is really up to.

Chapter Eighty-Six

The Wall

Once I wake up and my bedroom wall is different. Colder. Stone. My back hurts. I am on floorboards, a splinter sticking out of my hand. I open my eyes and the room is newer, the bed on the other side, a bed pan under it and the smell slinking towards me. I don't care. I fall back into sleep.

*　　　*　　　*

Gingerbread lands with a thump on my stomach, pads up to my chest and flumps down with her paws either side of my neck. Her purr is a mini-digger on concrete. She pats my jaw, claws in to start. I raise my hand and she leans into it, rubbing her chin on my knuckle. But then I think of Lana cuddling her, and how I led him to Lana. I tip Gingerbread onto the floor.

*　　　*　　　*

I sit up today. There's a point on my sternum where anger at Robert keeps flicking hard, like the switch on my gas fire. And something else. There's something else. Because there's something that keeps rising up, a reed twitching.

*　　　*　　　*

I smell his aftershave before the soup on the tray. I hear him clearing away the untouched minestrone from last night, then dragging over a chair. I reach out to the wall and touch its bumps, then I turn away from it. I count to ten, in Greek, then open my eyes.

'You stink, mate,' Satnam says, grinning at me with an uncertain smile. 'I know.' My voice cracks out like old vinyl under a needle. 'Sorry 'bout that. And I am so sorry. About everything.''I know.' My

403

voice cracks out like old vinyl under a needle. 'Sorry 'bout that. And I am so sorry. About everything.'

Satnam takes a can out of his pocket and sprays deodorant into the air. It forms a cloud of minty musk that tastes metallic in the mouth. 'Don't mention it, mate,' he says.

My legs feel empty as I swing them over the edge of the bed, like bendy straws. Greyness nibbles at the edge of my vision.

'Whoah, take it slowly,' Satnam says, reaching out to steady me.

I lie down, cuddling the pillow.

'How you doing?' he asks.

'All I can think of,' I say, 'is what I could have done differently. Then you wouldn't be hurt, and she wouldn't be . . . ' I stare down at the carpet, covered with ginger hairs.

'But she told you it wasn't down to you.'

'What are you talking about?'

' "This is not your fault".'

'It really is. If I hadn't tried to find the body, it never would have been there.'

He stares at me as if I've lost fifty points in IQ. 'That's rubbish mate, and you know that somewhere. You've got to let it go. She wouldn't want this; that's why she wrote it.'

'You are making even less sense than usual. Wrote what?' The thought that Lana wrote me a note, or anything, that I could keep and read through for always.

'On her arm. God,' he says, rearing back. 'Didn't they tell you?'

I shrug.

'She wrote it on her inner arm, with your dart. They found his blood mixed in with hers so I'm

404

betting she gave him a scratch with it, but that's what she wrote. THIS IS NOT YOUR FAULT. She meant you.'

'I read it as THIS IS YOUR FAULT. Are you sure?'

'Sometimes we see what we want to see,' Satnam says. He strokes Gingerbread and pats my knee. The door clicks closed behind him. I turn back to the wall.

*   *   *

Jane sits at the end of my bed. 'Are you going to get up?' she asks.

'Not yet,' I say.

'Then you won't want this message from Lana then,' she says blithely.

I lift my head.

'She said "it's not that bad" and "suck it up, Buttercup".'

'No, she didn't.'

'But she would if she saw you here, and so do I.'

The sun is trying to sneak through the gaps in the curtains. I sit up. 'What did she say?' I ask.

'She said she should never have left. That she had found Jackamore Grass's manuscript, and that it might help you find him.'

I stand up quickly and reel back. Jane reaches out and steadies me. 'Where is it?'

'That's the problem,' Jane sighs. 'She was very cryptic. She said she had hidden it in the strangest and messiest collection in the world. She seemed to think you'd know what she meant. Did you visit any museums or galleries together?'

I grin and lurch for the door. My legs feel like

405

twine. I cross the floor of my study, searching. No sign. Where could it be? Crouching down, I see something tucked between Bandit's legs. He seems to give me a glassy wink.

The book is as heavy as a fat toddler in my lap, heavier than it looks. It seems to breathe when I open it, sighing like a bellows. The pages are stained as if they've spent centuries brewing in vicars' tea; brown and thin, translucent at the edges, like onion skin. A living thing, tannin-fed. Five tiny red spider mites crawl over the surface, the ones I would find in exam papers.

I recognise the writing and it does not chill me.

It causes fire to spread from my shoulder to my fingers; fire that could break down water and melt down stone.

'And one more thing,' Jane says. 'She showed me that I should believe you.'

Chapter Eighty-Seven

Formal Hall

The Grand Hall is already full when I walk in. Students look up from their starters as I weave between the long tables and find my way up to the top table. A few nudge each other as I pass. I try and avoid eye contact. They must have heard rumours about the mad lecturer who had confined himself to his room for weeks.

I sit in the only empty seat at the far end of the table. The bald man who looks as if he's been kept in a jar of pickled eggs has claimed Robert's seat.

The ceiling arches up over us into a carving of the college crest. Lord Mortimer sneers down from the wall and I long to scrape the smug paint from his frame. I have an idea.

Standing up, I walk through the door in the back of the hall through to the Senior Common Room and keep in mind and body the mixed state of being alive and dead at the same time, of the feeling and heft of 1635, the same walls only younger. I open my eyes. I have done it—I'm in Mortimer's rooms. Alone. Footsteps pass outside. I don't have much time.

Lucy is hung on the wall in her different poses. Reaching up, I gently take each version of her down. I grab Jackamore from his cupboard and, touching the indentations in the wooden walls till I find a catch, slide back the panel. Mortimer's book lies face down in a cubby hole.

Closing my eyes, I visualise the layout of the college and where I was locked into the cellar. I pick up keys from the mantelpiece and pocket the box with Lucy's slippers and the locks of hair.

The paintings are heavy and lifeless as I heft them down the stairs. I'm holding her body in my arms again as I did in the boat. I try several doors and then one opens—Mortimer's own wine store by the look of it. Casket after casket in the corners of the room. I lay the paintings against the wall, near each other, safe from the eyes of that bastard. Tomorrow I will go back, find the portrait of Jackamore and make sure it is hung where he'll not be forgotten.

*   *   *

Students shout to each other and scrape cutlery on college plates. I knock back a glass of wine and the walls of the hall soft en. The Mistress smiles at me for the first time.

A gilt-edged plate is slid in front of me. On it are two slabs of chicken slathered in gravy so thick that I can draw my face in it with my finger and it doesn't slink back to one liquid.

'Are you going to eat that?' Alice Henry, a classicist with a Caesar haircut, says, pointing at my plate.

I push it towards her.

*   *   *

There is always more port to be had in Cambridge; that much I've learnt. In the Senior Common Room, I take a schooner from the sideboard and get frowned at by Anwar. I move over to stand with the Mistress and Pickled Egg man, whose name slides from my brain like yolk down a wall.

'It is fantastic to see you again, Stephen,' Claire says, keeping her voice low. 'I can only begin to imagine how difficult this has been for you. I am truly sorry that the college has not been more supportive since you arrived. I hope you can forgive us.'

I nod. Because I can. I can nod, and I can forgive. Sometimes I don't want to do either.

'Do you mind if I sit down? I'm knackered,' I say. The banquette lets out a puff of dust. The paintings on the wall take a while to stop swinging. Maybe I won't have more port.

'I've been talking to some others and, do say if this is a bad time, but we were wondering if you

408

would be interested in taking over the Moore Lecture later on this month. It is a prestigious event; usually the speaker will have been at the university for years but you are Robert's most obvious successor.'

'He was going to talk on Free Will and Determinism, wasn't he?'

It is Claire's turn to nod. Her curls bounce.

Something constricts inside me, something near my heart, or what's left of it. 'I can't do it. Not on that subject. I have always thought that we had free will, and then this happened. I can't go anywhere near it, now.'

'That's a pity.' Her eyes are soft grey with green lace. 'Have a think, why don't you. You may change your mind.'

'I don't think so.'

'Why? Because you have no free will?' Her mouth twitches.

Tara Yarrow taps Claire on the shoulder. She glances at me and wrinkles her nose. 'It may not be the time, Mistress, but I was wondering if anyone had been given Robert Sachs's rooms yet.'

Claire opens her mouth to speak.

'And if not, then I think I should get them, having put up with him all this time. To think what he must have been doing up there.' He shudders. 'It doesn't bear thinking about.'

'But you'd want to be in the rooms where these unthinkable things took place?' I say, crossing my legs. 'That's very brave.' My voice is crisp with sarcasm.

He ignores me. 'And he never stopped talking, or having arguments. His snidey voice would slide down the stairs like children on a tea tray.' He lowers his voice and peers over his shoulder. 'I'm sure he was having someone staying there as well.'

I snap my head up. 'Who would he talk and argue with?' I ask.

'I couldn't say. Some woman. Wasn't my place to go spying on the man. I never liked him. I really do deserve to have the rooms after what I've put up with.' Now he turns to me, sticking out his jaw.

God, these people are awful. I stare up at the ceiling.

'More port?' the butler says, holding out a decanter.

'Go on, then,' I say.

Chapter Eighty-Eight

Harry and the Tattoos

'Harry Zappa and The Onion, how can we hurt you today?' says The Onion.

'Hello there, good morning. I picked up an urgent message from Harry, asking me to come and meet him. He said he might have some information for me. Oh, I'm Stephen Killigan,' I say.

'You need to be here quicker than it takes to tattoo a star on the back of a slapper.' The Onion slams down the phone.

*　　　*　　　*

I walk as fast as I can, past the Reality Checkpoint lamp-post. That's a joke. There is no particular reality to check, just whatever is in front of you at

410

that point. Whatever you have to compare it to is flawed; you have to go with whatever makes the most sense. Occam's razor. I wonder if anyone's ever topped themselves with it. Of course they have. Sometimes the simplest option, death, is best.

No. That is never true.

*　　　*　　　*

Harry Zappa is waiting for me when I arrive, putting together a machine. He shines one of the parts with a cloth. Glances up at me. 'So how's your tattoo going?'

I show him, peeling back my sleeve. 'Lots more to do. And I think I need another one, on the other arm.'

'A new start?'

'Not exactly.' I show him the picture of what I want. Schrodinger's cat, with a message on the box that contains it.

He whistles. 'Not sure I'd like to carry that around with me all the time.'

'You're not me,' I say.

'Good job for both of us.' He selects one of the bottles of red ink. 'I could get going with that while you talk if you like.'

I open my mouth to say I can't afford it at the moment but he puts his big hand on the arm of the chair.

'Complimentary. Gratis. I don't want your money.' He plugs in another machine and the needle pumps in and out faster than I can see. 'I have a feeling this was partly to do with me. Or I could have stopped it at least.'

Everyone seems to think that. As if all of our

411

egos cry out to be important enough to be blamed.

The first scratch starts in the crease of my elbow. The pain is intense this time, my skin vulnerable. But it is good to feel the pain. It is nothing compared to what they would have gone through.

The Onion comes in with three huge mugs of coffee on a tray. She hands me one of them and settles with hers in the other chair. 'We've been thinking of you, ever since we saw that photo of the little boy's wrist in the paper. There have been a lot of enquiries, as you'd imagine. Some people even wanting to get copies of them done: "I want an S shape, yeah? On each wrist, yeah? Cause I'm called Sarah, all right? And I'm really dark, okay?" Her voice is sharp, sarcasm oozing out the juice of a cut onion. She nods for Harry to take over and brings the mug to her lips. The fairground horse on her arm shakes its mane.

Harry finishes a letter and takes a gulp of his coffee. 'And then yesterday we had a visit from this man. He was nearly as tall as me and looked me dead in the eye. Not many do that, not for any good reason, they just don't, but he did. And then he asked if I was in contact with you.'

'What did you tell him?'

'Nothing, obviously. We are very discreet.' He scratches the next letter into my forearm. The veins stand out blue and alarmed.

'Unless we don't like someone,' The Onion chips in. 'In which case we'll spill everything. And I didn't like him at all. Not many people make my skin crawl, but he did.' The snake seems to shiver round her neck.

'He didn't believe me anyway. In fact he told me to remind you,' Harry Zappa continues, 'to

412

consider looking in the mirror. And there was another thing.' If Harry could ever look sheepish, it was now. 'He said that he had won.'

The Onion stands up and shakes her head. 'And I told him to get out.' She leaves, muttering.

Harry Zappa finishes my new tattoo and reaches over to take a photo for his wall. It doesn't do his art justice: my Schrodinger's cat is ginger and at once lies lifeless from one angle, sprightly and alive from another. I rotate my arm from the elbow and both versions appear to merge into one mixed-state-moggy. Beneath her, is the message I'll carry with me. THIS IS (NOT) YOUR FAULT.

*   *   *

Towards the bottom of Mill Road, I stop by a pawn shop. It's the first time I've thought of buying something to do up for weeks. I could do with selling some of my junk, to try and buy the painting of Jackamore. In theory I have all this gold and investments but that will just draw attention to me in this century, and this is where I want to be most of the time. The rest of it, I want to roam.

I can get away with paying a few thousand for the bastard. He will hang in my room and be a constant reminder of what he has cost me.

They've got one of the first Space Invaders machines; I've always wanted one of those. It could go in the space next to my—no, that's not why I'm here. At least they were buying the odd stuff I collect. The dusty window has a carefully stacked and placed array of rare records; pianolas; lawn mowers; moustache holders; spectacles; turn-of-the-last-century cosmetics and a selection of stringed instruments laid out as if ready to play with themselves, the curvy pin-ups of the orchestra, fine hair and hips and . . .

My hand is on my chest. My wrist feels my heart's beat, and my heart its own reply in my wrist.

S shapes lie on either side of the bodies of the violins, violas, double bass . . . and cello. The cello lies on its side on a chaise longue, its spike wrapped in silk so as not to damage the upholstery. A spike.

Only, of course, it's not an 'S', it's a stylised 'f'. Nothing is as I thought. And the mirror image is on the other side. Mirror images. Cellos. Two sides. Twins.

I twist away, feeling the past sidling up to me, sense impressions of Mill Road as it was nudge me to come their way: horses' hooves on the streets, the smell of sweat and frying kidneys, the gossip of passing people and I want to run headlong into it. But I can't. Not this time.

Chapter Eighty-Nine

Bernard Hermann

Julia Sachs stares at us from the doorway. A smile starts in her eyes and ticks the edges of her mouth. 'Inspector, Sergeant, Dr Killigan. A pleasure to see you. Please come through,' she turns and leads us through into the lounge. She points at the sofa, sits down at the piano and starts playing. I recognise it—the Faure from the concert.

The three of us remain standing. Pemberton ducks beneath the chandelier but still sends it swinging. Jane catches my eye and gestures towards the cello. It leans against the stand. The sides of the instrument are smooth, curved, the wood shiny red-brown. And in the top, the carvings on each side are the ones on Miranda and Rhys and Lana. I want to take the cello and stab her with it.

Pemberton moves out of the way of the swaying crystals. 'Julia Sachs. You are being arrested on the charge of murder. You do not have to say anything but it may harm your defence if you do not mention, when questioned, something which you later rely on in court. Anything you do say may be given in evidence.'

Julia continues to play. 'You've charged my brother and I believe he has confessed to each of the murders and that he acted alone. There is nothing more to say. I am entirely innocent of any wrongdoing.'

Pemberton has been putting on his gloves and now crosses the room to the cello. 'So you will not mind if we take the cello for forensic tests. We will also be searching your cellar, where we believe Rhys's and Miranda's bodies were kept before you disposed of them with the aid of two other people.'

Julia watches, her cheek twitching as Pemberton begins to bag up the instrument. She dashes forward and holds out her hands, grabbing at it. Pemberton moves it away and she pushes him. Jane grabs my wrist to stop me helping. The cello smashes against the stone surround. Strings break and flail, the wood cracks. Julia shrieks, a high C.

She holds the remnants in her arms, rocking.

'Julia, why did you kill Miranda?'

She is silent for minutes. I watch them wind round on her clock. 'I wanted her to hurt,' she

415

says, at last. 'She did not have any worries, and she wouldn't have. People do anything for the beautiful.'

'So you wanted to destroy her beauty?'

'I was just doing what nature does anyway. It removes beauty when it is no longer useful. I was halting it in its tracks, before it had a chance to take hold.'

'But what about Rhys?' I ask.

'Rhys's voice was the most pure it would ever be. The perfect time to leave. And I loathed his smug, perfect face. We wanted victims for the four masks, each one beautiful in death. And it was Jackamore's idea that we went for your girlfriends and again that in the end we had five—the perfect fifths. The f holes on the wrists were my idea, even though Jack performed the cuts. I preferred it on the ones still alive. I wanted to hear them scream like Hermann violins.'

'So you silenced Rhys,' I say.

'I did.'

'Do you consider that you were doing them a favour?'

Julia laughs. She strokes her own cheekbone. 'That is a very leading question, Sergeant. You'll have to do better than that. She made me angry. Miranda. The *beauty queen*. There was nothing beautiful about her. She was simply young and symmetrical. She couldn't even sing. No one looks at me but I've seen her at concerts, men of all ages, perverts they are, staring at her. Wanting her. No one looks at me that way anymore. Apart from the exceptionally old.'

'And your brother,' I say to her.

She ignores me and turns to Jane. 'Have you

416

noticed that yet? Do you remember the moment when you first became invisible? That your worth and presence has died with your looks.'

'That's where I have the advantage,' Jane says. 'I never had them in the first place. I've got nothing to lose.'

Julia Sachs walks over to the fireplace and picks up a photo of her and Robert. She is luminous. Stunning. I would have stopped in the street to stare at her. *He* looks as if he has everything he ever wanted. Maybe she *is* all he wanted. And he would do anything for her, and she, beauty that she was let him.

'What about Robert?' I say.

Jane nudges me and whispers: 'I told you to stay quiet. It won't help the case.' To Julia she says, 'What was your brother's role? To take the blame?'

'I called him after killing her. And he was there after I killed Rhys. Right here. In this room.' She lights a cigarette. 'He sorted it out. With Jackamore.'

'Has he always sorted things out for you?'

'Of course. What else are big brothers for?

'Did you do the experiment to show that beauty was transitory and that it could be found in the most ugly places?'

'Is that what you took from this?' She laughs and laughs. Her hair falls onto her cheekbones. 'Well that is precious. The aesthetics is all down to Robbie—he has always tried to justify what I did. He never had the courage to do anything truly. He needed me to excite him. In every way. Does that surprise you?' she says to Jane. She closes the lid of the piano, walks across the room and picks a rose out of a splayed bunch in a white vase. She sniffs, deeply. 'He always gave me roses, you know. I called him my Beast.'

Chapter Ninety

Going Home

Iris pushes her glasses back onto her nose and dunks a Garibaldi biscuit. 'This is advanced stuff, you know,' she says. 'You could get yourself caught up in a pickle if you get it wrong.'

'What kind of pickle?'

'You might not be able to get back. You were lucky, in a way: Jackamore was forging a path in the timelines and you were able to fall through in his slipstream to jump between two points. That's how you could get back to take those paintings—nice work by the way. I read about him in the papers. He'd been grooming kids for years then, according to his books?'

I nod. 'Can we get back to the point?'

'Anyway, Jackamore has disappeared as he always does. But that means you have to feel out a specific time as you would search in between the layers of a lady's petticoats.' Her eyes shine. She looks as if she is remembering something. Or someone. She shakes it off.

'Just how old *are* you Iris?' I ask. 'You do know that women haven't worn bloomers and petticoats in some time.'

'More's the pity,' she says. 'They were fun. Anyway. Your task now is to divide the tissue paper into layers and get between the right sheets.' She sucks the softened currants out of the biscuits and spits them onto the grass. 'Do you know which date you're aiming for?'

'Yes.' Some dates just stay in your head, like the list of stamps at the front of the library book. Another sheet might get licked in place on top, but it's still underneath, sometimes in ink, sometimes by hand. 'Eighteenth March 1985.'

She jumps up like a mouse surprised. 'Well the eighteenth is in a couple of days; you aren't good enough to pick out days from the chaos yet, only years, and not specific ones. Still, you've got to try. I'll have a go with you, just for fun mind.'

I choose easy dates first, ones recently gone which Iris assures me are just as hard to get to as others, but they feel safer, or at least known. The first time I end up slamming into a wall at a punk gig that sent me careering, covered in spit, back to the fourteenth century and then on again to the nineteenth where I was criticised by a preacher for an immoral absence of beard. Iris claims she went nowhere but I watch her fade and then return like a hologram.

It gets easier. I butter toast in the kitchen and can slip in and out of any year on this day for the three hundred years that the building has been standing. Things haven't much changed. Although I think there might be less sex going on in the rooms.

I've waited for 18th March to roll round and here I am on a British Rail train, trundling up north, eating a ham sandwich that's curled and brown at the edges like a foxed book. I'm going to try and save my mother. That's a statement isn't it? And it is not accurate. As a philosopher it is important to get the language right. I'm going to save my mum.

419

The girl in the seat opposite me has dyed black hair and a black net top. In my pre-teen mind, the eighties were the colours of the Rubik's Cube, bright and primary and glaring. But they're not. Neither are they the pale pastel of faded photos and Deirdre Barlow's face-filling spectacles. The eighties spill past but while there are more perms and fewer telephones, they are the same colour as every year there has ever been and people talk about house prices and having no money like they always will.

It makes me a bit uncomfortable, actually, the idea that I could have wrongly perceived the event. Because, if I allow myself to think that, what I have been seeing in my mind all these years is merely a conjunction of memory, imagination and angles of vision and what I see is not what I saw.

Walking up from the station I sniff up the brine and ice-cream, the sound of gulls and ghost trains. I am a ghost in my own town.

I cannot resist going to the house. I'm not risking anything: there are no guests in, I'm not back from school for an hour, Da is on a clock job in Hull and Mum will be leaving work in half an hour and making her way down to the sea. Whoever is with her in the waves will follow. Let it be Jackamore; I'll push his head under the waves and hold him. He can time travel if he likes, centuries can peel past, but there will always be sea to drown him in.

The doors to the rooms have been thrown open and I sit on my old bed. The duvet is spattered with stars.

As I walk past Mum and Da's bedroom, I see something move. Da is on the bed, shaking. He has not seen me. Maybe he can't see me.

420

He looks up and a cry comes from his wide open mouth but he doesn't move. He doesn't even ask who I am. There's a letter in his hand. I take it. It's in Mum's writing and smells of her perfume where her wrist slid across the paper.

I can't stay. I'm sorry.

That's all it says.

'Sorry for what?' I ask.

He rocks on the bed and stares up at me, empty; a man who once controlled time with his hands and heart.

I turn away from him and run down the stairs, counting my steps as they echo throughout the house.

The hill down to the sea is steep and I stumble, stubbing my toe on cracked-up pavement. I check my watch. And run faster.

On the promenade, four old men stand close together on the checkerboard in their own endgame. I rush down the white steps onto the sand. The quicker I move the surer I sink.

Mum is wading out. Her long white dress dips into the sea. The water climbs up her.

I throw off my shoes. The sea claims my feet. 'Mum, stop,' I cry out but she keeps moving away from me. I don't know if she can hear me above the gulls and the merry-go-round that mocks from the prom. 'Stop. Now.'

The water is up to my waist and the cold causes my breath to stop but I keep moving, part running, part swimming. The sand keeps shifting, the shelf drops away.

She swims now. Her hair is wet and darker, the red curls dragged out by the tide. I am only two arm reaches away.

She turns her head and holds out her hand, her palm flat, forbidding me to move forward. 'You can't save me,' she says. 'I don't want you to. Please leave me be.'

I see me on the shoreline, small and dark haired, arms in the air, seeing me in the sea, tall and dark haired, reaching for his mother.

She backs away and, breathing out, keeping her eyes on the beach, sinks under the surface.

I dive, arms outstretched. Her white outline is suspended in the sea but my hands close on water. I plunge down again and again, lungs burning. I could just sink too and join her, but I can't even see her. She's gone.

*   *   *

I wade back to the beach, numb.

The me on the beach points to the sea with my yellow net, screaming.

Da crouches by the rock pool, rocking, holding onto me and holding me back from running into the waves. 'This is your fault,' he says to himself. 'This is all your fault.'

*   *   *

A woman in a café brings me a towel with my tea. When she touches my shoulder, tears drop onto the table top. I need to change my tattoo. I am a philosopher; my job is to seek the truth, and I have based everything on a lie. I thought I could have stopped her, stopped time. But you can't change time or people—both shift in their own paths. I can't save people, not yet anyway, I'm only a beginner. I can't change things for Lana. But I'm not done with Jackamore.

Chapter Ninety-One

I Can Do It Too

On the way out of Rhys Withins's birthday party, having given the mother an almighty clue that the piano player was her son's murderer. I pick up the family portrait from the hallway and place it under my arm. It will be my first acquisition for my new place, my next adventure. As I step out of the doorway, a hand grips my arm.

Stephen Killigan grins at me but his eyes are iced. His fingers circle tightly around my forearm. 'Bet this wasn't part of your plan, Jackamore,' he says.

No it was not. And as a result, I can feel my heart beat again. 'No, it was not, Mr Killigan.'

I feel the curve of my own knife at the base of my back, in between the notches of my spinal column. I would know that knife anywhere, the way it graces flesh with its signature and flesh falls away at its touch. And now it caresses me. Blood runs.

Stephen pushes me down the steps and into the street that runs along the back.

'You've managed to control it then. Your skill. Do you know, Stephen, I am feeling something, a swelling, like the swelling of a body after death, which, I imagine, is often called pride. Have you ever watched a body, Stephen? Stood in vigil as it turns from sunset red to dusk to twilight to black midnight? It is something all humans should do.' I do not know

423

what he is going to do: after all this time, someone else is in control.

'Down here,' he says. We stand by a wall, the Cam metres away. It is one of the locks, keeping back the water but for only so long; at some point the river has to be levelled.

Somewhere among the backyards and washing lines, a dog barks and a baby wheedles.

'Now you are the one with the choice,' Stephen says. The point of the knife goes further into my skin. 'Die by your own knife, the one you used on Rhys and Miranda, or by your own rope. The rope you used to kill Lana.' He is trembling. His adrenal glands are pumping epinephrine into his bloodstream; his pupils dilating; his lungs, heart, alimentary canal all reacting to the fight and the fear, just as mine are.

I look in his eyes and take a step back against the wall. He has it: there in his glare is the willingness to kill. I would call his bluff otherwise. But it is present, under the surface of his skin, like the gradients present in a flat map.

'I think the Jack of Diamonds, the rope, would be most fitting,' I say. 'You aren't here for the other victims. Only Lana. And she is only here because of you. Remember this moment. Remember that this is when you are alive, when you are on the brink of someone else's death.'

Stephen laughs. It is a laugh I recognise as mine: one that does not touch the sides or eyes. That is the best result of this pseudo-experiment of Robert's. A young man has been stripped of his heart just as authentic features are taken out of a house and replaced with fakery. He has been emptied, cleared and will kill as a result. Now that is the beauty of murder.

'I can just leave, Stephen—you know that, don't you? At any time I choose I can step into another time far quicker and slicker than you. You are getting better but you have barely shed your baby wings. Where shall I go next? I will give you the great honour of choosing my next destination. But make it a good one for murder, full of people willing to listen to the voice in their heads.'

Stephen is still laughing. It irritates my ears. 'You said to me once that I should not love, as that will hold me back.'

'I did. And I was right. Look at you now.'

'Do not,' he shouts, his blue eyes flaring, 'speak to me as if you were a proud father.'

'I have every right—' I stop speaking. Out of the shadows a small figure shuffles forward. A figure I know well.

'Hello Jackamore,' she says.

'Good afternoon, Iris,' I reply. 'I thought you could no longer join us.'

'I've been practising,' she says. 'It is good to see you again.'

I twist to talk to Killigan. 'I know what you are trying to do. But I did not love her.' She looks at me calmly. 'I do not love,' I say. I concentrate my mind on travelling but she keeps on looking at me and memories come, locking me to her and now.

I can't travel. The knife is in the epidermis now. The pain is sharp and real. And if this is the time that I die then so be it.

Still holding the knife to me with one hand, he loops the rope round my neck. If I move, I know the Laundy will be glad to sink further into me. I count my pulse. 80. Iris watches and I watch her. He pulls the noose tight around my throat. I grab at the rope,

425

try to insert a finger between it and my larynx but he is stronger than he appears. My vision is blurred and we are flicking through time and the sound that comes from my throat is a strangled gargle and there are stars that I have not studied in front of my eyes and if this is the time to go, goodbye—

The rope goes slack. 'Hold him,' Stephen says to someone I can't see. He can't do it; of course he can't. There are arms on me and shouting and the memories of Iris slip off like a shroud from a corpse and I
am
free.

Chapter Ninety-Two

Beauty and the Beast

Somewhere above us, cell doors open. They don't clink; glasses clink: prison doors clang, crank and grate. Robert winces. He sits on the edge of the thin mattress, looking at the stains on the inside of his coffee cup. 'It's a bit Dr Lecter, isn't it? Visiting me in my cell?'

'You can't derail me, not anymore, Robert. Why are you still protecting her?' I ask. 'And him.' I put my hand to the bruise that spreads from my cheekbone to my jaw.

He puts down the cup and looks at me. 'You look thin,' he says. 'And older. But there is something about you. Your eyes give me vertigo. It is a shame a portrait wasn't made of you before all this started. To compare to now.'

I touch my face before I can stop myself. Sitting

down, I look around the room. It is painted the grey of long-dead fish. On the wall next to me are letters to Julia from Robert, all in violet writing, the characters falling over themselves, I can't tell whether they've been returned to sender or if he never sent them; and a small shelf, with a gold-framed picture of Julia, smiling and holding a rose. Anger burns up my stomach. 'Tell the police what you know about Jackamore. You could be out of here in a couple of years.'

Robert smiles. It's an open smile that finds his eyes and lights them. His face has changed as well as mine. The wrinkles have softened, loosened. 'Tell me, how is college?'

'I've been given your rooms. I'm not sure I want them.'

'Keep on being honest, Killigan. It's one of the most beautiful things about you.'

'How can you still talk about beauty?'

'You may insist on denying the beauty of the murders but you cannot deny the beauty of my actions, surely?'

I'm not going to give him anything.

'Perhaps you've never loved someone enough to do anything for them.' He twists his ring round his right ring finger. 'In which case I feel sorry for you. Julia is an extraordinary woman. You don't know her. She is intelligent, charming, talented—she can pick up any instrument, make it bend to her and sing out her wishes. Even as a girl.' He opens the drawer by his bed, takes out two photographs and hands me one in which two fair-haired children hold hands, twin heads turned to each, smiling as if they are the only people in the world. 'She was beautiful. So was I, hard to believe I know. People

427

stopped us in the street to stare. We were very popular.' Robert's eyebrow lifts as he holds out the other photo. A man stands by a pond, his hand up to his eyes, squinting in the sun. 'My uncle. She wouldn't let him near me. She sacrificed herself for me. Now I can sacrifice myself for her. In that there is symmetry. Elegance. Purity. Selflessness. Selflessness has an aesthetic purity.' He moves about the room as if he were in a lecture hall not a prison cell with flat-eyed walls. 'I should write about that; it's not like I haven't got time.' He stretches up to reach a book on a shelf and something cracks. He pings up an eyebrow, and the old Robert is, for the moment, back. 'Although not as much as you have.'

'How much do you know about what happened? When you were at Oxford.'

'When your roommate leaves the study room in your camel overcoat at four and comes back with it smelling of dung and blood three minutes later, you know something is awry. And when he offered me the chance to travel in time, I tried, but I could never leave Julia behind.'

He flicks through the book then throws it on the bed. 'I never asked Jackamore any more than is necessary—that is one of the conditions of our friendship—but even he went too far, killing someone in the college.'

'Do you regret any of this?' I ask.

'I did not want them to die, but the only thing I would really change is for Julia to have been kept safe. That would have been perfect.'

'The "perfect" murder. You don't really believe that, do you? I thought that was all bluster, before you decided to try and frame me.'

428

'You can't blame me for that, surely?'

'I can. I do.'

'How churlish.' He smiles and sucks on the end of his fountain pen, blowing out imaginary smoke. 'Why did you really come here, Stephen? It wasn't to see me.'

I lean forward, 'Tell me more about Grass.'

'Well, it is green, unless parched. And stretches over the earth like a canvas ready for rolling . . . ' He sees my face. 'Oh all right, then. You are no fun anymore. You want to know more about Jackamore. May I ask why?' He tilts his head to one side and the smile slips off his face. 'You loved Lana. I understand that.' He rubs the knuckle of his ring finger. His forehead ripples. 'And I want to help you. But it's a question of loyalty. Jack helped me help Julia. It isn't his fault it went wrong.'

'It's not mine. He wanted you to be found out.'

'We all want to be found out by someone, Stephen. I found you out. As soon as I saw you, I knew. You are a fraud, a beautiful fraud. You pretend to be the ebullient trickster; and inside, and I know you inside, you are clinging to the edge of your bed, rocking. The boy who became a philosopher because he cannot bear to think, not about what really matters. You cannot run for ever, Stephen.'

I check out of the window and down the corridor. No sign of the guard; no suicide watch for another half hour. I launch at Robert, grab him by the collar and push him backwards. His head smacks against the wall.

'I am not running from anything. You are the one sprinting from your responsibility: you called Jackamore Grass—you owe me, and the victims.'

Robert peels my hand from his shoulder; his amber eyes look on me with pity. 'I'm sorry, Stephen. I don't know what I can do.' He gazes at the picture of Julia and does not say goodbye.

Chapter Ninety-Three

The Beauty of Murder

It started with a phone call.

'Jackamore?'

'I have been in Cambridge for over a year. You have not replied to my invitations.'

'I don't have time to explain. I need to see you, now,' Robert says. His speech is rushed; his consonants huddle together as if backing away at knifepoint.

'The last time we saw each other, Robert Sachs, you said you never wanted to see me again. Which is it to be, seeing me or not seeing me?'

'No games, Jack.'

'You only call me that when you are trying to appear sincere. What is—'

'Twenty-two Madingley Road. Come through the gate in the back garden.' He is out of breath. Beyond his voice is the sound of water running.

I twist the telephone rope around my wrist. I do not approve of new telephonic devices. They have no cables, no wires. I like everything to connect. Join to something else, and for me to be the one to sever it. 'I owe you less than nothing, Robert. You are in debt to me for spending away my faith in you. You let me down.'

'How can you say that? Just because I would not—' Robert's voice winches higher. 'We are not all like you, Jackamore. Fortunately.'

'Do not ring me here and call me that.' I look around. A man peers up from his place at the desks. He has taken his shoes off under the table. That is not in the rules. There are notices stating that this is not acceptable.

A familiar female voice murmurs in the background.

*　　　*　　　*

The beauty queen lies dead on the carpet. Her arm is bent above her head as if still waving to the clapping crowd. Blood blooms beneath her. Her once-white dress is a mess of red.

'Make her vanish, Jackamore?' he says.

I look around the living room. Photos of the two of them throughout their lives. No one else. This is their own world and they will build up a universe of lies to protect it. A cello leans against the piano. The shaped holes to each side possess an appealing symmetry. 'Why did you kill her?' I ask.

'She was beautiful. And she laughed at me,' Julia says. Her face is Botox still.

'Is there another, or others,' I ask, 'that you would kill for similar reasons? Because that is what I am giving you permission to do. Would you like that, Julia?' I ask, placing my hand on her shoulder. Robert flinches and steps between us.

She nods and there is a microflash of a smile on her lips. 'There is a child,' she says. 'A choir boy.'

I nod. I need to act. Soon the beauty queen will be stiff with rigor and more difficult to play.

431

'You will have to change the carpet,' I say as I leave. 'I suggest a red one.'

Chapter Ninety-Four

The Masks and the Ends of Time

All four masks are in my bag. I am amazed that Jane let me take them, but she too wants them destroyed for good. Each one is wrapped in muslin and I swear I can feel them breathing and whispering, billowing out the cloth. It is as if I am carrying four heavy ghosts.

'Are you sure you are all right to be left out here?' the boatman says as we approach the hut. It's a short row from the train station: days ago I could have driven but now the fens are flooding again. 'It's a bit creepy—isn't that where that girl was kept for ages? By that queer what killed the beauty queen.'

'That's not what happened. And don't use that word.'

He blows out cigarette smoke. 'Didn't mean to offend, I'm sure. Terrible business. The boy and those girls. And their poor parents being hounded by the press. It's a shame, it really is. I don't know why they do it, those journalists.' He glances suspiciously at my notepad and my heavy rucksack. 'Hey, you're not one, are you?'

'No. I'm a lecturer.'

'Right. Well that's all right then. That's as far as I can get,' he says, pointing to the field beyond. It's too shallow from here on as they've stopped the flooding. 'I'd come back for you later, but there's the first part of that new Swedish murder on the telly.'

I wait until he is out of sight and then wade through the calf-high water towards the hut and beyond until I find a small swelling in the land that is relatively dry. In two days' time, when forensics have finished for good, they will turn the flooding machines back on and, within weeks and years, the wetlands will be back, taking back what was once their own. Balancing the rucksack on my legs, I reach in and take out the top mask, the one placed on Rhys's face, and a hammer. I place the mask on the ground, and whack at it. The stone mask cracks into two pieces. Both lie with dull mud eyes.

Miranda's mask smashes into five satisfying pieces, Dawn's into three.

Then there is Lucy's and Lana's.

I hold the mask they shared up to the sky and picture Lana's face, her real one, her first-thing-in-the-morning face, her pillow-marked and bare and slightly salty to the tongue face that twisted into a grimace when I tickled her armpits in an intimate alarm, her eyes gummed at the corners and a faint line of dribble down to her dimples.

This is the mask that means I can't see that face again.

This is the mask that galvanised me into searching out the face behind it, causing her to be killed in the process.

I was clay and it fired me.

I lay it on the ground and raise the hammer—

and let it thud on the ground.

All I can see is her face. I can't destroy that, but I can't take the mask home with me.

I trace the outer edge of the mask where her hairline would be and bear it held to my chest back into the water until I am up to my knees. Bending down, I hold the mask to the meniscus, and let go. For one moment it stays and I think it will float then water comes out of the eyes and it sinks, slowly, rocking and I can't see it and I hope it can't see me. The other pieces of mask are scattered around her and there they can stay, to be swum through by fish and speared by reeds for centuries until someone decides to drain again, as they will, as they always will.

A sob swells up inside me and bursts as I turn.

I feel the water on my leg, cool and reacting to the warmth of my leg, my leg reacting to it, and then I peel deeper: the atoms mix with the atoms in my leg until there is no separation and as me I am water and the sky is reaching into the water and flooding me and and all is me and the squawk is me and the flying is me.

Time is water and I can part it where I want and walk through a dry canyon, picturing the when I want to be in.

The hut is still on the bank, but there is now no water in what was once the river. It looks small and vulnerable, like a child left out on the moor. Yet it will survive floods and kidnap and death within and near-murder.

Bill sits on a stump round the back, knotting a net. 'You're back, then,' he says, looking up and squinting. 'I thought you'd show up again one day. You left your clothes.'

'Did you miss me?'

'Miss the big fish we couldn't eat? Of course we did. The girls were heartsore for days after you

434

left,' he says. He grins. He has one fewer tooth than before. 'We wondered what'd happened to you, that's for sure. Martha thought you'd be all right. Said you had a good head on your shoulders. I said you'd be lucky if you hadn't got yourself caught in a lobber pot and hung up in the rafters of an alehouse.'

'You were both right, in a way.'

He reaches out and places his hand on my shoulder. 'You look older, boy.' I want to cry.

'I am older, Bill. Nothing can stop that.'

'What happened, lad?' His tone drops.

'I lost someone. And they are not coming back.'

He grasps my hand. His rough, warm fingers grip me. 'When you lose so much it is easier to let go. Don't lose hold of *everything*, Stephen. Something always comes out of death. Believe me. Mary is my second wife. I nearly didn't get there.'

Two faces appear at the window of the hut, there's the sound of scuffling and the girls run out. They pull at my arms and, tucking their knees up, swing backwards and forwards. 'Mind,' I say, 'you'll have one off and I won't be able to conduct a great symphony again.'

'A what?' asks Bill.

'A symphony. It's like a book, only music. Although it is possible that it hasn't been invented yet.'

'Students,' is all he says, shaking his head. 'Well, he says, 'are you coming in then?'

*   *   *

Mary serves up a stew with vegetables that dissolve on the tongue and hunks of bread so filling that

435

I can barely eat. Every few minutes Bill grabs her hand and looks at her as if expecting her to disappear at any minute and my heart feels like it's being squeezed in the hands of a butcher.

'I found the man who killed that girl uncovered at the levelling site.'

Bill cuts off a small chunk of cheese and sniffs it. 'Good for you. And for her. They will find judgement in the world to come if not in this.'

'I'm about to make sure he finds it very soon indeed,' I say.

He shakes his head but says nothing.

'The draining is affecting this area then? The river has dried up. I thought it would be safe,' I say, mopping up the last of the stew.

Mary glances at Bill and holds up her hand. 'Do not talk about the Level—Bill was in the last riot.'

Bill grimaces and points to the gap where one of his front teeth used to be. 'Mary tried to plug it with a wooden peg but it kept falling out. It don't trouble me; it's easier to sup my soup through.' He demonstrates by taking a spoonful of stew and noisily sucking it.

Mary takes a cloth off the table and throws it at him and he spills the liquid down his shirt. He gets up and goes out to the other room.

Mary leans forward. 'He will not tell you himself, he has too much pride, but we are moving to live with my father in Ely. The murder of that girl has given them the excuse to drain further, "to uncover the secrets of the fens". Bill can't be a tenant land farmer and learn a new skill at his age.'

'I'm sorry,' I say.

Bill comes back in, whistling. 'I'm going out in the boat tonight, if you want to go back to the

436

stone city.'

'The Stone City?'

'That's what I call it. I see boats, great big ones some of them, carrying the stone they use to put up the new buildings. They heave them out and next you see them being made into points and spires and halls and I have to say it is impressive—all I can do is fish. But I could not live there. Cities sing sad songs underneath, and this one is more sad than most. They say the fens are cold, but that stone takes more sun than the sky has got to warm it, and it doesn't give it back.'

I could stay here—learn how to fish and make nets and—but that will not exist anymore. Not in the same way. Murder has a long arm span: it affects everyone. 'I need to get back.'

Mary stands to clear away the plates. As she passes by my chair, she bends to kiss the top of my head. 'Goodbye,' she says.

*   *   *

I feel like a canal lock losing its level as I wave Bill away. He looks round before rowing round the bend in the river, holds up his hand and I can't see him anymore.

Sepulchre's clock tower rings out midnight. The kitchen light is still on.

'I said I would return,' I say at the bottom of the steps.

Simon spins round. His face is freckled with flour. He drops the bowl he is holding and it smashes on the floor. Bending to pick the pieces up, he holds my gaze.

'You look like you've seen a ghost,' I say. 'I'm

not going to hurt you. I've come to tell you that the artist *was* responsible for Lucy's death, and where he lives.'

'What do you want me to do?'

'Whatever you consider necessary,' I reply. 'He is currently finding favour with the court, as are his paintings. I suggest you stop that going any further.'

He looks pensive for a second, then a change of thought flashes across his eyes. 'What happened to the cat?' he asks.

'Do you want her back?' I ask. Please say no, please say no.

'Is she content?'

'I'm looking after her,' I say. 'I've called her Gingerbread.'

He nods and picks up his pastry pin. I read out Charles Witt's address as Simon walks to the door. 'Thank you,' he says.

I wave away his thanks and half expect my body to become transparent. There is justice; there is revenge and there are the areas of grey that ghosts are grown in.

*   *   *

I stand behind one of the columns supporting the walkway and breathe my way into the right brain state that allows me to travel, taking in the sensory input around me and in me, and allowing everything to flood me:

438

The stone is the white of wishbones and gristle,
the smell is of whitebait and marshwind and
    samphire,
the sound is of water and blood in the ears
the taste is the salt and umami of tears
the touch is the touch of the touch of a mother
in the now there is me and there is no another.

There is the lurch of landing a fish. I turn on the spot. Electric lamps; air that clears the lungs not chokes them; CCTV camera that can't quite see me; and the scaffolding that is now only halfway up the gate. I'm home.

Indigestion sends a wave of acid up my oesophagus and a migraine migrates across my vision but travelling is getting easier every time. I don't know how I feel about that. It means I'm becoming more like Jackamore, and that is what he wants.

I knock the knocker to the Mistress's Lodge. And again, harder.

Anwar the butler answers, frowning. He is carrying a glass mug of hot cocoa.

'Thank you very much, that's exactly what I need,' I say before he can speak, taking the chocolate from him. I take a large mouthful and, as I swallow, feel the friction of whiskey goad my throat.

Anwar gasps and opens his mouth.

I speak before he can. 'I know it's late. And I'm sure I'm not that popular round here, but I think the Mistress will want to speak to me. It is about the college finances. I believe I've found a way to solve them.'

The Mistress ties the belt to her silk dressing

gown and sits down artfully on the edge of a grey French armchair. 'This had better be good,' she says. 'I have an eight o'clock breakfast tomorrow where I have to prostrate myself before the rich colleges and beg for a handout. Your escapades with Robert Sachs and his sister have hardly helped.' She sighs towards the door. Where's Anwar? I ordered more cocoa.' She stares pointedly at the empty glass next to me.

'This is more than good, Claire. If I am right then you should have enough money to spruce up the college and set up a fund for state-school students.'

'But we don't intend to set up a fund for state-school students.' She blinks once then stares, wet-eyed, for an unnerving amount of time, like a Siamese cat.

'You do now,' I say. I take a form out of my pocket and unfold it. 'I had this run up by Tara Yarrow; I met her in your study that time, do you remember? It states that you pledge to establish a scholarship for twenty state-school candidates a year, rising after five years given good investments, to twenty-five. And a programme for making sure state schools get through the door.'

'You realise this isn't strictly binding,' the Mistress says.

'Professor Yarrow said it would be "as hard to get out of as the Mistress out of her Spanx after the Christmas feast".'

The Mistress raises her chin and sits up straighter. Her robe moves as if she is sucking her stomach in. 'Show me what you've got, then we'll see if I sign.'

440

'How much further,' she says, as we weave past boxes and walk down more stairs to get to the basement. 'I didn't know half of this was here.'

Some of the corridors have no lighting so I hand her my phone, set onto torch, and she points it in front of her feet, leaving me to trip and stumble over crates. At last we reach it, at least I think so: it is hard to navigate from memories of a dead century, and I begin to heave away the dust-covered boxes blocking the door.

'There it is,' I say, mid-sneeze, and take the bolt cutters out of my back pocket. They're not needed. The lock falls apart in my hand.

The room is dark and swagged with cobwebs that cling to the lips. I walk straight into a stack-up of chairs and tables, banging my shin.

'This isn't a convoluted attempt to get me alone in an old stationery cupboard is it, Dr Killigan?' she says. Her white face peers round the doorway.

'No. That would never be a possibility.' A shudder passes over me that I hope she didn't see. I have had enough of that.

'Quite right, it wouldn't,' she replies, although there's a twitch of her lips as she says it. 'So what's in there, then? It must be some kind of treasure to be worth that much.'

I fumble out lecterns and music-stands and benches and boxes, moving all the time, making a channel through like when the police have to tunnel through cardboard and books to reach a corpse buried under a lifetime of detritus that they couldn't throw away.

In the corner, leant against the wall, are the

441

portraits. I carry each one through to a corridor that has a light switch and show her the pictures. There is Lucy, standing, lying, partially and fully nude; a different aspect of her in each of the pictures. The torchlight is harsh, but shows up the cracks, the faded paint. The outside wall the paintings have been laid against is damp to the touch, and I want to cover Lucy over, apologise for the conditions she has been kept in.

'These are awful,' the Mistress says. 'There is no quality to them at all. And I don't even know the artist. And I don't think much of their model.' Even in the dark I can tell she's scowling.

'The information you are missing is that these,' I point to Charles Witt's pictures of horses and fruit; and fruit and flowers; and flower-strewn horses; and horses with flute-players, 'were made by a man who confessed on paper to killing the model, his muse that you were so sisterly about. She was also a Sepulchre College servant to a pederast Master who assisted in covering up the crime. This is Charles Witt's painting of her. Between that and the Master's diaries, with her missing shoe and the lock of hair that was missing from her body when she died, you should be able to get the macabre to pay out the cash for the cleaning of the college.'

She flicks through the diary and grimaces at the contents. She then touches the broken surface of the artwork, her fingertip lingering on Lucy's face. Her face is lit by the torch's brash blue light. 'We'll auction off the paintings, with a publicity drive behind it, sell rights to the image, allow them to film here in college. It's got nudity and a murdered woman. It's perfect,' she says.

'I thought you wanted the college to "veer clear

442

of negative press at a time of recession".'

'But this is the past, Stephen, don't you see?

'Even a past with a corrupt college Master with a tendency to paedophilia?'

'Well we'll cover over that bit,' she says, looking through the paintings. She stops at the portrait of Jackamore. 'This one has good form, and technique,' she says.

'You don't want to sell that one,' I say, quickly. 'It's nothing to do with the murder so you won't get much money in an auction.'

'He's handsome. Who he is?' she asks.

'A librarian.' That still smarts and always will— that he was there all the time, skulking in the stacks under our noses.

She stands up, dismissing him. 'We'll get something for it, if it's by this Witt killer. "Killer Witt", that's not bad.'

'Then you'll sign?'

'I'll sign.' She scribbles her signature and dates the document. 'And you'll say nothing about the Master's involvement—after all it is not in the college's interests.'

'I promise that I won't say anything,' I say. And I won't. But you can be sure I'll send all the evidence to the press.

443

Chapter Ninety-Five

Final Time

I'm in London. Present day. Though, as I walk through Trafalgar Square, the layers of Londons-gone flex and pulse beneath my feet; in some streets the feeling is so strong that I'm convinced that all I have to do is close my eyes and reach out my hand and be in a time of hat-doffing. But I don't try. I have a pocket full of money, a painting to buy and a hot-dog stand nearby.

'Lots of onion please mate, mustard and ketchup.' Fried onions linked like a magician's rings are heaped onto the hot dog. The smell makes my stomach heave.

The auction room is packed, and hot. An electric fan turns its head from side to side, blowing into the faces in the front row. Bidders wave glossy catalogues at each other.

By the lectern is the first portrait, covered over by a blue dust sheet. Iris Burton is already here: sitting in the back row, legs up on two other chairs, reading a broadsheet that tickles the head of the man in front. Seeing me, she swivels her legs round and pushes her glasses up her nose. They slide down again, the chain tinkling.

'Thanks for coming,' I say, sitting down. 'You didn't have to.'

'Of course I didn't have to; what a ridiculous platitude. I want to see you win. Besides, I had other business in town,' she says, wiggling her eyebrows in what, I think, is supposed to be a display of enigmatic secrecy.

'Well ta anyway.'

'Nice write up for you,' she says, tapping the paper.

LECTURER BRINGS KILLERS TO JUSTICE, the headline states.

'Better than them saying you've got cellulite.'

'It's not right. Inspector Horne has painted me as a hero.'

'While still managing to take plenty of credit herself, I see. She didn't mention that it was you who found Mortimer's diary. Or Lana who unearthed all the documents that would convict Jackamore if he were ever caught, and would have had Witt hanged at the time. I don't suppose she'll be enlisting your help in other ancient cases?' Iris raises her eyebrows and takes a custard cream out from a clingfilmed pack of five. She nibbles at the edges and grimaces. 'Stale,' she says.

'I'll help her if I can. And I don't know why you are sniffy. She did as much as I did.'

'I'd like to see *her* trying to time travel.'

I imagine Jane throwing herself in the river and clambering out, hair covering her face, bellowing for Sergeant Pemberton to get her a towel. I'd like to see that too.

'She believes me now, after Jackamore's book and the paintings and the DNA that links him to crimes across time. Her chief is happy to put the paradox of a child being dead and alive at the same time down to errors in pathology, and the press are happy too as they get to discuss a series of blunders and a scapegoat—that's weeks of righteous indignation without lifting an inky finger, but she's also been contacted by people high up in the Met and secret services who are aware of him. She doesn't get why I need the painting though.'

Iris snorts. 'You don't need the painting. You know what he looks like.'

'I want it hanging in front of me every day.'

'I wouldn't trust her too much. She didn't exactly summon all of Cambridge's police service to find him.'

'He had already gone, Iris. He could be any when.' Anger pokes at a raw point in my chest.

'And she already had Robert and Julia Sachs. Everyone is satisfied that way: the police have a result and can put away files in a filing cabinet and the press can be morally outraged at how unnatural it is for a woman to kill. It's an abomination, you see. In the media's eyes.' Iris's own eyes flash. 'At some point people won't make the assumption that women are the nurturers, and that not nurturing means you are not feminine. And that not reproducing is considered selfish. Then they might consider that women can easily kill. You can be more than one thing at once.'

'All right, all right,' I say, 'back in your box. I thought you didn't approve of the paradox.'

Iris sticks out her tongue.

The auctioneer, a woman, in her forties, I'd say, with eyebrows plucked into steeples, steps forward. 'My name is Cynthia Slider and, on behalf of Planter and Harness, I'd like to welcome you to this auction of rare and notorious paintings. Discovered in forgotten vaults of Sepulchre College, Cambridge, they are the works of three previously undiscovered artists of the mid-seventeenth century. One of whom has been unveiled as a killer, with portraits of his victim, a housemaid and muse, that were painted shortly before her untimely death.'

A titillated ripple rides the room.

She continues. 'The murderer, Charles Witt, only son to a baron who supported, and is said to have collaborating in hiding, Charles I during the Civil War, was himself murdered, although his killer was never caught.'

Twin stabs of guilt and shame make my stomach clench. This is my fault. And then I see Lana's writing down to her wrist: THIS IS NOT YOUR FAULT.

Cynthia Slider plays with her long silver earring and strokes her earlobe. An assistant hurries over and lifts the sheet from the easel. Charles Witt's earlier works are up first. A succession of commissioned portraits is paraded: his father and mother and uncles and children and dogs and anyone that could be persuaded to sit for him. I like the one of a horse standing with one leg raised. His ears are flat against his head and he looks as if he would like to kick the painter in the face with a shiny hoof.

Hands rise, heads tip, programmes flick to indicate interest. Auction house employees stand with phones to their ears, nodding occasionally and murmuring with the dropped jaw of the southern posh. They're upper-class call-centre workers, I suppose.

The paintings go for around a thousand pounds each, pushed up each time the auctioneer highlights Witt's inhumanity. Waving her gavel, she says: 'He is thought to have suffocated Lucy Miller, a beautiful, innocent girl, and cruelly disposed of her body in the marshes of the Cambridge fens. It was only by chance that her body was found and he was apprehended, and when he was he laughed and laughed.'

'How do you know all that then?' I call out. 'Given it's nigh four hundred years ago. Got witness statements, have you?'

Cynthia glares at me, wrinkles up her lips and turns to the next painting. 'This is one of the more confrontational paintings that Charles Witt produced. It is thought to be one of the earliest examples of the form by a British artist and gives perhaps an insight into his disturbed mind at the time of the murder.'

The assistant parades a still life, with a skull next to a vase of what looks like phlox. Witt wouldn't know what to do unless someone else showed him, copying Dutch innovators and Jackamore's cruelty.

I wipe my hands against my jeans. He's up next, just before the portraits of Lucy. Hopefully everyone else will be thinking of those and holding fast to their money rather than bidding for a picture of an unknown man.

'Next we have the most accomplished of Charles Witt's paintings,' the auctioneer says, reading from her notes.

Iris pats my arm. Her fingers are dry and scratchy and comforting.

'We do not yet know the subject, but the anonymous man is rendered in great detail, with an attention to the facial expression that suggests an intriguing character. There are rumours that he was intimately involved with the murder of the muse.'

Oh, don't say that. People in front of me sit up a little straighter. Heads bend to see the description in the catalogue. Fuck off, everyone, he's mine.

448

The assistant walks shyly down the centre aisle, her head down, holding the portrait of Jackamore Grass as if she were about to be given away by him. She places him on the easel. He leans against it, arms folded. That smirk on his face. The triumph. His tongue is dipped into the space between his lips and his teeth, mocking me. Saying, 'Come on, then.' This is no picture of Dorian Gray. The Jackamore I've met has marks and lines on his face that have been carved in by acts and thoughts and choices.

'Would you sit down, please, sir?' says a young man in a suit that overshoots his shoulders.

I am standing up, pointing. Iris tugs on my elbow and pulls me back to my seat. Disapproving murmurs settle around us like leaves.

'I have a number of bids on the books already so let us start the bidding at one thousand pounds.'

Shit.

No hands go up. That's more like it.

'Then how about eight hundred. Eight hundred pounds for an early seventeenth-century masterpiece.'

When did it become a masterpiece? Because she said so? That's art for you.

A woman in the front row with hair the colour of Marmite sticks her hand straight up.

'An enthusiastic first bidder. Thank you,' says Cynthia. 'Shall we say nine hundred next?'

The price is met, and then another, flying one after the other like shuffled cards. 'One thousand five hundred, two thousand . . . ' The bids shift from someone on a phone line to several in the room, to me, lifting my forefinger in the air and hoping no one will bid again. The phone bidder ups the price. My heart is racing itself to an attack. My budget is

£3,000—that's the last of my inheritance from Ma.

Iris leans over. 'I could buy it for you. No one knows me.'

I have to quash a sob. I've turned into a wuss. 'That is lovely of you, Iris. But no. If I'm going to get this I'll get this on my own.'

'Three thousand pounds, do I hear three thousand pounds?' Cynthia says.

'You do,' I call out.

'Thank you, sir,' Cynthia says. The bidding goes up. And up. 'Three thousand five hundred?'

Silence in the room. People look round to me and raise their eyebrows.

'Three thousand five hundred,' says the curly-haired girl on the phone.

Iris looks over to me. 'You sure?' she whispers, reaching into her pocket.

I nod.

Jackamore is taken away. His snide smile lingers in my mind.

*　　　*　　　*

I stand outside on the pavement, still waiting for Iris. I didn't want to stay to see the portraits of Lucy being sold. The macabre desire for someone else's death gives me shivers today despite the heat.

People bustle past, some apologising, others huffing. Across the road, a tall man with his back to me talks on a phone. There is something about him, the turn, the nose. Jackamore? I start to cross but a bus chugs in the way. When it passes, he has gone.

'I got you a consolation prize,' Iris says. She holds out a tiny picture of the mask.

450

Chapter Ninety-Six

Jane puts the phone down. Pemberton watches, waiting.

'She's dead,' she says. 'That was the hospice. She went last night, in her sleep.' Jane tries to keep her tone flat but her voice cracks.

'I am sorry, guv,' Paul says, pulling up a chair. He reaches out a hand but does not actually touch her.

Jane takes a picture of Marion out of her top drawer. 'I said I'd go back and see her, Paul. I promised her, and I didn't.'

'You've been busy.'

'I'm always busy. I could have gone. I should have gone.'

Pemberton looks down at his hands. 'It's hard,' he says, quietly. 'When people close to you are ill or dying. You think your life will change completely, but you still have to make sure there's milk in the fridge and turn up at work and drive the car in a straight line.'

'That's the first time I've heard you talk about personal things. Who are you talking about?'

'My wife. She died.' Pemberton rubs the gold ring on his right ring finger.

She had never even noticed it before. Jane shuffles through conversations with Paul, his words, his clipped behaviour. 'All this time I thought you were an arse. When I was the biggest arse there has ever been. I've never even asked about your family,' she says. 'I am sorry. Has there been anyone else?'

He smiles, a little. Shakes his head. 'I can't imagine that.' He twists the wedding ring round and round.

'I can't imagine ever thinking like that,' Jane says. 'So as detectives we must make a good team.'

'We will, guv,' he says.

A rap at the door. The chief enters, rubbing his neck. 'So what's next for you, then, Jane?' He laughs for no reason and his neck rolls jiggle. He has the forced jollity of a Butlins entertainer who never made the big time. Jane takes a mouthful of tea to stop herself screaming in his fat face. That would be understandable to anyone who knew him, his wife especially—Jane met her at the Christmas bash and got the impression that, beneath the Laura Ashley frocks and Rigby-and-Peller-pinioned tits, there was a woman desperate to take a Breville to the chief's massive head—but it would not be, perhaps, the best career move.

'I thought I'd take early retirement, sir, and live in the South Pacific.'

'You thought wrong, Jane.' His laugh is even more forced. 'And not for the first time. But I will say now that I am hearing very good things about you. You are getting excellent press and that has not gone unnoticed.'

'That's mainly because the labbies have been blamed for cock-ups in identifying Rhys's tissue in the path lab. When we know that's not true.' Hana is livid. She's asked Jane to testify for her if it comes to a tribunal. The chief won't like that. Tough. She smiles at him, sweetly.

He sweeps past that one. 'In fact I've had a conversation with the chief super and he hinted that it would not be a bad thing if you pursued this line of investigation.'

'Could you be more specific, please?' Jane asks.

452

The chief circles his jaw. He has one long red hair like a strand of saffron in his otherwise salt and pepper beard. Jane longs to take tweezers and pluck it right out. That'd make his eyes water even more than they are already. She wonders if she should feel bad for disliking him so much. And decides, on reflection, she shouldn't. 'Cases from history: known or unknown. Goes down a storm with the public; strange really, seeing as they should be concerned with solving crimes in their own times, but that's Mr and Ms Normal for you.'

'I'm sure quotes like that would go down a storm as well.'

His eyes lurch round the room, as if on the scout for recording equipment. Now that's an idea: *no I've no idea how that got out, sir; no I don't know how the device ended up in my pocket—funny that. We must have a mole.* Maybe not. Not since Belinda Millins was shown to heave leaked information to journalists and interested parties. Shame. She made great coffee.

'Well, I'll leave you with that thought,' he says. He nods at Pemberton then turns back to Jane. His right eyelid scrunches up.

Jane waits till he leaves the room. 'Was that a wink? Did he just wink at me?'

'It looked more like a tic to me, guv. Either that or a squint,' Pemberton replies.

'Did you just slag off a superior officer, Pemberton?'

'I may have done, ma'am.' He is blushing; big red patches stripe his face.

Jane feels an urge to hug him. She looks down at the picture of Marion. 'Well done, Pemberton. Well done.'

That night, Jane runs the bath and watches the mirror mist over with steam. She unfastens her bandage, closes her eyes and

stops.

Marion's words play back in her head.

'Live well,' she writes in the condensation in the looking-glass with her finger.

The strapping peels to the floor and she stands, naked as a raw apple core. Letting out a long, slow, Shiraz-scented breath, she plucks a towel and wipes down the mirror. She hasn't seen her face properly in over a year, aside from in a pocket-watch-sized hand mirror, and then only to apply make-up to an eye, her nose or an eyebrow. She touches her cheek and the hollow underneath, carved out by lack of sleep. In the nineties she used blusher to create that effect.

But her face was never the problem.

Trembling, holding onto the towel rail for support, she looks down.

Her chest is flat and puckered, and seems to be chewing on itself. The image in her head is of how she used to be—36D and glad of it. It is like holding a map of concentric rings and contours only to look down at your feet and be in the sea. The radiation burns to the right are still livid, the skin dipping where her nipple would have been. The other looks as if a white flap has been pulled up over her chest and left there, like the roll of fat at the top of tights. She is not the Frankenstein's monster patchwork she had imagined; the scarring is healing and in time she may consider a reconstruction, but, for

454

now, she will be as the fens, with all the mountains and mysteries under the surface.

She steps back from the mirror to see her whole body rather than a Picasso of assorted parts. Ugly and beautiful and mis-shaped and perfect.

'Hello again,' Jane says.

Chapter Ninety-Seven

The Pre-ordained Lecture in Free Will and Determinism

Iris pats me on the back. 'You'll be great,' she says. 'I know it.' She winks and opens the door into the lecture hall, letting out a blast of chat, gossip and blather. Gingerbread looks up at me and gives a silent miaow.

'You can go home, you know,' I say to her. 'You don't have to follow me in.'

She nudges her head against my leg.

The noise dims as we enter. A few of my students, all sitting in the front row, start clapping. Gingerbread leaps onto the stage as if she knows exactly where she should be. She stares at the front row, then bends over to lick her privates. Laughter breaks the tension.

Professor Ian Reynolds, chair of the philosophy faculty, specialist in the philosophy of mind and mariachi bands, stands up at the lectern to introduce me. 'Stephen Killigan joined us only six months ago and has already made his mark on the university. Accused of murder and vilified by the press, he in fact helped to discover the actual killer

455

and uncover a paedophile ring from nearly three hundred and eighty years ago. ' My face now has more blood than my brain. 'The faculty is delighted to welcome him to give the annual Moore Lecture on Philosophy.'

More clapping, my students have progressed to whoops. I look behind me as if expecting someone else to appear. I hold up a hand. 'Thank you but I'm so used to being hated that I just get confused when people are lovely.' The front row laugh.

I glance around the hall. Iris is wearing her peacock hat near the back; Jane has her arms folded in the middle of the third row, straight in front of me. Seeing them both makes me at once relax and want to be brilliant.

I rustle my papers and the last few whispers are swallowed. 'Many of you, including our friends from the press over there,' I point to the reporters standing at the back, 'want to hear about all the things I've been up to. I found a body, which seemed to set off a chain of events that were linked by some key factors: the beauty of the victims and the masks they were wearing. And that appears to be the case. My former colleague, Professor Robert Sachs—'

A hiss skittles across the room.

'Some of you sympathise with him, I know. He convinced me that there is true beauty in flaws, the cracks that run down glass, the colour of spores, what is underneath the mask.'

The boy in the tweed suit from Robert's lecture nods from the same row as he was before and wipes his knuckle under his eye.

'But Robert stood on this very spot and told us, beautifully, eloquently, persuasively, that murder was noble, and with it, perfection could be achieved. That there was a perfect victim—beautiful, pure, honest. The victims in this case, Miranda, Lana and Rhys, were all very attractive, beautiful in different ways and they were murdered for it. He did not hold the knife or strike with the cello—his sister did—but he covered it over and made it a study, a subject, beautiful as an act in itself, lying just as an undertaker makes up a face with fillers and tape and thick make-up to make a mask that only vaguely resembles the person who once lived and is now in decay.'

A flash of red at the door.

The flick of coat tails like the turning of a page.

A latecomer I didn't hear come in.

I twist my head.

Lana stands against the window, smiling at me.

And then she is not. There is only window.

The reverse image of the Lana that wasn't there ghosts in my eyes when I close them.

I turn back to the audience.

'They enraged Julia Sachs because they had what she didn't. Or that is how she perceived the situation. They were qualities to her, universals, abstracts: Beauty, Purity, Youth. Qualities she felt she no longer possessed and so she removed them from others. The world kills beauty, youth and innocence so she is simply carrying out the world's wishes. That is what she believes. The fact that this is premature did not occur to her. Really of course she was a sociopath who could not bear to be invisible, but she saw it as destiny.

'Destiny suggests that there is an overarching force at work, something beyond, an omnipotent Rod Hull with his hand up the universe's Emu.'

457

Laughs from the hacks at the back and the academics at the sides. The rest don't get it. I'm old.

'But it could have been any one of you. Each of you possesses a kind of beauty, or youth or something that she didn't even know she wanted till she saw it in you. You,' I say, pointing at a girl with red hair on the row in front, 'could have been walking your dog one day past her house one Friday; she saw you and your natural hair colour was an affront to her.'

The girl blushes and scratches her head.

'Whereas you,' I nod at Aidan from my tutorial group. 'You would make her livid with your smooth skin and way with words.'

He points at himself, his eyebrows skybound. He seems touched that someone would notice him enough to kill him.

'She came into contact with them due to factors beyond her control; and they died because she lost her temper. That spoils the notion of being an Agent of Destiny,' I say in a booming voice.

Giggles bounce across the hall like rubber balls.

'In philosophy we talk about determinism. Determinism in philosophy, as different from that in physics, Newtonian Determinism—'

Satnam whoops and waves his arms.

'—thank you to Mr Rai, Isaac Newton fan at the back there and the best friend a man could hope for—'

Satnam stands and bows.

'Determinism in philosophy, however,' I continue, 'is concerned with human choices and actions and their relationship to causal sequences, raising questions about the freedom of these

458

choices. Everything that happens is detemined by antecedent events, that's the thesis, inevitable cause and effect. Metaphysicists bicker about the extent to which this is true and how much freedom we have. If taken to the incompatibilist extreme that there is no free action in a deterministic universe, then humans are, as seventeenth-century theologian Jeremy Taylor put it, "nothing but tennis-balls of destiny".' Cause and effect. If I had not found Lana's body then Lana would be alive.

I feel as if my heart is being squeezed. Breathe. Breathe.

Silence in the hall.

Jane leans forward, hand on her heart. Iris waves.

And start again. 'But we must not fall prey to the fallacy named "retrospective determinism" by Henri Bergson. The fact that an event has taken place can lead to us to look backwards in an attempt to find a necessary cause when there isn't one. In our desire to link effect to cause, we lose the wondrous variety of paths that have taken us to that point. Boettner, the twentieth-century theologian and reformer, describes predestination and free will as the "twin pillars of a great temple, and they meet above the clouds where the human gaze cannot penetrate" which is a fancy way of saying that the choice you made over which pair of pants to wear in the morning, or whether to wear any, and I know you filthy lot are trying to divine the choice *I* made, is a mystery based on a whim driven by upbringing, advertising, availability, current weight, psychological state, how many times they've been turned inside out already and many other factors. Boettner may not have had that

459

example in mind, but he should have.'

More laughter. I've got them back. I carry on with the lecture, plotting a course that avoids topics that make images of Lana and Mum materialise in my mind: First-Cause theories, Kant, Mill and Hume, responsibility, indeterminacy in quantum physics for Satnam's sake, the possibility of never knowing whether any choice, including your reality television vote, is your own—

'But what do you think?' a reporter asks.

'Questions at the end, mate,' I say. 'If you can wait eight minutes.'

Another journalist sticks up her hand. 'But doesn't it bother you that there are things we'll never know? Like whether you caused your girlfriend's death by chasing the beauty queen's murderer.'

The audience murmurs.

The heating system shivers.

'You haven't got the hang of this lecture lark, have you? You're supposed to listen not ask questions,' I say, placing my hands on the lectern, hoping my heart doesn't show through my shirt.

The audience looks up at me, expectantly. They want to know.

'Okay,' I say, holding up my hands. 'Questions are good. Philosophy is about asking questions—it is human to want to know more, to penetrate above the clouds and that is what each of us should do: keep going, keep asking questions of mysteries.

'I'm not going to talk about my private life—I'm not that much of a fool—but I will say that there are many things we'll never know, but if we insist on looking back we'll trip over ourselves. Besides, most of the time there are as many answers as questions,

460

some of them contradictory. I keep coming back to Schrodinger's cat.' I point to Gingerbread, who has settled in a croissant shape on my knapsack. 'This is Gingerbread. She found me one evening and has decided not to throw me back yet. Don't worry, I'm not going to put her in a box with a decaying radioactive thing and a canister of gas. For one thing, they don't stock radioactive isotopes at Robert Sayle's.'

They laugh again. I step down off the stage and pace in front of the first row.

'We are many things at one time. Beautiful, ugly, happy, sad. We want people to be in boxes and for things to be simple, to know the answer once and for all, to label the box with dead or alive, good and bad. Guess what: you can't. Conflicting states may both be true. And this is not chaos; it is balance. Contradiction and paradox are at the heart of humanity: just as out of destruction can come life, so the most beautiful qualities—love, loss, grief—can come out of death and murder. It is our choice how we deal with events, how we act after someone has died, or been taken from us. Our actions make us. That there couldn't be any other way does not diminish the value of having done what was the most difficult thing to do. There is no beauty in murder and loss, only in coming out of the aftermath stronger and more alive. And that is the paradox we live in and the choice we can make. It is too easy, too passive, too cowardly to say that all is inevitable. "Whatever will be, will be" leads to no responsibility. You must risk and jump and love and lose. Sartre says we are "condemned to be free" and that just about sums up me. Thank you.'

Silence. Applause. Several stand, then several

461

more. Gingerbread stretches out a leg and sighs back to sleep.

Chapter Ninety-Eight

The Cabinet

'This is a very fine collection you have here, Mr Sylvester,' I say, putting down my glass of port and running a gloved finger down the glass. The room, a front parlour reserved for visitors and open caskets is kept curtained with heavy fabric, lit only by three gaslights.

Arnold Sylvester dusts the top of the cabinet with a fine white handkerchief. When he shakes it out, it is as pristine as when he began. 'Thank you, Mr Grass. And from a man of your standing and experience, that is high praise indeed.' He raises his glass to me and bows his head once, believing me to be an expert in the subject. Which, in many ways, I am. I have more remembrances of death than most.

Sylvester unhooks a key from the wall and holds it out to me. 'Please. I would be most honoured.'

I rest my cane against the panelled wall. There is nothing like a cane. This one is topped by a silver spade. I had considered a skull, but that is too prosaic, too expected. But I must not forget the rest of late Victorian dress on a man; the way it makes me stand as if the whole British colonial world were inside my top hat.

The key slips as easily into the lock as a knife into a heart. His compiled items are few in number but fascinating: a child's death mask; a human tallow candle in a trepanned skull; a photograph of two entwined skeletons in a shallow grave. They will complement my growing museum. 'I'd like to add something, if I may,' I say, turning to him.

'Certainly, certainly.' His eyes widen. There is such glee in them. His eagerness is touching.

Walking over, I take Mr Magic's hand from my bag. It has been aged, leathered. It sits well on the top shelf, just as his counterfeit body lay well in its cold coffin.

Sylvester stares at me; his fingers tap against his thumb in turn. Tap, tap, tap.

'There's room for one more, I think, to make it complete before I take it over. I do like for things to be complete.' I take out my cards and fan them out in my hands. 'Choose Hearts and I take out your heart; Spades, I bury you alive; Diamonds, I hang you with a noose in the shape of that stone; Clubs; I poison you with red clover.'

His brows meet each other. 'I do not understand.'

'You will have what you always wanted: to be your very own memento mori. I can make this happen for you. You are very fortunate: not everybody receives this opportunity. Choose a method and I will do the rest.'

There is no comprehension in his eyes. I open my suitcase. The knives smile in the dim light.

He backs away to the door. It is locked, of course. The key is safe in my pocket. He bangs at the door for his servants. They will not be on their way, having been chloroformed before I pushed the doorbell. He glances at the cabinet.

'Where would you like to be?' I ask. 'Top shelf, next to the hangman's ponytail?'

He whimpers. A sound somewhere between 'no'

463

and a moan emerges from his dry-lipped mouth.

'Oh come on, show some fight, would you? Where is the challenge otherwise?' Although not too much of a fight. My shoulder is still recovering from being dislocated in the fight with Stephen Killigan. It is good to feel the pain, the red heat of inflammation in the tissue.

Sylvester lunges at me. I throw the cards into the air and he swipes them away. One of them catches between his fingers. The Jack of Clubs.

He stares at it. He is trying to remember what Clubs signify. Remembering, he laughs. 'How are you going to poison me? I can't be forced.'

'Now that is not true. But it is not necessary. You drank willingly.' I indicate the poisoned bottle of port.

He does not answer, because he cannot. The poison has already clutched at his oesophagus and squeezed his throat. His choice. He scrabbles at my feet, digging nails into my ankle. He is turning a shade of blue that would suit the sky.

Reaching into my top pocket, I note the time on my watch. Twelve fifty-five post meridiem. In one hundred and twenty-nine years, Stephen Killigan is finishing a lecture on free will and determinism. All I know is that he had every choice along the way and he made all the ones he was going to. He may see that as a problem; as far as I'm concerned, nothing matters, I have proved that, so I may as well do as I wish. One day he will know this, and I will be there to observe his face.

Chapter Ninety-Nine

The Portrait

I walk the long way back from the lecture, following the river just as Gingerbread follows me. The colleges are grey ghosts in my peripheral vision. The sky cannot decide whether to spit at me or shine.

A bicyclist screeches to a stop in front of me. A basket full of books nudges my ribs. 'Watch where you're going, would you?' the girl on the bike says. She tuts and chucks her scarf round her neck.

My heart is in a fist. Everything reminds me of Lana. Even a rude girl in a scarf on a bike.

I keep seeing her. And sensing her. In the glass of bookcases. In the smell of apples in a box. In the edge of my eye when I smile. I reach into my coat pocket and touch my mother's gold ring and Lana's dart. I know I will grow around the loss, become its lining. In time I will see more of what I have than what I haven't but I know it will never go away. And I don't want it to.

*   *   *

'It's all ready for you,' Earl, the new porter, says, sliding out Robert's nameplate and replacing it with mine. He chucks the plate into a box of Robert's belongings. 'Mind out for the fire—the chimney spits like a Chelsea player.'

Stepping into Robert's rooms feels strange, as if trying on a man's discarded shoes. All of his books have gone and the shelves have been swept clean. The place even sounds different as I walk through into his study. My study. The mini fridge is unplugged and no longer humming out white-goods noise. There are still a couple of signs that Robert existed: his velvet drapes are still up, and the filmy netting over the windows. Raindrops run their fingers down the glass.

On the wall, grey smudges frame pictures that are no longer there.

Earl knocks on the door. 'I forgot to say that the police inspector lady called—dropped your coat off and a cake. And Dr Sachs's lawyer got in touch, got us to leave a few bits and bobs.' Earl points to a large rectangular parcel leant up against the fireplace. On top of it is balanced a large envelope and Robert's bone letter opener.

I take my coat from the back of the door and put it on. Walking over to the fire, I tip the contents of the envelope onto the mantel and the smell of violets breathes out along with folded papers, an old pamphlet and a rose's worth of browning petals.

'Dearest Stephen,' the letter says, full of ink blots and crossed-out words.

I realise all this started for you with a missive from me and thus it is fitting that I write again. I told you almost everything when you visited. I was not sure at that point if it was in my interest to help you further and, as you know, I never attempt anything that is not in my interest.

I almost didn't write this, and I still may not send it—sometimes all we have is the option of not doing what is inevitable—and I know

I am waffling, putting off what must come. I was never that interested in ethics but I have, rather embarrassingly, been thinking things through. Even that pleases me aesthetically, the guilty finds himself in his cell, thus removing any benefit from any self-awareness that has resulted. And so it is still about me, so I've learned nothing.

I have not heard from Julia. I could ask where she is, but can't yet bring myself to: whatever the rights or wrongs, I let her down. I shouldn't have given so much away to you. I love her. There is always someone you can't face in the mirror.

I am sorry. For everything. Everything. *This business (what a euphemism that is) has taught that* there is much I do not know, and even more that I do not understand. *That is not something you will extract from my lips in public, and I will deny it, dear boy, if accused thereof.* (The only statements I can make now are in parentheses and even that is posture. It always was. You know everything is fake about me, but then all beauty is in the arrangement).

There is one tiny tenet I cling to when lying on this thin and ridiculous bed *— if in doubt, do something: the only thing to regret is doing nothing.*

Enough pseudo-parental advice. This letter is accompanied by a number of items I want you to look after: my recipe for mayonnaise (I never did get to teach you); the rose; a pamphlet and a painting. The only prudent thing to have on my wall is a picture of lovely Lucy,

467

who shows in-depth knowledge of the politics
of the day while wearing nothing but a pair
of cami-knickers: the portrait would be more
fruitful in your hands. I hope the pamphlet
helps. You know where I am if you need me.
   Yours, as much as anyone's now,
   Robert

I read it through again, and again. Then place the letter in my top drawer and pin up the recipe for mayonnaise. 'The secret is in the lemon,' it says.

I slice down the brown paper covering the painting with the letter opener. The paper peels back and for a moment my brain paints a picture of Lana on canvas and then I see what is actually there. My jaw grinds forward. It is the painting of Jackamore by Charles Witt. He poses, life size, against brown velvet drapes, long fingers curled round his lapels, his eyes mocking me. His top lip sneers.

I punch his fucking face in.

The canvas buckles and tears; the rip spreads to his cheek.

Earl coughs. He's still here, frowning at the painting. 'Don't blame you, looks a nasty sort. Wouldn't like him on my wall. Sorry—he's not a relative, is he?' He wobbles his jowls in a fake shudder, then a real one shivers up over his shoulders.

'No relation. Just a reminder.'

Earl brushes his palm up and down the back of his neck and looks back down the stairs. 'You all right now then? You going to be all right putting that up with your . . . ' He nods at my injured arm.

'I'll be fine,' I say. 'Thanks, I owe you a pint.'

468

I wait till he's stomped all the way down the stairs then, standing on a chair, lift the painting of Jack onto the wall. He hangs there, now.

Picking up the chapbook, I go over to the dark bay window. The book is a crinkled brochure for *The Cabinet of Curiosities: A Victorian Gentleman's Memento Mori Museum*. When I open it, the smell of a dentist's chair leaks out. On the inside cover is a title, a date and, beneath a list of grotesque exhibits: the name of the curator. Jackamore Grass. There he is, in 1883, waiting for me.

Grabbing the drapes with my right hand, I yank them off their hooks. Rain zig-zags down the window. The sun tears a hole in a cloud and sunlight spreads over the carpet, coating Jack with amber wax. Time to begin.

Acknowledgements

The Beauty of Murder is set in a fictional Cambridge—streets aren't where they should be and a new ancient college sits in the city centre (so watch out when travelling). It is no reflection on the beautiful and inspiring locations in the novel that my imagination twists to the dark side.

Huge thanks to Jean, Chris and David Benedict; all of my family; Mumrah and Liono; the fabulous Judith Shaw; Matt, for everything; Liz and Peter; James; Jacqueline; Sue; Richard; Daniel; Barny; Tris; Beth and Zeph; Lin and John; Tom, Chris, Shirley and Anne; Karen and Leon; Ruth and Jesper; Josie; Katie; Lou and Stephen; Hope; Stavroula; Heidi Heelz; Paul Deadman; Toby Amies; Fiona; Michelle and Sid; Kirsty and Ben; Emilia and Dom; Anna and Blair; Nicky and Danny; Keith and Gene; Jackie, Helen and Conor; Deborah, Bob and the banana bread at Retreats for You; Peter Mould; everyone at The Stables Theatre; Black Phoenix Alchemy Lab; the Hunterian Museum; Hoagies; Imogen Salt; Claire Massey; Nicholas Royle; Helen Searle; Carole Baldock; Bill Cummings; Ruth Padel and all at Loutro; Aitor Basauri and fellow clowns; Nicola Lees, WFTV and the 2012 mentees; Richard Fell; my teachers at Corfe Hills and King's; Todd Kingsley-Smith, Kerrith Bell and all at the Hastings outpost of the University of Sussex Creative Writing Certificate; New Writing South; Alice Jakubeit; Patrick Knowles for his gorgeous artwork; Diana Beaumont; my agent, Rupert Heath, for his faith, acuity, wit and YouTube links;

my editors, Genevieve Pegg and Eleanor Dryden, for their insight, guidance and support; Laura Gerrard, Angela MacMahon, Louisa Macpherson and all at Orion; the city of Cambridge and the town of Hastings for being weird, wonderful and stimulating. And to everyone who knew it would happen one day and/or read the novel at its various stages—thank you so very much. I owe you a pint. Or cake. The choice is yours.